"A story of love, hope, redemption, and rediscovering who you ...
meant to be . . . will resonate with readers who love a tale full of heart
and soul."
—Camille Di Maio, bestselling author of *The Memory of Us* and
The Beautiful Strangers

"Infused with honesty, friendship, and a touch of romance. Davis
creates nuanced and well-developed characters . . . a carefully woven
tale that the reader won't soon forget."
—Emily Cavanagh, author of *The Bloom Girls* and *This Bright Beauty*

"Brimming with compassion and a refreshingly grown-up romance . . .
an uplifting tale about starting over and how letting go of our nevers
just might be the only thing that lets us move forward."
—Emily Carpenter, author of *Until the Day I Die*

"Heartfelt and beautifully written."
—Diane Chamberlain, *USA Today* bestselling author of
Pretending to Dance

"A beautifully crafted page-turner . . . Part contemporary women's
fiction, part historical novel, the plot moves seamlessly back and
forth in time to unlock family secrets that bind four generations of
women . . . This novel has it all."
—Barbara Claypole White, bestselling author of *Echoes of Family*

"Everything I love in a novel . . . elegant and haunting."
—Erika Marks, author of *The Last Treasure*

THE
LAST
OF THE
MOON
GIRLS

THE
LAST
OF THE
MOON
GIRLS

BARBARA DAVIS

LAKE UNION
PUBLISHING

Published by Lake Union Publishing, Seattle

www.apub.com

Amazon, the Amazon logo, and Lake Union Publishing are trademarks of Amazon.com, Inc., or its affiliates.

ISBN-13: 9781542006491
ISBN-10: 154200649X

Cover design by Micaela Alcaino

Printed in the United States of America

For the women . . .
Healers of hearts,
Workers of light,
Makers of magick.

Love works magic.
It is the final purpose
Of the world story,
The Amen of the universe.

—Novalis

PROLOGUE

A body that's been submerged in water undergoes a different kind of decomposition: harsher in some ways, kinder in others—or so I've been told. We Moons wouldn't know about that. We choose fire when our time comes, and scatter our ashes on land that has been in our family for more than two centuries. Mine are there now too, mingled with the dust of my ancestors.

Can it really be only weeks that I've been gone? Weeks hovering between worlds, unable to stay, unwilling to go, tethered by regret and unfinished business. The separation feels longer, somehow. But it is not my death I dwell on today but the deaths of two young girls—Darcy and Heather Gilman— more than eight years ago now. They'd been missing nearly three weeks when their bodies were finally pulled from the water. It was a ghastly thing to watch, but watch I did. They were dragging my pond, you see, convinced they would find what they were looking for. And why not, when the whole town was looking in my direction? Because of who I was—and what I was. Or at least what they imagined me to be.

Memory, it seems, does not die along with the body. It's been years since that terrible day at the pond, and yet I remember every detail, replaying them again and again, an endless, merciless loop. The police chief in his waders, his men with their boat. The ME's van looming nearby, its back doors yawning wide in anticipation of new cargo. The bone-white face of a mother waiting to learn the fate of her girls. Whispers hissing through the crowd like electric current. And then, the telling shrill of a whistle.

A hush settles over us, the kind that carries a weight of its own—the weight of the dead. No one moves as the first body appears, the glimpse of an arm in a muddy brown coat, water pouring from the sleeve as the sodden form is dragged up onto the bank. A bloated, blackened face, partly obscured by hanks of sopping dark hair.

They're careful with her, handling her with a tenderness that's gruesome somehow, and agonizing to watch. They're preserving the evidence, I realize, and a cold lick goes down my spine. So they can make their case. Against me.

A short time later a second body appears, and there comes a broken wail, a mother's heart breaking for her darlings.

And that's how it all unraveled, the awful day that set up all the rest. The end of the farm. And, perhaps, the end of the Moons.

ONE

Althea Moon was dead.

That was the gist of the letter. Dead in her bed on a Sunday morning. Dead of a long and wasting illness. Dead and already cremated, her ashes scattered at the rise of the full moon, as laid out in her will.

The room blurred as Lizzy scanned the letter through a film of tears, the terse lines smearing on the page. *With your mother's whereabouts currently unknown, you have been deeded sole possession of Moon Girl Farm. I am forwarding this parcel in accordance with your grandmother's final wishes.*

There was a signature at the bottom. *Evangeline Broussard.* The name wasn't familiar, but it was clear that the woman—whoever she was—knew more about Althea's last days than she did. She hadn't even known her grandmother was sick.

Lizzy swallowed past the bite of tears, the mingled tastes of guilt and grief salty on her tongue as she reached for the parcel that had accompanied the letter. It was wrapped in brown paper, and somewhat worse for wear. She stared at the words stamped across the package in red ink: RETURN TO SENDER. Apparently it had been mailed to her old apartment, returned by the new tenants, and then re-sent to her office.

She'd meant to send Althea one of those change of address cards, but like so much of late, it had fallen through the cracks. She held her breath as she tore away the wrapping, then exhaled sharply when she caught a glimpse of heavily tooled black leather. She knew the book well. It was the journal Althea had given her on her sixteenth birthday—the journal *all* Moon girls received on their sixteenth birthday.

Her fingers quivered as she ran them over the cover, the ribbed spine, the pages with their coarse deckle edges, knowing the feel of them by heart. There were eight more just like it back in Salem Creek, locked away in a bookcase in her grandmother's reading room, each named for the author who had penned it. *The Book of Sabine. The Book of Dorothée. The Book of Aurore.* On down through the generations. Presumably, the ninth—*The Book of Althea*—had now taken its place among them.

They were a tradition in the Moon family, a rite of passage as each member committed to the Path. Painstakingly penned volumes of remedies and recipes, sacred blessings and scraps of womanly wisdom, carefully preserved for future generations. And here was hers, turned up again like the proverbial bad penny, as blank as the day she'd received it.

She opened it gingerly, staring at the inscription. *To Elzibeth—It's Time to write your story.*

Not Elizabeth. *Elzibeth.* She couldn't even have a normal name.

At sixteen, she'd wanted no part of the tradition—or any other part of her family's strange legacy. She'd wanted to be normal, like *other* people. And so she'd put the journal in a drawer and ignored it.

Holding it now, after so many years, felt like an indictment, a reminder that in spurning this sacred family custom, she had turned her back on everything her grandmother had lived, taught, and believed. She could have pretended for Althea's sake, gone along with what was expected of her and filled the journal with silly scribblings. Even normal girls kept diaries—pink things with hearts on the cover and flimsy brass locks to keep snoopers at bay. But she'd been too stubborn to go along, determined to break with the Moon tradition and map her own future. She'd done it too, if the shiny new plaque on her office door was any indication—from freshman at Dickerson to intern at Worldwide to creative director of Chenier Fragrances, Ltd., all in the space of eight years.

But six months after her coveted promotion, she was still trying to wrap her arms around the new position and the recent flurry of changes in her life. There hadn't been time to tell Althea—at least that's what she'd been telling herself. The truth was their communication had grown increasingly spotty over the years. Not out of laziness, but out of guilt. It felt wrong to crow about her success when her grandmother had been forced to watch her own life's work—her beloved farm—wither and die. Instead, she'd convinced herself the checks she sent from time to time would atone for an eight-year absence, for letters that went unanswered and phone calls that came only rarely. They didn't, of course. Nothing could. And now it was too late to tell Althea anything.

She tried to digest it—a world without Althea Moon—but couldn't manage it somehow. How could such a woman, so rich in wisdom, life, and love, who seemed to have sprung from the very soil she loved and tended, ever be gone?

She'd never mentioned being sick. Not once in all her long, newsy letters. Yet Evangeline Broussard's letter had mentioned a prolonged illness. Why would Althea have kept such a thing from her?

"Ah, you're here—finally."

Lizzy blinked back a fresh sting of tears, dismayed to find Luc Chenier hovering in her office doorway. He'd just had a haircut, and looked even more devastating than usual in his ubertailored black Brioni. He knew it too, which used to annoy her when they were seeing each other, but didn't anymore.

She sniffed away the remnants of her tears. The last thing she needed was to be caught crying at her desk by the man who'd just green-lighted her promotion—or to be peppered with uncomfortable questions, which she would be if he thought for a minute that she was holding something back. She glanced up at him, hoping to appear unruffled as she swept the journal into her lap and out of sight.

"Did you need something?"

He turned on the smile, recently whitened by the look of it. "I came looking for you at lunchtime, but they said you had a meeting."

"I was with marketing, trying to nail down the concepts for the new print campaign. We're not quite there yet, but we should have—"

Luc cut her off with the wave of a hand. "Come out with me after work. I was going to take you to lunch, but dinner's better, don't you think?"

No, she didn't think, though it didn't surprise her that he did. He was used to getting his way. And why wouldn't he be? The man positively oozed charm. It didn't hurt that he looked like Johnny Depp without the eyeliner, or that he'd retained a hint of his mother's French accent. But those things had quickly lost their appeal.

They'd done their best to keep things quiet. No office flirtations or public displays of affection. No lunches that didn't include a spreadsheet or a PowerPoint handout. But the night her promotion was announced they'd gone to Daniel to celebrate, and run smack into Reynold Ackerman, an attorney from legal, who happened to be there with his wife, celebrating their twentieth wedding anniversary. That was when she knew she had a choice to make—end things or become the office cliché.

She'd ended it the next day. Luc had taken it well enough, perhaps because they'd established ground rules early on. When the time came, either party could walk away. No tears. No recriminations. But lately, he'd been signaling that maybe they should pick up where they'd left off. A nonstarter, as far as she was concerned.

"So tonight, then?" he prompted from the doorway. "We can do Italian."

"I can't. I'm sorry."

"I'll book us a table at Scarpetta. The cannoli alone—"

"My grandmother died," she blurted. "I just got the letter."

Luc had the good grace to drop the smile. He stepped into the office and closed the door behind him. "I'm sorry. I didn't know she was sick."

"Neither did I." The words stung more than Lizzy expected, and she found herself having to look away. Crying on each other's shoulders hadn't been part of their arrangement, and she wasn't about to start now. "Apparently, she'd been keeping it from me."

"I don't remember you talking about her much. Or any of your family, for that matter. Were you close?"

"We were," she said evenly. "She basically raised me."

"Tough break."

Lizzy stared up at him from her desk chair. *Tough break? That's what you say to someone when a person they love dies?* And yet she shouldn't be surprised. She'd seen him deal with death before.

They'd been seeing each other on the quiet for several months when Luc's mother, and Lizzy's mentor in the world of fragrance, finally lost her battle with cervical cancer. Lizzy had watched him at the funeral, shaking hands and accepting condolences, playing the dutiful son. But as the afternoon wore on, she couldn't help thinking that that was precisely what he was doing—playing a role. Initially, she had attributed the lack of grief to the lingering nature of his mother's illness. He'd had time to prepare, to make his peace and say goodbye. Now she wondered if she'd given him too much credit.

"I'm sorry for your loss," he said finally, reaching across the desk to lay a hand over hers. "You'll want to go home, of course, for the funeral."

Lizzy slid her hand free, tucking it in her lap and out of reach. "There isn't going to be a funeral. They've already scattered her ashes."

Luc's brows shot up. "What—without you?"

Lizzy nodded, unwilling to say more. When it came to family, she preferred to keep the details to a minimum. If you wanted to be taken seriously—and she did—there were places you just didn't go.

"We don't make a fuss in my family," she said, blinking back a rush of tears. *Unless you consider having your ashes scattered in a lavender field on the first full moon after your death making a fuss.* "Besides, it was my fault. I forgot to send a change of address when I moved, so there was a mix-up with the letter. She died two months ago. When I didn't respond, the funeral home must have gone ahead and taken care of her ashes."

Luc nodded, as if it all made perfect sense, then frowned suddenly. "Still a bit odd, though, right? Moving ahead without you?"

Lizzy avoided his gaze. "It's sort of a family tradition. There's . . . timing involved. Anyway, it's done."

"Just as well, if you ask me. I've never been big on funerals. All that grief in one place." He paused, feigning a shudder. "It's a wasted emotion when you get right down to it. The person who died has no idea you're grieving, because, well, they're dead. And everyone else is just standing around mumbling platitudes and eating deviled eggs. And then there's family, which is a whole other can of worms. Always messy—or as my mother liked to say . . . *compliqué.*"

Compliqué.

Lizzy nodded. It was the perfect descriptor for the Moons. "Yes. We're quite . . . messy."

"How long since you've been back?"

"Never. I left eight years ago and never went back."

Luc whistled softly. "That's a long time, even by my standards. Your mother's gone?"

Lizzy knew what he was asking—was her mother *dead*? The truth was she had no idea. No one did. And that was almost the same thing. "Yes. She's gone. Everyone's gone."

Luc stepped around to her side of the desk, propping a hip on the corner. "My poor little orphan," he said softly. "You're not alone, you know. My mother loved you—so much that she made me promise to look after you. She said, *Luc, Lizzy is going to be brilliant one day, and I want you to take care of her.* It's as if in leaving me this company, she left me you too."

Lizzy resisted the temptation to roll her eyes. "You can't leave a person in a will, Luc. And I've been on my own for a pretty long time."

He stood, and moved to the window. "How long will you need? Three days? Four?"

She frowned. "For what?"

"I don't know. Bereavement, I guess. Whatever you need to do. I'm guessing there's financial stuff to handle, a house to sell."

"It's a farm, actually. An herb farm. But I don't need to go back. I can handle everything from here."

"Seriously?" He smiled, as if pleasantly surprised. "And here I was thinking you were the sentimental type."

Lizzy shook her head, desperate to end the conversation before she said something that raised Luc's carefully groomed brows again. "It's just . . . a lot of stuff. Memories I'd rather not dredge up. Like you said, it's . . . *compliqué.*"

His smile widened, straddling the line between arrogance and condescension. "My mother was the sentimental type. She used to say we all need to go home from time to time, to remind us where we came from. I think she was half-right. We do need to go home from time to time, but only to remind us why we left in the first place, so we can get clear on what we *do* want. Because in the long run, that's all that matters—what we want from life and what we're willing to do to get it. Maybe that's what you need, Lizzy, to go spend some time with your memories. Things might look different when you do."

Time with her memories.

Lizzy dropped her eyes to her lap, unwilling to meet his gaze. He had no idea what he was asking. Not that he should. How could anyone imagine the kind of memories they were really talking about?

"It's fine, really. I'm fine. I can make it work long-distance."

Luc eyed her skeptically. "Suit yourself, but you don't sound fine. Maybe there's something to be said for processing your loss, putting a period to things, as they say. I could go with you, make things easier."

And there it was, the real motive behind his sudden concern. "We've been over for months, Luc."

"I'm aware."

"Then why make the suggestion?"

"Would you believe I was being noble?"

"No."

Luc dropped the smile, apparently accepting defeat. "Still a crummy time to be alone. At least let me take you to dinner. I promise to stick to business, if that's how you want it."

"Thanks. But I think I just need to be by myself."

Lizzy watched him go, pretty sure he was miffed. But he'd been right about one thing. She *did* need time to process, to digest the fact that she was suddenly alone in the world, and what that meant. Althea was dead, and her mother had apparently fallen off the face of the earth—either literally or figuratively. And there'd be no more Moons after Elzibeth—of that she was certain. For all intents and purposes, she had just become the last Moon girl.

TWO

Lizzy kicked off her shoes and made a beeline for the kitchen. She'd managed to finish out the day, smiling through a steady stream of condolences as news of her loss spread through the office. Now all she wanted was a large glass of wine and to be alone with her grief.

She opened a bottle of chardonnay and poured herself a generous glass, then paused to water the herb pots she kept on the sill. *Rosemary, for remembrance. Basil, for courage. Thyme, for warding off nightmares.* It was the catechism of her childhood—the catechism of all the Moon girls.

On impulse, she plucked a basil leaf from the plant on the sill and rolled it between her palms, releasing its savory-sweet fragrance—peppery, anise-like, faintly minty. It was one of her favorite aromatics, perhaps because it reminded her of happy times spent cooking in her grandmother's kitchen. But this time another memory surfaced—an older memory.

Althea had been out surveying the damage after an unusually late frost when Lizzy came up from behind. She couldn't have been more than seven at the time, but she had known instinctively to keep still, mesmerized by the strange intensity in her grandmother's face as she knelt beside a clump of blackened basil plants and, with eyes closed, passed her calloused hands over them. She had murmured something then, tender words Lizzy couldn't make out. It was the first time she'd ever seen her grandmother's gift in action, but she'd never forgotten it. Or the sight of those same plants the next day, healthy and green, and without a trace of frostbite.

It had been Althea's most startling gift—the ability to raise a nearly dead herb or flower with a touch and a few gentle words. That, and an uncanny knack for growing things that had no business flourishing in stingy New England climes. Whispers about her grandmother's green thumb had been commonplace in Salem Creek. Some chalked it up to magick, others to a strict reliance on her almanac. Whatever it was, it was widely accepted that the rocky soil of Moon Girl Farm could refuse Althea Moon nothing.

Who would tend that soil now that she was gone?

The question needled as Lizzy carried her chardonnay to the living room. It would belong to someone else soon. The house and barn, the herb fields, her grandmother's apothecary shop, all passed out of the family and into the hands of strangers. She had always known it would happen, that one day Althea would die and something would have to be done with the farm. She just hadn't given much thought to what that something might look like—or that it might fall to her to carry it out.

She'd have to work out the logistics, find a Realtor willing to handle the sale long-distance, then contact an estate dealer to handle the contents of the house. There wasn't much of any real value. But what of Althea's personal belongings? Her clothes, her books—the collection of journals kept under lock and key in her reading room? Could she really trust the handling of *those* to a stranger? And if not, who did that leave? Certainly not her mother, whose recklessness had sent the final dominoes toppling. But Rhanna was another story—apparently one without an ending, since no one had heard from her in years.

Lizzy felt numb as she perched on the arm of the couch, emptied of anger and blindsided by the events of the day. The sun was beginning its descent, sliding into the cracks and crevices of Midtown Manhattan's jumbled rooftops, like one of those sepia postcards drugstores stocked for tourists. Three months after trading her tiny loft for a place in the East Tower, she still wasn't used to the view. Or any of the other perks that came with her posh new address. Luc had assured her that she would grow into her new surroundings, but as she glanced around the room, she recognized nothing. The furniture, the art on the walls, even the reflection staring back at her from the darkened window seemed to belong to someone else—a stranger *pretending* to be Lizzy Moon.

Over the years, the city had polished her rough edges, leaving no sign of the girl who'd run barefoot through her grandmother's fields, gathering herbs until her fingers were stained, her nails gritty with New England soil. But then, that was why she'd come to New York: to rid herself of that girl. To live like other people. A plain, round peg in a plain, round hole. No surprises. No suspicions. No secret book with her name on it. Just . . . normal. And it had worked, mostly. She'd come a long way since leaving Salem Creek. But was there such a thing as *too* long? Was it possible to walk away so completely that you lost yourself in the process?

She drained her glass and headed to the kitchen for a refill. She was on the verge of a good wallow; she could feel it. But she couldn't afford to become nostalgic, or forget what had ultimately driven her from Salem Creek.

Eight years ago, a pair of teenage girls had failed to return home at curfew. Hours turned to days, days to weeks. Heather and Darcy Gilman had simply vanished.

It had taken less than twenty-four hours for Althea's name to be raised as the likely culprit. It was hardly a surprise. Anytime anything went wrong—an early blizzard, a freak high tide, an outbreak of measles—the Moons were somehow to blame. Many claimed to speak in jest, but for those in certain circles, the rumors held a ring of truth. What Salem Creek lacked in worldly pretentions, it more than made up for with arcane superstitions and gaudy displays of religious fervor. The disappearance of the Gilman girls proved no exception.

A hotline had been set up and the press descended. Vigils were held, complete with Bibles, candles, flowers, and teddy bears. And then, just when the furor was beginning to die down, there'd been a knock at the door. Someone had called in an anonymous tip, claiming to have seen Althea dragging the girls, one at a time, into the pond, and then burying something nearby.

A warrant had been issued, a pair of small straw poppets found. Voodoo dolls, the paper had called them, because they bore an eerie resemblance to the missing girls, right down to the color of the coats they'd been wearing the night they disappeared. But they hadn't been buried as the tipster claimed, only left out under a full moon, along with a small cloth bag of salt and caraway seeds. A protection ritual, Althea had explained to police, an *offering* to help guide the girls safely home to their parents.

They'd searched the pond next. An hour later, the bodies of Heather and Darcy Gilman had been dragged up from the bottom while half the town watched from behind a line of yellow crime tape. The ME's findings hadn't been long in coming: a fractured skull for one girl, a broken neck for the other. Both homicide.

Decades-old rumors resurfaced with a vengeance, sometimes whispered, sometimes not. Spells, potions, naked rituals held at full moon. Virgin sacrifices. Many circulated by people who'd known Althea all their lives. There wasn't a shred of real evidence, which was why no case had ever been brought, but that hadn't stopped the tongues from wagging. Or prevented the good people of Salem Creek from holding a candlelight vigil—one nearly half the town had shown up for—to pray away the evil in their midst. Innocent until proven guilty—unless your name was Moon.

And now the woman they'd suspected of murder was dead. Had there been a sigh of relief? A day of feasting proclaimed by the mayor? *Ding-dong, the witch is dead?*

Yes. Definitely wallowing now, and maybe just a little bit tipsy. She should probably scare up something to eat, but the idea held little appeal. Instead, she headed down the hall with her purse and her newly filled glass, intent on a long, hot soak before bed.

She tossed her purse on the bed and peeled out of her clothes, then turned to retrieve her wineglass from the nightstand. The contents of her purse had spilled out over the comforter, including the journal Evangeline Broussard had sent along with her letter. The sight of it hit her like a blow to the solar plexus, the kind that doubled you up even when you knew it was coming.

Althea was gone.

Grief overwhelmed her as she sagged onto the bed and picked up the book, her tears so hot and jagged she nearly missed the sheet of paper that slid from between the pages and into her lap. She blinked at it, her tears shuddering to a sudden halt. The words were splotchy in places, but there was no mistaking Althea's taut script.

My dearest Lizzy,

If you're reading this letter, you know that I'm gone, and why I asked for your book to be sent. Your happiness was all I ever wanted—and all I want for you still—but it would be a lie to say I didn't hope that happiness would be found at Moon Girl Farm. I've never stopped wishing you home, wishing that one day you would come back to the land we both love so well, and to the Path the Moons have walked for generations. You showed such promise as a girl, so many gifts. But you were afraid of being different—of being special. You wanted so badly to be like everyone else that you were willing to throw away those gifts. But gifts like yours can't be thrown away. They're in you still, waiting to be called up. Waiting for you to come home. Ours is a long and undiluted line, but I fear that line will soon be broken, our legacy lost forever. You're all that's left now, the last and best of us. But there are still things to learn, things there wasn't time to share before you went away. Broken things that need mending. Hidden things that need telling. The books are here, the teachings of all those who came before you. And you are their steward now, the keeper of our secrets. It's my hope that one day your book will be there too, shelved beside mine, so that gifts like ours will not be lost to the world. But that choice is not mine to make. It's yours. We all of us have a story—one we tell knowingly or not with our hours and our days. But as I said all those years ago, no one should write your story but you. Whatever you choose, know that you are always in my heart, and that this is not goodbye. There are no goodbyes, my Lizzy, only turnings of the Circle. Until then . . .

A—

Lizzy was still crying as she folded the letter and slid it back between the blank pages of the journal. They were the kind of words that should never have to be written, the kind that should be said only face-to-face. Not that her grandmother's letter held many surprises. She had always known what was expected of her—the same thing that was expected of every Moon girl. She was meant to produce a daughter and train her in their ways, to ensure that the line remained unbroken, because that's how it had been done for generations.

There were no Moon men. No brothers or sons, or husbands either. It hadn't been planned that way—or if it *had*, no one ever said so aloud. The Moon girls had just never been the marrying kind, preferring to keep their own company, raise their own daughters, and focus their energy on the family farm.

But precious little had remained of the farm by the time Lizzy left for school—or of the family for that matter—and she doubted the eight years she'd been gone had done much to repair that. Besides, she had a life. One she'd worked hard to build. Let someone else rebuild the farm, someone who actually wanted it.

But Althea's words echoed back to her. *The books are here, the teachings of all those who came before you. And you are their steward now* . . .

Once again, it came down to the books. That's why Althea had arranged to send her journal. It wasn't just about her story. It was about *all* their stories, and the duty that now fell to her as keeper of the Moons' secrets. Always, always duty.

Yes, she could find a Realtor to list the farm. She could even locate someone to clear out the furniture and her grandmother's personal effects—but not the books. She had no idea what to do with them—it wasn't the kind of thing anyone had ever talked about—but disposing of them was out of the question. Theirs was a subtle form of magick—quiet magick, Althea had called it. None of that nonsense with cauldrons and candles for the Moon girls. No summoning spirits or casting curses. No covens or midnight bonfires. Just healing work recorded for posterity, proof that they had lived, and done good in the world.

She'd have to make the trip to Salem Creek and box them up, even if all she wound up doing was shoving them in the back of her closet. At some point, she'd need to think about what would happen to them when she was gone—when there would be no one left to pass them on to—but not yet.

Althea saw her as the last and best of the Moons. But she wasn't. Her *gifts*—if that's what they were—were different from Althea's. She wasn't a healer or a charmer. She made perfume. And since her promotion to creative director, she didn't even do much of that. The truth was that, beyond a functioning reproductive system, she had little to offer the Moons. No remedies to share, no wisdom to impart, no sacred rituals to pass on to the next generation.

But she would go back for the books—for Althea's sake. And maybe Luc was right. Maybe she did need to spend some time with her memories, to look that other Lizzy Moon in the eye one last time before she walked away for good.

THREE

The sign for Moon Girl Farm was so faded Lizzy could barely make out the letters as she turned into the drive. It had taken six hours in a steady drizzle, the last of which had been spent winding along the frost-heaved backroads of rural New Hampshire, but she'd finally made it.

She had called Luc before 6:00 a.m., when she knew he'd be at the gym and unlikely to pick up. Her message said only that she had changed her mind about going home, and would call him when she had some idea how much time she would need. She had then turned off her phone, nixing any chance of a return call.

At the top of the drive, she cut the engine, reminding herself as she got out of the car that this was something she had to do, one last duty to be discharged before she could finally bolt the door on this chapter of her life. But even now, with a knot the size of a fist forming in her stomach, she could feel the pull of the place, a connection to the land that seemed to have been sewn into her soul.

There had always been something otherworldly about the farm, a sense that it had somehow been carved out of time, and stood apart from the rest of the world, like Brigadoon—a place that existed only in her imagination. And yet here it was. Her childhood, preserved in time, like a living thing suspended in amber.

There'd been nothing but open pasture on the outskirts of Salem Creek in 1786, when a pregnant Sabine Moon had fled France for the newly formed United States with nothing but a handful of jewels sewn into the hem of her skirt. And she'd put those jewels to good use, trading them for an eight-acre parcel of land, where she would set up a small but soon-to-be-thriving farm.

She'd been spurned by the villagers, who were wary of a woman brash enough to buy land without the help of a man, and then farm it herself. A woman who wore no ring, and offered no explanation for her swollen belly. Not to mention the bastard daughter she eventually paraded beneath their noses. And then two years of drought decimated the town's crops—all except Sabine's, which continued to flourish. And so began the whispers about the strange ways of the Moons, the women who never married and bred only daughters, who grew herbs, and brewed teas, and made charms.

Even now, no one was really sure what the Moons were, though there had been plenty over the years willing to venture an opinion, throwing around words like *voodoo* and *witchery*. Not that the good people of Salem Creek professed to believe in witches. Those superstitions had died more than a century ago, along with practices like pricking and dunking.

But the Gilman girls had acted as a touch paper, reigniting speculation and long-buried wives' tales. The murders went unsolved but the whispers lived on, while Althea's beloved farm withered for want of customers. Rhanna had been the first to go. Lizzy had moved to New York City a short time later, a twenty-eight-year-old freshman bound for Dickerson University—and a life as far from Moon Girl Farm as she could get.

And now Moon Girl Farm was hers.

She sighed as she surveyed the grounds, struck by the glaring signs of neglect. Behind the house, neatly parceled flower beds had long since gone to weed, leaving a smattering of stunted blooms visible through the damp, green overgrowth. The herb rows had fared no better. But the neglect ran deeper than just the land. Beyond the ruined fields, the old stone cider house that served as Althea's apothecary had grown shabby as well. The slate-paved courtyard had once been filled with racks of potted herbs and bright summer flowers. Now crabgrass grew between the pavers, and the racks sat empty, the windows coated with grit. What must it have been like for Althea to see it shut up? To know her life's work was at an end? And to bear it all alone?

Across the fields, the old drying barn stood like a sentinel, its vivid indigo-blue boards now weathered to a dull blue gray, the hand-painted clouds and milky white moon decorating its west-facing wall faded to little more than ghosts.

The skyscape had appeared almost overnight, a manifestation of Rhanna's unpredictable and often outrageous muse. The fanciful artwork had caused quite a stir with the locals. An eyesore, some said, too hippie-dippie for the likes of Salem Creek. But the barn had eventually become something of a landmark, even appearing once in *Yankee* magazine as part of a feature on the hidden treasures of rural New England.

Even now, dulled by time and weather, the sight of it brought a smile. It had been her main haunt as a teenager—her alone place—cool and quiet, and blissfully off-limits to customers. It had also been an ideal place to set up a makeshift lab to work on her perfumes. Now, like the rest of Moon Girl Farm, it had become a shadow of its former self.

Lizzy shook off the memories as she headed for the car and her suitcase. She was hungry and tired after the drive, and still battling the remnants of a wine headache. There'd be plenty of time for recrimination after she'd scrounged up something to eat.

The elements had taken a toll on the house, the sage-colored boards weathered to a shade that was more gray than green, the window lintels sagging and porous with rot. And yet here it stood, weather weary, but proud somehow, as tenacious as the woman who had built it more than two hundred years ago.

The door groaned as Lizzy turned her old house key in the lock and pushed inside. She stood still for a moment, waiting for her eyes to adjust to the gloom of the entry hall. She'd forgotten how dark the house was, especially at the front, where the boughs of an ancient ash tree blocked the sunlight. But it was the stillness that struck her most, the sense that with Althea gone time had somehow stopped moving forward.

The parlor was exactly as she remembered: the tweedy settee under the front windows, the pair of worn wingbacks flanking the brick fireplace, the mismatched collection of pewterware on the mantel—and the portraits lining the opposite wall. They were crudely rendered, for the most part, the work of various amateurs over the years, but each framed face bore a striking resemblance to its neighbor. Dark hair worn plainly, skin pale enough to be called translucent, and the telltale gray eyes that marked all the Moon women.

She had grown up under those watchful eyes, their collective gaze so intense that she had often avoided the room as a child. *Each face tells a story*, Althea would say, before quizzing her on the names. Sabine. Patrice. Renée. Dorothée. Sylvie. Honoré.

The unexpected scuff of feet brought Lizzy up short. She turned sharply, surprised to find a mahogany-skinned woman standing at the base of the stairs. She was tall and strangely beautiful, with a high forehead, broad cheeks, and salt-and-pepper hair shorn almost to the scalp.

"She said you'd come," the woman said, after a weighty moment of silence.

"Who are you?"

"Evangeline Broussard. Evvie."

"You sent the letter."

"I did. Twice, as a matter of fact."

Lizzy lifted her chin, chafed by the unspoken censure. "I moved."

Evvie seemed in no hurry to respond. She regarded Lizzy through narrowed eyes, sweeping her from head to foot. "You forgot to tell your gran."

Lizzy closed her eyes briefly, startled by the mingled tang of vinegar and spoiled peaches that seemed to radiate from the woman.

Disapproval.

It was a thing she had. The ability to read a person based on scent, like reading an aura, but with her nose instead of her eyes. It had started around the time she hit puberty, a common time for such gifts to ripen, Althea had explained.

The episodes had been overwhelming at first: jumbled scents that hit without warning, and rarely made sense. It took a while, but she'd eventually learned to decipher what was coming through, and even use it to her advantage, like a radar ping alerting her to possible threats. But her skills had grown spotty since moving away, as if leaving the farm had somehow diminished her reception. Now, suddenly, she was picking up a signal again, and that signal was disapproval.

"I meant to let her know, but I . . ." Lizzy let the words trail, annoyed that she felt the need to explain herself to a stranger. "What are you doing here?"

"Could ask you the same."

"Yes, but I'm asking. And since this is my grandmother's house, I think I'm entitled to an answer."

"I was her friend," Evvie answered flatly. "Who else would've written that letter?"

Lizzy tipped her head to one side, trying to read this strange woman. She had a peculiar lilt to her voice, her words rising and falling like the notes of a song. It was lovely and musical—and slightly unsettling. Or perhaps it was the woman's copper-flecked green eyes that made it difficult to meet her gaze straight on. "I assumed Evangeline

Broussard was someone who worked for Althea's lawyer. Or the funeral home. I didn't expect to find you here."

Evvie grunted. "Makes us even, I guess. Why are you here? Now? After all this time?"

Lizzy groped for an answer, but the truth was she didn't have one. At least not one she felt comfortable sharing. "There are some things of my grandmother's I wanted to take care of personally. Things I know she'd want me to have."

Evvie's eyes narrowed again, but she made no reply. Instead, she offered the barest of nods before turning away, her battered UGGs scuffing the floorboards as she headed for the kitchen.

Lizzy followed, noting for the first time that Evvie was wearing one of Althea's floral aprons. "Are you cooking something?"

"Supper."

Lizzy watched as she lifted the lid from the soup pot simmering on the stove. After a taste, she pulled a jar of something from a nearby cabinet and sprinkled a pinch into the pot.

"You live here?" Lizzy asked as the truth slowly began to dawn.

Evvie turned, still clutching her spoon. "I do. Unless you're here to give me the boot."

Lizzy stifled a sigh. She was too tired to do battle, especially with a stranger. "I'm not here to give you the boot. I didn't even know you were here. Were you . . . her caregiver?"

Evvie laid down her spoon and wiped her hands on her apron. "She didn't pay me, if that's what you're asking, but I suppose I was. It's what friends do for each other—give care."

Lizzy felt her cheeks warm. "I didn't mean . . . I'm sorry, I'm just trying to understand."

"You hungry?"

Lizzy blinked at her. "What?"

"Hungry?" Evvie repeated, as if speaking to a particularly dull child. "Are you hungry?"

"Yes, I guess . . ."

"Good then. Set the table."

They ate in silence at the kitchen table—a rice dish of some sort, made with tomatoes and beans, and plenty of spice. It was delicious and exotic, full of ethnic flavors Lizzy couldn't place. And thankfully it contained no meat, sparing her the potentially awkward vegetarian discussion.

"She never told me she was sick," Lizzy said when the silence grew heavy. "I would have come if she had."

Evvie nodded as she drizzled a wedge of corn bread with honey. "She knew that. It's why she didn't tell you. Even at the end, when I begged her to let me call you. She was a stubborn old thing. Said you were too. Somehow, I don't have trouble believing that."

Lizzy looked down at her plate, toying with her food. What was it about the woman that made her feel like a naughty schoolgirl?

"She wanted you to *want* to be here," Evvie said finally, licking honey from her fingers. "And if you didn't, she wanted you to be happy wherever you were. That's how much she loved you. Enough to let you go."

Lizzy put down her fork and wiped her mouth. "I didn't just leave her, Evvie. I went away to school—like I'd always planned to do. I never hid the fact that I wanted out of this town. When I got accepted to Dickerson, I knew it was time. Althea was sad that I was leaving, but she understood."

"She knew that if she tried to keep you, she'd lose you for good. And I guess she knew best, 'cause here you are—finally."

"Then why the shot about me leaving?"

Evvie turned coppery green eyes on Lizzy. "I didn't take a shot. Least not the way you think. It isn't the leaving I have a problem with. I get that part well enough. It's the staying gone that gripes me. Everyone's got a right to go looking for themselves, but once they manage it, they should come back home and deal with what's past, look things squarely in the eye." She paused, pushing back her plate, then fastened her eyes on Lizzy's face. "Or maybe you haven't really found yourself."

The remark chafed, as it was almost certainly meant to. But there were things Evvie didn't understand.

"There was a reason I wanted out of Salem Creek, Evvie. Something happened—"

"I know all about those girls," Evvie said, cutting her off. "And what people thought, and what they said, and how they treated your gran. I know about your mama too, how she lost her mind that day in the coffee shop and said those awful things about cursing the whole town. How she packed up her clothes and hightailed it out of here, leaving everything in a shambles. I know it all."

Lizzy only needed to meet Evvie's eyes to see that it was true. She did know it all. Or almost all. "Is there still talk? About Althea, I mean. Do people still think—"

Again, Evvie cut her off. "I didn't hear it through the grapevine, if that's what you're asking. Your gran filled me in. As for this town, I don't know what they think. I can tell you no one's ever uttered a word where I could hear it, but then they wouldn't be likely to."

The sudden intensity in Evvie's voice took Lizzy by surprise. "Why not?"

"They know better, I expect." The ghost of a smile appeared, showing teeth as white and even as a well-knotted string of pearls. "I think they're a little scared of me. Not too many faces like mine in Salem Creek."

It was Lizzy's turn to smile. She had no trouble believing people in Salem Creek were afraid of Evvie. She was nothing if not formidable. And yet there was something about her that was inexplicably comforting, a curious sense of the familiar.

"Tell me about my grandmother," she said softly. "How long was she sick?"

"Dishes."

"I'm sorry?"

Evvie pushed to her feet, scraping her chair across the oak floor-boards. "We can talk while we do up the dishes. Bring your plate."

Lizzy finished clearing while Evvie filled the sink. It felt strangely good to be back in the kitchen where she and Althea had spent so many happy hours, like stepping into a pair of old slippers you hadn't worn in a long time, and for a moment she could almost forget the terrible chain of events that had changed their lives forever. Almost.

"So my grandmother . . . ," Lizzy prompted, accepting the dripping plate Evvie was holding out.

"Her liver," Evvie said, fishing another plate from the soapy water. "It just gave out. She finally broke down and went to the doctor, but there wasn't much they could do. Sometimes we just wear out. And she didn't want any heroics. You know how she was. Never one for a fuss."

"Were you here when she . . ." Lizzy let the question dangle, unable to say the word out loud.

"I was."

"And her ashes—that was you too?"

"Mmm-hmmm."

Lizzy put down her towel, her throat full of razor blades as she captured Evvie's soapy hand. "I don't know what to say except thank you. For being her friend. For being here. For doing the things that needed doing. It should have been me. It should have been family."

Evvie looked up from the sink, her chin wobbling as she blinked away a film of tears. "It was," she said thickly. "Family isn't always about blood. Sometimes you just recognize someone. That's how it was with your gran and me. We were kin. A special kind of kin."

Anyone looking at Evvie, at her mahogany skin and copper-flecked eyes, would have a hard time believing she could be any sort of kin to Althea. And yet Lizzy had no trouble believing it.

"I'm glad she had you, Evvie. That she had someone with her who loved her."

Evvie's face softened. "You go on up now. I'll finish here. You look done in."

Lizzy nodded. *Done in* didn't begin to describe how she felt after the events of the last twenty-four hours. She dried her hands, and was about to head to the hall to retrieve her suitcase when Evvie stopped her.

"Almost forgot. I'm in your old room, so you'll need to use Althea's. Bed's been stripped, but there are sheets in the hall closet. I'll move your clothes and things in there tomorrow." She paused, running a critical eye over Lizzy's skinny jeans and trendy black boots. "You'll need real clothes around here."

Lizzy accepted the critique of her wardrobe but balked at the idea of sleeping in Althea's bed. It felt wrong somehow, intrusive and disrespectful. "I'll use Rhanna's old room. It'll only be for a few days."

Evvie shook her head. "Can't. Rhanna's room is more storage than bedroom these days. Besides, your gran would be happy to know you were in her room."

"I don't think—"

"Go on now," Evvie pressed softly. "She'd want you there."

Althea's room was at the head of the stairs. Lizzy closed her eyes briefly as she took hold of the knob, steeling herself for the flood of emotions she knew waited on the other side of the door. She lingered in the doorway, picking out small, familiar details: the volume of Rumi that had been Althea's favorite, the bit of stag antler they had discovered one day while walking in the woods, the carved wooden bowl of wishing stones on the nightstand.

In the end, it was the dressing table that finally drew her into the room. It had been her favorite spot in the house as a child, the place where her love affair with fragrance had begun. Geranium, jasmine, patchouli, sandalwood—an endless array of scents to blend in fresh, new ways, like an artist's palette for the nose. As far back as she could remember, Althea had spun tales about the strange talents of the Moon women, each uniquely gifted with her own quiet way of being useful in the world. And one day, while sitting at this dressing table, Lizzy had discovered her own brand of quiet magick—the glorious, mysterious alchemy of fragrance.

She had known instinctively that fragrance was its own kind of medicine, that its natural abilities to elevate mood and evoke emotion could be enormously effective in restoring a sense of well-being. She had also gleaned—thanks to her unusual gift—that every person possessed their own distinct scent, like fingerprints, a set of olfactory markers that acted like a kind of signature. It was a discovery that eventually became the foundation of her entire career.

On her fourteenth birthday, she had announced her intention to bottle Althea's love for the land. It was an impossibly childish idea—capturing emotions like fireflies in a jar—but Althea hadn't discouraged her, despite the fact that she hadn't a clue where to begin. She had simply followed her nose, eventually settling on lavender because it smelled like earth, and bergamot because it smelled like sunshine, and together they smelled like Althea. A few months later, she made good on her intention, unveiling a simple, dual-note fragrance she'd named Althea, after the woman who had inspired its creation.

She'd found the bottle in one of the dusty secondhand shops downtown, and saved her lunch money for two weeks to afford it. It was still on the dressing table, square with a heavy base and a long, tapered stopper. It had been refilled many times over the years but was empty now, save for the sticky brown resin at the bottom. She lifted the stopper anyway, hoping for a telltale whiff of her grandmother, but was disappointed to find only the cloying tang of oxidized oils.

A fresh wave of grief washed over her as she returned the bottle to the dressing table, the ache of Althea's absence moving through her like a physical pain as she wandered to the low-ceilinged nook that had served as a storage larder before Althea fitted it with shelves and a chair for reading. Over the years, her grandmother had acquired many cherished possessions, but none more cherished than her books. Her guilty pleasures, she had called them, perfect for whiling away the frigid New England winters.

And then there was the bookcase: glass-fronted with three tiers, and doors that locked with a tiny brass key. Lizzy bent down to peer through the glass. The books. As a girl, she'd been in awe of them, or at least of what they represented. All those Moon women—spinsters to the last—sitting by their fires night after night, scribbling secrets meant only for walkers of the Path. And now, like Moon Girl Farm, they belonged to her.

She found the key right where Althea always kept it, in the drawer of her dressing table. There was a whiff of leather and old paper as she opened the door, and for a moment she caught herself holding her breath, like a child expecting to be caught with her hand in the cookie jar. Except there was no one left to scold her. She ran a finger down the row of ribbed spines, the leather cool against her fingertips, then dropped to her knees and slid the first book free.

The Book of Sabine. The woman who had started it all.

Lizzy turned the pages slowly. The ink had faded to a muted brown, the nib strokes spidery and fine, making them hard to decipher. The mix of English and French hardly helped. Not that she needed to read any of it. She knew it all by heart. Sabine's betrayal by the man she loved, and her flight to avoid persecution. The struggle to survive in a strange land, with an infant daughter on her hip. Her edict that no Moon allow themselves to be enslaved by marriage, lest they be betrayed and the line ended. It was the stuff of family legend, told and retold down through the generations.

She slid the volume back onto the shelf, running an eye over the others. So many Moons, each with a story to tell. *Patrice*, the first Moon girl born on US soil. *Renée*, the only Moon to have ever produced a son. The poor thing had lived only a handful of hours, unlike his twin sister, *Dorothée*, who had managed to thrive. Whispers about the boy's death had persisted throughout Renée's life. *Sylvie*, who'd scandalized the town by living openly and unabashedly with a woman named Rachel Conklin. *Aurore*, who had shocked the neighbors with her daily walks in the woods, wearing nothing but her shoes. *Honoré*, who after four stillborn girls had finally given birth to Althea at age forty-four. And of course, the most recent addition, *The Book of Althea*.

They were all there—plus one more. Lizzy frowned at the final volume, not black like the others but a deep-wine calfskin, embossed with flowers and vines. She had never seen it before. Was it possible Rhanna had left a book behind after all? It would be just like her to break with tradition and use such a vividly colored book, one final gesture of defiance.

What kinds of things might her mother have recorded? An apology, perhaps, for her reckless behavior and poor choices over the years? Lizzy doubted it. Remorse had never been Rhanna's strong suit. Still, she was curious.

She pulled the odd volume from the shelf and laid it in her lap. The book was thick and oddly lumpy, fastened with a small brass hasp. Lizzy flicked it open and folded back the cover, expecting to see her mother's round, backward-slanting hand. Instead, she found a square of folded waxed paper tucked between the cover and first page. She teased open the folds, surprised to discover a carefully pressed sprig of rosemary. She blinked at it, then looked down at the open page and the tidy script running across the top—Althea's script.

Rosemary . . . for remembrance.

My dearest girl,

You must forgive me, dear Lizzy, for the secret I have
kept. I had my reasons for not wanting you to know I
was ill. I didn't want you to come back because of me,
because you felt some sense of duty. I made so many
mistakes with your mother when she was young. I was
determined to make her honor my path instead of her
own, when I of all people should have known better.
I never wanted to put that kind of burden on you. I
wanted you to be free to spread your wings—and fly
home only if that's where your heart led you. If you're
reading this, perhaps it has.

My Circle will close soon—as all Circles must—
but there is time yet, and so I have picked up my pen.
Because it is our way to teach, to reach back into history and pull out what should always be remembered.
We must never forget who we are. How far we've
come, and what we've had to endure at the hands of
those who fear what they do not understand.

You know Sabine's story, that she came from France, alone, with a child in her belly, fleeing the authorities. But it wasn't for any crime that they wanted her. It was for what she believed and the Path she walked. It wasn't long after the burning times, and there were some—many in fact—who held tight to their superstitions. They were useful, you see, trotted out now and then, against women who dared to speak up, and claim what was rightfully theirs.

This was how it was for Sabine. Her lover was engaged to marry another. When he learned about the child, he denounced her, accusing her of unspeakable things. A warrant was sworn. They would not have burned her. Such things had ended by then. But they would have made a case against her, for indecency or thievery, or some other thing. And they would have arrested her—or worse. And so she fled and began again. She learned to do for herself and her child. Without a man, and without a care for the opinion of others, depending on her farm and her gifts to make her way in the world. And she passed on those gifts— her knowledge of herbs and healing—and made her place in the world helping others.

That is who we are, Lizzy.

Fighters. Mothers. Healers.

There will always be those who are afraid, who will make up stories to cover their fear. They'll point fingers and call names. And yes, they'll lie. But we can't let that change who we are, or dim the light that is in us.

You were such a clever child, so bright and obser-vant. You never missed a thing. And that nose of yours. You were special, gifted in a way your mother never was—in ways I never was, come to that. I knew it early on, could see it shining out of you long before you knew yourself. And then, when you began to suspect, you fought it. You wanted a life that looked like everyone else's. Pony rides and Christmas trees, sleepovers with girlfriends. I can hardly blame you for that. Salem Creek isn't an easy place to be different. And there's nothing on earth quite so cruel as a child who's discovered someone is uncomfortable in her skin. I don't imagine your mother's escapades helped matters either, always kicking up some fuss or other in hopes of drawing attention to herself. She never cared that it drew attention to you too. Attention you never wanted.

You preferred being alone. You had your books and your oils and your perfumes. And you pretended it was enough. It wasn't, though, and that was hard to see. You were so beautiful, but you were always hiding, trying to make yourself invisible.

And then . . . those poor girls.

It was an agony to know the people of this town thought me capable of such a thing. Murder. Why? What would I have to gain by taking the lives of two beautiful young girls? But there's no reasoning with people once an idea takes root. The whispers caught fire, and that was that. But it was harder still to watch what all their talk did to you. Every day, I saw you pull away a little more, knowing there was nothing I could do. And then when your mother left, I saw how badly you wanted to go too, to be away from it all.

I didn't blame you—will never blame you—for leaving for school. You've grown into a special woman, just as I knew you would, living the life you've carved out for yourself. I'm so proud of you for that—for making your own way in the world.

You're like Sabine in that way. You have her will and her strength. I was not so strong when I was young. I fell in line and walked the path already paved for me, too timid to stray, to find a way to be both what I wanted and what was expected of me. I hadn't your spirit back then, though I sometimes wish I had. So much becomes clear when looking over one's shoulder. I have no regrets, or if I do, they're few, and faded with time. But I understand now that there are an infinite number of paths in this life. Some are well traveled, others must be forged. But none should be walked with a guilty or bitter heart.

Which is why I've written this second book—a Book of Remembrances—not for posterity, but for you, my Lizzy. So you will remember how things were before it all went wrong—the happy times we shared when you were a child, the lessons I taught you, and your love of the land. Those things will always be your heritage. And so I ask you to read the remaining pages, but to do so slowly, as I taught you to do when you were young and hungry to know too much all at once. Absorb the words a little at a time, and hold them close. Then come back to the book when you are ready. Trust me in this, sweet girl. You will know when it's time.

A—

FOUR

Lizzy swam up slowly from sleep, fully dressed beneath the softly worn quilt she must have pulled over herself during the night. She hadn't bothered to change clothes, or even to go looking for sheets. She had simply curled up on the bare mattress with Althea's book and started to read.

The Book of Remembrances.

Even now, after her death, Althea was still teaching, reminding her who she was and where she'd come from. But there had been one passage in particular that had struck her in a way she hadn't expected. So much so that she'd gone back and read it over several times.

I was not so strong when I was young. I fell in line and walked the path already paved for me, too timid to stray, to find a way to be both what I wanted and what was expected of me. I hadn't your spirit back then, though I sometimes wish I had.

Had she imagined the tinge of regret? A wistfulness for something lost or left undone? It was hard to imagine Althea wanting anything more than the life she had. She always seemed to be right where she belonged, in love with her work and the bright, sprawling fields of Moon Girl Farm. And yet her reference to *falling in line* seemed to hint at a disappointment of some kind. And there was the mention of *a bitter heart*, though that was easier to explain. If being branded a murderer and losing everything you held precious wasn't cause for a bitter heart, Lizzy didn't know what was.

The book sat on the nightstand. Lizzy laid a hand on the cover, wondering what else Althea had to say. The temptation to keep reading last night had been almost overpowering, but she had been urged to *absorb the words a little at a time, and hold them close.* And because it was the last request her grandmother would ever make of her, she would honor it.

She went to the door and peered out into the hall. There was no sign of Evvie, but she did find a folded pair of soft green corduroys, a white cotton blouse, and a pair of battered lace-up boots. She smiled as she ran a hand over the scuffed boots, strangely glad to see them, like old friends she'd left behind but not quite forgotten. She had to admit, it would feel good to lose the heels and office attire for a few days.

After a quick shower, she made her way downstairs. Evvie was seated at the table, scanning the morning's copy of the *Chronicle* through a pair of bright-blue drugstore readers. She twitched the corner of her paper down as Lizzy entered the kitchen, giving her outfit a quick once-over.

"Better," she said flatly. "Like you belong here."

"Thanks. Is there coffee, by any chance?"

"Just tea," Evvie said, retreating behind her paper. "And a plate of eggs in the oven."

Lizzy didn't have the heart to tell Evvie she usually skipped breakfast. Or that she didn't function particularly well without her morning coffee. She pulled the plate from the oven, eyeing the mound of scrambled eggs and home fries with dismay. It was more food than she was used to eating in a day, let alone for breakfast.

Evvie eyed her with raised brows. "You don't eat eggs?"

"No, I do. I just don't usually eat breakfast. And this is a *lot* of breakfast."

"Hmmm." Evvie looked her up and down again. "Could do with a bit of meat on your bones, if you ask me. Don't they feed you in New York?"

Lizzy let the remark pass, opting to change the subject as she sat down with her plate. "Tell me your story, Evvie. How you met my grandmother and ended up living here."

Evvie plucked the readers from the end of her nose and laid them on the table. "My bees."

"Bees?"

"Look out the window."

Lizzy craned her neck to peer out the back window. It took a few seconds, but eventually she spotted a trio of pastel-hued boxes to the left of Althea's greenhouse. Apiaries, she believed they were called. "You raise bees?"

"Don't raise 'em. Just look after 'em. I make jewelry too. Bracelets mostly."

Lizzy nodded, trying to imagine what taking care of bees might entail, then realized Evvie hadn't actually answered the question. "What have bees got to do with my grandmother?"

Evvie pushed back from the table, crossed to the stove, and put the kettle on. "My sister," she said, pulling a mug from the cupboard. "Can't remember why now, but she was up here a few years back and stumbled onto your gran's shop. When she came home, it was all she could talk about, the kinds of things she made and how special it all was—how special *she* was. So I wrote to her about putting some of my honey in her shop, and she said yes. After that, we wrote back and forth." She paused, smiling wistfully. "That woman loved a good letter."

Lizzy smiled too. "Yes, she did."

Evvie reached for the kettle as it began to whistle. When she had finished brewing the tea, she carried two mugs back to the table and produced a small jar of honey from her apron pocket. "Moon Girl Farm Honey," she said proudly. "From right out back."

Lizzy accepted the jar, stirring a spoonful into her mug as Evvie settled back into her chair. "You were telling me how you got to the farm."

"Two years ago, she invited me for a visit." She paused, shrugging as she spooned a hefty dollop of honey into her own mug. "I never went back."

"Back where?"

"Baton Rouge."

"But the accent—it's not just Southern. There's something else."

"*Kréyol la lwizyàn,*" Evvie pronounced over the rim of her mug. "Creole. My mama's people came from the West Indies."

"Do you still have family there? In Baton Rouge, I mean."

Evvie shook her head. "Not anymore. My sister remarried. Moved to Texas, of all places. Then my husband passed. Wasn't much reason to stay after that." Her face darkened briefly, and she looked away. "So here I am with my bees and my beads, getting on with what time I have left. And you—why are you here? The real reason. Last night you said there were some personal things you wanted to take care of, but I expect there's more to it than that."

Lizzy looked at her barely touched breakfast. She'd been hoping to keep her plans to herself awhile longer, until she had a firmer grip on the logistics, but under the circumstances that didn't seem fair. Evvie deserved to know what was coming, so she could make plans.

"I'm here to put the farm on the market," she said quietly. "I'm going to sell it."

"I figured as much."

"It isn't about the money, Evvie. There's just no reason for me to hold on to it. I know what Althea wanted, but what would I do with a farm?"

"Same as she did. Grow things. Make things. Help folks."

"I already have a job—one I worked hard to earn—and it's in New York."

Evvie folded her hands on the table, lips pursed, as if deliberating what to say next. "Your gran told me about you," she said finally. "How you were something special. She couldn't stop bragging about you—not just your gifts, but who you were and what you'd made of yourself. You had a dream, and you chased it. She was proud of you for that, even if it did mean leaving her. She knew you had some things to work out, but she never lost faith that you *would* work them out one day. And that you'd be back."

Lizzy set down her mug, determined to make herself clear. "Yes, I'm back, but not the way you mean. There's nothing for me here."

Evvie grunted, a sound Lizzy was starting to recognize as skepticism. "You came all this way just to stick a sign in the ground, and then scurry back to New York?"

Lizzy didn't like the word *scurry*, but couldn't argue with the premise of the question. "Yes. Mostly."

"You have someone there?"

"*Have* someone?"

"Someone," Evvie repeated. "Someone who makes you soup when you're sick, holds your hand when you're sad. Someone who *means* something."

Lizzy considered lying, but knew better than to think she could get anything past Evvie. "No. I don't have anyone who fixes me soup."

But then that was the deal she'd struck with herself. No one to fix her soup also meant no one to ask awkward questions about her family, or wanting things she wasn't free to give. No strings. No hassles. No baring her soul. She'd never learned the art of opening up to another person. Alone was what she'd learned instead, and what she'd gotten good at. Alone was safe.

"I'm too busy for a relationship right now," she told Evvie evenly.

Evvie responded with another grunt.

The gesture irked Lizzy. "I know you and Althea were friends," she said, pushing back her plate. "But there are things you don't understand about the Moons. We're not like other people. We don't do the whole love-and-marriage thing."

"That right?"

"Yes, that's right. I don't expect you to understand—"

Evvie stood, collecting Lizzy's abandoned plate. "I understand more than you think. I also hear what you're *not* saying—that this is none of my business."

"No," Lizzy shot back. "That's not what I'm saying. I'm saying there are things you don't know. Things we don't talk about."

Evvie clamped her lips tight, swallowing whatever she'd been about to say. "How long you planning to stay?"

Lizzy was both surprised and relieved that Evvie had changed the subject. She'd already said more than she should about the Moons. "I don't know yet. A week, maybe. I thought I'd walk the property this morning and get a feel for what needs to be done before I can list with a Realtor."

Evvie scowled as she placed the empty plate in the sink. "Almost forgot. There's a man coming by later to do some work on your gran's greenhouse. It's in awful shape, but he swears he can fix it."

"Does that really make sense? Spending money on repairs when the new owners will probably just knock it down?"

"Probably not, but your gran set it up before she died. She loved that greenhouse."

"I know she did," Lizzy said somberly, opting to let the matter drop. "Thanks for breakfast. I'll be back in a bit."

Lizzy stepped out the back door and headed for the greenhouse, as good a place as any to begin her tour. Evvie's assessment of its condition had been generous at best. Several of the glass panes were cracked; others were missing entirely. Inside, the tables were mostly bare, strewn here and there with rusty tools and stacks of empty clay pots. In one corner, several bags of potting soil had split open, spilling their contents onto the packed earth floor.

She walked the lavender fields next, or what remained of them. Hidcote, Grosso, Folgate, Lavance. They had all grown here once upon a time—Althea's pride and joy. Now, only stunted patches of green remained, leggy and budless after too many untended winters. The sight made her heart sink. Why hadn't Althea picked up the phone and asked for help?

The question quickly segued to another. *Would* she have come? If Althea had in fact picked up the phone, would she have dropped everything and returned to the farm? She wanted to believe the answer was yes, but she couldn't help wondering. The truth was she'd never considered such a scenario, preferring to pretend Althea would live forever, because anything else was simply unthinkable.

She arrived at the apple orchard a short time later to find that it had fared only slightly better. While the trees themselves seemed not to have suffered, the ground was riddled with last year's fruit, left to decay where it had fallen, luring swarms of greedy yellow jackets. A small wooden shed stood beyond the last row of the trees, its shingled roof sagging and green with moss. In better days, it had been used to store bushel baskets and picking poles for the locals who would descend each fall to pick their own apples—back before the Gilman girls went missing.

Strangely enough, speculation about Althea's role in the disappearance had initially been a boon for business, luring curiosity seekers eager to purchase a vial of lavender oil in exchange for a glimpse of the woman suspected of murdering two teenage girls. For nearly three weeks speculation grew and the money had poured in. For those who knew Althea, locals who'd come to trust her remedies and charms over the years, the talk seemed ludicrous. But even they began to doubt when the swollen bodies of Heather and Darcy Gilman were recovered from the pond and zipped into heavy black bags. Overnight, the avalanche of customers slowed to a trickle. Eight years later, the memories were still fresh, a wound that had never quite scarred over. But how could it when the questions continued to fester?

Lizzy turned away from the orchard, heading for the woods and the trail Althea had walked nearly every day. She had made it a point to spend time among the trees every morning. Her prayer time, she'd called it, which made sense. The woods had been her temple, sacred in a way no stone edifice could ever be. But she would never walk here again, never forage for mushrooms and wild herbs, never return from her walk with some feather, or bird's nest, or bit of horn she'd discovered along the way.

A warm breeze suddenly shivered through the trees. Lizzy lifted her nose, catching the unmistakable scents of lavender and bergamot. It was only a whiff, the kind that clings to scarves and sweaters long after the wearer has shed them, but the sensation was so palpable that it felt like an actual presence, and for an instant she half expected to turn and find her grandmother standing behind her with an old willow trug tucked into the crook of her arm.

It was just wishful thinking, wasn't it? Sensing a loved one's presence after they were gone? Believing they were still nearby, watching over those they held dear? She'd heard of such things, everyone had, but she'd always chalked them up to grief. Now she wasn't so sure. What she'd just experienced—a fleeting but bone-deep certainty that she wasn't alone—was hard to dismiss. And she wasn't sure she wanted to.

Lizzy forced her feet to move, knowing all at once exactly where she was going—perhaps where she'd always intended to go.

∾

Lizzy slowed as she caught her first glimpse of the pond. The last time she saw it, there were policemen in wet suits and divers' masks crawling through the cattails and common reed along its banks. But before that—before the Gilman girls and the body bags—her mother had come here to swim during the sticky New England summers. Once, she had even been invited to tag along.

It was one of the rare times—perhaps the *only* time—Rhanna had invited her anywhere, and for a few brief weeks, Lizzy had been foolish enough to think things between them might change, that at long last Rhanna was ready to actually *be* her mother, instead of leaving those duties to Althea. But that was the summer Rhanna abruptly stopped swimming, and that had been the end of that. She left a few weeks later.

Not that she'd been surprised. It was always Rhanna's way, to live her life in fits and starts. She'd never had any real roots to Moon Girl Farm. Staying had merely been the path of least resistance—three meals a day and a roof over her head, and the freedom to come and go as she pleased. She had steered clear of the day-to-day work of the farm, choosing to busk on street corners instead, crooning folk ballads for whatever passersby might toss into her battered guitar case, or to read cards at the downtown market, wearing a head scarf and enormous hoop earrings. It had never earned her much, but it kept her in cheap booze or whatever else she happened to be into, and for Rhanna that had been enough.

Lizzy shrugged off the memories and inched closer to the bank. The ground felt spongy, the damp grass slick under the soles of her boots, and for a moment she imagined herself skidding headlong into the reeds. She dug in her heels, unwilling to go closer, her arms hugged tight to her body as she gazed past the reeds to the shiny-dark water beyond.

It had never been very deep. Just deep enough.

The thought brought a shiver and the sudden chill of memory. Sodden hair dark with mud and a tangle of slimy weeds, a face rendered unrecognizable by weeks in the water. That was the Moons' legacy now—those girls and that day. And it would continue to be their legacy, as long as there was one person alive who remembered it.

Harm none.

It was their creed, and one her grandmother had taken very seriously. It was why they were vegetarian, because *harm none* meant animals too. How could anyone think her capable of harming two young girls?

Lizzy squeezed her eyes shut, remembering the moment WKSN news had broken into the season finale of *The Good Wife* to report that two local girls had gone missing, and that police suspected foul play. No one could have predicted what happened next. How events would unfold to implicate an innocent woman, to rob her of friends, livelihood—and eventually her family. A guilty verdict without a trial.

How had her grandmother lived with it?

Worse still—how had she died with it? Knowing there would always be some who chose to believe the whispers? In her *Book of Remembrances*, Althea had written of the Moon line, of her fear that it would soon be broken. Couldn't she see that it was *already* broken? That there was nothing to salvage, no way to clean up the story Salem Creek had already written?

You're all that's left now, the last and best of us.

The words returned to taunt Lizzy. She might be the last, but she certainly wasn't the best. If she were, she wouldn't be in such a hurry to be rid of Moon Girl Farm. She'd stay and make things right. Fight to clear Althea's name. But was that even possible?

As far as she knew, the police had failed to come up with a single viable lead, content in the absence of any real evidence to let the court of public opinion decide. And the public—or most of it at any rate—had been only too happy to oblige. That there'd been no trial, no conviction, no sentence, was immaterial. People knew what they knew, and that was that.

But if it was true that there would always be someone who remembered the day the Gilman girls came out of the water, it might also be true that someone, somewhere, remembered the day they'd gone into it. Perhaps someone who knew something they didn't realize they knew. And maybe that was reason enough to try.

FIVE

Andrew Greyson stepped over the low stone wall separating his family's land from the Moons', determined to finally begin the greenhouse repairs he'd promised to start nearly six months ago. He hated that Althea had died before he could make good on his promise, but winter had gone on forever, and then there'd been a backlog of renovation clients that needed placating. He thought there'd be more time—she'd always been such a tough old bird—but things had gone quickly at the end, which he supposed was a blessing.

And yet here he was, toolbox in hand. Because a promise was a promise, especially one made to a dying woman. And Althea wasn't just any woman; she'd been part of his life for as long as he could remember, going back to the weekends he'd spent at the farm, helping his father, who, when not running the local hardware store, had enjoyed playing handyman. When Andrew moved back from Chicago four years ago and found his father in failing health, it had seemed natural that he'd step in as Moon Girl Farm's handyman.

There wasn't much he hadn't patched or mended over the years. He knew every inch of the place: every leaky faucet, rickety gate, and tricky fireplace flue, not to mention the groaning furnace and fritzy wiring.

He'd done his best over the years to help hold the place together, but two hundred years of damp springs and snowy winters had taken an inevitable toll, meaning long-term repairs needed to happen sooner rather than later. Unfortunately, they wouldn't be cheap, and although Althea had never said so directly, he suspected money was scarce.

It would be sold eventually, perhaps as a fixer-upper, though as an architect specializing in the renovation of historic properties, his advice would be to raze it all to the ground and start from scratch. And yet the thought rankled. Something about the place—its history and its secrets—had gotten under his skin as a boy, and had never quite let go of him.

Okay, not something—someone.

Elzibeth Moon.

Lizzy.

She'd been part of his life for years too, though that particular street ran in only one direction. Nearly twenty years later he could still see her, emerging from the woods in a shower of autumn leaves, her dark hair caught on the wind, like something from another world, and so damn beautiful she'd made his throat ache. Until that moment he'd had only a vague awareness of her, the memory of a young girl peeling apples in her grandmother's kitchen, all knees and elbows and enormous gray eyes. And then that day in the woods, when he realized the skinny little girl had become a young woman of strange and startling beauty.

She'd gone still at the sight of him, eyeing him like a skittish colt. There'd been a flash of something quick and sharp as their eyes locked. Recognition? Defiance? All these years later he still couldn't say. The encounter hadn't lasted long—the space of a few heartbeats—but in those few taut moments, without so much as a word or a nod, she had bewitched him. And had then proceeded to treat him as if he were invisible. At school, in town, even at the farm, she'd gone out of her way to steer clear of him. And who could blame her, when he'd stood there staring like a lovesick calf?

It wasn't until she left for school that he'd finally taken his father's advice to *stop mooning over that girl and go live up to your potential*. And so he'd packed his car and headed to grad school. He'd done well for himself too, graduating top of his class with a job waiting at one of the most prestigious architectural firms in Chicago. But the Windy City had quickly lost its shine, and when his father finally came clean about the cancer, returning to Salem Creek had been a no-brainer.

He had assumed Lizzy would do the same when Althea got sick, but she hadn't. He got it, sort of. She'd never been comfortable in Salem Creek, and the witch hunt that had ensued when the Gilman girls disappeared certainly hadn't helped. He was a Granite Stater down to his bones, but he wasn't blind to the sometimes priggish beliefs of small New England towns, or the damage those beliefs could do when turned on an entire family.

The last he heard she was in New York, making perfume. Good for her, if she was happy. God knows she deserved it after all the crap she'd endured.

He'd been walking mindlessly, lost in his memories, but now, as he approached the place where the path forked off to the right, he registered the crunch of footsteps. He halted, turning toward the sound. For one addled moment, he entertained the possibility that he had stumbled through some sort of time warp, that the years had rewound themselves, hurtling him back to that chance meeting so many years ago. His next thought was that he'd lost his grip on reality. It wasn't until she turned to face him that he realized she was actually there, staring back at him as if no time had passed at all. His breath caught as their gazes locked, as if he'd just been sucker punched. Was it any wonder people believed what they did about the Moon girls?

SIX

Lizzy went still as she approached the fork in the path, startled by what she assumed was a squirrel scurrying about in the underbrush. She peered through the trees, scanning left, then right, as the sound drew closer. She saw him then—Andrew Greyson—coming through the trees, wearing jeans and heavy work boots, carrying a battered red toolbox.

Her breath caught as their eyes locked and an eerie sense of déjà vu crept over her. What was he doing here? Now? Again?

She eyed the toolbox in his right hand. Evvie had said someone would be coming by to repair the greenhouse. That it turned out to be Andrew Greyson shouldn't really surprise her. He'd been a kind of fixture around the farm when they were kids, and even at school, always turning up at awkward moments, like some jock in shining armor, always bent on rescuing her, whether she wanted him to or not.

There was the time he'd ambushed her at homecoming assembly. She'd been sitting by herself, as usual, when he dropped down beside her, grinning goofily as he held out an open pack of Twizzlers. Every eye in the gym had suddenly fixed on them. At least that's how it felt at the time. She'd wanted to crawl under her seat. Instead, to the delight of his jock pals, sitting two rows up, she'd bolted. Unfortunately, it hadn't deterred him. He kept turning up, tagging along with his father when he came to repair a faucet or a bit of fencing, appearing out of nowhere to offer her a ride home when the sky opened up one day and rained pea-size hail all over Salem Creek. And then the night at the fountain, when Rhanna had made a drunken spectacle of herself in front of the whole town, he had turned up again, to rescue her from the hecklers. It still baffled her. He'd been one of the hottest guys in school, honor student, captain of the football team, the clichéd big man on campus. She couldn't imagine what he'd want with someone like her. Maybe it was pity. Or curiosity. The Moons were nothing if not curious.

And now, here he was again.

He was taller than she remembered, and harder somehow, but still ridiculously good-looking—his russet hair cropped close to his head, his face lean and tanned. The last time Althea mentioned him, he was in Chicago, designing swanky homes for well-heeled corporate types. But that was before his father died. Was he here to stay then, or had he merely returned as she had, to tie up loose ends?

"Hello," he said stiffly. "You might not remember me. I'm—"

"Andrew. From next door."

He nodded, shifting the toolbox from his right hand to his left. "I didn't know you were back. I'm sorry about your grandmother. I know you used to be close."

Lizzy bristled at the suggestion that that was no longer the case. "We were still close."

"Right. I didn't mean—"

"She wrote me that your father died. I'm sorry. I remember him being a nice man. Nice to Althea."

"Yes, he was, and thank you. I was on my way over to do some work on the greenhouse."

"Evvie said you'd be by. Well, not you, but someone."

An awkward silence spooled out as the small talk dried up. Andrew shifted the toolbox again and took a step forward, as if planning to accompany her back to the house. Lizzy turned away, heading down the path at a clip. She had a decision to make, and she didn't want company. Andrew Greyson's least of all.

Back at the house, she found Evvie seated at the kitchen table, surrounded by saucers filled with an assortment of colorful beads. She was stringing a necklace, threading a series of marbled blue spheres onto a thin leather cord. After a moment, she looked up.

"How was your walk?"

"You said someone was coming to work on the greenhouse. You didn't say it was Andrew Greyson."

Evvie shrugged. "Didn't think it mattered." She peered at the beads she'd just strung, adjusting several before looking up. "*Does* it matter?"

"I was just surprised to see him. I didn't know he was back."

"Almost three years now. Came back when his daddy got sick, and never left. Truth be told, I think he was looking for a reason."

"A reason?"

"He knew where he belonged. Chicago never really agreed with him. Salem Creek did. Simple as that. How was your walk?"

Lizzy blinked at her. She had a habit of doing that, changing the subject so abruptly you weren't sure you'd been following the actual thread of the conversation. "I ended up at the pond," she said quietly. "Seeing it again, after all these years, started me thinking. All the hideous things people said, the things they believed . . . I can't help wondering if that's why Althea got sick. Maybe she just . . . gave up."

Evvie laid down her cord of beads and shot a look over her glasses. "Your gran never gave up on a thing in her life."

"You weren't here, Evvie. You can't imagine what it was like, the way people looked at her after they pulled those girls up out of the water. And the worst part is nothing's happened to change their minds. The people who believed it then still believe it."

"Maybe. But there's nothing to be done about it now. Once folks make up their minds, there's not much chance of changing them. Not without proof."

"What if there *was* proof?"

Evvie lifted her head. "Where are you going with this, little girl?"

Lizzy scooped a bead from the saucer, letting it roll against the flat of her hand, deep sea-blue flecked with gold pyrite, like a tiny world resting in her palm. *Lapis lazuli, for revealing hidden truths.* She dropped the bead back into the saucer and met Evvie's gaze.

"Last night you asked me why I was here, and I said I came back to handle Althea's personal effects, but the truth is I wasn't planning to come at all. Then I found a note from Althea tucked into the journal you sent me. She said I was the best of the Moons, and that there were things that needed mending. Maybe that's why I'm here—to mend things."

"Mending things," Evvie repeated thoughtfully. "What does that look like?"

Leave it to Evvie to jump straight to the thorny part of the equation. "I don't know, exactly. But there's got to be something I can do, some way to find out what really happened, and clear Althea's name."

Evvie slid her glasses off, a crease between her brows. "You think so?"

"I don't know, but it's worth a try. Eight years isn't that long. Someone in this town knows something, maybe something they don't realize they know. Asking questions might jog some memories."

"Might jog a lot of things."

Lizzy glowered at her. "What does that mean?"

"It means there are two sides to every sword. You'll be digging those girls up for everyone to look at all over again. Folks might not take kindly to that."

"Maybe not, but I can't tiptoe around the truth because it might make someone uncomfortable. I did that once. I stuck my head in the sand and let this town bully my grandmother. I'm not doing that again."

Evvie smothered a snort. "Your gran said you were feisty. She wasn't lying."

"Do you think I'm wrong?"

"No, I don't. In fact, I know you're dead right. But what you're talking about—poking around, asking a lot of questions—could get messy, and the odds of getting at the truth are pretty low."

"I know. But when I leave here, I'll at least be able to say I tried."

Evvie returned her glasses to the end of her nose and picked up the half-strung thong of beads. "Any idea where you might start?"

Lizzy blew out a long breath, mulling the question seriously for the first time. "I hadn't really gotten that far, but I suppose the police station is as good a place as any. I need to get a sense of where the police left things, and how open Chief Summers might be to reopening the investigation."

"Him," Evvie grunted.

"I know. Good luck getting any help on that front. But I need to try. I'll go tomorrow—before I lose my nerve."

"Your gran would be proud."

Lizzy's throat tightened. How she wanted to believe that. "Would she?"

Evvie reached across the table to give her fingers a squeeze. "Don't you ever doubt it."

~

Lizzy had plenty to think about as she slipped out the mudroom door with a pair of secateurs in her pocket and a basket over her arm. Evvie was right. Things would get messy when people found out she was back, and intent on raking up the murders.

Salem Creek had always prided itself on its reputation, proud to be dubbed a "true slice of Americana" by *Yankee* magazine, and perennially named to *New England Journal*'s "Best Tiny Towns" list. But a pair of dead girls had put an end to that. She couldn't imagine the locals being particularly happy to be reminded of Salem Creek's abrupt fall from grace—or that the blame had been laid squarely at her grandmother's door. But now that the idea of clearing Althea's name had taken root, there was no walking away. There were broken things that needed mending—and no one left but her to see to them.

As she crossed the yard, she spotted Andrew down on one knee in front of the greenhouse, rooting through his toolbox. He lifted his head. Their eyes met briefly. Lizzy looked away, quickening her pace on the way to what remained of Althea's wildflower garden. She'd spotted a few blooms among the weeds and thought it might be nice to bring a few inside.

The pickings were slim, not enough for a full arrangement, but they would do for a few small jars on the kitchen sill. She foraged through the overgrowth, gathering speedwell and crane's-bill, wild clary and musk mallow, dropping the blooms into her basket. She would have liked a few cornflowers—the deep blue would be a nice contrast to the pinks and fuchsias—but there were none to be had.

It made her sad to see this particular garden so neglected. Althea had always had a particular affinity for wildflowers, perhaps because they gave so much and asked so little. For those on the Path—often dubbed pagans by the uninitiated—everything was sentient, fully aware of its role in the divine circle of birth, growth, life, and death. Althea had taken comfort in that, in the tides and seasons that made up their year, the belief that nothing was wasted or useless, that everything had a time and a purpose, and when that time was over, that purpose fulfilled, their essence lived on, and embraced some new purpose.

It was why the Moons chose to scatter their ashes on their own land, so that a part of them would always live on in the soil. Lizzy had never given much thought to the custom but took comfort in the knowledge that Althea had become an enduring part of the ground beneath her feet. Still, she deserved better than a dismal patch of weed-choked earth.

54

She ran an eye around the garden. It wouldn't take much, a few hours and a handful of tools. Maybe it was silly—like Andrew repairing the greenhouse—but it felt right somehow, a labor of love for the woman who had raised her when her mother couldn't be bothered.

Before Lizzy could talk herself out of it, she was crossing the field toward the drying barn, where Althea kept an assortment of rakes and spades. She dragged the crossbar from its bracket and yanked at the door. It gave finally, with a rusty groan. She stepped inside, inhaling the ghosts of a thousand harvested flowers. They were gone now, the drying racks and screen frames all empty, but their memories remained, hovering like spirits in the cool, dry air.

It took a few seconds for her eyes to adjust, but eventually she was able to make out shapes in the gloom. The tools she had come for hung just inside the door, but she ignored them, moving instead to the long wooden counter along the back wall, where she used to make her perfumes.

It was an amateur's work space, a dusty collection of borrowed supplies and makeshift equipment, but seeing it again made her strangely nostalgic. The truth was she missed those early days of trial and error, the delicious serendipity of discovering something new and utterly unexpected. There weren't many surprises at Chenier. In fact, she rarely set foot in a lab these days, spending the bulk of her time on conference calls or in meetings, collaborating with people who didn't know a floral from an oriental.

Lizzy pushed the thought aside. She'd been incredibly lucky to catch the eye of Jaqueline Chenier straight out of school, and land a job most thought her too young and inexperienced to handle. She should be grateful—and she was. She *absolutely* was. But she'd be lying if she said there wasn't a certain wistfulness to being back in the barn.

Tools, she reminded herself sternly as she stepped away from the counter. She'd come for tools, not a walk down memory lane. She grabbed a pitchfork and was reaching for a hoe when a shadow darkened the doorway. She turned, startled to find Andrew silhouetted in the opening.

"You shouldn't be in here."

She stared at him, pulse skittering. "That's the second time you've snuck up on me today."

"I didn't sneak up on you—then or now. And I'd appreciate it if you'd put that thing down. You're making me nervous."

Lizzy glanced down at the pitchfork she was holding, dismayed to find it pointing straight at Andrew, as if she were preparing to run him through. She lowered it slowly, annoyed with herself for being so skittish. "Did you need something?"

"Yes, I need you to come out of there, please. It isn't safe."

Lizzy performed a quick scan of the barn, finding nothing that looked remotely hazardous. "What do you mean, it's not safe? It looks fine."

"Well, for starters, this door is about to come off its hinges. You're lucky it didn't flatten you when you opened it. And there"—he paused, pointing to the apex of the roof, where a slice of sunlight was visible through a chink in the boards—"we had a storm back in April, pulled up part of the roof, and damaged several trusses. Plus, the loft and stairs are ready to give. That's not from the storm, just good old-fashioned dry rot. New England barns are built to last, but not forever. Also, we had a colony of bats last summer, and they tend to come back."

Lizzy eyed him as she edged toward the door. He smelled of amber and sandalwood, of crisp fall days with the hint of smoke underneath. The combination caught her off guard—not flagrant, but subtly masculine, nudging at memories she preferred to keep buried. He had always smelled like that. Always.

She tipped her head back, noting the smear of caulk in his hair as she sidled past. "Bats don't scare me. In fact, I find them rather cute. But I draw the line at collapsing roofs."

Andrew followed her out, easing the door closed behind him. "It's on the list."

"The list?"

"Things I promised your grandmother I'd do. I wanted to get them done before . . ." He looked away, shoulders hunched. "I ran out of time."

Lizzy swallowed the sudden lump in her throat. "Me too."

"She was quite a lady, your grandmother. I had just started working when my father was diagnosed. I was new to the firm and had just landed this big project, so he kept it to himself. Didn't say a word about being sick until the very end. But your grandmother knew—or guessed. She cooked for him and kept the house clean, drove him to treatments, and made him this special tea to ease the nausea. Stubborn old goat. I didn't find out until the doctors pulled the plug on his chemo. But Althea was there for all of it. I owe her for that."

Lizzy managed a fleeting smile, a mix of pride and grief. "Althea didn't tell me she was sick either. I didn't find out until she was gone."

"I wondered why you didn't come to see her. I'm sorry. I know it's hard. I was furious with my father for not telling me, but he honestly thought keeping me in the dark was the right thing to do. Your grandmother must have thought so too."

Lizzy pretended to study the barn door, eager to change the subject. "It's nice of you to want to help, but the new owners will probably have their own ideas about what to fix."

Andrew stiffened. "You sold the farm?"

"Not yet, but eventually."

His shoulders seemed to relax, though not completely. "Yeah. About that. There are a few things you should know."

"Such as?"

"The place is going to need work before a bank will think twice about financing, and I'm not talking about a coat of paint and some tulips in the window boxes. The house wiring's tricky on a good day, and the plumbing isn't much better. The furnace is hanging by a thread, and every roof on the property needs replacing."

Lizzy stared down at the toes of her boots, registering this unwelcome bit of news. One more complication she hadn't planned for. And couldn't afford. "I had no idea things were that bad. I don't suppose any of that's going to be cheap. I'm not exactly rolling in cash."

Andrew shot her a crooked smile. "I'm afraid not. But I know a guy. Friend of the family. Lives close by. Will work for food and the occasional kind word."

Lizzy squared her shoulders. "Thanks, but I couldn't accept that. A few panes of glass is one thing, but I can't let you rewire the house and redo the plumbing."

"Historic renovation is sort of my thing. Why not let me help?"

Lizzy held up a hand, cutting him off. "No. Thank you. I'll figure something out. Maybe I can find a cash buyer to take the place as is." She lifted her chin, meeting his gaze squarely. "I don't mean to sound callous, but why would you want to waste your time? We hardly know each other."

He offered a half smile and a bit of a shrug. "Because I told your grandmother I would, and a promise is a promise. I owe her."

"You can't owe her. She's gone."

"Then I guess I owe you."

Lizzy found herself at a loss for words. She couldn't help thinking about her conversation with Luc two days ago, his glib assertion that when he inherited Chenier Fragrances, Ltd., he'd inherited her too, as if she were some shiny trinket in his mother's jewelry box. And here was Andrew, telling her a promise he made to Althea was a promise he now owed to her. The contrast was hard to ignore.

"You don't inherit promises," she said quietly. "It doesn't work like that."

He shrugged, smiling again. "My promise. My rules. I'll nail the door shut before I leave, just to be on the safe side. I've got a load of wood coming next week. As soon as I finish the greenhouse, I'll get started on the loft."

"I just told you—there's no money to pay you. And I can't ask you to work for free."

"Your grandmother was a special woman, Lizzy. She had a great big heart, and she used it to take care of people. Not everyone understood that, and toward the end, even the people who knew her forgot it. I'm not one of those people. I'm repairing the greenhouse and the barn for the same reason you're about to carry a pitchfork into that wreck of a garden. I can't bring Althea back, or change how things went down, but I *can* do this for her—I can look after the things she cared about."

Lizzy fought the urge to look away, rattled by the sudden intensity in his voice. Or maybe it was his kindness that made her feel so defensive. He'd been with Althea at the end, where she should have been. He had to have an opinion about that.

"It isn't that I don't care, Andrew. I do. But I can't stay. I know what you think. I know what Evvie thinks too. But I have a job—in New York." She shook her head, hating that she felt the need to defend herself. "Althea *was* Moon Girl Farm. I'm not. That's why I'm selling. Because it should belong to someone who'll love it the way she did."

Andrew scrubbed his knuckles over the stubble along his jaw, as if weighing his next words carefully. "What about Rhanna? She doesn't want it?"

Lizzy stiffened at the mention of her mother's name. "We haven't heard from her in years. I think it's safe to say she isn't interested."

"Sorry. I didn't know. Althea didn't mention her much."

"The last we knew she was in California somewhere, singing for her supper."

And god only knew what else.

She didn't say the last part out loud. She didn't need to. Everyone in town knew Rhanna's story. The drinking and the drugs. The revolving door of one-night stands. The frequent run-ins with police. And

Andrew knew better than most, since he'd seen it firsthand. Lizzy tightened her grip on the pitchfork, trying to fend off the memories. They came anyway.

A crowd at the Dairy Bar on a sticky summer night. Families with children. Kids from school looking for a place to hang out on a Friday night. A ruckus at the back of the line. People scurrying, moving like a school of minnows, across the parking lot and around the corner.

She had followed them, because that's what you did when people started running. When she rounded the corner, there was a police car in front of city hall, blue lights strobing dizzily. A burst of laughter. A smattering of catcalls. A prickle of dread as the crowd peeled apart. And then Rhanna, stripped down to her panties and knee-deep in the fountain, belting out "Me and Bobby McGee" at the top of her lungs.

One of the officers kicked off his shoes and waded in after her, chasing her around in circles until he was red-faced and panting. It had taken a full fifteen minutes, but finally she was hauled from the fountain, high as a kite and still singing as they wrapped her in a blanket and folded her into the squad car. A wave of relief had washed over Lizzy as she watched the black-and-white pull away. The spectacle was over.

Only it wasn't.

There was a boy from school, a football player named Brad or Brett, who spotted her in the crowd. He rounded on her, pointing with an outstretched arm. *Hey, that's her kid! Maybe she's next! What are you gonna sing, sweetheart?* More laughter. More pointing. She had wanted to melt into the pavement then and there, to run, to die. But her feet wouldn't move. And then, out of nowhere, there was a hand on her elbow, steering her through the crowd, down the street, around the corner.

She finally yanked her arm free and stood glaring at her rescuer—the boy from next door, whose father did odd jobs for her grandmother, the guy with the grin and the Twizzlers.

He'd meant to be kind, to spare her from further humiliation, but his face, thinly lit from the streetlamp overhead, was full of pity, and she had hated him for it. She'd told him so too, before leaving him standing alone on the sidewalk.

She'd been humiliated twice that night. The first time by a crowd of jeering onlookers, the second by someone trying to show her kindness. Strangely, it was the latter that stung most, which was why, from that day on, she had redoubled her efforts to avoid him. Growing up a Moon had prepared her for pointing and whispers. Kindness, not so much. And here he was, being kind again, looking at her the way he had that night under the streetlamp, dredging up emotions she'd just as soon not feel.

"I have to go," she said, hoisting the pitchfork up onto her shoulder. "I have things to do."

Let him think what he wanted. If she'd learned anything over the years, it was not to let herself care what anyone else thought. But as she turned and walked away, she couldn't help wondering what he'd think if he knew she was planning to pay the police chief a visit.

SEVEN

July 19

Lizzy drove slowly through Salem Creek's downtown district, strategizing how best to approach Chief Summers. Not much had changed since she'd left, not that she was surprised. Progress came slowly to small New England towns. No malls or big-box centers needed. Which was precisely how the locals liked it. Sleepy streets lined with small mom-and-pop shops, window boxes brimming with geraniums, hand-lettered chalkboards advertising daily specials, and water bowls on the sidewalk for thirsty pups. It was New England charm at its best, even if it did tend toward shabby in places.

But progress hadn't halted completely. There was a new farm-to-table café on the corner of Elm Street, and a bookstore where the dry cleaners used to be. The library had a brand-new addition, and a tattoo parlor named Inky's had taken over the old Cut & Dry Salon.

She turned onto Third Street, lined with a sprawl of redbrick buildings that housed Salem Creek's public safety complex. As expected, the lot in front of the police station was nearly empty. Aside from the odd double homicide, Salem Creek enjoyed a fairly low crime rate.

The desk sergeant glanced up as she pushed through the tinted glass doors. "Can I help you?"

"I was hoping to speak with Chief Summers."

Lizzy glanced at his name badge. Sergeant Oberlin. He was rake thin, all but swimming in his crisp black uniform, his cheeks pocked with recent acne scars. He ran his tongue over his teeth, surveying her with a comical air of self-importance. "Is it regarding a police matter, ma'am?"

"This is the police station, isn't it?"

The sergeant colored slightly. "Yes, ma'am."

"Good. And yes, it is a police matter. It's regarding a murder. Well, two murders, actually."

Oberlin's eyes shot wide. "Murders?"

Lizzy smiled blandly, satisfied that she had his full attention. "It's about an old case—the Gilman murders."

"Can you spell that?"

Lizzy fought the urge to roll her eyes. Before she could respond, a beefy captain with hair the color of steel wool appeared behind the counter. "I've got this, Todd. I'm sorry, Miss . . ."

"Moon," Lizzy supplied. "Elzibeth Moon."

"Yes, of course. Miss Moon. Did I hear you inquiring about the Gilman murders?"

"You did. I'm here to speak with Chief Summers about the investigation."

"The . . . investigation?"

The blank look on the captain's face confirmed what Lizzy already suspected. There *was* no investigation. "Is the police chief in?"

The sergeant cleared his throat, managing a tight smile. "I'm afraid the chief is tied up right now, but if you'll share the nature of your inquiry with me, I'd be happy to pass it along."

"That won't be necessary," Lizzy told him, strolling to the row of plastic chairs along the wall and dropping into one. "I'll wait."

This clearly wasn't the hoped-for response. "But Miss . . . ?"

"Moon," she repeated coolly. "I'm Althea Moon's granddaughter, and I'd appreciate it if you'd tell the chief I'm here to see him at his earliest convenience."

The captain seemed to sense defeat. Lizzy watched him disappear through the same door he'd used to enter, wondering how long he'd be gone before returning with a new excuse. Instead, Randall Summers appeared.

Lizzy stiffened instinctively. He was tall and square, but no longer the well-cut figure he'd been when she left. He was thicker through the middle now, his navy blazer snug across the chest, his khaki slacks worn low, to compensate for a budding paunch. And his hair was a peculiar shade of blond, no doubt straight out of a box purchased at the drugstore. He reminded her of an aging game show host.

"Miss Moon," he said, offering a nicotine-stained smile as he pumped her hand. "No one told me you were back."

She looked up at him, unsmiling. "Should someone have told you?"

"No, I just meant . . . with your grandmother dying, we sort of expected you to turn up. Then when you didn't, we assumed . . ."

He let his words trail, leaving Lizzy to wonder exactly who *we* might be, and what they had assumed. "I only arrived two days ago. I'm here because I have some questions about where the Gilman case stands."

Summers shot her an oily grin. He reeked of breath mints and last night's merlot. "Let's step outside, shall we? I need a smoke, and you can't do that indoors these days."

Lizzy followed him out onto the front walkway. He fished a pack of Marlboro menthols from his jacket pocket, along with a heavy silver lighter, then held the pack out to her.

"No. Thank you. I don't smoke. The Gilman investigation," she prompted when he had taken his first long drag. "Where do things stand?"

Summers looked faintly annoyed as he pushed out a column of smoke. "They don't stand at all, Miss Moon. There is no investigation, as such."

"But you never found the killer."

He threw her a sidelong glance as he took another pull from his cigarette. "No one was ever charged, that's true."

Summers's inference was clear. As far as he was concerned, he *had* found the killer; he just hadn't been able to make the case. Now, with Althea dead, he considered the matter put to bed.

"So that's it? You're done looking?"

He narrowed his eyes on her, his ruddy cheeks more florid than they'd been a moment ago. "It's been eight years since those girls came up out of your grandmother's pond, Miss Moon. Eight years, an anonymous tip, a pair of voodoo dolls, and an empty vial from your grandmother's shop in one of the girl's pockets. That's where we are. No prints, no murder weapon. Just two dead girls and your grandmother's pond. Where else do you suggest we *look*? Or maybe you have a crystal ball we could borrow."

Lizzy held his gaze, unflinching. If he was trying to push her buttons, he was wasting his time. There wasn't a cliché she hadn't heard over the years—and learned to ignore. Nor was she surprised by his attitude. He'd never hidden his belief in Althea's guilt, or his feelings about the Moons in general. Prejudices that were likely greased by his priggish wife, Miriam, who served as organist at the First Congregational Church and had been in the front row of the so-called prayer vigil for Heather and Darcy Gilman, throwing around words like *heathenry* and *godlessness* for the TV cameras.

"Can you tell me the last time you made any kind of inquiries? Spoke to anyone about what they might remember around the time the girls went missing?"

"It's been . . . some time."

"Does that mean months? Years?"

Summers flicked his cigarette into the parking lot and squared his shoulders. "This is Salem Creek, Miss Moon, not New York City. We're a small town, with a small police force, and even smaller coffers. That means we have to pick and choose how we allocate our resources. And if you'll pardon me for being blunt, I have better things to do with those resources than squander them on an eight-year-old case that's every bit as cold as those girls."

Lizzy gaped at him, stunned by his callousness. As far as he was concerned, the Gilman girls were nothing but a case number, something to be checked off a list, a matter of resources spent. She pulled in a breath, counted to ten. She'd come to ask for his assistance. Losing her temper wouldn't help.

"I'm sure it's terrible for you, Chief Summers. But I have no budget. And, as you might guess, I have my own reasons for wanting to know what happened to those girls. I'd like to think that as the chief of police, getting to the truth is just as important to you as it is to me."

"Of course it is. I take my duties to this community very seriously."

"Then you won't mind if I do a little asking around on my own, about what people may remember from that time?"

"As a matter of fact, I do mind." He was simmering now, throwing off the scent of hot metal as he struggled to tamp down his anger. "This town was turned upside down when those girls disappeared. It was like a circus. Media crawling all over the place, talking about serial killers and god knows what else. It was five years before you could sell a piece of property in this town. And don't pretend you don't know what I mean, because we both know you do. Call it superstition, but when people get a whiff of that sort of thing, they run the other way. It's taken years, but things are finally back to normal around here, and I don't need you poking your nose in, stirring up things folks would just as soon forget."

"And what about the Gilmans? How do you think they feel, knowing whoever killed their daughters is walking free? Do you honestly think they give a damn about their property values?"

"I assure you, Miss Moon, if I could have brought a case against the killer, I would have done so years ago. I understand your stake in all of this, but it's pointless now, isn't it? Your grandmother's gone, and so are those girls. And nothing you or anyone else does is going to bring them back. Sometimes justice takes care of itself. Why not do us all a favor and leave the dead buried?"

It took everything Lizzy had not to fly at him. He'd as good as admitted that Althea had done him a favor by dying, bringing things to a tidy end. And maybe it *had* ended for him. But it hadn't for her. "I'd like to speak to the detective in charge of the case."

Summers let out a sigh, clearly weary of the conversation. "As I've already stated, the case was closed years ago. As for Roger Coleman, he left the department a few years back. Bit of an odd bird, Coleman. Pot stirrer, some would say. I don't think anyone's heard from him since he moved away."

"Moved away where?"

Summers shrugged. "No idea. He stopped being my problem the day he turned in his badge. Now, if you'll excuse me, I have a luncheon with Mayor Cavanaugh. He's retiring after seventeen years, and I'd like to pay my respects."

He was reaching for the door when Lizzy stopped him. It was a long shot, but she had to ask. "I don't suppose you'd let me look at the case file?"

"You suppose correctly." He nodded then, coolly polite, and was gone.

Lizzy didn't realize she was trembling until she got back behind the wheel. Summers had been about as helpful as expected, and twice as loathsome, but she hadn't come away empty-handed. She had a name— Roger Coleman. Now all she needed to do was find him.

Her cell phone went off as she pulled out of the parking lot. Luc. She clicked the hands-free to answer. "What's up?"

"I was going to ask you the same thing. How's it going?"

"It's going."

"When are you coming back?"

"I just got here."

"I know. I just figured you'd be itching to get out of there." He chuckled dryly. "Ghosts of your past, and all that."

Lizzy blew out a breath. *Ghosts indeed.*

"There's been a development, Luc. Two, actually. This trip might end up taking a little longer than I expected. Apparently, the house needs a ton of work. According to Andrew, I'll be lucky to sell it at all."

"Who's Andrew?"

"A neighbor, and a friend of my grandmother's. He's also an architect. He rattled off a list of repairs as long as my arm. I'm not sure how I'm going to swing any of it."

"So don't. Knock it all down and be done with it. You can sell it as unimproved property. Plus the taxes go down. Boom, problem solved."

Problem solved? Selling the farm was one thing. Razing it to the ground was something else entirely. "I grew up here!"

"And if I remember correctly, you couldn't wait to leave."

His response chafed. Not just his words, but the callous way he'd flung them at her. "You don't have a sentimental bone in your body, do you?"

"I never claimed to. It's part of my charm. But while we're on the subject of sentiment, Andrew the Architect wouldn't happen to be one of the developments, would he?"

The question took Lizzy by surprise. "Why would you ask that?"

"Just curious." There was a long pause, the sound of desk drawers opening and closing, and then finally, as an afterthought: "I miss you."

"No, you don't."

"How do *you* know?"

"You just told me you didn't have a sentimental bone in your body."

Luc conceded the point by changing the subject. "You didn't answer the question. This Andrew who's being so helpful—are we talking old flame or what?"

"No, we're not. He's just someone I used to know. He's doing some work for my grandmother."

"Your grandmother's dead."

Lizzy bit back a sigh. "It's a long story, and I really don't feel like getting into it now."

"Fine. Just as long as he's not thinking of poaching my new creative director. You mentioned a second development, and you've assured me it isn't Andrew. So what is it?"

Lizzy bit her lip, kicking herself for not having been more guarded. What was she supposed to say? *I'm trying to clear my grandmother of murder?* "It's nothing," she said finally. "Just some legal stuff I need to clean up." *Okay, so not a complete lie. Technically, a double murder did qualify as legal stuff.* "Like I said, it might take longer than I thought."

"Are we talking days? Weeks?"

"I don't know. But I have some time saved up, and I'm going to need to use it."

Luc was silent a moment. Lizzy could hear the steady tap-tap of his pen on the desk, his go-to gesture when annoyed. "I think you need to keep all this in perspective," he said finally. "Just do what you need to do and get out of there. I promise it'll be a relief when it's over, like closing one chapter so a new one can begin."

Lizzy's knuckles went white as she tightened her grip on the steering wheel. "Is that how you felt when your mother died? Relieved?"

More silence. More tapping. "People die, babe. It's a fact of life. There's no reason to feel guilty about selling something that belongs to you. Get on with it, and come home."

Maybe it was the way he insisted on calling her *babe*, when she'd asked him a hundred times to stop, or his complete lack of empathy, but Lizzy suddenly needed to end the call. Now, before she said something she couldn't take back. "Look, I need to go. I'm in the car and traffic is crazy."

"Lizzy—"

"I'll call you when I know more."

EIGHT

Lizzy was still stewing over her conversation with Luc when she turned into the drive and spotted a white utility pickup parked near the top. The words ANDREW GREYSON, ARCHITECT were emblazoned on both doors. She remembered Andrew saying he had ordered some wood for the barn. Presumably, he'd come to deliver it. She shielded her eyes as she climbed out of the car, scanning the property for a glimpse of him. Instead, she spotted a man in worn gray coveralls coming toward her.

He was tall and burly, and looked vaguely familiar. Lizzy racked her brain, finally coming up with a name. Or at least a last name. The Hanleys had been neighbors once upon a time, their land bordering Moon Girl Farm to the north. Not that they'd ever been a particularly neighborly family. Especially the old man, who drank heavily and was rarely seen in town.

There'd been two boys—Hollis and Dennis—a year apart in age and thick as thieves. She'd never known them well enough to tell them apart, but if she were guessing, she'd say it was Dennis—the older brother—now coming toward her. He hadn't changed much over the years. A bit thicker through the neck, perhaps, but his hair was still the color of young corn, his eyes the same unsettling pale blue.

Lizzy offered a polite wave as he approached. Hanley ignored the gesture as he marched past, leaving a pungent *sillage* of copper, salt, and stagnant water in his wake, like a mud flat at low tide. How was it possible no one else smelled it? She took shallow breaths as she watched him gather up an armful of lumber, presumably for the barn repairs Andrew was planning.

She forced a smile as he hoisted a half dozen two-by-fours up onto his shoulder. "If you tell me how much I owe you, I'll write you a check."

Hanley shot her a glare, sidestepping her again. "Didn't send no invoice. Just told me to drop the stuff off."

Lizzy watched as he headed back to the barn and dumped the wood onto the existing pile in front of the door. He was huffing by the time he returned. She waited for some sort of acknowledgment that he was through. Instead, he slammed the tailgate, climbed into the truck, and left her standing in a cloud of dust.

Lizzy watched as he disappeared down the drive, unable to shake the stench of him. Or the hard glint in his eyes when he'd looked at her. There might be a tattoo parlor and a brand-new café downtown, but Dennis Hanley's snub made it clear that some things in Salem Creek would never change.

She was still scowling when she spotted Evvie prowling what remained of the vegetable garden in her faded chintz apron. The garden was nothing like it used to be, but it had fared better than much of the farm, and still boasted a decent selection of berries and vegetables.

Evvie dropped a fistful of string beans into her apron pocket and looked up, appraising Lizzy through narrowed eyes. "You look like someone ran over your best pig."

Lizzy scowled at her. "I look like . . . what?"

"It's something my daddy used to say. It means down in the mouth. I take it things didn't go well with the chief."

"That's one way to put it. Apparently, the case was closed years ago, and he has no intention of reopening it. His exact words were *sometimes justice takes care of itself*."

Evvie's expression hardened. "How did you leave it?"

"I told him I was going to do a little asking around."

"I'm sure he loved hearing that."

"Not really, no. He made it pretty clear that he'd like me to leave it alone. Gave me some line about property values and scaring people off. I asked to talk to the detective who was in charge of the investigation—Roger Coleman was his name—but he's apparently moved away. According to Summers, no one's heard from him since he quit the force."

Evvie grunted, scraping dirt from under her nails. "Shows how much he knows."

Lizzy caught her by the wrist. "What does that mean?"

"It means there's someone who knows exactly where that man went, and he happens to live right next door."

Lizzy looked in the direction of Evvie's crooked thumb. "Andrew?"

"Mmm-hmmm. Came over one day a couple years back and asked your gran if she had a problem with him renovating the detective's new house. Said he wouldn't take the job if she didn't want him to. He meant it too. But you know Althea. She said the man was just doing his job, and that he'd never been anything but polite while doing it."

"So he took the job?"

"Far as I know. But if you want to know for sure, go knock on his door and ask."

~

Things had definitely changed at the Greyson place. The bedraggled hedge that had once threatened to swallow the house whole had been yanked out, replaced by a terraced garden blooming with dahlias, helenium, and bright-orange daylilies.

The house itself was also undergoing changes. There was an addition going up on one side, with large windows, a fieldstone chimney, and a wraparound deck that would look out over the hills when it was finished. Andrew had obviously decided to put his own stamp on the place when his father passed away.

Lizzy followed the walkway to the front door, surprised to find it standing open. The sound of hammering echoed from somewhere inside. She knocked, then called out over the steady banging. "Hello? Andrew?"

The hammering stopped. Andrew appeared moments later, clearly surprised to see her in the doorway. "Hey." He paused, wiping his face on his sleeve, then brushed a smattering of sawdust from his hair. "What's up?"

Lizzy hesitated as she noted the state of the house. The furniture had been removed, the floor strewn with heavy canvas drop cloths. "I can come back if you're busy."

"Don't you dare. I was looking for an excuse to knock off. Come on in."

The air was sharp with the smell of freshly cut wood and the sticky-sweet fumes of varnish. "You're remodeling," she said, as she moved deeper into the room. "I noticed the gardens out front. They're beautiful. I'd put down some fresh mulch, though. It'll cut down on the need to water, and help keep the weeds down."

"You sound like your grandmother. She wrote it all down for me, by the way. In fact, the whole thing was her design. I'm a wiz with walls and wiring, but when it comes to the outside stuff, I'm clueless. You want the tour?"

Lizzy followed him into the kitchen, where the new floorboards were littered with sawdust. It was large and open, with a cooking island in the center and wide windows that opened out onto the new deck.

The appliances were state-of-the-art stainless, the lighting updated with recessed canisters, the cabinets fashioned of some satiny dark wood.

"It's going to be gorgeous when you're finished," she told him, running an admiring hand over one of the cabinet doors. "I love the wood."

"I still need to decide on the granite. Care to weigh in?" He pulled a trio of samples from the top of the refrigerator and held them out. "I've narrowed it to three."

Lizzy glanced around the kitchen, then back at the samples. After a moment she took the middle sample—the lightest of the three—and held it up against one of the cabinet doors. "This one," she said, handing it back. "The creamy background will brighten up the room, while the dark veins pull the wood and stainless together."

"Done, madam. But be warned, I may consult you again when it's time to choose the hardware. Oh, speaking of which, did Dennis deliver the wood for the barn?"

"He did. Though I wasn't a hundred percent sure it *was* Dennis. I never could tell the two of them apart."

"Yup. Definitely Dennis. He works the night shift at the meatpacking plant, but does delivery and odd jobs for me a couple days a week."

"He's not very friendly, is he?"

Andrew shook his head. "I'm afraid not, but don't take it personally. He's been worse since his brother died."

"Hollis died?"

"Two years ago. Car crash out on Route 125, not long after he got back from Afghanistan. Poor guy couldn't catch a break. He was always a little slow, but Dennis looked out for him. They enlisted together and assumed they'd be stationed together, but it didn't work out that way. Hollis had a rough time on his own. Came back a mess. I think Dennis feels responsible for the way things went. I'm pretty sure that's why he took the job with me, so he could help Hollis's wife."

"Oh no. He was married?"

"He was. Married Bonnie Markham's youngest daughter, Helen. The baby was barely a year when he died. A little girl named Kayla. She's about three now, I think."

Lizzy shook her head, grieved by the thought of a little girl growing up without her father, a young wife without her husband. "How awful. But it's good of Dennis to look after his brother's family. I wouldn't have thought him the type, but then I should know better than to judge."

She glanced at the granite sample still in her hand. She'd forgotten she was holding it. She handed it back, feeling timid suddenly. "I came to ask for a favor."

"Okay, shoot."

"I went to talk to Randall Summers today about the Gilman case."

"Seriously?"

The look on his face said it all. "I know. Why dredge all that up again? I swear, I never meant to. But now that I'm here, all I can think about is how awful it must have been for Althea, knowing people believed her capable of . . ." She looked away, leaving it to Andrew to fill in the blanks. "I thought he might be able to tell me something new."

Andrew pursed his lips thoughtfully. "I get you wanting to clear Althea's name. I'm just surprised you thought Summers would be willing to help. He's certainly been no friend to the Moons over the years."

"Maybe, but I had to start somewhere. And you're right. He isn't willing to help. He hung around just long enough to tell me I was wasting my time. Then he hurried off to some luncheon with the mayor."

"Of course he did."

"Why *of course*?"

"Summers has been counting the days until Cavanaugh either retires or dies. And last week it became official. The mayor's packing it in, heading to North Carolina and the grandkids. Your chances were never good, but with an election looming you've got zero chance of getting help from Salem Creek's finest."

"Which brings me to the favor I mentioned." She stepped away, wandering toward the window to peer out. "I asked to talk to the detective who headed up the case. Summers told me he left the force several years ago and moved away. He also claims no one knows where he went. But Evvie thinks you might."

"Roger."

Lizzy turned away from the window, suddenly hopeful. "Yes! Do you know how I can get in touch with him? An address or a phone number?"

Andrew scrubbed a hand through his hair, clearly weighing his response. "I have both, though I doubt he'd be thrilled with me for sharing either. He's a private investigator now, works for his brother in Dover. I could give him a call, though, ask if he'd be willing to speak with you. He might not be. I have a hunch his memories of the Salem Creek PD are far from happy."

"Call him. Please. I just want to ask a few questions, see if anything new comes up. It'll probably come to nothing, but it's worth a conversation."

He studied her a moment, head tilted to one side, as if trying to work out a riddle. "I'm curious about something. Earlier, you said you never wanted to dig all this up. Now you're talking about kicking over rocks and turning Salem Creek upside down. That's quite a swing."

"I know it is. And I wish I could explain it. The truth is I don't know what happened. I was so angry when I left. So angry I swore I'd never set foot in this town again."

"Yet here you are."

She nodded. "Here I am."

"It's a long way from New York. In more ways than one."

Lizzy shrugged, knowing her answer would sound ridiculous to someone like Andrew. Or anyone, really. "I feel safe in New York. I know that probably sounds strange, but it's easier to be anonymous there, just another face in a crowd of millions, where everyone has a story, but no one has time to ask. I'm sure that makes no sense to you. You've never wanted to disappear, to just be invisible, but I have—and still do sometimes."

"Well, I can tell you one thing for sure. The last thing you'll be, once you start asking questions about those murders, is invisible."

"I know that. But sometimes you have to come out of hiding, don't you? To stand up for what's right? I can't help thinking that maybe if I hadn't tried so hard to be invisible when the feeding frenzy started, it might have made a difference. Instead, I hid and just let it all happen."

"Lizzy, you can't blame yourself for what happened. This is Salem Creek. People don't get murdered here; they die of boredom and old age. This town lost its mind when those girls turned up dead. They were afraid, and fear makes people do crazy things, sometimes shameful things. What happened to Althea was like a brush fire. It swallowed this town whole."

"It certainly swallowed my grandmother."

"And you."

"Yes," Lizzy said quietly. "And me."

"You're not afraid of reigniting it?"

"I am, actually. But not as afraid of leaving here knowing I didn't even try to get to the truth. Althea deserves that, even if I *am* eight years too late."

"I'll call Roger in the morning. I can't guarantee anything, but he's a decent guy. He took the job seriously, but he and Summers were always butting heads. No one was surprised when he left to join his brother's law firm as an investigator. He could be helpful, but like I said, I have no clue how he'll respond. Given his history with Summers, he might want to steer clear."

Lizzy nodded. Only a fool would want to wade back into such a grisly mess. "Thank you. No matter what he says, I appreciate your help. I'll wait to hear from you."

NINE

Lizzy's stomach knotted as Andrew turned onto Dover Point Road. Roger Coleman had agreed to speak with her, but with two stipulations: Andrew would be present for the interview, and he would under no circumstances be expected to interact with Randall Summers. It seemed Andrew had been right about the friction between the detective and his ex-chief.

She wasn't sure what her reaction would be to seeing the detective again. She wasn't crazy about the idea of being face-to-face with the man who had knocked on their door with a search warrant in his pocket. But it was too late to back out now. They were pulling into a narrow drive lined with tall, wind-battered pines.

The lot was deep and shady, a pie-shaped parcel snugged up against the shore of Little Bay. The house was a small one, a single-story, slate-blue cape with crisp white shutters. In the side yard, a sailboat sat up on blocks, presumably in some stage of repair.

Lizzy left her purse on the seat and got out. She wasn't prepared when Roger Coleman suddenly rose from an upended milk crate beside the sailboat's hull. She braced herself as he approached. She remembered him being tall, polite but imposing, with dark, close-cropped hair and a sharp, narrow jaw. He hadn't changed much over the years. He was still tall, still angular, and still a little imposing, despite the fact that his hair was now threaded with silver, and he had traded his crisp khakis and blazer for loose-fitting jeans and a holey T-shirt.

Andrew was all smiles as he extended a hand. "Still working on the old hulk, I see."

Roger grinned as he pumped Andrew's hand. "She'll be ready for canvas soon. With any luck, I'll have her in the water before the docks come out." His chest puffed proudly as he hiked a thumb over his shoulder. "I even got around to naming her."

It was a smallish boat, not more than thirty feet, with a single mast and a faded blue hull. Lizzy squinted to make out the letters stenciled across the stern. SLEUTH JOHN B. It was a play on the old Beach Boys song, and fitting given his profession, though it was hard to imagine a man of Coleman's considerable height folding himself into what would have to be a very tiny cabin.

Lizzy brought her eyes back to Coleman. She dipped her head when Andrew introduced her, unable to muster a smile as she extended her hand. She caught a whiff of polished shoes and freshly ironed cotton, which fit perfectly with a by-the-book detective. But there was something else, a faint trace of wet leaves, that felt at odds with the rest. It was a dark, slick smell, one she'd always associated with grief or sadness, but when she forced herself to meet his gaze, she saw nothing that hinted at either. Perhaps her radar was off.

"Thank you for agreeing to see me, Detective."

Coleman studied her with eyes that were neither silver nor green, but somewhere in between. Lizzy remembered those eyes: sharp and unsettlingly steady, in no hurry to move on until they'd taken full measure. "Roger," he corrected evenly. "It's just Roger."

He invited them inside and poured them each a glass of iced tea, then gave Lizzy a quick tour, pointing out the renovations Andrew had completed two years ago. The wall he'd knocked down between the living room and kitchen, the pass-through window out onto the porch, the bank of skylights in the living room.

When the pleasantries were complete, they wandered out onto the deck. Behind the house, the bay stretched lazily in the afternoon sun, silvery and still at nearly high tide. Lizzy lifted her face, grateful for the breeze coming in off the water.

"So," Roger said when they had all settled into chairs. "Andrew tells me you're on a mission."

Lizzy glanced at Andrew, who was swirling the ice in his glass and gazing out over the water. He had set up the meeting and agreed to accompany her, but it was her show now.

"Yes, I suppose that's what you'd call it." She paused, not sure how to begin. "My grandmother didn't hurt those girls," she said finally. "But someone did, and if there's a way to find out who it was, I want to try."

He studied her again with those gray-green eyes. "You realize the odds of turning up anything new are slim—that all you're likely to do is remind everyone what they thought, and why they thought it?"

"I do."

"And you still want to do this?"

"I do."

"Even if you learn something you don't want to know?"

She knew what he was asking. In his mind, there was a chance that in her search for truth, she might actually uncover evidence that implicated Althea rather than exonerating her. But he didn't know what she did—that Althea was incapable of harming anyone, let alone a pair of young girls.

"I won't."

He nodded coolly, willing for now to accept her at her word. "Well then, what do you want to know?"

"Why did you leave the department?"

Roger blinked back at her, clearly surprised by the question. "Because it was time."

It was evasive, a polite way of telling her it was none of her business. But if she was going to trust him, she needed to know his story, and understand what had prompted him to walk away from what had surely been the biggest case of his career. "So you retired?"

"Officially? No." He squinted out over the water, where a red-and-white sailboat bobbed lazily at anchor. "I quit. Because I was no longer able to be effective."

"I don't know what that means."

"It means Chief Summers and I had different ideas about the department's responsibility to the public. He wanted to make the Gilman case go away, and I wanted to keep digging until we solved it."

Coleman's matter-of-fact tone surprised her. "You don't think he wanted to solve it?"

"In the beginning, maybe. When he was getting tons of press. Big man with his name in the paper, always available for an interview. Then the coverage turned ugly, and he slammed on the brakes. He started cutting man-hours, hamstringing us on resources, wouldn't sign off on sending stuff to the state lab because it wasn't in the budget. And the press was strictly off limits. All statements had to be cleared by him. It felt funny. He'd always been a bit of a tyrant, but this felt like something else."

"What did it feel like?"

"Like there was something going on that the rest of us didn't know about."

"Did you confront him?"

"You don't *confront* Randall Summers. But I did voice my concerns."

"And what happened?"

He shrugged. "I bought a sailboat and went to work for my brother."

"Ah . . . right."

"Don't get me wrong. I like the work I'm doing now. It's useful. But law enforcement was in my blood. I know it sounds corny, like I'm some kind of Boy Scout or something, but it's how I've always felt about the job. I think it's how most of us feel. We're proud of what we do. Because we believe we're making a difference." He paused, looking back out over the bay, at a father and son horsing around in a bass boat. He was smiling when he turned back, but it faded quickly. "Some of us give our lives to the job. The job doesn't always return the favor."

Lizzy glanced back into the house. She hadn't noted it until now, but there was no sign of a woman about the place, and no ring on his finger. Single? Divorced? She recalled the trace of wet leaves she'd picked up earlier, and found herself wondering if Roger Coleman had given up something—or someone—for the job, and if the choice had been worth it.

Andrew had been idly swirling his tea, ice cubes rattling rhythmically against the glass. He set it down now, and leaned forward, elbows on knees. "Would it be breaking any rules to discuss where the case stood when you left? Neither of us wants you to go against your principles, but Lizzy has her own sense of duty. She'd like to know that she's done everything she can to clear her grandmother's name. She did go to Summers first, but he wasn't much help."

Roger nodded slowly. "I'd like to say that surprises me, but it doesn't. The man doesn't give a damn about public safety. He sees being police chief as a gig, a stepping-stone to bigger things."

Andrew caught Lizzy's eye with a look that said *I told you so.* "Mayor Cavanaugh just announced his retirement."

Roger's lips thinned. "Then you can bet the VOTE SUMMERS yard signs are being printed as we speak. Not that it was any big secret. We all knew he was angling for mayor, or higher. We could see him working it, milking the high-profile cases to get his name in the paper. He was all about the show. Unless it made him look bad. Then he wanted no part of it."

Andrew's brows knitted. "You think the Gilman murders made him look bad?"

Roger blew out a long breath. "The Gilman murders made everyone look bad. People in Salem Creek aren't used to seeing that kind of thing on the local news. So when they do, it doesn't take long for the finger-pointing to start. And the fingers weren't just pointing at

Summers. Cavanaugh was taking heat too, and Election Day was right around the corner. It was in everyone's interest to make it go away."

"Not everyone's interest," Lizzy shot back. "But he did get his way. There was never a resolution. No arrest. No trial. Nothing."

Roger looked at her over steepled fingers. "You have to consider the evidence we had. Or, rather, didn't have. We had the bodies and an anonymous tip, but nothing that linked your grandmother directly to the murders. No motive. No weapon. And no concrete forensics to speak of. Say we go ahead and make an arrest to tamp down the noise. Then we go to court. Only we can't make the case and your grandmother's acquitted. The last thing Cavanaugh wants while he's out stumping for votes is for people to remember that two girls died on his watch, and that his police chief let a killer walk free." He paused, shrugging heavily. "Sometimes, when you can't make a case, it's better to do nothing than to poke the hornet's nest. Strategy must have worked. He's still there."

Andrew sat up straighter in his chair, as if grasping the full import of Roger's words. "You think it was Cavanaugh who asked Summers to slow-walk the investigation?"

"No," Roger replied flatly. "I think Cavanaugh told him to bury it completely. Summers probably wasn't too keen at first. A conviction would have made him a hero, a champion of law and order. But when he realized a conviction wasn't likely, he changed direction quick. I suspect there was some back-scratching involved. Cavanaugh wanted the story to go away so he could win reelection, and Summers wanted a hand when it finally came time for the mayor to head south."

Lizzy stared at him, stunned. "So he just dropped a murder investigation?"

"Starved is more like it, but it amounts to the same thing. He claimed it had to do with budgeting, but none of us bought that. Here's this huge case, and all of a sudden my guys can't get the overtime they need to do the legwork, can't get approval for labs that might help us nail down how long the girls had been in the water, or whether either of them had been poisoned. Nothing but alcohol came up on the tox screens, but that's not unusual when a significant amount of time has passed before samples are collected. Fermentation skews everything. Toss in a couple weeks of submersion and things get really messy."

"What about the Gilmans?" Lizzy asked, eager to change the subject. "Weren't they demanding answers?"

"They were—or at least Fred Gilman was. But Summers managed to convince him the investigation had hit a dead end and that was that. Not that Gilman ever changed his mind about your grandmother's guilt, but that was fine with Summers. He didn't care what people believed, as long as he and Cavanaugh didn't get their hands dirty."

Lizzy stared at him, astonished. "Didn't get their hands dirty? My grandmother was getting death threats, Detective. We were terrified every time she left the house."

"I know. Things got . . . out of hand. It was bad enough when word leaked that we'd found the vial in Heather's pocket. Blue glass, just like your grandmother used, but with no label. When she verified that the girls had visited her shop the afternoon they went missing, well, it was inevitable that people would jump to conclusions. As far as anyone knew—including us—Althea was the last person to see the girls alive."

"Assurance," Lizzy told him quietly. "That's the name of the oil blend she made up for Heather that day. She wanted to make a boy fall in love with her. That's why she came to the shop, for a love potion. But Althea didn't believe in love potions. She thought they were manipulative, so she sold Heather the Assurance oil instead, to dab on her wrists. It's a combination of cedar and carnation oils, used to inspire confidence. Not a sedative, and not remotely poisonous. But my grandmother told you all of that."

Roger nodded. "She did."

"But you didn't believe her."

"The neck of the vial was cracked when we retrieved it from Heather's pocket. There was nothing to test, no way to verify its contents. We thought a sedative of some kind might account for how someone your grandmother's age could have overpowered two young girls. We were doing our jobs, Ms. Moon."

"I was there the day you came with your men," Lizzy said softly. "I let you in."

"Yes," Roger said, the slight inclination of his head an acknowledgment that they'd officially crossed into uncomfortable territory. "I remember."

Lizzy stood abruptly and moved to the railing, the combination of anger and memory making her vaguely queasy. Andrew must have sensed her mood because he was suddenly beside her, sliding a hand over hers on the railing. He said nothing, but the question in his eyes was easily read.

Are you okay?

When she nodded that she was, Andrew turned back to Roger. "You bring up a point that's always bothered me, Roger. Althea Moon was five feet two, tops, and I doubt she weighed a hundred pounds soaking wet. Is it likely that she was strong enough to inflict the kinds of head injuries the girls sustained?"

"Only Darcy, the younger of the two, sustained a head injury," Roger explained gravely. "Blunt force trauma to the left temporal and parietal areas. Subdural hematoma. Gruesome stuff. But the ME couldn't be certain as to her definitive cause of death. There appeared to be some pulmonary hemorrhaging, which is sometimes seen in drowning victims. Hard to say, though, after so much time in the pond. Heather was strangled. Crushed trachea, two broken cervical vertebrae. Lungs looked clear, which means she was dead when she went in."

Lizzy couldn't help feeling a grudging respect for Roger Coleman. Eight years had passed since the Gilman girls were murdered and he still remembered their names, referring to them as Darcy and Heather, rather than mere faceless victims.

Andrew had fallen silent, his brows pinched, as if trying to work out something in his head. "Was there a time lag between the two deaths?" he asked finally.

Roger shrugged. "The level of decomposition was similar for both girls, but that has more to do with how long they were in the water than with actual time of death. It's likely they died in close succession, but we can't know for certain. There's a lot we can't know for certain."

"I'm just thinking out loud here, but leaving size out of the equation, how likely is it that Althea could have killed them both? I mean, a woman in her sixties against two young girls? You'd think at least one of them would have gotten away. Unless they were tied up. They weren't, were they?"

"Not when they went in the water. The divers scoured the pond for rope, tape, anything that could have been used to bind them, but they came up empty."

"Then how could she have pulled it off?"

"That's the question, isn't it? In fact, it's one of the things that kept nagging at me."

Lizzy's head came up sharply. It was the first sign he'd given that he had doubts about Althea's guilt, and she seized on it. "You don't think she did it."

"I didn't say that."

"But you had doubts. You just said you did."

"Not initially. The bodies were discovered in your grandmother's pond, weighted down with rocks, and if there's one thing this job teaches you, it's that there's generally a reason the obvious suspect is the obvious suspect. But it isn't my job to decide who's guilty and who's not. It's my job to follow the evidence. And in this case there were some things that just didn't add up."

"Like what?"

"Like why our tipster didn't come forward when we asked him to contact us again. Not even when we upped the reward. And then there's motive. I couldn't for the life of me figure out why your grandmother would have wanted to harm two young girls, and then dump them in her own pond, where she had to know they'd eventually be found.

People have said a lot of things about Althea Moon over the years, but no one ever said she was stupid."

"No," Lizzy said evenly. "She wasn't. So who?"

Roger shook his head. "That's the other problem. It's much harder to prove someone *didn't* do something than to prove they did. For better or worse, big cases tend to take on a momentum of their own. The evidence points in a certain direction, and that's the direction everyone looks. The media, the public, and, yes, sometimes even the law. It takes something substantial to shift that momentum in a new direction, and we just didn't have that. We didn't have anything."

"So you were fine with letting everyone believe Althea was guilty?"

Roger rose stiffly from his chair. "Come with me, Ms. Moon."

Lizzy caught Andrew's eye as they followed Roger into the house. They passed through the kitchen and living room, then down a short hall lined with three doors, two of which stood open. The first was a small guest bath. The second appeared to be Roger's bedroom, furnished with only a bed, a bureau, and a treadmill stationed in front of the window.

The last door was closed. Roger said nothing as he pushed it open, stepping aside so Lizzy and Andrew could enter ahead of him. The room was small and dim, the blinds closed against the afternoon sun. There were no furnishings of any kind, just stacks of cardboard storage boxes on the floor in the center of the room.

Lizzy looked from the boxes to Roger. "What's all this?"

"This," Roger said wistfully, "is my career. Or was. Personal notes on every case I worked as a detective." He stepped into the room, making a beeline for a pair of boxes set slightly apart from the rest. "And these," he said, laying a hand on the top box, "are the Gilman files."

Lizzy eyed him warily. "Should you even have those?"

"They're not official police documents. Just stuff I kept together so I could work the case from home. Notes mostly." He lifted the lid and pulled out a handful of small black notebooks. "I've been accused of being a pack rat, but the truth is, I think better on paper."

Lizzy stepped closer, peering into the carton at the jumble of note-books and file folders.

"There must be hundreds of pages here. What is it all?"

"Notes on basically everything I could remember at the end of every day, stray thoughts, offhand remarks I wanted to follow up on. Impressions I jotted down after interviews and daily briefings. Anything I thought might eventually fit somewhere."

"How on earth did you find time to do all this?"

"Like I said, some of us give our lives to the job. My wife and son were killed not long after I made detective. They were on the way back from my son's tae kwon do match in Manchester. The roads were icy, and the car jumped the median into oncoming traffic. I was supposed to go with them that night, but I was stuck in an interview. Maybe if I'd been driving . . ." His eyes flicked briefly from hers. "My son was eleven."

Lizzy's throat went tight. Apparently her radar was spot on. A wife *and* a son. How was it possible to even survive such a loss? To keep putting one foot in front of the other when you've lost everything that mattered?

"I'm so sorry."

Roger hunched his shoulders, clearly uncomfortable with his grief. "After that, there was just the job. And my notes. Anyway, it's all here."

Andrew moved closer, craning his neck to inspect the contents of the carton. "I can't believe you saved all this."

"My brother's a criminal attorney. The first thing he told me when I joined the force was never get rid of your notes, because you never know when a case is going to come back to bite you in the ass. I never forgot it. You have no idea how many times some tiny detail has ended up shining new light on a case. Not that this is likely to be one of those cases. God knows I've spent hours looking for something I might have missed. Unfortunately, I never found it."

Lizzy's admiration for Roger Coleman ticked up another notch. "You seem to have taken the case very seriously."

"I took all my cases seriously, but I admit this one hit me hard. I know what it's like to lose a child, but I never had to wonder what happened to my son. For better or worse, I knew. The Gilmans didn't. And they still don't. I can't imagine what that must be like, to wake up every day and know my child was gone and have no idea how or why. It's also why I agreed to talk to you. It struck me when Andrew told me you were thinking about digging all this up again that maybe the Gilmans weren't the only ones who deserved answers."

"Thank you, Detective."

"Roger," he reminded again. "I've got seventeen years under my belt as a detective, and in all that time there were only three cases I couldn't close. This was one of them. I'm telling you this because I need you to understand that my only stake in all of this is getting at the truth, and that anything I may find is in that interest alone. I don't work for you."

"I understand. I'll wait to hear from you. In the meantime, I was thinking of talking to the Gilmans."

Roger's face darkened. "You're certainly welcome to try, but I doubt you'll get very far. The last time I had contact, Fred Gilman nearly tore my head off, and Mrs. Gilman looked like a ghost. Not that I blame either of them. He wanted someone's head on a pike, and she just wanted it to be over. They needed closure, and I couldn't give it to them."

"Maybe we can still give it to them," Lizzy said quietly. "If I can just make them see that that's what I want too, they'll talk to me."

"Maybe so," Roger said, though he sounded less than convinced. "I was sorry to hear about your grandmother, by the way. She seemed like a good woman, despite what was happening in her world. I wish our paths could have crossed under different circumstances."

Lizzy met his gaze squarely. "She didn't hurt those girls, Roger."

"You have no idea how much I'd like to believe that, Ms. Moon."

"It's Lizzy," she corrected. "And I'm guessing it's not half as much as I'd like to prove it to you."

TEN

Lizzy was quiet on the ride back. She could feel Andrew's eyes sliding in her direction now and then, but she was too busy digesting what she'd learned about Randall Summers's negligent handling of the investigation to make conversation. And yet, in a perverse way, it gave her hope. She'd been operating under the assumption that the police had simply run out of leads, when the truth was the investigation had been quietly and deliberately quashed.

It was clear now why Roger had walked away from a nearly twenty-year career with the Salem Creek Police Department. She barely knew the man, but she'd seen enough to know he wasn't the type to stomach collusion and blatant malfeasance, which was what Summers's actions amounted to. Which was why she believed him when he said he'd comb through his notes in search of some previously missed clue. Not because he wanted to help her, but because he wanted to get to the truth. Because that was how he was built.

"Here we are," Andrew said, as they pulled into the drive. "Home again." He put the truck in park and turned to look at her. "You haven't said much since we left Roger's. Are you okay?"

"I'm fine." She was clutching her purse with one hand, the door handle with the other, ready to be alone with her thoughts. Instead, she sagged back in her seat. "It's just a lot to take in, you know? To find out the chief of police was willing to let my grandmother take the fall for something she didn't do because he wanted to run for mayor one day. What kind of man does something like that?"

"The ambitious kind."

Lizzy shook her head, unable to comprehend it. "Someone needs to know."

"Who? Summers doesn't have a boss, unless you count Cavanaugh, and I think it's safe to say he's not going to be helpful."

"The governor, then. Or the media. Someone."

Andrew looked away, his hands still on the wheel. "I get that you're angry, Lizzy, but how many fights are you willing to jump into?"

"As many as it takes."

He blew out a breath, slow and thoughtful. "Okay. But maybe take them one at a time. Focus on what matters right now."

"I want to talk to the Gilmans."

Something like a wince crossed Andrew's face. "You're probably the last person the Gilmans are going to want to talk to. Why not wait and see what Roger comes up with?"

"And if he comes up with nothing?"

"I don't know. I'm just not sure dragging the Gilmans through it all again is a good idea."

"I'm trying to find out what happened to their daughters. You don't think they'd want to help me do that?"

"In their minds, they already know what happened, Lizzy. As far as they're concerned you'll just be trying to clear Althea. You should also know the Gilmans split up a few years back. Fred's still around, but I'm pretty sure someone told me Susan moved away."

Lizzy was sorry but not surprised. She'd heard about marriages unraveling when a child died. Wives blaming husbands. Husbands shutting down emotionally. It was hard to imagine going on when a piece of your heart had been torn away forever. But then the Gilmans didn't have to imagine it. It happened.

"You don't think I feel awful about what they went through? I was there to see Susan Gilman's face the day they pulled her daughters from our pond. I watched her die inside as the coroner's van drove away. But Althea's dead too. And I'm all that's left, the only one still here to care about *her* memory. Is that wrong?"

"No. It's not. I'm just saying give it some thought. And if you do decide to talk to them, try to remember that their grief is different from yours. Maybe not as fresh, but every bit as raw."

Lizzy nodded, grabbing for the door handle, then paused. "Thank you for making today happen, and for going with me. Even if nothing comes of it, it was kind of you to help."

"You're welcome."

She watched from the top of the drive as Andrew pulled away. Maybe he was right. Maybe she should leave the Gilmans alone. What right did she have to tear the scab from a wound that was barely healed? Salem Creek had moved on. Perhaps it was time she did the same, just put the farm on the market and let it all go.

Evvie was in the kitchen when she came in, pulling something golden and fragrant from the oven. The smell of warm blueberries hung in the air. Lizzy looked at the pan on the stove and thought of Althea. No one made blueberry cobbler like Althea, but this one looked—and smelled—awfully close.

"You made cobbler," she said, smiling at Evvie. "I love cobbler."

"Your gran told me."

"We used to pick our own blueberries, then come home and make a big mess. By the time we finished, my fingers and lips were blue. It's my absolute favorite dessert."

"She told me that too."

She looked at the pan of gooey, browned goodness, then back at Evvie. "Did you . . . you made this for me?"

"Thought you might need a little pick-me-up after talking to that detective. There's ice cream in the freezer."

"Vanilla?"

"What else?"

Lizzy blinked back an unexpected rush of tears. It had been an emotional day, and her nerves were raw. "Thank you, Evvie. This was so kind of you."

Evvie nodded, acknowledging the thank-you, but her expression was all business. "You going to tell me what happened?"

Lizzy went to the freezer and pulled out a half gallon of Hood vanilla, then grabbed two bowls from the cupboard. "He wasn't what I expected. He's . . . sincere."

"There's a word you don't hear much anymore."

"No, but it fits. He cares about the truth. Which is more than I can say for Summers."

Evvie dished up the cobbler and handed the bowls to Lizzy, who added a healthy scoop of ice cream to each before heading for the kitchen table.

"He agreed to help," she said, dropping into a chair. "He's got two boxes of notes from the investigation in his spare room, and he promised to go through them again, in case he missed something. In the meantime, I'm thinking of talking to the Gilmans."

Lizzy had expected a look of disapproval, but Evvie simply nodded. "You'll have to settle for the daddy," she said through a mouthful of cobbler. "The mama took off a few years back, and no one's heard a peep from her since."

"Andrew told me."

"Can't blame her. Word is Mr. Gilman's no prize. Can't imagine he'd be any better after what happened. And who'd want to live in a place where everything you looked at reminded you of what you'd lost? Not me, I know that. He's still here, though. Lives over in Meadow Park now, the trailer park out by the fairgrounds. And I'm pretty sure he still works at Mason Electric."

Lizzy spooned up a bite of cobbler, but paused before putting it in her mouth. "The detective doesn't think I'll get very far. Neither does Andrew. And I'm starting to think they're right. Fred Gilman will take one look at me and see Althea—the woman he thinks murdered his little girls."

"He might just. And he'll probably be mad. But you knew you were going to make folks mad when you decided to do this. Are you having second thoughts?"

"I don't know. Maybe. I think about how I'd feel if I were in the Gilmans' shoes, and someone came along and made me relive it all. It seems cruel, especially when it's not likely to amount to anything. I'm just wondering if it's worth it."

Evvie lifted her apron and dabbed the corner of her mouth. "You might be right. It might come to nothing. But what if you're wrong? What if there was something somebody forgot to tell the police? Something that could have made a difference? Neither of them was in a good place back then. But time's passed. They can look at it now, through clearer eyes. Maybe there's something, some tiny bit of a memory stuck way down deep, and you showing up could shake it loose."

"That's a lot of maybes, Evvie. What if I'm just stirring up trouble for trouble's sake?"

"Trouble." Evvie scowled at her. "That's what you're worried about? Stirring up trouble?"

"I'm trying to do the right thing. To be compassionate."

"You want to do the right thing? Help those little girls move on."

Lizzy tipped her head to the side, eyes narrowed. "What did you say?"

"I said you need to help those girls move on. You're worried about Mr. Gilman, but have you ever thought those girls might rest easier if someone caught whoever hurt them? That all this time they've been hovering between this world and the next, waiting for someone to figure out what really happened? And your gran—she might just feel like she's got some unfinished business herself, things tethering her to this place, instead of where she's meant to be."

Lizzy lowered her spoon back to her bowl. "The other day—" She broke off, waving the thought away. "Never mind. It was nothing."

"Doesn't look like nothing from where I'm sitting."

"All right. The other day, when I was coming back from the pond, something weird happened. All of a sudden it was like she was with me. It was so real I felt like I was going to turn around and find her standing there." She forced herself to meet Evvie's gaze. "I smelled her, Evvie. The perfume I used to make for her—I could smell it."

"They say smells can trigger memory."

"They can," Lizzy agreed. "The olfactory and memory centers of the brain are closely connected. But this didn't *feel* like a memory. It felt . . . real." She rolled her eyes and heaved a sigh. "Listen to me, carrying on like a crazy person. It is crazy, right?"

Evvie's mouth softened, not quite a smile but close to it. "Maybe. But sometimes the craziest things are the truest of all. Just because we can't explain a thing doesn't mean it's not real."

Lizzy stared at her, still trying to wrap her head around this enigmatic woman, with her all-seeing eyes and strange half smiles. "Sometimes you say things, Evvie. Things that make me wonder if you're . . ." She caught herself, waving away the rest of the thought. "Never mind."

Evvie pushed back her chair and stood. "Come with me. There's something I need to show you."

Lizzy followed her to the backyard, past the greenhouse with its newly replaced glass, and the vegetable garden with its chicken wire fence and gate, finally coming to a stop before Evvie's pastel-colored bee boxes.

Lizzy eyed them warily. She'd never developed Althea's fondness for bees, or anything with wings and a stinger. She held her breath as Evvie laid a hand on the lid of one of the hives, a smile softening the corners of her mouth. Lizzy held her breath. She didn't know a thing about beekeeping, but even she knew you were supposed to wear some sort of protective gear—a smock, gloves, one of those pith helmets with the netting. Evvie had none of that. She just stood there, barefaced and bare armed—and began to sing.

The hairs on Lizzy's arms prickled to attention. It wasn't a tune she recognized. The words were foreign and had a faintly French lilt. She stood spellbound as Evvie closed her eyes and let her head fall back, holding perfectly still as the song poured out low, lush, and achingly sweet. And then she slowly began to raise her arms, holding them out to her sides. An invitation, Lizzy realized. She was calling them to her.

One by one the bees came, hovering around her like a soft, humming cloud, eventually lighting on her arms, her neck, her cheeks. It should have been terrifying, but somehow it wasn't. It was lovely and magical, and suddenly Lizzy understood.

She's one of us.

It explained so much. The inexplicable sense of the familiar she'd felt almost from the beginning; those sharp, all-seeing eyes; her remark about family not always being about blood. Of course she and Althea had hit it off. They were sisters under the skin, walkers on the same path.

"Come meet my bees," Evvie said, as if nothing remotely extraordinary had occurred.

Lizzy eyed the humming bodies still clinging to Evvie's arms and shook her head. "Thanks. I'm good."

"They're happy. They won't hurt you."

Lizzy sucked in a breath, holding it as she inched closer. "Aren't you supposed to have one of those smoker things?"

"Don't need one."

"You're not afraid of being stung?"

"Nope."

Lizzy couldn't stop staring. Magick or not, it was hard to comprehend what she was seeing. "The song you were singing just now—what was it?"

"It's called 'Galine Galo.' It's a Creole lullaby."

"You sing lullabies to your bees?"

"They like it."

Lizzy cocked an eye at her, skeptical. And yet it was plain that Evvie's song had not only attracted the bees, it had lulled them. They seemed almost . . . affectionate. "Have you always been able to do this?"

"Long as I can remember."

"How on earth did you know to sing to them?"

Evvie shrugged. The bees on her shoulders stirred, then resettled. "Don't know. Just did. My mama used to sing that song to me when I was little, and it always calmed me. Guess I figured if it worked for me, it would work for them." She paused, pursing her lips to blow gently on one arm. "Go on," she said softly, clearly talking to the bees. She turned to the other arm and blew again. "Go. Go. I've got work to do, and so do you."

Lizzy watched, fascinated as the bees obeyed. When the last bee departed, Evvie bent to remove the lid from an old enamel washtub at the base of the hive. Inside was an assortment of tools. She pulled out a curved blade and set to work, prying one of the frames free, carefully lifting it out, shaking off several clinging bees.

Lizzy was surprised to find herself relaxing as she watched Evvie work. The bees seemed unfazed by this invasion of their habitat, treating Evvie not as an intruder, but as a guest.

"Do they ever sting?"

Evvie glanced up from her work. "Every once in a while, but it's usually my fault when they do. I've broken their rules."

"Bees have rules?"

"Of course they have rules. Every living thing has rules. A big one with bees is that you don't wear anything with a strong scent. It stirs them up, makes them nervous."

"I guess that makes sense. Could I learn how to do it? The singing thing, I mean. Not that I want to. I'm just curious."

"Doubt it." Evvie pressed her lips together as she mulled the question further. "It's like you and your nose. Your gran told me how you're able to read people. It wasn't something you learned. It was something you were born with—a gift."

"Althea used to call it that too, but it hasn't always felt that way to me. Sometimes I know things I'd rather not know. Like what someone's thinking when I'm around."

"If you've been given a gift, there's a reason. The magick goes where it's best used."

Lizzy nodded absently, wondering what use there might be for a woman who sang to bees. "I suppose. But it still seems a little dangerous. What if something happened? What if they all decided to get mad at the same time?"

Evvie looked up from the frame she'd been examining. "Bees are like people, little girl. They attack when they feel threatened—when they're afraid. It's the same for us. It's always the things we fear that sting us in the end. The things we hide from or push against. When we drop the fear—the resistance—things take their course in a more natural and painless way."

"You sound like Althea now, with her nature metaphors, always trying to teach me something."

Evvie slid the gooey frame back into place and wiped her hands on the front of her apron. "I'd say that's just about the nicest compliment I've ever gotten."

"I found a book," Lizzy blurted. "In the bookcase in Althea's room—one she wrote just for me."

Evvie nodded, her expression wistful. "She finished it the day before she passed. I helped her press the flowers and herbs. And locked it up with the others when she finished it. She knew you'd find it when the time came."

"How could she possibly know that?"

Evvie smiled one of her enigmatic smiles. "She raised you, little girl. And loved you with her whole soul. That kind of bond doesn't end just because one of you stops breathing. That book was a labor of love, a way to keep teaching you after she was gone."

"I thought she left you here for that."

"Don't be silly. There's only ever one queen in a hive. And that was Althea."

Lizzy couldn't help asking the obvious question. "What happens when the queen dies?"

Evvie looked at her a long time, her eyes softly probing. "Depends," she said at last. "Sometimes the queen nurtures her own replacement. But if the death is sudden and the hive is unprepared, the drones band together to nurture a new queen. She's carefully prepared, fed, and pampered, until she's ready to assume her new position as head of the hive."

"And then what?"

"As queen, her sole responsibility is to ensure the survival of the hive."

"You mean reproduce," Lizzy replied matter-of-factly.

"Yes. Her job is to populate the hive, and eventually give birth to her successor. If she fails, the hive may wither and die—unless the beekeeper steps in."

Lizzy took a moment to digest this, aware that their conversation had gone beyond beekeeping to something much closer to home. "Is that why you're here? To step in?"

Evvie smiled sheepishly. "Something like that. Your gran hoped I'd be able to smooth things a bit when you came back."

"What if I hadn't come back? I wasn't going to."

"Silly girl. You were always going to come back. You just didn't know it. She did, though. That's why she wrote the book. Because she knew it would be hard. It was never easy for you here, growing up the way you did, with no friends and no real mother to speak of. And then those poor girls turning up dead. They blamed her, but you took your share of fire. Still, here you are, back in Salem Creek, thinking of kicking over a hornet's nest. That's brave."

"Or maybe it's just crazy." She shook her head, staring off into the woods. "I could call Roger Coleman and tell him to forget it, just let the whole thing drop and go back to New York."

Evvie's brow puckered. "Could you?"

Lizzy struggled to find an answer. She wasn't like Luc. She couldn't just get on with it and feel relieved that it was finally over. Because it wasn't over. And wouldn't be until everyone in Salem Creek knew what really happened the night Heather and Darcy Gilman disappeared. But was she prepared—truly prepared—to pay the price for that truth? She wanted to say yes, to believe she was up for whatever the Gilmans or the rest of the town could throw at her. She wanted to, but she wasn't sure.

As if in answer, the air around her seemed to ripple, the subtle breeze freshened with the scents of lavender and bergamot. The fragrance was unmistakable, like the brush of fingers against her cheek, and suddenly she knew what she needed to do.

. . . *come back to the book when you are ready. Trust me in this, sweet girl. You will know when it's time.*

Bluebells . . . for truth.

My dearest Lizzy,

If you're reading this, you have been pulled back to these pages, perhaps because you're wrestling with a choice, searching your heart for what's right. I knew that if you came back, this day would come, and that it would not be easy. The truth seldom is. Which is why we spend so much time hiding from it. But the truth is incapable of real harm. It is we who do harm, when we refuse to face what is real, because it's uncomfortable or inconvenient.

When you were a girl, you were such a sensitive little thing, afraid of the dark, and the monsters you swore lived under your bed. Nearly every night you would wake, soaking wet and rigid with terror, certain you were about to be dragged off into the dark and devoured. You would come wailing down the hall, begging me to save you, to hide you, and I would let you climb in with me. I would soothe you, and promise that the monsters would never get you.

And then one night I realized I was helping you keep your monsters alive, by coddling and protecting you. I knew if I let you climb in with me again that the next night, or the one after that, you would be terrorized all over again. And so I carried you down the hall—do you remember it? You fought like a hellcat the whole way. But I made you go in, and I flipped on the light. Then I took you by the hand and made you look under the bed and in the closet, in every drawer and corner of that room, until you saw for yourself that the monsters weren't there, that they'd never been there.

You never had the dream again. Because you understood that what isn't real can't hurt you. Illusions have no power—unless we insist on clinging to them. Then they become a warped kind of truth, a story we settle for because we prefer to remain in the dark with the monsters we know, rather than face new ones.

That's why the worst truths—the ones that do the most harm—are those we refuse to face. We prefer falsehoods and half-truths, inventions meant to gloss over things we don't wish to see. But knowing half a thing is to not know it at all. We tell ourselves the price of truth is simply too high, that it's better to leave a thing alone in the name of peace than to inflict pain in the name of truth. But that kind of peace comes at a price.

We must never forget that there's always another side to the coin—that on the other side of every lie is a truth that has gone untold. And there is always a cost to such things. We all of us come to a place in our lives when the things we dread inevitably come for us. Not the childish things that lurk in dark corners or under beds, but the kind that live in our heads and our hearts. The grown-up things. The kind that cut deep when they're finally revealed. And then we must choose—do what's hard and topple the lie, or simply allow it to stand.

You have always had a good heart, my Lizzy—a kind heart. But it is never a kindness to allow a lie to stand, however hard the pursuit of the truth may be. In the end, light is the only thing that has ever chased away darkness—the only thing that ever will. Seek truth in all things, my dearest girl. There can be no healing without it.

A—

ELEVEN

July 22

It was nearly five when Lizzy pulled into the parking lot of Mason Electric. She'd purposely waited for closing time but found herself hesitating as she reached for the door handle. Once she approached Fred Gilman, there'd be no going back. But Althea's words thrummed in her head. *Seek truth in all things. There can be no healing without it.*

So be it.

The door chimed softly as she stepped into the lobby. A young woman in cat-eye glasses and a lime-green sundress glanced up from the counter with a polite smile.

"Can I help you?"

"I was hoping to speak with Fred Gilman. Is he in?"

"Sorry. He's out on a job. But if you leave your name, I'll have him call you."

Lizzy wasn't sure whether to feel relieved or disappointed. "No. Thank you. No message."

She was preparing to leave when she noticed two men in gray work shirts huddled around the watercooler behind the counter. One of them, the taller of the two, locked eyes with her over his paper cup.

"What do you want with Fred?"

Lizzy eyed the name patch on his shirt—JAKE. "I want to talk to him. On personal business."

"No," he said flatly. "You don't. I know who you are, and I know all about your business. Hasn't your family caused enough trouble in this town?"

Lizzy fought the urge to step back, registering the caustic combination of lye and hot tar. Not exactly a promising sign. "I didn't come to cause trouble. I just need to ask him a few questions."

Jake leaned across the counter until his face was inches from hers. "Leave the man alone. He doesn't need your questions. None of us do."

"Jake!" The woman in the cat-eye glasses slapped a manila folder down on the counter. "Get back to the warehouse where you belong. You too, Tommy." When the men were gone, she turned back with an apologetic smile. "Sorry about them. Fred should be back shortly. You can wait if you want."

"No. No, thank you. I'll catch up with him another time."

She had crossed to the door when she felt a pair of eyes between her shoulder blades. She glanced back to see that Jake had reappeared, his eyes flinty as he watched her go.

Back in the car, she sat with both hands curled tight around the wheel. She'd known better than to expect red-carpet treatment, but she hadn't prepared for open hostility. And she'd yet to ask a single question. What would happen when she really started digging?

Before she could consider the question, a utility pickup with a ladder rack on the roof swung into the lot and parked several rows over. She hadn't seen Fred Gilman in years, but there was no missing the man's telltale gait, shoulders bunched close to his ears, arms nearly stationary as he crossed the lot, like a man bracing himself against a storm. She reached for the door handle, then changed her mind. Following him inside would just lead to another run-in with Jake, squelching any hope for a productive conversation. She'd have a better shot if she waited for him to come out.

Ten minutes later Gilman reappeared with Jake at his side. She hadn't counted on that. She slouched down in her seat, praying she wouldn't be spotted as they crossed the parking lot together. They lingered for what felt like an eternity, in deep conversation. It wasn't hard to guess what they were discussing.

When Gilman finally climbed into a battered green Subaru and started the engine, she followed him out of the lot, maintaining what she hoped was a discreet distance, slowing when he slowed, turning when he turned. She felt ridiculous, like an obsessed stalker or inept spy. If he spotted her, would he call the police? And what if he did? She wasn't breaking any laws, and she had every right to ask her questions.

They had just passed the fairground entrance when he turned off into Meadow Park. His driveway was the third on the right. She sped past as he pulled in, circling the block several times to allow him time to get inside. Ambushing the man in his driveway wasn't likely to earn her any points. On the third pass, she pulled in behind the Subaru.

Fred Gilman's home was a yellow-and-white single-wide with a weathered wood porch tacked onto the front. The postage stamp–size lot was brown with neglect, barren but for a straggly hedge running down one side. No flowers in the yard. No mat on the porch. No wreath on the door. The home of a man who lived alone.

Lizzy held her breath as she mounted the porch steps and knocked on the dented aluminum door. There was a moment of fumbling with a lock before the door finally inched back. Gilman stood blinking at her through the opening, a frozen dinner half out of its box in his hands. He looked weary as he peered out, and a little annoyed—until he recognized her.

His face hardened as he backed away, clearly bent on slamming the door in her face. But she'd come too far to leave empty-handed. Reflexively, she wedged her foot between the door and the jamb. An ambrosia of mothballs, burned coffee, and dirty carpet wafted through the opening. Lizzy suspected the odors had more to do with Fred Gilman's living conditions than with the state of his emotions, but it was enough to make her take a small step back.

"Mr. Gilman, I'd like to speak to you."

Gilman glared at her. "Stay away from me."

"Please. I think you'll want to hear what I have to say. It's about the investigation into what happened to your girls."

His face suddenly went slack, and for a moment he stood blinking at the frozen dinner in his hands, as if wondering how it got there. Finally, his eyes snapped back to hers. "You have one minute to say what you came to say, and you can say it from right there on the porch."

Lizzy felt her shoulders relax. "You've heard, I'm sure, that my grandmother died." She waited for a response, but his face was disconcertingly blank. "I know what you think, Mr. Gilman. You believe Althea hurt your girls. But it isn't true. I have reason—good reason—to believe the investigation was mishandled. I've asked the police to look at the evidence again, but in the meantime, I was hoping you and your wife might remember—"

"My *wife*," Gilman spat, "lives in Massachusetts now."

"I'm so sorry, Mr. Gilman. Truly sorry, for everything you've been through. But I'm sure you'd want to know the truth."

"You have nothing to say that I want to hear. My girls are dead. My wife's gone. Isn't that enough for you?"

"Mr. Gilman, please, if you knew my grandmother at all, you'd know she could never hurt your daughters. All I need is something to go on, something that might convince Chief Summers to reopen the case."

Gilman's face had gone a blotchy shade of red. He locked eyes with her. "I know all I need to about the Moons. And so does the rest of this town. They don't want you here any more than I do. Yet here you stand on my front porch, asking for my help. You've got some brass. But then your lot always did. Well, I say good riddance to your grandmother. Got what was coming to her, if you ask me. Maybe you will too."

His words, a blend of menace and thinly veiled disgust, sent a chill down Lizzy's spine. Had he just threatened her? She couldn't say for sure, but it was clear that she'd get no help from him. She turned and headed back down the steps.

"And don't go bothering my wife if you know what's good for you." The words hit Lizzy in the back as she reached the driveway. "She's got nothing to say."

~

Lizzy replayed the conversation in her head on the drive home, not that it had *been* much of a conversation. She hadn't learned anything she didn't already know. Still, she couldn't shake the feeling that there was more to Gilman's rancor than met the eye. He clearly didn't want her dredging up the past, and especially not with his ex-wife.

She's got nothing to say.

Maybe that was true—and maybe it wasn't. Was it possible Gilman had something to hide? She shuddered at the possibilities, but it happened, didn't it? You heard about it on the news, saw it in the papers. Parents capable of the unthinkable.

Lizzy brought herself up short. She was grasping at straws now, concocting a plot that felt like it had been lifted from an airport novel, and on nothing more than speculation. She knew better than most the wreckage wrought by false accusations. She needed to rein in her imagination, to follow the facts rather than her emotions. But where did that leave her? Roger had been swift to point out that there was a reason the obvious suspect was typically the obvious suspect. But what if there *were* no obvious suspects? No obvious motive, no clear-cut opportunity? You had to start looking at the not-so-obvious suspects, didn't you?

Lizzy was surprised to find herself back home so quickly. She'd been so caught up in her thoughts that she'd made most of the drive on autopilot. She spotted Andrew's truck in his driveway as she drove past. Maybe a male perspective was what she needed.

She got out of the car, cut across the yard, and knocked. Andrew answered moments later, sporting loose-fitting sweatpants and a damp towel draped around bare shoulders. The mingled scents of amber and smoke came off him in waves.

"Hey. I thought I heard a knock. What's up?"

Lizzy's gaze slid down his bare torso, then shot back to his face. "I just got home and saw your truck. Is it a bad time?"

"It's a great time, actually. I was just about to fix some supper."

"Oh, sorry. I'll come back if you're cooking."

"Who said anything about cooking?"

"I thought you did."

Andrew motioned for her to follow him to the kitchen. "I can boil water, scramble eggs, and butter toast. Beyond that, I'm pretty much a ready-to-eat kind of guy. Plus, the stove's not hooked up yet." He paused, opening the fridge door with a flourish. "Which is why I hit the market this afternoon. I was thinking of having a little picnic."

Lizzy eyed the collection of deli containers and what appeared to be a rotisserie chicken. "Looks like quite a feast."

"Join me?"

"Oh, no. I don't want to intrude. We can talk tomorrow."

"Stay. There's plenty. I'll warn you, though, this isn't New York City. The fare isn't exactly trendy, and we'll be sitting on the floor."

He shot her a grin. Lizzy found herself grinning back, wondering why she hadn't noticed his dimples before now. "Personally, I've always thought chairs were overrated."

"Great. Give me a minute to throw on a shirt. You can go ahead and pull that stuff out of the fridge if you want. Paper plates are in the cabinet next to the sink."

He reappeared a short time later wearing torn jeans and a faded Patriots T-shirt. "Never let it be said that I forced you to dine with a savage."

While Lizzy busied herself with the food containers, Andrew spread a paint-spattered drop cloth on the floor of what she assumed was the breakfast room. When the food was ready, they settled down to their makeshift picnic, sitting opposite one another with their paper plates and plastic utensils.

Lizzy watched with mixed emotions as Andrew struggled to dissect the chicken with a plastic knife, wondering when the best time might be to mention that she was a vegetarian. "Not to criticize, but a real knife might come in handy."

Andrew grimaced, still wrestling with the chicken. "Don't have one." Another few minutes and the drumstick came free. He offered it to Lizzy.

She waved it off with a shake of her head. "No meat for me."

"Sorry. Didn't know that."

"No reason you should. Why don't you have a knife?"

"Most of the downstairs stuff's in storage. I wasn't thinking when I packed up the kitchen. I just wanted everything out. It's a hassle, but it's easier in the long run. You're not tripping over things, worrying about protecting the furniture, moving stuff from room to room. I've got a bed and a dresser upstairs. And my drafting table. That'll do until it's finished."

Lizzy took in the room, the empty walls and bare floor. "When will that be?"

Andrew shrugged as he reached for a carrot stick. "Depends. Spring, maybe. I'm fitting it in between clients, so it could be a while. And it's just me, so there's no rush. You're the first person to see it, by the way. I don't entertain much. Come to think of it, why did you drop by?"

Lizzy spooned a blob of potato salad onto her plate and handed him the container. "I went to see Fred Gilman today. You were right. He all but slammed the door in my face."

"You can't be surprised."

"No, but I can't help wondering . . . How well do you know him?"

"Gilman? Not well. He was a customer of my father's. Why?"

"I was just wondering if there might be a reason he doesn't want me snooping around. Maybe he knows something he doesn't want *me* to know."

"By *something*, you mean . . ."

"It happens."

"Lizzy, think about what you're saying."

"I have been thinking about it. I thought about it all the way home. He wasn't just upset, he was hostile. He doesn't want me anywhere near this."

Andrew set down his fork, scowling. "What did he say?"

"That Althea got what she deserved, and maybe I would too. It was probably just the anger talking, but there was something, I don't know, sinister about the way he said it. He also warned me to stay away from his wife, which I thought was odd since they're not together anymore. Why would he not want me talking to her?"

"Maybe it's as simple as wanting to protect her. Just because two people are apart doesn't mean they've stopped caring about each other."

Lizzy nodded, accepting the remark at face value. When it came to marital dynamics, she had little to go on. "I suppose so. That's why I came over. I needed you to tell me I was imagining things. I just thought after so much time he might be willing to at least listen."

"What are you going to do now?"

Lizzy pushed her potato salad around her plate. "I have no idea. Talk to Mrs. Gilman, I suppose. If I can track her down. I need something I can take back to Summers, something he can't ignore."

"Good luck with that. Cavanaugh just endorsed him as Salem Creek's next mayor. There's zero chance of him touching this now."

"Then I guess I'll have to force his hand."

"Lizzy." Andrew folded his paper napkin and laid it aside. "I get you needing to do this. In fact, I admire the hell out of you for it, but maybe you should slow down, give Roger time to get through his notes. If there's something to find, he'll find it. And then he can deal with Summers, and you're out of it. In the meantime, maybe I could do some poking around, see if anyone knows how to contact her."

Lizzy managed a smile. She didn't want to seem ungrateful, but he was doing it again, stepping in to protect her, like he had the night Rhanna went wading in the fountain. Only this time he had more to lose. "Andrew, I'm grateful to you for putting me in touch with Roger, but this is my fight. I'll be gone in a few weeks, and you'll still be here. Your business will still be here. The last thing you need is to get mixed up in this."

"I'm not worried about what this town thinks."

"You should be," Lizzy replied, thinking of the men at Mason Electric, of Jake and his buddy, and how they'd bowed up at the mere sight of her. Fred Gilman was right about one thing. No one wanted her here. And if Andrew was seen as choosing the Moons over Salem Creek, no one would want him here either.

"I shouldn't have involved you," she said, setting aside her plate. "I knew better."

"You didn't involve me, Lizzy. I involved myself."

"Why?" The word was out of her mouth before she had time to think about where it might lead, but now that it was out, she was curious. "Why did you agree to help me—when you're clearly not convinced I should be poking around in this? You're always doing that, you know? Helping me. And it's not just making the call to Roger. It's the greenhouse, and the barn, and all the other stuff."

Andrew arched a brow. "Other stuff?"

"In school. The Twizzlers at the assembly. The ride home the day of the hailstorm. We barely knew each other then. Come to that, we barely know each other now." She paused, ducking her head. "I always wondered . . . Was it because you felt sorry for me?"

Andrew stared at her, as if genuinely astonished. "That's what you thought? That I felt sorry for you?"

She responded with a half-hearted shrug. "I wasn't exactly Miss Popular in school. All I wanted back then was to be invisible. I thought I was doing a good job of it too. Except you kept turning up, being all nice. For the life of me, I couldn't figure out why. I still can't."

Andrew paused, picking up his napkin again, and slowly wiped his hands. Finally, he looked up. "Why is a boy *ever* nice to a girl? I wanted you to like me. I still do."

Lizzy blinked at him, cheeks tingling. There were no dimples this time, no sign that he was teasing. There were only his words hovering between them, and something warm and unfamiliar unfurling beneath her ribs. She'd had her share of adult relationships, but she'd skipped over this part of adolescence, the giddy flutter of first attraction, the breathless tug of young heartstrings. There'd been no point back then. And there was certainly no point now.

She scrambled to her feet, careful to avoid Andrew's eyes, and headed for the front door. "I'm sorry. I didn't realize it was so late. I need to get home before Evvie starts worrying."

Andrew stood and followed her to the door. "Lizzy . . ."

She turned, her hand already on the knob.

"You could never be invisible to me. Not then, and not now."

Lizzy nodded, cool and careful as she registered what he was trying to say without actually saying it. "It isn't about me liking you, Andrew. It never was. But the stakes are higher now. For both of us."

TWELVE

Andrew watched, cursing himself as Lizzy moved down the front walk. What was he thinking? She'd come to him for help, and instead of offering advice, he'd babbled on like some lovesick teenager and run her off.

Again.

She'd always been skittish around him. Around everyone, really. Why should things be different now? Could he blame her for keeping her guard up? Eight years might seem like a long time to most, but not in a town like Salem Creek, where minds changed slowly—if at all. Though he supposed she knew that better than he.

It had taken less than twenty-four hours for things to get ugly after the Amber Alert went out for Heather and Darcy Gilman. By the next morning the town's whisper mill had sputtered to life, grinding out a series of ridiculous and baseless speculations. In small New England towns where nothing much ever happened, gossip was a favorite pastime, like high school hockey or cornhole contests at the Sunday barbecue. And like good barbecue, the locals lapped it up.

By the time the girls' bodies were recovered from the Moons' pond, the torch-and-pitchfork brigade had begun to clamor for their own brand of justice. After Rhanna's coffee shop escapade, several churches banded together to organize a midnight vigil—*to pray away the evil dwelling in our midst, and see the Lord's will done.*

Flyers had gone up all over town the day before, in shopwindows and on telephone poles, inviting the faithful to gather and pray for the soul of their God-fearing town. The name Moon wasn't mentioned that night. There was no need. Everyone understood.

All three local news channels had covered the event, complete with plenty of B-roll capturing a sea of righteous faces lit by flickering white candles. When the story was picked up by the larger news outlets, a feeding frenzy ensued, and Randall Summers had been forced to issue a statement urging patience while law enforcement did its job—a hedge against the possibility that such talk might be seen as a call to action by those looking to take matters into their own hands.

Even now, the thought of it made Andrew sick. He'd had every intention of attending that night, prepared to tell every last one of them what they could do with their so-called prayers, but his father had urged him to stay away, explaining that the surest way to fan the flames was to point fingers and pit neighbor against neighbor. He promised that right would win out in the end, that the truth would come to light and the Moons would be left alone. His father hadn't been wrong about much in his life, but he'd been wrong about that. Salem Creek had never forgiven the Moons. Not for the murders of two young girls, but for the sin of being different.

The day after the vigil, Rhanna had skipped town—proof of the power of prayer, the candle wavers had claimed. Althea had done the only thing she could: keep her head down and fight to hold the tattered remains of her business together. And Lizzy had retreated to the barn, out of the reach of customers and curiosity seekers. And him.

He'd hung around after undergrad at UNH, taking postbacc classes and helping his father with the store, inventing one lame excuse after another to put off applying to grad school. Not that he'd actually fooled anyone. Still, he rarely saw her. Unless he manufactured a reason to walk over to the farm, which he'd done with embarrassing regularity. She'd been a riddle he needed to solve back then, the answer to some question he'd yet to fully form. He'd never walked in her shoes—the *other* in a world that rewarded sameness and conformity. Instead, he'd been president of the student council, a high school all-American, the son of a respected businessman, who graduated with a fistful of scholarships to his name. It was the kind of white-bread existence guys like him tended to take for granted. But Lizzy had lived a very different reality.

Her family's history, their choice of livelihood, even the way she looked, was so far from conforming to the norm that she was punished for it. But instead of lashing out, or embracing what made her different, she had withdrawn. And when that didn't work, she left.

It was Althea who had broken the news. He'd gone over to the farm on some made-up errand for his father, hoping to catch a glimpse of her. Her car, a battered blue Honda Civic, was gone. It should have been his first clue. She'd stopped going into town by then. He was pretending to check the flue in the parlor fireplace, trying to think of a way to bring Lizzy into the conversation, when Althea finally volunteered the truth. She was gone, off to New York to study fragrance.

After that, it didn't take his father long to convince him that it was time to quit moping over a girl who didn't know he was alive and get himself to graduate school. Eight weeks, maybe ten, and he'd left town, bound for Chicago and the Illinois School of Architecture, vowing that his days of pining for the illusive Lizzy Moon were over.

Now he was back—and so was she.

THIRTEEN

July 23

Evvie was pulling a pan of lemon–poppy seed muffins from the oven when Lizzy came down the stairs. She straightened, the fragrant steam fogging her glasses. "You're up early."

Lizzy checked the clock above the sink. It was just after six, early even for her, but after a night of jumbled dreams in which Fred Gilman's face kept morphing into Andrew's, she was more than ready to be up and moving. "I had a rough night."

"That's what happens when you skip supper. Sit, and I'll fix you some breakfast."

"I didn't skip supper. I ate with Andrew—sort of. I wanted to talk to him about Fred Gilman."

"I wondered where you'd got to, then I dozed off. Next thing I knew it was nearly midnight. How'd the meeting go?"

Lizzy put the kettle on to heat, then fetched the tea canister from the cupboard. She really did need to get some coffee in the house. "It went just like everyone said it would. I didn't get past the front door."

"And how was supper?"

Lizzy willed her face to remain blank. She didn't want to think about last night's conversation with Andrew. "Supper?"

"You said you ate with Andrew."

"Oh, right. It was just a spur-of-the-moment thing. We had a kind of picnic on the floor. Did you know he's remodeling? He's put a new deck on, replaced all the windows, and is redoing the entire kitchen. I actually helped him pick the granite last time I was there."

Evvie's gaze slid to Lizzy's. "That right?"

Lizzy was spared a response when the kettle began to shriek. Evvie snapped off the burner. "I'll do the tea. You go get my paper off the stoop."

Lizzy did as she was told and headed for the foyer. A draft of morning air greeted her as she stepped out onto the front steps. The birds were up, warbling in the treetops. She stood there, in the shade of the sprawling ash boughs, relishing the chorus of bright, sweet notes. Chickadees, siskins, pine warblers. Althea had taught her to pick out their songs.

She was about to bend down for the paper when she spotted something hanging from one of the lower branches. Curious, she left the *Chronicle* on the step and padded barefoot across the grass to peer up into the tree. Her stomach dropped when she realized what she was looking at—a crude straw doll wearing a black dress and pointy hat, dangling from a length of filthy rope.

She gave the rope a tug. It came free more easily than she expected, tumbling limply into her arms. She stared at the note pinned to the doll's throat.

Thou shalt not suffer a witch to live.

She knew the quote—all the Moons did—from the book of Exodus.

A shiver crawled up Lizzy's spine as she stared at the scrap of white paper. It was heavy and slightly slick, the kind of paper that came on large rolls and was sometimes used by restaurants to cover tables, or by preschool teachers for finger painting. The verse was scrawled in rough red letters, in what looked to be crayon. She peered over her shoulder, scanning the yard, the street, but there was no sign of the culprit. Not that there was likely to be.

Halloween—Samhain—had been a particular favorite for the local children. Althea had always taken it in stride, even managing to chuckle at some of the more imaginative pranks. She'd found the toilet paper pentagram in the front yard particularly amusing. But that was years ago. Was it starting again? Or was this something else? Something more sinister?

"I wondered where you'd gotten to." Evvie stood in the doorway, untying her apron and tossing it over her shoulder. "What's that you've got there?"

"Nothing," Lizzy said, shoving the hideous straw doll behind her back. "A prank, probably."

Evvie's eyes narrowed. "Let me see that."

"It's nothing."

"Well then, there's no need to hide it. Give it here."

Lizzy stared at Evvie's outstretched hand. There'd be no slipping past her, that much was clear. "It's probably nothing," she said again, wanting to believe her own words as she handed the doll over. "It used to happen all the time after the murders. One time someone carved a pentagram into the hood of Althea's car. Another time we found a dead cat on the back stoop. But nothing ever came of it. This was just somebody trying to be cute."

Evvie's jaw hardened as she held up the doll, giving it a shake for emphasis. "This doll is not *cute*, little girl. This note is not *cute*."

She turned then and headed back into the house, leaving Lizzy on the steps.

Lizzy sighed, following her inside. "Please don't make this a bigger deal than it is."

"A bigger deal?" Evvie jabbed a finger at the scrawled note. "What do you think this means? Coming the day after you paid that man a visit? I'll tell you what it means. It means someone isn't happy about you coming back here and dredging up the past. This wasn't some young'un from down the street. This was someone grown. Someone dangerous."

"Or maybe it's just someone who wants us to *think* they're dangerous." Lizzy paused for a deep breath, groping for some way to talk Evvie off the ledge—and maybe herself too. "Look, I know how scary this must look—"

"Do you?" Evvie parked her hands on her hips, eyes flashing. "Because where I come from, we take nooses pretty seriously."

Lizzy dropped her head, properly chastened. "Yes, of course you do. But this isn't that, Evvie. No one's planning a lynching."

"We don't know what anyone's planning, and we're not going to find out. You need to call the police."

"Evvie, the last thing I need right now is the police involved in this. At the moment only a handful of people even know I'm back. The minute I pick up the phone and tell them about that note, it'll be all over town. And there goes any chance I have of getting anyone to talk to me. Please don't say anything. At least not yet." She reached for Evvie's hand, giving it a squeeze. "Please?"

"Fine." Evvie pushed the doll back into Lizzy's hands. "But get rid of it. Like my mama used to say, we don't need no bad juju hangin' around. And say what you want, but that right there is some bad juju."

Lizzy breathed a sigh of relief as she carried the doll to the mudroom, where she wouldn't have to look at it again until she decided what to do with it. For now, she was grateful that she'd managed to buy herself some time with Evvie. It was entirely possible that the thing had been intended as a prank. It certainly wouldn't be the first time. But she wasn't ready to rule out the possibility that someone—Fred Gilman, perhaps—was behind the hideous straw effigy.

~

Lizzy squinted at the power bar on her cell phone. Sixteen percent remaining. She reached for her charger, plugged it in, scrubbed at her eyes, and kept scrolling. Researching old newspaper articles on a three-by-five screen was far from optimal, but given Althea's distrust of technology—including the internet—she hadn't seen much point in bringing her laptop.

She'd hoped something might jump out at her, something everyone had missed eight years ago, that might point her in a new direction, including where Susan Gilman might have gone when she left Salem Creek. But three hours of exhaustive searching had turned up nothing. There'd been no shortage of material, articles sourced from the local paper as well as out-of-state publications, each headline more gruesome than the last: Parents Beg for Safe Return of Missing Daughters. Grisly Scene at Moon Girl Farm. Bodies of Missing Girls Recovered from Local Pond. Double Homicide Rocks Quiet New England Town. Still No Arrest as Gilman Girls Are Laid to Rest.

But harder to take than the headlines was the endless barrage of photos, grainy black-and-white images carefully placed to tug at readers' emotions. There was the idyllic family portrait—mother and father in back, daughters in front, dressed in what appeared to be Easter outfits—as well as several shots of the girls when they were older.

The sisters were strikingly similar in appearance, pretty in the way most girls are pretty in their teens, fresh-faced and free of concern. But there were differences too. Darcy had wide eyes and a winning set of dimples. Heather had the same eyes, but the dimples were missing. Probably because she wasn't smiling in any of the photos. And there was something else about Heather that was different: a flinty sort of defiance peering back at the camera, in stark contrast to her younger sister's wide-open gaze.

There were photos of the parents as well, most of them taken during press conferences or interviews. Susan Gilman looked virtually catatonic in all of them, as if sleepwalking through a nightmare, which she had been. And there was Fred, the grieving father, glaring straight at the camera. He looked washed-out and gaunt, but with the same hard edges she'd seen in him yesterday.

She studied his face, the pinched lips and flared nostrils, the almost palpable anger staring back at her from the photo. Was it the face of a grieving father, or a man capable of harming his own daughters? Was it possible to be both? And if so, how could she prove it?

The question continued to nag as Lizzy closed the browser and set her phone aside. She'd spent the entire morning online, with zero to show for her efforts, when she should have been calling Realtors or going through the attic. But both options left her cold. She needed to move her body, to clear her head and work off some energy. Perhaps she'd go back to the wildflower garden for an hour, and do some weeding.

She was halfway down the stairs when she heard Andrew's voice, along with Evvie's, coming from the kitchen. After her abrupt departure last night, she would have preferred to keep some distance between them, but there was no way to get to the mudroom door without passing through the kitchen.

They stopped talking the minute she entered the room. Not a good sign. Andrew turned to face her, the straw doll clutched in his fist. "Were you planning to mention this?"

Lizzy's head swiveled in Evvie's direction, but she was already holding up her hands, absolving herself before Lizzy could get a word out. "Don't go laying this at my door. I told you to get rid of it. It's not my fault he saw it when he came in."

"I found it this morning," Lizzy explained wearily. "In the tree out front. I know it looks bad, but we don't really know what it means."

"Yesterday you paid Fred Gilman a visit. Today you find this. You don't think the two are related?"

"I get how it looks, and that the timing is suspicious, but if Fred Gilman wanted to hurt me, he had the perfect opportunity last night when I was standing on his front porch. Can you honestly see him climbing a tree and hanging that thing up in the dark?"

Andrew blew out a long breath. "You can't ignore this, Lizzy. It isn't like having your car keyed. You need to report it."

"I'm not ignoring it. And I will report it—eventually. Though, after what Roger told me about Summers the other day, I don't trust the police to lift a finger when it comes to the Moons. All I want right now is time to do what I need to do without the police muddying the water. Now, can we please drop it? If anyone needs me, I'll be in the wildflower garden, pulling weeds."

She turned and walked out, leaving Andrew and Evvie to stare after her, knowing full well they'd have plenty to say once she was out of earshot. She didn't care. Bad juju or not, it was going to take more than a straw doll to scare her off.

FOURTEEN

July 26

Lizzy had to circle the block three times before she finally located a parking space near the ReadiMaxx office. She was far from eager to sit down with "Southern New Hampshire's Premier Residential Specialist," but she'd already wasted an entire week. It was time to talk to someone, to get some idea about what to expect given the farm's run-down condition. Not to mention the stigma of two dead girls turning up in the pond.

The news wouldn't be good—she was prepared for that—but at least she'd have some idea about what her options might be. She had some money in savings, but nowhere near enough to pay for the laundry list of repairs Andrew had rattled off. Maybe she could take out a small mortgage. Nothing huge, just enough to pay for the most urgent repairs, and swing the property taxes until the place sold. But what if it didn't? What if finding a buyer took years rather than months? She'd be risking foreclosure.

The thought made Lizzy's stomach churn as she dug in her wallet for coins to feed the meter. A nickel and two pennies were all she came up with. She scanned the businesses along Center Street, looking for somewhere to change a ten-dollar bill. Her choices were slim: the post office, a chiropractic clinic, a flower shop that was apparently closed on Mondays—and the coffee shop.

She eyed the sign queasily. Brewed Awakenings. The scene of Rhanna's infamous last stand—still here. Which was more than she could say for her mother. But then there'd been no staying in Salem Creek after that particular spectacle.

Rhanna had spotted a pair of women staring at her over their lattes, and had proceeded to stage a meltdown of epic proportions, railing about pious old biddies who simpered about turning the other cheek on Sundays, then turned into vipers the other six days of the week. She might have gotten away with it if she'd stopped there. But Rhanna had never been one to do things by half. Instead, she walked to the center of the shop, raised her arms above her head, and in the name of all the Moon girls, living and dead, had called down a curse on every breathing soul in Salem Creek—as if such a thing were actually possible.

The so-called curse had produced the desired effect, emptying the shop in a matter of minutes. But there'd been undesired effects as well, like the police showing up to investigate a threat reported by a half dozen townspeople. In the end, nothing came of it. There were no laws on the books regarding curses, threatened or otherwise.

Word of the incident spread like a wildfire, and the outcry for something to be done about *that Moon woman and her girls* quickly swelled. The day after the vigil, Rhanna packed her van, pocketed Althea's emergency cash from the stoneware jug on top of the fridge, and disappeared, leaving her mother and daughter to deal with the fallout.

And now, eight years later, one of those Moon girls was about to walk into the same shop and ask for change. The thought made Lizzy's palms clammy. Perhaps she'd just risk the ticket. But that was ridiculous.

Instead, she turned and made herself push through the door with its tinkling brass bells.

The shop hadn't changed much over the years: black-and-white floor tiles, scarred bistro tables lined up along yellow walls, potted ferns suspended from macramé hangers. Lizzy scanned the chalkboard menu while she waited in line, but her gaze kept straying to the woman working the register. She wasn't wearing a name badge, but she looked vaguely familiar.

Lizzy watched as she rang up the man ahead of her, barked out his order to the barista—*maple scone and a half-caf macchiato for Brandon*—then opened a roll of quarters while he slid into the pickup line. She was still fumbling with the change wrapper when she closed the register and finally looked up. "What can I get for you, hon?" Her smile wavered, the crumpled coin wrapper in her fist forgotten. "Lizzy Moon . . . It is Lizzy, isn't it?"

Lizzy squared her shoulders, trying to read the woman's expression. Was it fear? Disdain? In the end she decided it didn't matter. "Yes, it's Lizzy."

The woman's face softened. "I heard you were back. I was so sorry to hear about your grandmother passing. She was a fine lady. A fine, fine lady."

"I'm sorry," Lizzy said, flustered at this unexpected show of kindness. "I thought you looked familiar, but I don't remember your name."

"I'm Judith Shrum. I was a customer of your grandmother's. Always knew just how to fix me up. Good as any doctor, if you ask me." She leaned forward, dropping her voice to a whisper. "All those busybodies flapping their yaps about those poor girls. They had no idea what they were talking about. Anyone who knew Althea Moon—I mean *really* knew her—knew she wasn't capable of such a thing. Even their mother knew it."

Lizzy seized on Judith's words. "Mrs. Gilman?"

"Susan. Yes, poor thing. We were friends, though we don't see each other much since she moved. Not that I blame her. She had a hard time of it. She told me once that she never felt right about what people were saying about your grandmother, how it just never sat with her. It seemed like—" She went quiet as a girl in a smudged apron and Brewed Awakening T-shirt sidled past with a spray bottle and cloth, resuming only when she was sure the girl was out of earshot. "It always seemed to me like she had her own ideas about what happened."

"What . . . kind of ideas?"

Judith shrugged. "She never said. It's only a feeling I had. And then one day she just stopped talking about it. Stopped talking about everything, really. Like she'd tuned out the whole world. Again, not that I blame her. I did wonder, though, if her going quiet had to do with Fred. Bit of a bully, that one. I was sad when she moved, but I'm glad she's away from him."

Lizzy peered over her shoulder, relieved to find that there was no one lined up behind her. "Do you still see her?"

Judith shook her head wistfully. "No, but we still talk. She lives in Peabody now. She's a hairdresser. Doing all right for herself too. She was seeing someone last time we spoke, which made me glad. She deserves some happiness after everything, a fresh start with fresh memories."

Lizzy nodded. She understood better than most that sometimes a fresh start meant leaving a place. She also knew how hard it could be to look old memories in the eye. Was it fair to force herself into Susan Gilman's world, to rip the scab off a wound that might finally be healing? She'd made that mistake with Susan's ex, and it hadn't gone well. But if she passed along her cell number by way of Judith Shrum, the decision would be Susan's to make. Perhaps the years had rendered her more willing to share her ideas about the fate of her daughters.

~

An hour and a half later, Lizzy left Chuck Bundy's office with a virtually untouched vanilla latte and a throbbing pain behind her right eye. As expected, the prospects for an easy sale were far from rosy, though he'd been careful to remind her several times throughout their conversation that he was speaking only in hypotheticals as it related to her particular property.

She'd gotten a crash course in real estate, learning the many pitfalls inherent in the sale of distressed properties, and how price could vary wildly based on the number of comparable listings currently on the market. When asked about the possibility of a quick sale, he'd been coolly evasive, suggesting they set up a time for him to come out and look around. Once he knew what he was dealing with, he'd give her a list of options, and they'd come up with a battle plan.

In the meantime, he'd given her some homework: documents she needed to locate; calls she needed to make; forms she'd need to procure, sign, and record with the county. He'd offered her a toothy smile as she left the office, assuring her that there was no such thing as an unsellable property, but now, as she drove home with terms like *market saturation* and *stigmatized property* rattling around in her head, she wasn't so sure. Nor was she looking forward to explaining it all to Luc, and telling him she would be delayed. Again.

She was considering just how long she might be able to put off that conversation when her cell phone rang. She eyed the number on the hands-free display, wondering if she'd actually conjured Luc, but the area code was 978 rather than 212—not one she recognized.

"Hello?"

"Miss Moon?"

"Yes."

"It's Susan Gilman. Judith gave me your number."

Lizzy was so surprised she could barely speak. "Thank you so much for calling. I know this is awkward, but I was wondering if you'd consider speaking with me. We could meet for coffee."

"It would need to be here in Peabody," she replied after a lengthy pause. "I can't meet you in Salem Creek."

"No, I understand. I'd be happy to come to you. Name the place, and I'll be there."

"I'm not sure I can tell you anything that will prove helpful, but if you have questions, I'll answer whatever I can. I could meet you after work."

"Thank you, Mrs. Gilman. I can't tell you how much I appreciate this."

"Today then. After I finish my shift. There's a bookstore at the mall—a Barnes & Noble. I'll be in the café at six."

~

The café was packed when Lizzy arrived at ten minutes to six, students and business types mostly, hunched over laptops, earbuds plugged in. It took several passes before she spotted Susan Gilman seated at a corner table, and even then she had to do a double take.

The years had changed her, but not in the way they had changed her husband. Her hair, always mousy and lank, was now a pale shade of blonde with rose-gold highlights, and her makeup looked as if it had been applied by a professional. In her boots and skinny jeans, she looked chic, almost edgy.

"Mrs. Gilman?"

Susan looked up from her magazine without smiling. "I go by Ames now, my maiden name. It was just . . . easier. But please call me Susan."

Lizzy nodded, understanding why her online searches had come up empty. "Thanks so much for agreeing to see me. Can I get you a coffee?"

"Thanks, I'm all set. My last appointment canceled, so I've been here awhile." She gestured toward the vacant chair and waited until Lizzy was seated. "I hear you paid my ex-husband a visit."

Lizzy opened her mouth, then closed it again, surprised that she knew about her visit to Fred Gilman's trailer.

"Don't look so surprised. We both know how that town works. Judith's husband works at Mason Electric. It didn't take long for word to spread that you'd shown up looking for Fred. So how'd it go?"

"Not well. I'm pretty sure he was trying to scare me off."

Susan nodded grimly. "Big man, my ex."

"Did he ever try to scare *you*?"

"He didn't have to try. It came naturally."

"Was he . . . abusive?"

"If you're asking did he hit me—no. He got his point across in other ways."

"What other ways?"

Susan lifted her mug, cradling it between her palms. Her hands were shaking. "There are all kinds of ways to be abusive, Ms. Moon. Ways that don't leave scars for the neighbors and the police to see."

"Did you ever call the police on your husband?"

Susan peered over the lipstick-stained rim of her mug. "And say what? That he was being mean to me? That I was being punished for burning his toast or forgetting to buy new laces for his boots? No, I never called the police. I drank instead. Not too much, just enough to numb myself. Then a little more when that stopped working."

Lizzy was getting a depressingly vivid picture of life as the wife of Fred Gilman. "What about Heather and Darcy? Were they scared of their father?"

"Scared? Of Fred? God forbid."

Something new had crept into Susan's expression, something deeper than sadness, and far more brittle. Lizzy remained quiet, waiting for her to say more. She didn't, choosing instead to pick at the frosty maroon polish on her left thumbnail.

Lizzy shifted in her chair, feeling the woman's pain, but needing desperately to get to the truth. "Susan?"

"Hmm? Oh, right. Were the girls afraid of him. That would be a huge no. Maybe if they had been, they'd still be here. Heather would have gone to prom, and Darcy would have gone to nursing school. I'd have grandkids and scrapbooks full of vacation snaps. But I kept quiet, so none of that happened. Fred got his way like he always did. And look where it got him, where it got all of us. As far as Fred was concerned, those girls could do no wrong. He absolutely refused to see it. And he certainly didn't want to hear it from me."

"Didn't want to hear what?"

"That Heather was out of control. That Darcy was right behind her. That if he didn't rein them in, something awful was going to happen. And something did." Her voice broke then, splintering with emotion. She looked away, fanning the tears that had pooled in her eyes. "I'm sorry," she said finally. "It's just so hard to have been right. You know how you get that feeling, and you just know something bad is coming. And then when it does, you keep kicking yourself because you knew. You knew, and you didn't stop it. I live with that."

Lizzy was groping for a response when she caught a whiff of something murky and dank, a combination of mildew and freshly turned earth. The mingled aromas of coffee and baked goods were so prevalent in the café that she hadn't noticed it until that moment, but the layers of emotion were unmistakable now. Loss. Regret. Soul-crushing grief.

Before Lizzy could check herself, she had reached for Susan's hand. "What happened wasn't your fault. A mother can't protect her children from everything."

"No. Not when you're not allowed."

"Not allowed? I don't understand."

"Fred wouldn't let me discipline them. Not for anything. That was his job, he said. His girls, his job."

"He wouldn't let you discipline your own daughters?"

Susan glanced up from her thumb, where she'd been at work again on her polish. A tear spilled down her left cheek. "That's just it. They weren't mine. Not legally."

Lizzy blinked at her. In all the coverage of the Gilmans eight years ago, that little detail had somehow escaped notice. "He was married before?"

"Christina. His high school sweetheart, if you can believe that. She died in a fire. Faulty wiring or something. Fred had taken the girls to his mother's for supper. By the time he got home, it was over. They found her in the bathtub. They think she must have been trying to protect herself from the flames."

Lizzy suppressed a shudder, trying not to picture the scene. "How old were the girls when you and Fred married?"

"Heather was three. Darcy was a year and a half."

"You raised them."

Susan nodded, brushing away another tear. "I'm the only mother they ever knew. Except I was never really allowed to *be* their mother. Fred never let me forget they were his girls, or that I was an outsider."

Lizzy felt her anger at Fred Gilman bubbling up all over again. "But he married you."

"Turns out he didn't want a wife so much as a housekeeper. Lucky me. I qualified for the job. By the time I realized what I'd signed up for, I was too in love with his daughters—our daughters—to leave. I'd have no right to them if I left. I'd never see them again."

"You never formally adopted them?"

"No." She wiped at her eyes, smearing her mascara. "I wanted to, but Fred wouldn't even discuss it. They had a mother, and I wasn't her. It didn't matter that they didn't remember anyone but me singing them to sleep, or holding their heads when they were sick. *He* remembered."

"That sounds a little . . ."

"Obsessive?" Susan supplied bitterly. "Only because it was. It was like she was a saint or something. It didn't help that the girls were the spitting image of her—Heather especially. Every time he looked at her, he saw Christina. I think that's why he couldn't deny her anything. Even when he should have. I tried to tell him. I warned him that she was growing up too fast, that they both were, but he wouldn't listen. He'd just give me that look and tell me to mind my own business."

Susan's cheeks had flared a dark shade of red as she spoke. Lizzy was almost relieved. It was easier to witness her anger than her pain. Still, she needed to tread lightly if she wanted her to keep talking. "I know this is hard, Susan, and that it's the last thing you want to talk about, but I truly want to find out who hurt your daughters, and talking like this might help me piece something together that the police missed. Do you feel up to answering a few more questions?"

Susan was starting to look a little ragged around the edges, but she managed a nod. "Ask whatever you need to."

"You said Heather was growing up too fast. What did you mean?"

"Exactly what you think I meant. She was breaking curfew, sneaking around with boys, wearing trashy clothes, drinking. All the things a girl does right before she comes home and tells you she's pregnant." She paused, shaking her head. "Can you believe *that's* what I was afraid of? That she'd come home one day and tell us she'd gotten herself in trouble? Back then I thought that was the worst thing that could happen."

"Did your husband know all this was going on? The drinking and the boys?"

"Yes, he knew. I told him—or tried to. He wouldn't listen. The night they . . ." Susan closed her eyes briefly. "The night they disappeared, I wanted to call the police, but Fred wouldn't let me. He said we didn't need the police in our business, and that the girls would come home when they were ready. We argued. It was awful. I couldn't believe he was being so cavalier. When I couldn't take it anymore, I got in the car and drove around. I hit all the spots I knew the kids went, but there was no sign of them. I knew something was wrong. A mother knows. I went home and ransacked their rooms, looking for something—a diary, a phone number—anything that might help us find them. I found a box of condoms in Heather's nightstand. Three were missing. When I showed Fred the box, he told me he bought them. He bought our fifteen-year-old daughter . . ." Her eyes welled with fresh tears. "To keep her safe."

Lizzy stood and went to the counter, returning with a handful of paper napkins. She waited while Susan blotted her eyes and pulled herself together.

"I'm all right," she said finally, still clutching the crumpled napkins. "Please go on."

"Do you know any of the boys she was seeing?"

"I wish I did, but Heather and I were barely speaking at that point. You know how teenage girls are. As far as she was concerned, I was the enemy. And she'd gotten very good at covering her tracks. She'd even recruited Darcy as an accomplice."

"What about her friends? Did any of them know who she was hanging around with?"

"She'd split off from most of her regular friends by then, and was hanging with some new kids. Older kids I didn't know. I talked to several of the parents. Fred was furious. He accused me of trying to paint his daughter—*his* daughter, like I had nothing to do with raising her—as a tramp."

This brought Lizzy to the question she'd really come to ask, uncomfortable though it might be. "When I spoke to your husband the other day, I was struck by the fact that he didn't seem at all interested in finding out who really hurt your girls."

"Probably because he already knows—or thinks he does. In his mind, there was never anyone but your grandmother. But I always had my doubts. Two beautiful girls. Why would she do it? But Fred grabbed the story with both hands. He needed someone to blame. Someone who wouldn't make his precious Heather look like a bad girl—or him like a bad father. Your grandmother was the perfect scapegoat."

"Speaking of scapegoats, I've been wondering . . ." Lizzy broke off, not sure how to form the question. Bad-mouthing your ex was one thing. Admitting he might be capable of harming his own daughters was something else altogether. And yet it had to be asked. "Do you believe your ex-husband might be capable of violence?"

Susan had been staring at the wadded napkins in her hand. Her head came up sharply. "Are you asking me if I think Fred killed our daughters?"

"I suppose I am."

"Then no. My husband was a lot of things, but he would never hurt those girls. I know it sounds bizarre, but hurting them would have been like hurting Christina."

Lizzy nodded, not because she accepted Susan's answer at face value, but because she was right about it sounding bizarre. What she'd just described was a complete reversal of the usual paradigm: the overprotective, chastity belt–minded father at odds with the seemingly too-lenient mother. In this case, Fred Gilman had not only *not* threatened his oldest daughter with a chastity belt; he'd given her a box of condoms, all the while claiming to be worried about her reputation. It boggled the mind. Which brought up another question.

"I'm not making any judgments, Susan. I can only imagine how horrible that time must have been for you, but I do wonder why you never spoke up about your doubts. You were on the news nonstop, always being quoted in the papers, and I never once heard you contradict your husband's assertions that Althea was responsible for what happened to Heather and Darcy."

Another ragged breath. A fresh rush of tears. "I was afraid of him back then. Still am, I guess. And I was drinking. Not just enough to get numb anymore. Enough to get unconscious. It was the only way I could get through the days, through the pain, and the guilt, and Fred's constant rages. I kept my mouth shut and I drank. And I went on drinking. And Salem Creek went on believing your grandmother killed my daughters. I live with that too."

~

There was plenty for Lizzy to think about as she drove back from Peabody. The troubling dynamics of the Gilmans' marriage for starters. Not only had Fred Gilman been emotionally abusive; he'd been obsessed with his daughters as well—or at least with Heather, because she'd looked like his dead wife. And there was something about the condoms and his paranoia about Heather's reputation that didn't square. Yet Susan had been adamant when she said her husband was incapable of harming his daughters, which basically left her nowhere on the question of Fred Gilman.

But she *had* come away from the meeting with something—a pair of names scribbled on a paper napkin. Cynthia Draper and Jenny Putnam had been friends of Heather's until a few months before the murders. It might come to nothing, but it was a place to start. Teenage girls didn't take being dropped—*ghosting*, they called it now—lying down. They would have known exactly who had replaced them—and why. Now all she had to do was track them down and get them to talk.

FIFTEEN

July 27

Lizzy wasn't expecting to find Andrew on the front steps the next morning when she went out for the paper. She was used to him coming to the mudroom door. She was also used to seeing him in jeans, not a blazer and freshly ironed khakis. It was a new look. A good look.

She pulled back the door, running her eyes over him. "What are you doing here?"

"Good morning to you too."

"Sorry." She was annoyed to find herself rattled by the sight of him. "I'm just surprised to see you. I was expecting the real estate agent. He's supposed to come by this morning to discuss my options, none of which are likely to be good."

Andrew registered this without comment. "I just stopped by to tell you I'm heading out of town for a few days. And also to tell you the barn is now safe. Well, safe-ish. I replaced the cocked-up hinge yesterday, but I need to show you something if you have a minute."

Lizzy checked her watch. Bundy wasn't due for another twenty minutes. She grabbed her coffee mug and followed him to the barn.

Andrew lifted the crossbar and pulled the door back easily, nodding for her to go ahead of him. The interior was cool and dim, fragrant with the smell of fresh sawdust. He flipped on the light switch just inside the door. "There," he said, pointing to the loft. "I took down the old ladder, but I noticed the frame around the window is ready to fall in. I'd steer clear of it for the time being. I'll get to it as soon as I'm back from Boston."

Lizzy tipped her head back, eyeing the loft window. "Fabulous. What's in Boston?"

"Potential clients. They're interviewing architects to renovate their Back Bay townhouse, and I'm on the list. It's a big job, but it's right up my alley."

"That explains the clothes."

He grinned, grasping his blazer lapels and striking a pose. "You never get a second chance to make a good first impression."

Lizzy took a sip of coffee, cold now, but welcome after a week and a half without. "How long will you be gone?"

"A week, maybe ten days if all goes well. Anyway, that's the other reason I'm here." He reached into his blazer pocket and pulled out a business card. "I wanted to make sure you had my cell, just in case."

"In case what?"

He shrugged. "You never know. Evvie said you went to see Susan Gilman yesterday."

Lizzy ignored the proffered card, wandering to the workbench instead. "I did. Turns out she never believed Althea was guilty. She also had some interesting things to say about her ex-husband."

Lizzy filled him in on the details: the drinking, the boys, the condoms, Fred Gilman's disturbing relationship with his daughters, and the fact that Susan wasn't their birth mother.

Andrew's brows shot up at this last bit of info. "I didn't realize the girls were adopted."

"They weren't. Gilman's first wife died in a fire when Heather was three. Darcy was still in diapers. Apparently, he didn't handle it well. He refused to let Susan adopt them."

"And that ties back to the murders how?"

Lizzy shrugged. "I don't know. Maybe it doesn't. It just seems . . . odd. I did come away with something, though. The names of two of Heather's girlfriends. I thought I'd try to track them down. Girls talk to other girls."

"I don't suppose you'd be willing to wait until I get back from Boston?"

"Andrew, we've had this discussion. I need to do this, and I need to do it by myself. Besides, I don't have all summer. Luc's chomping at the bit."

"Your boyfriend?"

"No, he's . . . We . . ." She looked away, embarrassed by her fumbling. "He's my boss."

"Is that your *final* answer?"

Lizzy flashed him a look, annoyed that he'd picked up on her clumsy response. "I thought you had somewhere to be."

"Right. Guess I'm off to Boston."

She watched him go, already wishing she hadn't been so abrupt. The man was persistent, she'd give him that. But he meant well. He'd always meant well. He just didn't understand that for the Moons, self-reliance was genetic, a survival mechanism passed down through generations. Solitary meant safe.

Lizzy's cell was going off on the kitchen counter when she walked back into the house. Before she could grab it, the call went to voice mail. Seconds later, she heard the alert ping. She pulled up the message, listening as she carried her mug to the coffee maker for a refill.

"Hi, it's Catherine Daniels from Chuck Bundy's office. He asked me to give you a call and let you know he's not going to be able to keep your ten o'clock appointment. His little boy took a bad spill this morning, and he and his wife are at the ER, waiting to find out if he's going to need surgery. He said he'd get back to you next week to reschedule."

Next week?

Lizzy swallowed a groan. Everything was taking longer than she'd anticipated, and there were decisions that needed to be made, requiring vastly different sets of documents, phone calls, and legwork. She'd been counting on Bundy to nudge her in one direction or the other. Instead, she was in a holding pattern. Again.

But in the meantime, maybe there was a different kind of legwork she could begin. She picked up her phone, opened the Facebook app, and tapped in Jenny Putnam's name. There were five profiles listed, but only one Jenny Putnam in New Hampshire.

Seconds later, Lizzy was staring at a photo of a petite blonde in cyclist gear, with a number on her chest. According to her profile, she was married with twin girls—Bella and Shay—and still lived in Salem Creek. Her married name was Wittinger—husband, Donny—and she worked at New England Regional as a labor and delivery nurse. A quick call to directory assistance and Lizzy had a phone number.

She held her breath as the number connected, wishing she'd given some thought to what she would say if Jenny actually answered or, worse, if voice mail picked up. Maybe she should hang up, think it through, then call back. She was about to do just that when a woman answered.

"Hello?"

Her voice was thick and slow, as if she'd been asleep. "Mrs. Wittinger?"

"Yes."

"My name is Lizzy Moon, and I'm calling—"

"I'm sorry. You're . . . Who are you?"

"Lizzy Moon." Lizzy held her breath, expecting the line to go dead. It didn't.

"What do you want?"

"I was wondering . . . I spoke with Susan Gilman yesterday, and she gave me your name. I was hoping we could talk. About Heather."

"Why would I talk to you?"

"Because Heather was your friend, and whoever hurt her—and Darcy—is still free."

"I heard you were back."

Lizzy ignored the dry response. "I have a few questions. About things Susan told me. I was hoping we could meet somewhere. I could—"

Jenny cut her off. "I'm not meeting you anywhere. In fact, I'm not sure I want to talk to you at all."

"Please. I just have a few questions."

"You got my number from her mom?"

"No. Information. But she gave me your name. She thought you might be able to help."

Another pause, longer this time. The sound of ice dropping into a glass, then running water. "What do you want to know?"

Lizzy breathed a silent *thank-you*. "She said you and Heather had a falling-out."

"It wasn't just me. She stopped hanging out with all of us."

"Why?"

"Who knows? She'd been acting weird for a while—standoffish and kind of jumpy. Then one day she just stopped talking to us."

"She never said why?"

"She never said anything. It was like we were invisible."

"Did she start hanging out with anyone else?"

"Not at school. She kept to herself, sat alone, ate alone. Then she started skipping class. No one knew where she went. And after a while, we stopped caring. I know that sounds harsh, but if someone doesn't want to be your friend, you can't make them."

"No," Lizzy said, noting the tinge of petulance in her tone. "You can't. You said she'd been acting funny. Did you ask her why?"

"She'd get mad when I tried to talk to her about it. We used to hang out at her house after school because her mom baked all this amazing stuff. All of a sudden she wanted to hang out at my house, or at Cynthia's. It was like she hated going home. Maybe because of how things were between her and her mom. Heather called her Mrs. Nosy Pants, because she was always giving her the third degree."

"And Mr. Gilman? How did she get along with him?"

"Okay, I guess. He was usually at work when we were there. I know he gave her things. One time she wanted this cute little skirt from Forever 21, but her mom said it was too short. Next thing I know, she's wearing it. When I asked how she changed her mother's mind, she said she didn't. She got her father to buy it instead. She said she had him wrapped."

"Wrapped?"

"You know—around her finger. She bragged that she could make him do whatever she wanted."

Like buy her condoms.

Lizzy felt a wave of disgust. Susan had said the same thing. "Did she say why?"

"No. I asked, but she just clammed up. Like I said, she got really weird."

"Did you ever see her with any cuts or bruises?"

"You mean did her parents beat her?"

"It happens."

"No. I never saw her with anything like that."

"Did she have a boyfriend?"

"No. Not for a while. She and Brian Smith used to be a thing, started when they were in middle school, but that stopped around the time she ditched us. There was no one after that as far as I know, and then . . ."

Yes. And then.

"Did the police ever talk to you? Afterward, I mean."

"Yeah. Two guys came to the house and asked me some questions."

"Did you tell them what you told me? About Heather not wanting to go home?"

"No. I should have, I guess, but it didn't seem like anything back then. And I think I was still a little mad at her. But you think about things when you get older—when you have kids of your own—and you wonder if there was something you should have known, something you could have stopped. I don't know what happened to Heather, or Darcy, but it's hard not to think that the way she changed was a part of it somehow." She sounded tired suddenly, and sad. "I have to go now. I'm on tonight. I should be asleep."

"Yes, of course. And thank you. You've been a big help. I was hoping to speak with Cynthia Draper too. Would you happen to know how I might get in touch with her?"

"Cynthia died two years ago. Leukemia."

Lizzy's stomach sank. "I'm so sorry."

There was a beat of quiet before Jenny answered, "I should have said something back then, but I was pretty freaked out. Still am, I guess. My dad's in the Elks with Fred Gilman. He'd be wicked pissed if he knew I was talking to you. Anyway, I'm sorry about your grandmother. I remember her being nice."

Lizzy wasn't sure what she felt as she ended the call. Sadness, revulsion, and anger all seemed to be warring for a place in her gut. Jenny had confirmed Susan's version of things with startling clarity, painting a picture of Heather Gilman that asked more questions than it answered. Why had she cut her friends dead, and broken up with her longtime crush? And why had she suddenly stopped wanting to go home? Was it mere teenage angst, or something darker?

She pulled up Roger's number and hit "Dial." It rang four times before kicking over to voice mail. For a retired guy, he certainly kept busy. She left a message, saying she'd spoken to Susan Gilman, and wanted to run some things by him.

A knock at the door sounded as she hung up. She expected to find Evvie, her arms filled with the packages she'd gone to pick up from the post office. Instead, she pulled back the door to find a plumpish woman in sunglasses and a wide-brimmed straw hat.

The woman smiled nervously. She smelled of bread dough, warm and yeasty. A good smell. A safe smell. "I doubt you remember me. My name is Penny Castle. I work at Wilson's Drugstore, at the lunch counter."

Lizzy didn't remember her, but she smiled back. "What can I do for you, Ms. Castle?"

"Nothing, probably. But I thought I'd try. Your grandmother used to make me a tea for my migraines. It was the only thing that ever gave me any relief. When I heard you were back, I couldn't help hoping—well, praying, actually—that you'd come back to reopen the shop."

"I'm sorry, no. I only came back to put the farm up for sale."

Ms. Castle's face fell, but she nodded. "I can't say I blame you. Still, it's a shame. The end of an era, some might say. She had such a big heart, your grandmother. Never turned a soul away. Even the ones who couldn't pay. It wasn't fair, the way people . . ." She trailed off, pressing her fingers to her mouth. "I'm sorry to go on. It's just that she was such a good woman. You're like her, you know? Not just your looks, but the light in you. Althea had that. Anyway, thank you for your time, and I'm sorry to bother you."

Lizzy felt a pang of sympathy as she watched Penny Castle walk away. How many others were suffering for want of Althea's remedies? And where would they turn?

She was about to close the door when she saw Evvie's battered station wagon lumbering up the drive. Evvie climbed out, arms laden with packages, and a bag brimming with several loaves of fresh bread. A canvas tote dangled from her wrist.

"I stopped off at the farmers' market on the way back. How does spinach salad with fresh strawberries sound for supper tonight?"

Lizzy relieved Evvie of her packages and turned back toward the house. "It sounds good. It's already way too hot to cook."

In the kitchen, Evvie set about opening her parcels—beads she'd ordered from a supplier in Vermont—while Lizzy pulled out a colander and began rinsing the strawberries. They worked in silence for a time, but Lizzy couldn't get Penny Castle's face out of her head.

"We had a visitor while you were gone," she said at last. "A woman looking for some headache tea."

Evvie looked up, clutching a bag of what looked like green agate beads. "Happens sometimes. People hoping there might be some of your gran's remedies lying around."

"Her name was Penny Castle. She heard I was back, and hoped I was going to reopen the shop."

"And you told her you weren't?"

Lizzy blinked at her. "What was I *supposed* to tell her? By the end of the month, there will be a FOR SALE sign out front. It made me feel bad, though. She said some awfully nice things about Althea. About how she helped people, and never turned anyone away. Judith, from the coffee shop, said the same thing."

"There's plenty who think that way, little girl. You just don't remember. You'd rather focus on the ones who gave your gran a hard time."

"It wasn't *only* Althea who had a hard time."

Evvie nodded. "True enough. They came at you as well. But it wasn't all of them. There *were* kindnesses. People who spoke out, who never bought a word of the lies. Your gran remembered that right up until the day she died. Maybe it's time you remembered it too."

Calendula . . . for the healing of scars.

My dearest girl,

You've returned to the pages, seeking answers or comfort, perhaps both. How I wish I could be there to soothe you, the way I used to when you were little and smarting over some unkindness. You've been through so much in your short life. But then, being born into our clan, what choice did you have? You never wanted to be like us. Not when you learned the cost of it. I can't blame you for being bitter. You have a right to that, and more I suppose. Isolation can be a terrible thing. And what girl doesn't have her dreams? A white dress. A church full of flowers. Happily ever after. But we're warned early on that those dreams are for other girls. Normal girls. And we none of us were ever that. Our path was mapped out eons ago, not a better path, though a different one to be sure. And for most of us, it was enough.

But not for you, my Lizzy.

You were never comfortable in the Moon skin. You wanted something else. Anything else. I think I knew it before you did. And though I hoped you'd change your mind one day, I was determined to let you find your way. I never pushed. Your mother taught me only too well where that can lead. You were all that was left—my hope and my pride. And so, I gave you your head, as they say, hoping with all my soul that one day you'd find your way back to your roots—to our roots.

And then the girls went missing . . . It took twenty-four hours for the fingers to start pointing in my direction. I was the one. Because I had to be, didn't I? The crone living at the edge of town, who grows herbs and mutters spells. I poisoned them, strangled them, hexed them with my dark powers. But the police had no case, no way to bring me to their so-called justice. And so the people of this town punished me in the only way they could, with their tittle-tattling and their cold shoulders. They crossed the street when they saw me in town and chased me from their stores—and you watched them do it. Day after day, week after week. As if things weren't already hard enough for you, you had to end up with an accused murderer for a grandmother. You never spoke of it—you were far too stoic for that—but I could hear you through the wall at night, crying into your pillow, and it broke my heart to know what it was doing to you.

Time leaves its wounds on us all, battering us in ways we do our best to hide. But you could never hide anything from me. I saw the wounds, felt the pain of each lash you suffered in my name. And I watched the scars begin to form, and watched you hide behind them. Because you don't feel in the scarred places. There's no registering of pain, just numbness meant to protect against future cuts. You shut yourself off from it, erected a wall around the soft parts of yourself. And in my desolation, I let you. I watched you slipping farther and farther away from me—and from yourself—until I barely recognized the tender girl I'd loved and raised.

And now that you've been thrust back into all of that, your wounds, I fear, have reopened. But you must remember what it all meant, where it came from, and why. It wasn't about anger or even hate. It's never about those things. It's about fear. Of anything that doesn't fit into their tidy notion of what's right and good. We upset the balance, you see, because we walk our own path and live our own truth. It's always been a rough road for those who live differently from the herd. We're seen as Other, a threat to the proper way of things. And so they label us, and they lash out. Because as long as they're lashing out, they don't feel their fear.

Knowing this doesn't make the knives easier to bear, but it does help us understand—and perhaps forgive. And you must forgive, my darling girl, and give up your scars. Bitterness is a subtle poison. It lulls with its righteous indignation and its false sense of power, then turns on you and burns your heart to ash. But forgiveness is balm to the wounded heart.

And love. We must never forget love.

Not only as something we feel, but as who we are deep down in our marrow. Which is why fear must never be allowed to eclipse it. Like most things in my life, I learned this the hard way, and am sorry to say I had to learn it more than once. To love truly is to risk the deepest cut, but it's always a risk worth taking.

Forgive me, Lizzy, for my preaching. Now, when so many years have passed. There were things we never spoke of, things that might have made that time easier for you. But I was struggling with my own wounds then, and my own fears. And so I must say them now, in the hope that you'll remember them when you're tempted to harden your heart. Salve your scars with love, my girl, whatever comes, and keep your heart open. Love—even love that cannot be returned—is never cause for regret.

Love always,
A—

SIXTEEN

July 28

Lizzy stared at the desiccated flower resting in her lap, golden once, now nearly leached of color.

Calendula . . . for the healing of scars.

Once again, Althea had known exactly what to say, and when to say it. She'd been cautioned not to hurry through the book, to come back to its pages when she was ready. And this morning, when she opened her eyes, she had felt the familiar pull, beckoning her to read—to remember that fear often masquerades as hate, and that forgiveness is balm to the wounded heart. Could she forgive?

Evvie was right. Not everyone in Salem Creek had turned their backs on the Moons. There were some—people like Penny Castle and Judith Shrum, like Andrew and his father—who had refused to believe the whispers. But the steady stream of baseless lies was easier to remember, the betrayal carved indelibly on Lizzy's memory. That people who had known Althea all their lives could have abandoned her so completely was still incomprehensible. But they had, falling away one by one, leaving her to the mercy of public opinion. Except there'd been no mercy.

But what of the others? Those who had spurned the rumors but kept a careful distance? Who'd never quite found the courage to speak out? Who had simply remained invisible? Where did they fall on the scale of betrayal? Where did *she* fall?

The question continued to gnaw as she closed the book and went downstairs to make coffee. Evvie glanced up from her seat at the kitchen table, where she was painstakingly applying labels to about two dozen small jars of honey.

"Breakfast?"

"No thanks. Coffee's all I need." Lizzy filled the basket and pushed the brew button, then propped a hip against the counter to wait. "What's with all the jars?"

"Getting another batch of honey ready to take to Ben at the hardware store."

"Didn't you just do that a few days ago?"

Evvie dropped her gaze. "And what if I did?"

Lizzy cocked her head, studying Evvie through narrowed eyes. She was wearing lipstick, a shimmery shade of coral that set off her eyes. And dangly jade earrings. "Is there something you're not telling me?"

"Such as?"

"Such as why you won't look at me all of a sudden. Or why you went all moony just now when you said Ben's name."

Evvie glanced up, chin jutting. "I did no such thing!"

Lizzy propped her hands on her hips, grinning slyly. "If I didn't know better, I'd say you were sweet on old Ben. Why else would you be making another trip so soon?"

"It's got nothing to do with being sweet on anybody," Evvie grumbled petulantly. "He puts the jars out on the counter and his customers snatch them up. Can I help it if folks know a good thing when they taste it?"

"So the lipstick's just a coincidence?"

"Oh, hush up and drink your coffee!"

Lizzy swallowed a grin as she pulled a mug from the cupboard, then waited for the final drops to splutter into the pot. "Have you been out to the shop recently?"

Evvie seemed surprised by the question. "To the shop? Not recently. Why?"

"I was just wondering what was still out there."

"You're thinking about Penny Castle's headache tea," Evvie said knowingly. "Might be some left. Far as I know, it's just like your gran left it. She used to go out every day and putter around, not that many ever came to buy. But she went out every morning. Even after she got sick. After a while, it got to be too much. One day she locked the door, hung up the key, and that was that. We never spoke about it, but I know it broke her heart. This place, that shop and her herbs, were her life. And you, of course. But you were gone by then. The shop was the last of it."

Lizzy spooned a bit of sugar into her mug, stirring as she moved to the table. "Can I give you a hand?"

"I've about got it finished. But you can grab me that box off the floor, so I can pack it up and get it out to the car."

Lizzy fetched the box and began filling it. "Ben will really sell all this at the hardware store?"

"Every lick. Folks around here believe in buying local, even if it is from a woman with a funny accent and skin the color of old wood." She shot Lizzy a wink as she hefted the box up into her arms. "You could come."

"To the hardware store?"

"Might not be a bad thing to show yourself around. Let folks know you're interested in something other than Fred Gilman."

"Actually, I have something I need to do. Or at least try to do."

Evvie removed her glasses, giving them a wipe with her apron. "Another meeting with your real estate man?"

"That's next week—I hope. No, this is something else. A favor I owe."

She waited until Evvie's station wagon rattled down the drive, grabbed the key from the hook beside the mudroom door, and headed for the one place she still hadn't been able to make herself go—Althea's apothecary.

The squat stone cottage had been built as a cider house in the 1820s, fashioned of rough-faced granite fitted together like a jigsaw puzzle. Over the years it had served as many things: a dry cellar, a pottery shed, even a quilting room, but it had been relegated to storage when Althea decided to clear it out and set it up as a shop. She'd done a job of it too, creating something straight out of a fairy tale, complete with a curved stone path, ivied trellis, and flower boxes for the windows. In its heyday, it had drawn customers from all over New England. Now, the window boxes sat empty, the path grown over with weeds.

So many memories shut up in one place.

The key turned easily, but the door was swollen and required a series of lunges before finally yielding. Lizzy cringed as she stepped inside. The windows were rimed with grit, allowing only a murky wash of light to filter in, but it was enough to see that everything was coated in a fine layer of dust, the corners crisscrossed with cobwebs. She cringed as she crossed to the light switch, registering the queasy crunch of mouse droppings underfoot. She flipped the switch, and the overheads blinked on. A third of the bulbs were out.

Not much had changed in the years she'd been gone. She scanned the shop: the back wall lined with shelves, the glass-front cabinets flanking the front windows, the butcher-block worktable running down the center. And Althea's remedy book—a kind of cookbook filled with recipes for treating all manner of ailments.

Lizzy picked it up, experiencing the same wave of reverence she'd always felt for Althea's gift as a healer. For an instant, she caught the blended scents of lavender and bergamot, soft and fleeting, like a sigh hovering briefly in the air. A sign of welcome? A nod of approval? Or merely her imagination? Lizzy couldn't say. But as she opened the book and began to page through, she realized it didn't matter. What mattered was that she was here, hoping to do some good, and that, somehow, Althea knew and was glad.

The pages were chock-full of remedies. There were preparations for colic, for cramp, for night sweats and sore throats, for skinned knees and achy joints, and, finally, a recipe for migraine tea. But she didn't need a recipe; she needed the finished product.

There wasn't much left on the shelves: a handful of dropper bottles and a smattering of salve tins. She moved to the drawers, where Althea kept more-specialized remedies in sealed plastic bags, carefully labeled and filed alphabetically by condition. It took a few minutes to comb through the packets, but she finally found what she was looking for—migraine tea.

She squinted at the date on the label, but it was too faded to read. Time had definite effects on herbal potency, as did exposure to light and air, but these had been stored in airtight bags and kept in a dark cupboard. With any luck, they had retained at least some of their medicinal properties. And if not, they wouldn't do any harm.

She was about to leave the shop when she had an idea. She turned back, running her eyes over the shelves until she found what she was looking for: lavender and clary sage oils. She tucked the small blue vials into her pocket, already composing the instructions in her head on how they should be used. A few drops of each sprinkled on a warm compress, or added to a pot of boiling water to create a steam. A soothing and therapeutic complement to Althea's tea.

~

The lunch crowd was beginning to thin by the time Lizzy arrived at the drugstore. Penny Castle was busy behind the counter, clearing plates and topping off coffee mugs. She had just dropped off a check to a man in bib overalls and a Patriots cap when she spotted Lizzy.

There was a flash of surprise, followed by a smile. She pointed to an open stool. Lizzy stepped forward but didn't sit. Instead, she pulled a brown paper bag from her purse and handed it to Penny. "I found this in Althea's shop, and wanted to bring it by."

Penny's face lit as she peered into the bag. "My tea!"

"There were only three packages, but I brought them all. There's a chance it's lost some of its potency, so you might want to steep it a little longer than you're used to. I also threw in some aromatherapy oils I thought might help. There's a note in the bag on how to use them."

"I can't tell you how much this means to me. How much do I owe you?"

"Consider it a gift," Lizzy said, waving the offer away. "For old times' sake."

Penny reached across the counter to give Lizzy's arm a squeeze. "I know you're not staying, but it's good to see you back in Salem Creek. And to see that you turned out so much like your grandmother. She'd be so proud of you."

Lizzy felt a surprising lightness as she drove home. Not much had gone right since her return to Salem Creek, but bringing Penny Castle her tea had been both right and good. Such a small thing, a handful of herbs and oils. But for Penny, it wasn't small at all. It meant relief, a place to turn when conventional medicine fell short, which to someone in chronic pain must feel like a miracle. Was that how Althea felt every day—like a miracle worker?

The question was still with her as she made a quick U-turn and pulled into the Nature's Harvest parking lot. Evvie had said something the other night about her grandmother making peach ice cream every summer when she was a girl. It wouldn't be homemade, but it would be a nice treat after supper.

It was early afternoon, and customers were scarce. Lizzy headed for the freezer section, grabbed a gallon of Hood peach, and made her way to the checkout. She had just put the ice cream on the conveyer belt when she looked up to find the woman working the customer service desk staring at her.

She was thin and pale, with shoulder-length hair the color of dirty dishwater. Lizzy didn't recognize her, but her name badge read HELEN. Helen's eyes slid away when she realized she'd been caught staring, but they soon returned, lingering brazenly this time. Lizzy held the stare, trying to decide if what she saw in the woman's face was curiosity or aversion. Not that it mattered. She'd grown up with looks like that. All the Moons had. And yet it surprised her that one glance from a stranger could still make her want to slink away and hide.

SEVENTEEN

July 29

Lizzy breathed a sigh of relief as she left the county registrar's office. She was nowhere near through with the red tape, but at least she'd gotten the ball rolling. It had taken days to round up and sort through Althea's financial papers, which consisted of a battered accordion file, a pair of dog-eared ledgers, and a shoebox filled with canceled checks and loose receipts.

On the upside, in the drawer of Althea's writing desk, she had discovered a manila envelope containing property tax documents, a declaration of trust, a beneficiary deed, and a boilerplate "Last Will and Testament." Everything she'd need to handle the deed transfer—and apply for a mortgage if it came to that. Of course Althea had seen to it all.

She'd know more once Chuck Bundy came out and had a look around. *If* he ever came out. She had called his office this morning to touch base and had been dismayed to learn that he hadn't returned to work yet. His son had undergone a second surgery, and the possibility of a third hadn't been ruled out. She had asked that her good wishes be passed along. She could hardly begrudge the man time with his son, but she couldn't let this drag on much longer. If he didn't return to work soon, she'd have to find another Realtor. Maybe she'd talk to Andrew when he got back from Boston, ask if there was someone he'd recommend.

Her cell phone rang. She checked the display. Roger. It had been two days since she'd left the message about her conversations with Susan Gilman and Jenny Putnam, and she'd begun to wonder if he'd decided to steer clear of the case entirely, perhaps on the advice of his brother.

"Hey, Roger."

"Sorry for the delay. I was out of town wrapping up an investigation when I got your message. I take it you have some thoughts to share about Heather Gilman."

Was she imagining the impatience in his tone? Probably not. And who could blame him? He had *real* clients, the kind who paid for his services and didn't try to tell him how to do his job. "I do, actually. I sat down with Susan Gilman on Monday."

"So I gathered from your message. For the record, I sat down with her too, on *numerous* occasions."

"I know. I didn't mean . . . she's in a different place now, Roger. She's free to say things she wasn't back then. Did you know she had doubts about my grandmother's guilt?"

"I didn't," he said, after a brief beat of silence. "But her husband was vocal enough for both of them. The papers, the news, every day the same thing. *Why hasn't that woman been arrested yet? How many more innocent girls have to die?* And not once, during any of that, did his wife contradict him."

"Because she was scared. She told me flat out that he was a bully, and after my conversation with him, I can personally attest to it."

"You've spoken to Fred Gilman?"

In her eagerness to relate her conversation with Susan, she'd apparently forgotten to mention her visit to Meadow Park. "Yes. I went to his house, but he refused to speak to me. Though I definitely got the bully vibe. I can see why she was afraid of him."

"There was no domestic history. We checked."

"And we both know a man doesn't need to use his fists to intimidate his wife."

"All right. I'll grant you that. But there were no signs of violence in the home. No broken bones or black eyes, no frequent ER visits. Just the normal bumps and bruises. You're saying she thinks it was him?"

"No. Not exactly."

"Then what *are* you saying?"

The impatience was back, his tone brisk and snappish. Lizzy pulled into the first parking lot she came to—Stay-Brite Dry Cleaners—and put the car in park. She needed him to hear her out, so he'd have a clear picture of life in the Gilman house. "I'm saying there were things going on back then that no one knew about. Creepy stuff. Like a father giving his fifteen-year-old daughter a box of condoms without telling her mother. Heather was running wild, skipping school and drinking. But Mr. Gilman didn't want to hear it—and he didn't want anyone else to hear it either. Especially the police. That has to set off some bells."

"You just said his own wife doesn't think he did it."

"She doesn't. But wives aren't always objective, even under normal circumstances. And things in that house were far from normal."

"Sounds like *you* think it was him."

"I certainly think it's possible. Susan said her husband had a kind of obsession with the girls. With Heather especially. But everyone was so convinced it was Althea that no one else was even considered."

Roger blew out a sigh. "That isn't true. Just because we didn't broadcast our every move doesn't mean we weren't doing our jobs. I can assure you we looked at him. In fact, we looked at both of them. Both had alibis for the night the girls went missing. Fred was seen by several neighbors out in the garage, working on an old Mustang he was restoring, and it was Susan's turn to host her card club's weekly canasta game, which didn't break up until almost midnight. That's when she realized the girls weren't home. Unfortunately, she waited almost five hours before calling it in."

"Because Fred wouldn't let her call sooner. He didn't want the police involved, and still doesn't, apparently. You don't find that odd?"

"His daughters are dead, Lizzy. Murdered. I can't say I blame him for not wanting to dredge it all up again. That kind of pain never leaves you."

Lizzy bit her lip, recalling the death of his wife and son. "No. I suppose not."

"There's also the possibility that this is some twisted revenge scenario on Susan Gilman's part."

"Revenge scenario?" It was a possibility Lizzy had never considered.

"Years in an emotionally abusive marriage, taking crap from a man who puts his daughters ahead of his wife. She leaves him, tries to put it all behind her. And then, out of the blue, you show up asking all sorts of questions. Bam. She sees a way to pay her husband back, by hinting that he might have had some sort of fixation with his daughters."

"Sounds like a bad movie plot."

"If you're going to pursue the dysfunctional-family angle, you have to look at it from all angles. You can't pick up one end of the stick without picking up the other."

Lizzy considered this. No doubt he'd seen his share of acts over the years, but her gut—and her nose—told her Susan Gilman's pain was real. "She wasn't faking it, Roger. No one could fake that."

"At the risk of sounding jaded, people are capable of faking all sorts of things."

"Maybe. But not in this case. If anything, she blames herself for not being strong enough to stand up to her husband the night the girls went missing. If she had, maybe things would have ended differently—for the girls as well as Althea. And maybe there would have been more than one suspect on your list."

"Fred Gilman, for instance?"

Lizzy waited a beat before answering, trying to tamp down her frustration. "Tell me you wouldn't have taken a second look at him if you knew

Heather's home life was falling apart. I spoke with a friend of hers from high school—Jenny Putnam—and she backed up everything Susan said."

"We questioned her right after the girls went missing. We questioned several of Heather's friends. No one knew anything. At least not anything they were willing to share."

"Well, her memory seems to have improved with age. And maybe hers isn't the only one. I've been thinking about looking up some more of her classmates, maybe knock on a few doors, see what people remember."

There was a long stretch of quiet. The kind that meant the person on the other end was forming a response that might not be well received. "I'm not sure that's wise given what's already happened."

"What's . . . happened?"

"Andrew told me about the doll. He also told me you refused to call the police."

"I didn't refuse, Roger. I'm just . . . waiting."

"For what? A noose is a threat, Lizzy. There's no other way to spin it. And you're the one insisting there's a killer on the loose in Salem Creek. Why not leave the door-knocking to me?"

It irked her that he didn't believe her capable of talking to a few ex-cheerleaders. She was also worried that a detective—even one not in uniform—would make them skittish. The good people of Salem Creek might claim to believe in law and order, but they had an ingrained distrust of those sworn to uphold it.

"I'll make you a deal, Detective," Lizzy said, as she restarted the car. "I'll track down Heather's classmates and see what I can find out. If I stumble onto anything promising, I'll turn them over to you for the thumbscrews and rubber hoses."

He sighed, a sound of resignation. "You do realize that you nosing around isn't going to sit well with folks."

"I'm a Moon, Detective. We're used to most things we do *not* sitting well with folks."

EIGHTEEN

August 2

The school office was smaller than Lizzy remembered, a warren of closed doors, scarred desks, and hideous chairs stamped out of orange plastic. The smells were the same, though: a combination of coffee, scotch tape, and printer ink perpetually suspended in the fuggy air.

A woman behind one of the desks slid her glasses down her nose, brows raised. "Can I help you?"

"I hope so. I was wondering if the school might have back copies of old yearbooks lying around somewhere."

The woman blinked at her. "Old yearbooks?"

"I'm looking for 2012 specifically. I'm back for a visit and was hoping to look up some old acquaintances, but I'm afraid I need to jog the old memory."

The woman surveyed her with a bland expression. If she found the request suspect, she gave no sign. "You need the library," she said crisply. "They have a full set going back to 1973, when the school was built. Ask for Jeannie. She'll know where to find them."

Jeannie, as it turned out, ran the library like the Pentagon, requiring Lizzy to sign in at the front desk, including name, time of arrival, and the purpose of her visit. Standard procedure for all nonstudents, she explained brusquely. She was then asked about her intentions for the yearbook and informed in no uncertain terms that the books from the archives were for review on premises only, and never allowed off the property. Lizzy assured her the yearbook would be going no farther than the cafeteria. In the end, Jeannie relented, but only after Lizzy offered to leave her driver's license as collateral.

She was probably on a fool's errand, but she had to at least try.

She had jolted awake at 3:00 a.m. with an image in her head: a woman wearing a hairnet over a puff of mousy brown hair. The Lunch Lady—who smelled of violets and talcum powder, and had been kind to a girl who spent every lunch hour with her nose in a book. Sometimes an extra Jell-O had found its way onto her tray. Or a second cookie, when they were oatmeal raisin, because they were her favorite.

At first, she couldn't imagine why the memory had surfaced, but eventually it dawned on her. What better place to begin her search for Heather's high school friends than with a woman who'd spent virtually every day of the last thirty years feeding Salem Creek's teens?

Louise Ryerson.

Like most kids, Lizzy had known her only as the Lunch Lady, but Evvie had had no trouble coming up with her name, or confirming that she was still working at the school. Unfortunately, she hadn't been able to provide an address, and directory assistance had been no help. Which left calling on her during her work hours, and asking if she'd be willing to sit down and look at a few photographs. It was a long shot, she knew. Nearly a decade had passed since Heather Gilman and her friends had walked the halls of Salem Creek High, but maybe the yearbook would help her remember.

It was the start of August, when only summer classes were in session, and lunchtime to boot, leaving the halls eerily empty as Lizzy navigated her way to the cafeteria. A wave of déjà vu hit her as she stepped through the double doors, followed by a wave of nausea as she registered the stomach-churning pong of grease, ketchup, and overcooked vegetables.

Scores of teenage eyes followed her as she moved between the rows of long tables—curious stares, mostly, wondering who she was and what she was doing there. A parent, perhaps, or a substitute teacher. They were all so young, so animated and carefree. The way she'd wanted to be when she was their age.

She scanned the area behind the serving counter, where a pair of women in white coats were breaking down the steam table. If the clock above the door was right—and it always was—the bell would ring in four and a half minutes, signaling the end of lunch period. Until then, she'd find a quiet corner and do her best to blend into the woodwork—like old times.

It took less than five minutes for the lunchroom to empty when the bell finally rang. Lizzy approached the counter, yearbook tucked under her arm, and waited to be noticed. After a moment she cleared her throat. Louise glanced up vacantly through steamy glasses, as if surprised to find an adult standing in her lunchroom. Her brow wrinkled as their eyes met, but there was no flicker of recollection as far as Lizzy could tell.

"Mrs. Ryerson, you probably don't remember me, but I was a student here a long time ago. My name is—"

"Lizzy Moon," she said, her face lighting up. "You're Althea's granddaughter."

"Yes, that's right."

"I heard you were back. So sad about your grandmother."

Lizzy smiled benignly. "Thank you. I was wondering if we could talk."

"Talk?"

"I have some questions you might be able to help me with. I promise I won't take up much of your time. If we could just sit down for a few minutes . . ." She paused as a woman with hair the color of

Mercurochrome walked by with an armload of dirty trays, then continued in a lower voice. "I think you might be able to help me."

Louise nodded blankly as she peeled off her food-service gloves and tossed them aside. "All right then, if it won't take long. We can sit over here."

Lizzy followed her to one of the long lunch tables and settled across from her. "Thank you for doing this. I'd like to talk about the Gilman sisters."

The corners of Louise's mouth turned down. She'd changed surprisingly little over the years. Her puff of hair was nearly white now, and the lines on either side of her mouth had deepened, but her hairnet was still in place, and her face was still kind.

"Such a shame. That poor mother. And your grandmother. What this town put her through—an absolute travesty."

"Yes," Lizzy said, eager to get to the point. "Which is why I'm here. I know it's a long shot, but I'd like to find out what really happened if I can, and I think talking to some of Heather's friends might help me do that. The trouble is I don't know their names, or how to contact them. I was hoping you might be able to help me there." She paused, sliding the yearbook over to Louise's side of the table. "I brought this. I thought pictures might help."

She opened the book to the tenth-grade section, scanning the photos until she found what she was looking for—Heather showing just a hint of dimple as she smiled for the camera. "This is Heather," she told Louise. "Could you look at the pictures and see if anyone else jumps out at you? Someone who might have been her friend? A boy, maybe?"

Louise looked at the yearbook, then back at Lizzy. "That's been a long time ago now."

"I know, but could you at least look?"

"I suppose I could try."

Louise pulled off her glasses and gave them a wipe, then returned them to her nose and bent her head to the open yearbook. Lizzy sat with her hands pressed between her knees, silent but alert for even the faintest flicker of recognition.

It took nearly twenty minutes, but Louise finally reached the last page. She closed the book with a shake of her head. "I'm sorry. No."

"No?" Lizzy did her best to hide her disappointment. "No one looks familiar?"

"There's not a face that jumps out at me, except that Gilman girl's. And yours, of course. You were always such a pretty thing. Still are. But that's not why you came, is it, to hear me go on about you being pretty?"

Lizzy shook her head.

Louise met her gaze squarely, her expression one of genuine sympathy. "I know how badly you must want to get at the truth, and I wish I could help. Truly, I do. But after so many years, the faces blend together. The only reason I recognize that poor girl now is because her face was all over the news, along with her sister's. As for names, I was never any good with those."

"But you always remembered my name," Lizzy protested. "You remembered it today."

"Ahh . . ." Louise smiled, leaning in as if to share a great secret. "But you were never one to blend in. Even then, you were your own girl."

Lizzy wasn't sure how to respond. Louise had meant the words kindly, but to someone who'd spent her entire scholastic career trying to blend into the scenery, the news that she had failed so completely wasn't exactly welcome. She managed a smile as she reached into her purse for pen and paper.

"This is my cell phone number," she said when she finished scribbling. "If you happen to think of anything—anything at all—please call me."

She had picked up the yearbook and was preparing to leave when Louise put a hand out to stop her. "Before you go . . . I was wondering if I might beg a favor. Penny Castle told me you brought her some tea for her headaches, and I was wondering if there might be some of that baby soap your grandma used to make lying around—the kind that helps put them to sleep. It worked like magic for my little girl, and now my daughter has a little one of her own. Poor thing. She's a year old and still doesn't sleep through the night."

Lizzy knew the soap Louise meant. It was a blend of chamomile, lavender, and oatmeal Althea had whipped up out of desperation when Rhanna was a baby. She had dubbed it Sleepy Baby Soap, and it had quickly become one of her best sellers. But she'd just searched the shop yesterday, and there hadn't been a bar of soap anywhere.

"I'm afraid my grandmother left the shelves pretty bare."

"But you could make more," Louise suggested hopefully. "You must know how she made it. We've tried all the things from the store—the washes and the lotions—but nothing works. My daughter's exhausted."

Lizzy sympathized with Louise's daughter, but making soap wasn't just a matter of whisking a few ingredients together and then slopping it into molds. Good soap was an art form. There were techniques involved, the kind that required time and practice to master. And even if she did agree, there was the cure time to consider—at least four weeks. She doubted she'd even be here in four weeks.

"Soap has to cure, Mrs. Ryerson. It wouldn't be ready for at least a month, and I'll be gone by then."

"Oh, but it wouldn't need to be ready. It could—cure, did you call it?—at my house. You could make it, and I'll just pick it up. I can pay you now if you like. My purse is in my locker."

Lizzy couldn't help recalling the look on Penny Castle's face when she had delivered her migraine tea, and how it felt to know she had helped put it there. "We'll call it a gift instead. I'll order the ingredients and let you know when it's ready."

"My daughter will be so grateful. You don't know how much a small kindness can mean when you're at your wit's end."

But Lizzy did know. Louise Ryerson had taught her a long time ago that kindness could come in many forms. Sometimes as cookies, sometimes as soap. "I'm happy to help, Mrs. Ryerson."

Louise held up a finger. "Don't run off. I have something for you."

She disappeared through a set of swinging doors, returning a moment later with something wrapped in a paper napkin. "Oatmeal raisin," she said, with the same kind smile Lizzy remembered. "They were always your favorite."

NINETEEN

August 3

Lizzy scrubbed her hands on the seat of her jeans and reached for her water bottle. She'd been working in the shop since breakfast—scrubbing windows, purging shelves, cleaning up mouse droppings—and she was finally starting to see progress.

She had called Althea's supplier yesterday to order the ingredients for Louise Ryerson's soap, knowing she would have to clean the shop before any work could begin. She still wasn't sure why she had agreed to make a batch of soap—she had enough on her plate without adding someone else's expectations to the mix.

A bead of sweat traced its way down Lizzy's back. August had arrived with a vengeance, and the shop was sweltering. She'd need to bring a fan down from the attic—for the heat as well as the lye fumes. She ran her eyes around the shop as she drained her water bottle, trying to imagine Althea's apothecary stripped of its counters and shelves. What would the new owners do with it? A guest cottage with lace curtains in the windows? An artist's studio littered with half-finished watercolors? Storage?

The question shouldn't bother her, but it did. Generations of Salem Creek residents had sought healing here. Many had found it. Now, on her watch, that would end.

You're all that's left, the last and best of us.

Althea's words haunted her again. But they weren't true. At least not all of them. She *would* be the last, but she had certainly never been the best. For her, Moon was just a name, something she'd inherited along with her black hair and strange gray eyes, like her mother, and her mother before her.

Her mother.

That's where the Moons' unraveling had begun. With Rhanna. The drinking and the drugs, the steady parade of men and repeated run-ins with the law—a slow-motion mutiny against the life she'd been expected to live. The life all Moon girls were expected to live. Rhanna had never wanted any of it, not the farm, not the shop, and certainly not her family. The murders had given her just the excuse she'd needed to pull up stakes and disappear for good.

That was the part Lizzy couldn't forgive. Not the leaving—she'd done that too—but the complete vanishing act. No warning. No note. Just an empty dresser and a vacant corner where her guitar used to sit. It never occurred to her that Althea might be worried sick. But then Rhanna never thought of anyone but Rhanna. She was happy bouncing from one calamity to the next, and to hell with whatever mess she might leave behind—including the daughter she'd never wanted.

Lizzy had been five or six when she realized her relationship with Rhanna wasn't normal, when she started school and saw how other mothers—*real* mothers—looked and dressed and acted. Rhanna had never been the healthy-snack, Purell-packing kind of mom. She'd been too busy partying to bother with things like checking homework or shopping for backpacks. Althea had done those things.

In third grade, her teacher had invited all the moms to come in and help the kids decorate Christmas cookies. Rhanna had been the only no-show, leaving Lizzy with a dozen gingerbread men to decorate on her own. Mrs. Gleason had taken pity on her and stepped in, assuring her as they piped frosting onto the crispy brown men that something must have come up to keep her mother from being there.

What Mrs. Gleason didn't know was that two weeks earlier, Lizzy had dropped the take-home flyer into the first trash can she passed on the walk home. She couldn't bear the thought of Rhanna showing up in her tie-dyed T-shirt and stringy bell-bottoms, standing next to moms in pastel twinsets and neatly pressed khakis. Being teased for being stood up seemed infinitely better than being teased for having a hippie mom who reeked of pot and patchouli.

But that was water under the bridge. She was here, and Rhanna was somewhere else. Or maybe she wasn't anywhere. She'd probably never know, and it didn't matter. Not really.

A shadow suddenly darkened the doorway. Lizzy turned to find Evvie behind her, a grin on her face and a glass of lemonade in her hand. "As my mama would say, you look like you could use a good scrub."

Lizzy peered at her grime-streaked hands, then wiped them on the front of her T-shirt. "I'm afraid I'd have to agree with her."

Evvie stepped inside, running her eyes around the shop. "You've been busy, I see. Wish your gran was here to see it."

"Me too," Lizzy sighed, recalling the days when the shelves had been lined with an assortment of tonics and remedies, each bottle and jar hand-labeled in Althea's careful script. Now the shelves stood empty, and those days seemed a lifetime ago. She accepted the lemonade from Evvie, downing half of it in one go, then wiped her mouth, leaving a fresh smear of grit on her chin. "What am I doing, Evvie?"

"Don't you know?"

Lizzy blinked at her. "Honestly? No. I'm supposed to be getting the place ready to sell. Instead, I'm making soap for Louise Ryerson's granddaughter. It's crazy."

"It's not," Evvie shot back. "In fact, it's the sanest thing you've done since you got here. This place is in your blood, little girl. This shop, and this soil, and that house—it's all part of you. So is caring for people. That's all healing is—trusting the magick, and sharing a little of it when you can. Your gran knew that."

Lizzy shook her head. "I'm not Althea, Evvie. I don't have that in me."

"You do. You just forgot where to look. It's why your gran left you the book—to help you find it. And you will, when it's time. The best magick always takes us by surprise. We plan our lives like we're in charge, lay all the pieces end to end like we think they should go, and then *zing!* Something happens we never saw coming, and we end up somewhere else. Sometimes it's right back where we started."

Lizzy met her gaze squarely. "And sometimes it's not."

"Maybe," Evvie said thoughtfully. "The best thing any of us can do is get out of our own way."

"And trust the magick?"

Evvie's coppery-green eyes lit with a conspiratorial gleam as she reached for Lizzy's empty lemonade glass. "Something like that. Come on inside now, and get cleaned up. Feels like maybe you've got some reading to do."

Lilies . . . for rebirth.

My dearest girl,

I am back as you see, returned to the page to scribble down things that are on my heart, things I hope will help you after I am gone. But there is selfishness here too, make no mistake. I'm not so noble as I thought myself when I began all this. I vowed when I lost Rhanna that I would never press you into a life you did not want. But now, as my candle burns down, I find my regrets make poor companions. And so I must turn my thoughts to the future, Lizzy—your future— and try to sway you a little.

    I have placed a lily between these pages. As you might guess, it was not an easy flower to press, too fragile in many ways to survive the harshness required to preserve it. But in the right hands, with the proper care, even the most fragile thing can withstand hardship and, in the end, yield a new kind of beauty—and so many lessons.

Renewal. Rebirth. Reincarnation.

Different words that all mean the same thing—the return of life to a thing believed spent. The end. The beginning. They have always been one. A part of the Circle into which we're all born. It's been taught in many ways down through the years, in many traditions, but the promise is always the same: the hope of a life to come. It's the natural way of things—or the supernatural way if one prefers—an unimpeachable truth etched in blood and bone.

Because we are all a part of the One. And so we must have a care, remembering that nothing is ever lost. Its seed—its purest essence—is always there, waiting to manifest a newer and better version of itself. With us to guide the process, to nurture and protect, heal and bring forth. It is our purpose—our raison d'être. Yours and mine, and all the Moons before us.

Take from these scribblings what you will. They are the musings of an old woman who wishes with all her heart to see you happy, but longs to see her life's work carried on too. We each have many destinies to fulfill. Being your grandmother was one of mine, and I would be remiss to stop teaching you now, simply because my feet no longer leave prints in the earth. And so I will say what is on my heart, because it is what I have always done. One day, perhaps soon, you will find yourself at a place of choosing, torn between the life you were born to and the one you've made for yourself, between your duty and your dreams.

And yet the two are not so far apart as you think. Trust your heart. Trust the magick. It's in you still, tightly furled, waiting to be coaxed out into the light. You look around at what you've been left, which isn't much just now, I'll grant, and see only decline and decay. But nothing is ever too far gone, my Lizzy. Nothing is beyond rebirth.

A—

TWENTY

August 7

Lizzy came awake with a jolt, eyes wide in the cocoonlike darkness of Althea's room, wondering what had startled her from sleep. There was no light bleeding under the door, no footsteps in the hall, no sounds that should have awakened her. She closed her eyes again, listening to the quiet, hearing only the familiar sounds of a house settling in for the night.

When she was a girl, she used to lie in the dark and imagine the house as a living thing, listening to its ancient bones creaking at the end of a long day, the ticktock of its clocks, steady as a heartbeat, its dark windows looking out onto the street like so many sightless eyes. And the curtains, sighing in and out at the windows, as if the house itself were breathing.

They were stirring now, rippling on the barest of breezes. Lizzy watched the hypnotic push and pull, feeling the subtle tug of sleep returning. And then she caught it, a faint whiff drifting in through the screen—smoke.

Her pulse ticked up as she threw back the covers and scrambled to the window. To the east, toward the apple orchard, the horizon glowed an eerie shade of orange. The breeze came again, pushing into the room, the bite of smoke unmistakable now.

The orchard was on fire.

Panic prickled through her veins as she dragged on her dirty jeans and shoved her feet into the work boots at the foot of the bed, then bolted out into the hall to bang on Evvie's door. "Call the fire department! Tell them to go to the orchard!"

And with that she was gone, thundering down the stairs in her unlaced boots, out the mudroom door, and across the empty fields. The smoke grew thicker as she approached the orchard, the sky glowing a hideous red. She nearly stumbled when she spotted the flames, jagged bright tongues licking from tree to tree with astonishing speed.

A sob caught in her throat as she stood at the edge of the conflagration, nauseated by the smoke and the sickening crackle of timber being devoured. The heat was savage, kicking up a wind that scorched her cheeks and eyes. In some tiny but still-functioning corner of her mind, it occurred to her that she should move back, but her legs refused to obey. The orchard shed was already engulfed, its roof on the verge of buckling. Over the roar of the flames, she caught the sharp pop of a window exploding, and then the growing wail of sirens.

There was a distant flash of red lights from the street as the pumpers pulled up. The sirens had barely stopped blaring when a handful of firefighters rushed in trailing hoses. Lizzy watched numbly as one team fanned out to circle the shed, and another went to work on the trees. One of the men spotted her and broke ranks long enough to order her to clear the area. Moments later the shed gave way, caving in on itself with a dry groan and a roar of fresh flames.

At some point Evvie arrived in her bathrobe and UGGs. She wrapped an arm around Lizzy's shoulder and dragged her close, her face shiny wet.

"How could it happen?" Lizzy muttered hoarsely. "In the middle of the night—how could it just go up in flames?"

Evvie dragged her gaze from the flames, as if coming out of a trance, then lifted her eyes to the smoke-filled sky. "Clear as a bell," she pronounced ominously. "It wasn't an accident."

~

Lizzy wasn't sure who she was expecting when she answered the door the next afternoon, but it certainly wasn't a man flashing a badge. She stared at him, her eyes still bleary from smoke and lack of sleep. "I'm sorry. Can I help you?"

"Guy McCardle," he announced briskly. "With the Salem Creek Fire Department. We're here about the fire last night."

Over his shoulder, Lizzy caught sight of a white SUV at the bottom of the drive, its doors emblazoned with the letters SCFD. She hadn't expected anyone to bother about a shed fire, but she supposed there were procedures that had to be followed.

"Yes, of course. I'll walk you to the orchard."

"I've got two of my men headed there now, actually. But I do have a few questions." He stepped away, motioning for her to follow, then picked up the pace when she fell in beside him. "It's my job to investigate the origin and cause of last night's fire," he explained as they cut across the barren herb fields. "To process the scene and collect evidence, then conduct an investigation."

Lizzy eyed him dubiously. "I'm not sure there's much to find. It was just a shed, and there's not much left."

"You'd be surprised."

She was about to respond when she caught the stench of smoke and scorched apples on the breeze. She forced herself to keep moving, telling herself that nothing could be worse than actually watching it burn.

She was wrong.

Her heart sank as they approached the orchard, her throat raw as she took it all in: row upon row of ruined trees, their charred trunks and gnarled limbs reminding her of something from one of those gruesome fairy tales with the haunted forests and poison apples.

But somehow the shed was harder to look at, its blackened shell splayed like a dead thing at the edge of the orchard. There was something vaguely macabre about its remains, lying cold and wet in the afternoon sun, bits of wood jutting like blackened bones. It had endured countless New England winters, weathered scores of nor'easters, but had in the space of only two hours been reduced to cinders.

How?

The question hummed in her head as she scanned the rubble. There were remnants of a spade and several rakes among the ashes, their wooden handles burned away. Bits of shattered glass glinted among the soot. Lizzy shuddered, recalling the sickening pop of windows exploding over the windlike rush of the flames.

McCardle's men were already at work, one brandishing a camera, taking shots from various angles, the other walking gingerly around the perimeter of the rubble, eyes glued to the ground. Both wore latex gloves.

She turned to McCardle, who was scribbling something on a small notepad. "What are they looking for?"

"Evidence. Footprints, accelerant containers, a scrap of clothing, anything the culprit might have left behind. It's too early to say for sure, but it looks like the fire originated in the shed, with the trees catching later."

"But how did it start? No one's used the shed in years."

"That's what we're going to try to determine. Do you know if the structure was used to store chemicals of any kind? Paint, fertilizer, gasoline? Even oily rags can pose a danger if they're stored in a closed container."

"No. Nothing like that. It was just picking poles and apple baskets. A couple of old ladders."

McCardle tipped his head back, surveying the area overhead. "No power lines running to the structure, so it wasn't electrical. That's the first thing we rule out for a structure like this. Old wiring, dry wood, only takes a spark. Next, we look at the weather. Lightning strikes are more common than people think, but there weren't any storms in the area, which means we can rule that out as well."

Lizzy felt a prickle of dread. "What does that leave?"

"Arson."

The word seemed to hang in the air as one of McCardle's men approached. "Thought you'd want to take a look at this." He was holding what looked like a glass bottle top, broken off at the neck. A scrap of checked yellow cloth had been twisted into the mouth. A piece of dish towel by the look of it, partially singed. "Found it just off to the right there, outside the zone."

McCardle pulled a pair of blue latex gloves from his back pocket and wrestled them on with a snap at each wrist, then took the proffered bit of glass and fabric and raised it to his nose. "Kerosene," he announced, turning to Lizzy. "And an old glass milk bottle. Better known as a Molotov cocktail. Crude, but effective, although apparently not in this case, since the rag is still intact. Probably went out before impact."

"It was effective enough," Lizzy pointed out. "The shed's an ash heap."

"Which is why we'll keep looking. We'll sift through every square inch if we have to." He looked away briefly, handing back the broken bottle top. "Good job, Ward. Bag it for the lab."

Lizzy watched as Ward produced a heavy poly bag, slid the bottle fragment and rag inside, and zipped it closed. "What happens at the lab?"

"We'll do an analysis on the rag to confirm the accelerant, and run the bottle for prints. Sometimes we get lucky. Do you know anyone who'd have a reason to do something like this? Someone who might be harboring a grudge?"

Lizzy stared back at McCardle, beginning to grasp the gravity of the situation. She'd been holding on to the slim hope that the doll had in fact been a prank, rather than what it looked like—an outright threat—but there was no explaining this away. Was the timing a coincidence? Or had someone—Fred Gilman, perhaps—gotten wind of her sit-down with Louise Ryerson, and decided she needed another scare?

It was certainly possible. Someone from the school library could have mentioned her visit, or one of the kids from the lunchroom, though she doubted any of them knew who she was. Or who Fred Gilman was, for that matter.

The truth was, Fred Gilman wasn't the only one who had a problem with the Moons. The icy stares she'd been receiving since her return were proof of that. It was tempting to jump to the most obvious conclusion, but bringing Fred Gilman into it without any kind of evidence would be rattling a door she wasn't ready to open. The locals were already taking sides. Accusation would only entrench them further.

"Ms. Moon?"

Lizzy had been watching Ward pick through the ashes. She dragged her gaze back to McCardle. "I'm sorry. You asked if I knew anyone who might have a reason to do this. I'd have to say no."

"So no recent altercations? An angry boyfriend? An argument with a neighbor?"

"No," she said, not quite meeting his eyes. "Nothing like that."

"Looks like we've got another one, boss." It was Ward, down on one knee this time, hollering over his shoulder. "No rag, but it's the same type of glass. I'm guessing this is the one that did the trick. Pretty smashed up, though."

"I'll be right there." McCardle closed his notepad and turned to Lizzy. "It appears our culprit was determined. Let's hope he was careless as well."

Lizzy nodded blankly, not sure how to respond.

"We should be able to wrap up our end of the investigation in a day or two, such as it is. Not much left of the structure. No witnesses. But until you're notified that we're through, I'd appreciate you steering clear of the area. It's natural after something like this to want to clean up, but we don't want to risk contamination until everything's wrapped up and we've turned our information over to Salem Creek PD."

"Of course, and thank you. If you don't mind, I'm going to leave you to it."

McCardle nodded curtly. "No worries. I know where to find you if I have any more questions."

~

Evvie was out back when Lizzy returned, filling the water bowls she kept positioned around the yard so her bees would have plenty to drink. She closed the hose nozzle and looked up. "Well?"

"They found a broken bottle with a rag in it."

"A torch?"

"Yes. Well, two, actually."

Evvie threw down the hose with more force than was necessary, muttering something that might have been Creole as she dried her hands on her apron. "You'll be calling the police now, I hope?" she said finally. "To tell them what's going on?"

"I suspect the investigators will be doing that shortly, which means it'll be all over town by tomorrow. There is one silver lining, though. If someone really is trying to scare me, it means I'm not the only one who's scared."

"Humph." Evvie cocked an eye at her. "You say that like it's a good thing."

"Scared people make mistakes, Evvie."

"They're also dangerous."

"They can be. But why set the orchard on fire when he could burn us all in our beds? Whoever is doing this is just looking to terrorize me, and sooner or later he's going to slip up. When he does, we'll finally get to the truth. Isn't that what we want? The truth?"

Evvie poked out her lower lip, clearly unconvinced. "Truth won't do you any good if you're dead. I just lost your gran. I don't want to be scattering your ashes next."

Lizzy managed a smile she didn't quite feel. If Evvie's intention had been to send a chill down her spine, she'd been successful. "Well, the police and the fire department are both on it now, so it's unlikely that you'll have to worry about my ashes anytime soon. And at this point, I'm not even sure what my next move is. Right now, I'm going upstairs and filling the tub, where I plan to soak until I no longer smell like a chimney sweep. And then I'll be heading to the kitchen to pour myself a hefty glass of wine and start the ratatouille. I'm in desperate need of some culinary therapy, and a night free of surprises."

TWENTY-ONE

An hour and a half later, Lizzy was waterlogged but soot-free, and the investigators' SUV was gone. In the kitchen, she opened a bottle of chardonnay and poured herself a glass, then pulled an eggplant, a green pepper, and several zucchini from the fridge. Cooking had always been a refuge for her, a calming, almost meditative act, and if there was anything she could do with just now, it was a little calm.

From the window over the sink, she could see the sun beginning to slide behind the treetops. The days were already growing shorter, the afternoon light taking on that soft, buttery hue that meant autumn wasn't far off. Soon the trees would turn, and the hills would go gold. Pumpkins would appear on doorsteps, along with cornstalks and bright yellow mums. She'd be back in New York by then.

A knock on the front door cut the thought short. She waited, expecting to hear the scuff of Evvie's UGGs. When she didn't, she wiped her hands, grabbed a sip of wine, and headed for the foyer.

She was surprised to find Andrew on the front steps. "You're back."

"Yes."

"How was Boston?"

"Good. It was . . . good."

"Does that mean you got the job?"

"Yeah. Yeah, it does."

Lizzy cocked her head to one side, studying him. He was acting strange—distracted and anxious. "Do you want to come in?"

"I'm uh . . ." He paused, shoving a hand through his hair. "I'm not alone."

"Sorry?"

"I picked up a hitchhiker," he said quietly. "Someone you know." He turned to glance at his truck, parked halfway up the drive. "It's your mother, Lizzy. She's in the truck."

A pall of white noise settled over Lizzy, like the thick, cottony quiet that surrounded you when you first took off in a plane, when the earth fell away and you seemed disconnected from the world, suspended between reality and whatever came next.

Her mother. In the truck.

It wasn't possible.

But a glance over Andrew's shoulder confirmed that there was, in fact, someone sitting in the passenger seat of his truck. Lizzy froze when the door opened and Rhanna climbed out. She was wearing a crocheted halter top and jeans worn to strings at the hem. A beaded purse slapped rhythmically against her hip as she advanced up the drive.

Lizzy remained rooted to the spot, breath held as confusion and disbelief spun into a wave of white-hot fury. She waited until Rhanna reached the walkway, then stepped around Andrew, effectively blocking her path.

"What do you want?"

Rhanna met her gaze without flinching. "I want to come home."

Lizzy stiffened. "Suddenly this is your home?"

Andrew cleared his throat, his discomfort plain. "Lizzy, she hitch-hiked all the way from California. It's taken her six weeks to get here."

"I don't care how long it took her to get here. I care *why* she's here. Now. After eight years."

"I came for Althea," Rhanna said softly. "And for you."

Lizzy folded her arms over her chest, eyeing Rhanna coolly. Her skin, once pale as milk, was nut-brown now, and leathery from too much sun, and there were threads of silver running through her dark hair. She'd also lost weight, enough to cause her clothes to hang limply on her slight frame. Was she sick? Was that what this was about?

"It's a little late to start thinking of me, Rhanna. And as for Althea, she's—"

"Dead," Rhanna supplied quietly. "Yes, I know."

Lizzy narrowed her gaze. She did know. That much was clear. What wasn't clear was *how* she knew. "How could you know about Althea? No one's heard from you in years."

"I had a dream," Rhanna said softly. "At least I think it was a dream. I woke up, and I could smell her perfume—the one you used to make for her. It was like she was in the room with me. And I just . . . knew."

Lizzy felt the ground shift. Althea's perfume. The same lavender and bergamot she'd been smelling since she returned to the farm. Rhanna had smelled it too. In California.

And now here they were, standing face-to-face, staring at each other across an eight-year void. Lizzy longed to look away. To *walk* away. To go back into the house and bolt the door. It was ironic. How many times had she grumbled that it should be Rhanna dealing with all this? And now she was here, all the way from sunny California, trying to nudge her way in.

Andrew cleared his throat, breaking the silence. "I'll get her bags from the truck."

"I never said she was staying."

"She's your mother, Lizzy."

Lizzy stared at him, stung by the rebuke. Had he forgotten her swim in the town hall fountain? The episode at the coffee shop? She glanced back at Rhanna in her bell-bottoms and beads, in her fifties now. A wilted flower child. And family, if blood counted for anything.

Was she really capable of turning her own mother away? Of treating her the way Salem Creek had treated so many Moons over the years—as a pariah? She was pretty sure the answer was yes. Rhanna had washed her hands of the Moons years ago. Now she could live with it.

"One night," she conceded frostily, stepping back to let Rhanna enter. "One. And then you're out."

Rhanna seemed almost wary as she stepped into the front parlor, arms pinned tight to her chest, as if she didn't trust herself to touch anything. "It's the same," she whispered, blinking back tears. "All of it—exactly the same."

The uncharacteristic show of emotion took Lizzy by surprise. Soppy had never been Rhanna's style. But then there were a lot of things about Rhanna that had changed. The way she smelled, for instance, like bonfires and tea leaves, rose petals and rain. The combination was as unfamiliar as it was unsettling—a blur of pagan and gypsy, layered with the loamy scent of wet earth—and sharply at odds with the woman she remembered.

"Andrew told me how it happened," Rhanna said quietly. "How Althea got sick, I mean. I would have come back if I'd known. I would have been here."

A nod was all the response Lizzy could muster. She'd said the same thing to Evvie the night she arrived, and wondered if Evvie had been as skeptical then as she was now. "What about you, Rhanna? Are you . . . well?"

"I'm well enough."

"Are you lying?"

"Would you care if I was?" Rhanna smiled sadly when Lizzy didn't answer immediately. "On second thought, don't answer that. I'm fine. Things have just been a little tight lately. And it's a long walk from Cali."

Lizzy was about to respond with something snarky when she heard the mudroom door bang shut.

"I thought I heard voices . . ."

Evvie's words dried up when she saw Rhanna. For a moment no one spoke. Lizzy watched as Evvie and Rhanna locked eyes, the air between them charged with unspoken questions. She could see by the look on Evvie's face that no introduction was necessary. No one looking at Rhanna could mistake her for anyone but a Moon. Still, she had to say something.

"Evvie, this is Rhanna—my mother."

～

Rhanna's bags turned out to be an army-green knapsack and a badly scarred guitar case. Andrew hovered in the foyer, the knapsack clutched to his chest, the guitar slung over his shoulder. "Where should I put them?"

Lizzy flashed him a look of exasperation. She wasn't anywhere near ready to think about sleeping arrangements. He of all people should know how this was likely to end. Which made it worse somehow that he'd been the one to drop her on the doorstep, like a stray puppy she was expected to keep whether she wanted it or not.

They were all looking at her now—Andrew, Evvie, Rhanna—waiting for her to say something that would ease the tension. They'd be waiting a long time. "Leave them right there," she told Andrew grudgingly. "Near the door. I've got the supper to finish." And with that, she turned and walked away, praying that no one followed her.

In the kitchen, she took a gulp of her now-tepid wine, then picked up her knife. She needed time to absorb this new development, and figure out what happened next. She had more than enough on her plate. She didn't need a drama queen with a predilection for meltdowns added to the mix. And that's precisely what she'd get if Rhanna was allowed to hang around any length of time.

While generations of Moon girls had grown up knowing the risks of making waves, Rhanna had honed the subtle art of not giving a damn, of poking a finger in the eye of convention, creating a scene, saying the unthinkable. Like the time she'd been suspended for reading tarot cards in the school talent show and predicting that her PE teacher would be discovered rolling a joint in the janitor's supply closet. Or the time she'd painted a peace sign with a middle finger in the center, on the wall of the First Presbyterian rectory. Recklessness and rebellion. Those were Rhanna's superpowers. And now she'd brought them back to Salem Creek.

One night, Lizzy reminded herself as she downed another sip of wine. That was all she'd promised. And what then? By the look of things, Rhanna didn't have two nickels to rub together. She had no job, and certainly no friends in Salem Creek. Which left . . . *what?*

The thought was interrupted by another smack of the mudroom door. She hoped it was Andrew leaving. Instead, she spotted Evvie through the kitchen window, heading toward the garden with a basket over her arm. Apparently, Lizzy wasn't the only one who needed a little alone time.

As if on cue, Rhanna wandered into the kitchen, trailing her fingers along the counter like a bored child in search of distraction. "Andrew's gone out to the garden with . . . Evvie, is it?"

"Yes," Lizzy answered tersely. "Her name is Evvie."

Rhanna was up on her toes now, craning her neck for a better view of the garden. "Now there's a sight for sore eyes. Andrew, I mean. Not Evvie. He was still at UNH when I left, but he turned out real nice."

Lizzy stopped chopping and turned to stare.

"What?" Rhanna pouted, all innocence. "I'm old, not dead."

Lizzy opened her mouth, then closed it again, and resumed her chopping.

"So what's the deal with her?" Rhanna asked, filching a bit of green pepper from the cutting board and popping it into her mouth. "Why's she living here?"

"The *deal*," Lizzy said dryly, "is that she was Althea's friend. She was with her till the end." She paused, looking up at Rhanna. "She's like us."

Rhanna's brows lifted. "By *like us*, you mean . . ."

"Yes," Lizzy answered pointedly. "I mean *like us*."

"Wow." The corners of Rhanna's mouth turned down thoughtfully. "There's something you don't hear every day." She reached for the glass of chardonnay on the counter, but Lizzy checked her, sliding the glass just out of reach. Rhanna sighed. "Is this how it's going to be? You treating me like I'm some unwanted guest who just turned up on your doorstep?"

"Isn't that what you are?"

"This is my home, Lizzy. I grew up here—just like you."

Lizzy stared down at her glass, twirling the stem between her fingers. "You grew up nothing like me."

"Lizzy . . ." Rhanna's eyes were soft, pleading.

Lizzy sidestepped her. "Let's not do this, okay?"

But Rhanna seemed determined to have her say. "What I did, when you were a baby, giving you to Althea—I know it seems horrible. But I also know I was right. I wasn't . . . equipped. I was selfish and thoughtless, and so screwed-up. That's why I did it, Lizzy. Not because I *didn't* care—because I *did*. I was afraid . . ." She closed her eyes, her slender shoulders sagging. "I was afraid I'd hurt you."

"Right," Lizzy shot back before swallowing the last of her wine. "You certainly wouldn't have wanted that."

They were still glowering at each other when Andrew reappeared. Lizzy turned, eyeing him frostily. "You're still here."

"Evvie asked me to bring you this." He handed her a trug of freshly picked lettuce. "She said she'd be in shortly to do the salad. Oh, and I'm supposed to tell you to set a fourth place for supper. She asked me to stay."

Lizzy eyed the basket, then Andrew, wondering how she'd managed to lose complete control of the situation. "Terrific."

"I carried your mother's things up. I didn't know which room she'd be in, so I left them at the top of the stairs." He paused, leaning in, dropping his voice. "I need to talk to you."

There were things she needed to say to him too, but now wasn't the time. She jerked her chin toward the counter, littered with chopped vegetables. "I'm a little busy just now. It seems I'm giving a dinner party, and I need to go kill the fatted calf."

Andrew let the prodigal-daughter reference pass. "After supper then. It's important."

An hour later, they were all seated around the kitchen table. Lizzy would have been happy to eat in silence, but Andrew seemed determined to draw Rhanna out.

"So I have to ask. What on earth possesses someone to hitchhike from California to New Hampshire?"

Rhanna flashed him a grin. "The same thing that motivates someone to hitchhike anywhere, I guess. Empty pockets. Or nearly empty. I had to sell my van to take care of some people I owed, which left me with exactly eighty-nine dollars, my guitar, and my thumb."

Andrew looked at her in astonishment, and perhaps the tiniest bit of admiration. "You left California with less than a hundred dollars in your pocket?"

"I've always been resourceful."

Lizzy rolled her eyes. "That's one word for it."

Andrew acknowledged the snipe with the barest of glances, then returned his attention to Rhanna. "What did you do in San Francisco? I remember you used to paint."

"I did, but I had to give it up. Couldn't afford the supplies. I sang in coffee shops, read cards, told fortunes. I didn't make much, but it was enough to feed me most of the time, and I had friends who'd let me crash on their couch when things got really tight. It was your basic 'Gypsies, Tramps & Thieves' existence, but it suited me."

Lizzy put down her wineglass with a snort. "And what about now? Does it suit you now?" She was glaring at Rhanna openly, disgusted by the entire performance, as if she were some fascinating bohemian simply marching to the beat of her own drum. Did she honestly believe anyone was going to buy that after the disasters she'd left in her wake?

Rhanna's smile slipped. "I've learned to take life as it comes."

"Better known as leaving your messes for other people to clean up."

Andrew caught her eye, as if hoping to stave off the scene he knew was coming. Lizzy met his gaze without apology. After years of not knowing whether Rhanna was alive or dead, she'd been blindsided by her sudden return. She was entitled to a scene.

She pushed back her plate, swiveling her attention back to Rhanna. "Do us all a favor and skip the clever banter. You might have been too stoned to remember how things were—how *you* were—but my memory's fine. Shoplifting from the drugstore. Passing out drunk at the Fourth of July parade. Picketing the VFW on Veterans Day. Every time I turned around, you were doing something to embarrass us."

Rhanna met her gaze, shoulders hunched. "Lizzy, please—"

"Please what? Please don't shame you like you shamed us?"

"I never meant—"

"Why don't you tell us what you're really after, Rhanna? Because we both know you weren't homesick. You took off and never bothered to let anyone know you were alive. Now, you show up expecting me to roll out the welcome mat. Did you really think that's how this would go?"

"Of course I didn't. I know what you think of me—what everyone thinks of me."

"Then why *did* you come?"

"I told you . . ."

"I know what you told me. Now I'm telling *you*—if you schlepped halfway across the country with your guitar on your back because you thought your ship had come in, you wasted your time."

Rhanna looked as if she'd just been slapped. "That's what you think? That I came here for money? You know me better than that."

If Lizzy hadn't been so furious, she might have laughed out loud. Know her? In what world would such a thing have ever been possible? When she was usually too drunk or high to remember her own name, let alone the name of her daughter?

Lizzy pushed her chair back and stood. "That's where you're wrong, Rhanna. I don't know you at all. I've never known you. You made sure of that."

TWENTY-TWO

Bloody hell.

Andrew stood at the edge of the orchard, his gut knotted like a fist. He had smelled the ash long before reaching the scene, had even imagined what he would find when he arrived, but nothing Evvie said had prepared him for what he was looking at: blackened trees, scorched ground, a heap of charred timber where the shed once stood.

Arson. Evvie had whispered the word out in the garden, explaining that the investigators had discovered a pair of kerosene torches among the rubble. The thought made his blood run cold. It could just as easily have been the house.

He'd touch base with Guy McCardle first thing in the morning. Randall Summers might not take his job seriously, but Guy was a straight arrow. If there was something to know, he'd know it.

He turned and headed east, the setting sun at his back as he walked the perimeter of the orchard, peering down each row as he went. Lizzy was here somewhere. He had known it instinctively when he left the house, ignoring Evvie's suggestion that he let her have some time to herself. They needed to talk, now, and not just about the fire.

He found her ten minutes later, sitting cross-legged with her back against an old stump, head bent, eyes closed. Was she crying? Praying? *Did* she pray? He'd wondered a lot of things about her over the years, but never that.

His chest tightened as he approached her. He'd run through a dozen conversations in his head on the way here. Now, suddenly, he didn't know what to say. She didn't lift her head, but he could tell she knew he was there. "Lizzy."

She looked up, fixing him with a withering stare. "What do you want?"

"I want to talk to you about this." He waved an arm, indicating the scorched ground and blackened trees. "Evvie gave me the *Reader's Digest* version while we were in the garden. I assumed you'd fill in the blanks at dinner, but you didn't say a word."

"Sorry, I was a little busy. Some guy decided to drop my mother on my doorstep without warning."

Andrew sighed, scrubbing a hand through his hair. "What was I supposed to do, Lizzy? Let her keep walking? She would have gotten here eventually. You realize that, right?"

"That isn't the point."

"It is, actually. She's not some drifter I just picked up. She's your mother."

"Stop saying that!"

"Okay. Okay. There's some bad blood between you two. I get it. I also get that this isn't really any of my business, but at the risk of stepping over the line, maybe it's time to work through your issues. For Althea's sake, if nothing else. She'd want the two of you to work things out."

"How would you know?"

"Because we talked."

Lizzy's eyes narrowed. "About me?"

Andrew suppressed a wince. He hadn't intended to mention his conversations with Althea. Especially the one they'd had about Lizzy's tortured relationship with her mother. He'd known instinctively that she wouldn't appreciate being discussed, even by her grandmother, but he'd opened the door now, and maybe it was time.

"Yes," he said carefully. "Sometimes we talked about you. We talked about Rhanna once too. About what happened before she left, and the effect it had on you. She made a lot of messes, that's for sure, but she did come back. That's got to mean something. Maybe she wants another chance. And maybe deep down you want to give her one."

Lizzy cut her eyes at him. "The only thing I want to give Rhanna is a ticket back to wherever she came from. Don't look at me like that. You *know* what she's like. You saw her that night in the fountain, making a spectacle of herself. That's who you picked up and brought here."

Andrew blew out a sigh. Yes, he'd seen her. Half the town had seen her. And the half that hadn't seen her had certainly heard all about it. And about every other damn thing she'd ever done. But he'd also seen Lizzy's face when Rhanna stepped out of his truck, that instant of recognition, of relief, before she'd retreated behind her outrage, and he couldn't help wondering if all that anger was masking something deeper, something she wasn't willing to acknowledge—pain. The kind people lived with when their hearts had been broken. Yes, there was history, and, no, he didn't know all of it, but surely thumbing three thousand miles across the country—even for a self-professed gypsy—counted for something.

"Maybe she isn't that woman anymore," he said quietly. "Maybe she's changed. People do, you know?"

Lizzy cocked an eye at him. There was a smear of soot on her right cheek, like an angry bruise. "She just hitchhiked across the country with a knapsack and a guitar. She had to sell her van to pay off some debts. She tells fortunes and crashes on couches. Does it sound like she's changed to you?"

"I think it's too early to tell. And she *is* here. I know you have every right to be angry, but I also know you're not the kind of person who could just toss her mother into the street. For starters, she's broke. And this is her home. She came home, Lizzy."

Lizzy kept her eyes on the ground as she scraped a streak in the soot with her bootheel. "She gave up the right to call this home a long time ago. And she's never been my mother. She had me when she was sixteen and handed me over to Althea before the midwife was done cleaning her up. We shared a house, toothpaste, shampoo. We were never mother and daughter."

"Maybe she thought she was doing what was best for you."

"Now you sound like her."

Andrew shrugged. He was annoying her now, and that wasn't why he'd come. He dropped down beside her, picked up a stick, and began to trace a circle in the ash. After all these years she was still an enigma, a puzzle he felt driven to solve.

"That bit before," he said finally. "About the dream. You asked how she knew Althea was dead and she said she had a dream. What did she mean?"

Lizzy's eyes slid away. "Nothing. She didn't mean anything. She just says things."

"I saw your face when she said it, Lizzy. It wasn't nothing."

He could see the wheels turning as she weighed her response, her lower lip caught between her teeth. Finally, she looked at him squarely. "Do you believe in ghosts?"

The question caught him off guard, or maybe it was the way she'd asked it, as if she were testing him. "If you mean do I think some part of us remains after we die, then yes, I guess I do. For a while, after my father died, I used to think I could hear him up in his room, crinkling the pages of his newspaper."

"You don't think it's just wishful thinking?"

He took his time with this one, sensing a new and more critical test. "I don't," he said at last. "I think most of us leave this world with unfinished business. Things we never said, chances we never took, wrongs we never righted. Maybe they keep us here. Like Jacob Marley and his chains, we're tied to this world by our regrets. We can't move on until we've cleaned them up, or at least made our peace with them."

There were tears in her eyes suddenly, trembling on her lashes, threatening to fall. She tried to blink them away, but it was too late. They spilled over, tracing a path through the streak of soot on her cheek. "Sometimes I wonder . . ." She shook her head and glanced away, letting the words dangle.

"What?"

"Nothing. Forget it."

"Talk to me, Lizzy. You wonder what?"

She pushed back her hair, leaving a fresh soot mark on her forehead. "Sometimes I wonder if Althea . . . if some part of her might still be here, trying to clean things up." She hesitated, eyes darting. "I feel her sometimes. I turn around, expecting her to be there. She never is, though."

"Just because you can't see her doesn't mean she isn't here."

"You believe that?"

"I do," he said matter-of-factly, because somehow it rang true for him. It would be just like Althea to hang around, to make sure the people she loved were okay, and, if possible, to put the broken pieces of her family back together.

"The thing Rhanna said on the steps—the perfume thing—it's happened to me too. Not always, but every now and then. And then there's this journal she left, with all these herbs and flowers pressed between the pages, like lessons she left for me. I know it sounds crazy, but it's like she's still here, talking right to me."

"It doesn't sound crazy at all. It sounds like Althea. She loved you. And if you ask me, there's no better reason to stick around than that."

The corners of her mouth trembled, not quite a smile. "Thank you for that. I thought you came out here to scold me about being a bad hostess. I wasn't expecting . . . this."

Neither was he. He'd come after her because he wanted to talk about the fire. And maybe about Rhanna, about what might actually lie at the base of all her anger. Instead, she had dropped her guard and, for the first time, allowed him to see her stripped of her armor. But now that she had, he found himself on shaky ground.

She was still looking at him, waiting for him to say something, her face all angles in the gathering dusk. She was a Moon through and through. Porcelain skin, hair the color of midnight, luminous quicksilver eyes. Like something from a grown-up fairy tale, but real enough to touch.

"We'd better go," he said, pushing to his feet. If he sat there much longer, he was going to say something stupid, something he couldn't take back.

TWENTY-THREE

It was full dark by the time Lizzy returned to the house. Dinner had been cleared away, the dishes washed and left to dry in the rack. She was glad, though she did wonder where Rhanna had gotten to. Perhaps she realized the Lazarus act wasn't going to fly and was already on her way back to California.

But a burst of muffled voices from upstairs put a quick end to that hope. Lizzy mounted the stairs with growing dread. The light was on in what used to be Rhanna's room, and whatever was going on didn't sound pleasant. The voices grew more distinct as she approached the landing: Evvie growling about hippies and flophouses, Rhanna snarling about being bossed around in her own room. Their heads turned in unison when Lizzy walked in.

"What's going on in here?"

Evvie's chin jutted like a sulky child's. "I'm trying to clear a place for her to sleep in all this mess." She paused, waving an arm at the stacked boxes and discarded household items crowding the room. "I finally get the bed cleared off, tell her there are sheets in the closet—"

"I haven't had a decent night's sleep in weeks," Rhanna bristled, matching Evvie sulk for sulk. "I don't need sheets. I need to crash."

Evvie folded her arms, eyes narrowed. "In this house you need sheets. Just like in this house we wash the dinner dishes and put them away when we're through."

Apparently, the battle had started in the kitchen. Not surprising, given Rhanna's aversion to all things domestic. Evvie had almost certainly made her opinion known. It wasn't in her DNA to hold back when something needed saying.

Lizzy closed her eyes, sighing. "I'll take care of it, Evvie."

Evvie shook her head. "No, ma'am. You've had enough for one day. You look . . ." Her eyes narrowed on Lizzy's sooty jeans and streaked face. "You've been out to the orchard, haven't you? I thought the man from the fire department told you not to bother anything?"

"I didn't. I just—"

"Wait." Rhanna held up a hand, cutting Lizzy off. "Why was there a fireman here?"

Lizzy swallowed a groan. She didn't want to get into this tonight. And she didn't want Evvie getting into it either. She shot her a silent plea to let her handle it, then turned back to Rhanna. "The shed burned last night. And part of the orchard."

Rhanna's face went blank. She looked at Evvie. "Burned?"

"Right to the ground."

"Do they know how it started?"

Lizzy waved the question away. "We can talk about it in the morning. Let's just make the bed, okay? You're not the only one who needs sleep."

But sleep didn't come easily when Lizzy finally slipped into bed. Snatches of her conversation with Andrew kept running through her head. He'd surprised her tonight. But then he'd always had a way of surprising her. Tonight was different, though. He hadn't batted an eye when she asked if he believed in ghosts. Instead, he talked about regrets and chains, about leaving this world with unfinished business.

Outside, the moon was high and full, splashing the bedroom walls with thin, milky light. Lizzy's eyes slid to the nightstand, to Althea's *Book of Remembrances*. She turned on the lamp, reached for the book, and flicked the button on the little brass closure. There was a whiff of something like licorice as she turned to the first unread passage, and a square of waxed paper containing a sprig of flattened leaves and tiny purple flowers.

Basil . . . for the mending of rifts.

My dearest Lizzy,

Of all the lessons I've recorded in this book, this will surely be the hardest for you to read. You have always been one to hold your wounds close, to chew on a hurt until all the flavor has gone out of it, and then to chew on it some more. But some wounds are more damaging than others. Some wounds sink down into the bone, festering out of sight, feeding on the anger until there's nothing left to knit back together. You become the wound, and it becomes you.

But healing comes when you let it. And it's time, little girl.

For years, I watched you nurse the rift between you and your mother, watched you feed it, and water it, and help it grow. And then when she left—the way she left—that rift grew some more. It was a betrayal. A final act of abandonment. And it hurt. Because you didn't think she could hurt you anymore. Believe me when I tell you I understand. No rift in the world runs so deep as one between mother and daughter. But bridges can be built across the widest chasms, even when all we have to build with are broken pieces.

You may not believe it now, but a time will come when you'll want to build that bridge, when you might even need to. It won't be easy, and if I know anything about you, it's that you'll fight it tooth and nail. Sometimes we find it hard to forgive someone else because we haven't learned to forgive ourselves. I can't tell you how to do that. But I can tell you there is no peace in blame. We must find a way to lay it down and be free.

Your mother was always different, from you and from me. From most of the Moons, I suppose. Nothing prepared me for her sullen moods and wild ways. I used to wonder if it was my fault, wonder if unhappiness could be passed down to a child, like blue eyes or a heart defect. She was such a restless spirit, but a sensitive one too. She claimed once to see things. She never said what, so I was never sure it was true, but there were times when she wouldn't sleep for days. She would wander the house like a ghost. I never knew what to do with her when she got like that. And then she'd come out of it, and go on one of her tangents, making a show of herself in some public place, like she was lashing out at the whole world. I didn't know what to do with her then either.

You were easier. But then, mothering isn't supposed to be easy. It's meant to stretch us, and Rhanna did that. And before it's over, I suspect she'll stretch you as well. Let her. Help her find her way back if that's what she wants. Maybe she'll help you do the same.

A—

TWENTY-FOUR

August 9

Lizzy tossed aside a wadded sheet of Bubble Wrap and began unpacking the supplies for the batch of baby soap she'd promised Louise Ryerson. The FedEx guy had delivered just after nine, and she'd wasted no time marching the box out to the shop, glad for an excuse to be out of the house—and away from her phone. Luc had been texting her nonstop, his messages growing increasingly impatient. At some point she would need to respond. Just not now, when she had a half dozen fires to put out, and no real endgame in sight.

Evvie had been sullen over breakfast, grumbling about Rhanna between bites of toast and scrambled egg. How sadly mistaken Rhanna was if she thought she was going to sleep till noon and then wander down for breakfast. They weren't running a hotel.

The criticism was perfectly valid, but the truth was, Lizzy was relieved that Rhanna hadn't come down for breakfast. She hadn't decided yet how much to say about the fire—or what might have incited it. The Gilman murders had rocked Salem Creek to its core, but Rhanna had taken them especially hard. She'd stopped painting, and started leaving the house at first light, staying gone until the wee hours, as if being in the house—or anywhere near the farm—had suddenly become unbearable. They never knew where she went, or what she did during those absences. Unless the police happened to bring her home, which they did from time to time.

No one was really surprised that Rhanna turned out to be a problem. She'd shown her colors early on. *Troubled*, the guidance counselor at Salem Creek High had labeled her in her freshman year. *Disruptive and a handful.* In her sophomore year she quit school to become a folk singer, only to turn up pregnant a few months later. There'd been a fresh round of whispers when she handed the baby off to Althea to raise. But it was her grand finale at the coffee shop that had left the entire town slack-jawed.

The last thing Lizzy needed was a repeat performance of her mother's greatest hits. And that's what would happen if Rhanna got wind of her recent preoccupation with Heather and Darcy Gilman, and then connected the dots to the fire. She had agreed to one night. As long as she stuck to that, she wouldn't need to say anything. Rhanna would leave and that would be that. But could she do that? Make her leave, today, with no money and no place to go?

Help her find her way back if that's what she wants.

Althea's words were still fresh. So were Andrew's. But what about what *she* wanted? Why should Rhanna be allowed to complicate things?

She was still wrestling with the question, head bent as she checked off items on the packing slip, when the shop door creaked open and Rhanna appeared. She was barefoot, dressed in a short denim skirt and a tie-dye T-shirt knotted at the waist, and carried a mug in each hand.

"I thought you might like some coffee." She held out one of the mugs, going out of her way to avoid brushing Lizzy's fingers.

It was a thing she had: an aversion to being touched. Haphephobia, they called it—an anxiety disorder usually associated with sexual assault and other physical traumas. But Rhanna hadn't experienced any physical trauma when her symptoms appeared. Lizzy had chalked it up to Rhanna's chronic need for attention, expecting that, like so many of her mother's ploys, it would eventually fall by the wayside. Apparently, it hadn't.

She was holding her mug with both hands now, inhaling the steam with an expression of pure bliss. "I take it Evvie isn't a morning person. I think I got five words out of her while the coffee was brewing. And that was her telling me to be sure to wash my mug when I was finished. What's with the accent?"

"It's Creole mostly. She's from Baton Rouge."

"Baton Rouge? How in the world did she end up here?"

"She keeps bees and sells the honey. Althea started carrying it in the shop. One day she invited Evvie for a visit, and they hit it off. She never went back."

Rhanna shook her head. "Leave it to Althea to buddy up with a Creole-speaking beekeeper from Louisiana."

Lizzy flashed her a look. "Was that snark?"

"No."

"Because I don't really think you're in a place to judge anyone. You weren't exactly the poster child for normal."

Rhanna pressed her lips together, managing to look chastened. "It wasn't snark, Lizzy. I swear. It's just that she's . . . unexpected."

Lizzy had to give her that one. Her own first impressions had been similar. Now, here she was, defending Evvie like a mama bear, wanting Rhanna to see her as she did: generous and wise—an extension of the Moon clan. "If we're talking unexpected, you should see her with her bees. She doesn't wear a stitch of protective gear. No gloves. No netting. Nothing. She just sings to them."

Rhanna squinted one eye. "Did you just say she *sings* to them?"

"I did. It's eerie, but beautiful too. They swarm all over her, and not one sting."

"Peter, Paul, and Mary . . . ," Rhanna said softly, as if unable to imagine such a thing.

The expression brought a smile to Lizzy's face. It was Rhanna's signature expletive—a hippiefied version of the ever-popular *Jesus, Mary, and Joseph*, which Althea had forbidden her to utter, asserting that the Moons did not take the name of anyone's god in vain. Apparently, she'd had no such compunction about taking the names of sixties folk singers in vain.

"You like her," Rhanna said.

"I do. And I'd appreciate it if you'd show her some respect. She was good to Althea, and she's been good to me." She took a sip of her coffee, eyeing Rhanna over the rim of her mug. Coffee. Chitchat. What was she up to? "I'm surprised to see you. I didn't think you were up yet."

"I've been up for hours, actually. I got some meditation in, did a little yoga, then went out to the orchard."

Lizzy paused, mug halfway to her mouth. "Why?"

"You said it burned. I needed to see it."

"You didn't believe me?"

"Of course I believed you. I just needed to see it for myself. To get a vibe, you know."

"A vibe?"

"It was on purpose, wasn't it? Someone set it?"

"You got that from a vibe?"

"No, from the way you were acting last night. I could tell there was something you didn't want me to know. So what's the deal? Why were you trying to keep it from me?"

Well, that certainly hadn't taken long. Lizzy blew out a breath. "Because I was exhausted and I didn't want you flipping out."

Rhanna nodded. "Fair enough. So what happened?"

"The investigators found two bottles in the rubble. One still had a rag stuffed into the neck. It was soaked with kerosene. That's all we know at this point."

It was mostly true. That *was* all they knew for certain. The rest was just speculation.

Rhanna was staring at her, horrified. "They have no idea who did it?"

"It was the day before yesterday. They're working on it."

"After all these years," Rhanna said softly. "They still can't leave us alone."

Lizzy lifted a brow. "It's *us* now?"

Rhanna's shoulders sagged. "You're determined to make this weird, aren't you?"

"I'm not *making* it weird," Lizzy replied. "It *is* weird. You. Here. Acting like nothing happened. And I'm supposed to just play along. Why? For Althea's sake?"

"Isn't that enough?"

"Althea's gone, Rhanna. And the farm will be too, in a few months' time."

Rhanna's shoulders sagged. "You're selling then? You've decided?"

"That's the plan. There's just one problem. The place is falling apart, and there's no money for repairs."

Rhanna peered into her mug. "It's hard to see, isn't it? Everything looks so tired. The gardens are all dead and wasted. I'm almost glad Althea isn't here to see it."

Lizzy shot her a hard look. "This didn't *just* happen, Rhanna. It's been happening for years. There was no money and no one to help her. And she *was* here to see it."

Rhanna set down her mug and stepped away. "I couldn't stay, Lizzy." The words tumbled out in a rush, as if she'd been holding them in since she climbed out of Andrew's truck. "I just . . . I couldn't."

Lizzy couldn't look at her. She reached for the sheet of Bubble Wrap on the worktable and began smashing the tiny blisters, one at a time, between her thumb and middle finger. Anything to keep from making eye contact. Perhaps because acknowledging her mother's regrets—her pain and her guilt—would mean acknowledging her own.

"I know," she said softly.

Rhanna looked away, sighing heavily. "You don't. You couldn't. Though I suppose you have your own reasons for hating this place."

Lizzy's brow furrowed. Something about the remark rankled. "I don't hate it. I never *hated* it. I just wanted a different kind of life. A normal life. And I have that. I live in New York now, and work for a perfume designer."

Rhanna turned back with a quiet smile. "Of course you do. You always knew what you wanted, even as a girl. And always so serious. You practically lived in that barn when you were a kid, always concocting something or other. I still remember how it smelled, the flowers and herbs drying in bunches or on screens, all the smells mingling together. I used to think of it as a single fragrance, but not you. You could pick each one out of the air—basil, tarragon, rosemary, sage. Do you remember?"

Lizzy nodded. "Yeah, I remember."

"So this job of yours—you'll have your own line of fragrances?"

"I don't actually design the fragrances. I work on the idea side, creative concepts, marketing campaigns, that sort of thing."

Rhanna's brows lifted. "Don't you miss it? The hands-on part, I mean? You used to love that stuff."

Lizzy couldn't argue with that. She *had* loved the hands-on part. But Chenier had a stable of highly paid *noses* for that part of the process. Her job was to put a face on their creations, to give each signature fragrance a distinct personality, then build a marketing campaign around it. It wasn't where she'd seen herself all those years ago, but the work wasn't without its rewards. And maybe someday it would turn into more. She was good at what she did. Very good. But she missed the creative part of the process, the delicious serendipity that had first drawn her to making perfume—the magick of scent.

"I enjoy what I do," she told Rhanna evenly. "I was lucky to get my foot in the door at Chenier five years ago. Now I'm their creative director."

Rhanna shook her head, her eyes suddenly shining. "It wasn't luck, Lizzy. You've had perfume in your blood for as long as I can remember. You were always experimenting with fragrances, giving them cool names. What was the one I liked?"

"Earth Song," Lizzy said quietly. "You liked the one called Earth Song."

"Yes! That was it. It was so calming. Cool and earthy, like a walk in the woods."

"Juniper, pink peppercorns, clary sage, and vetiver," Lizzy recited from memory.

"You actually remember it?"

"I remember them all."

Rhanna nodded. "I get it. Like my paintings. Each one special in its own way. I guess that's why the whole desk-job thing surprised me. I'd go crazy. But as long as you love it . . ." She let the words trail, quiet for a time, then narrowed her gaze on Lizzy again. "You do love it, right? New York and the title, and everything?"

"Of course I do," Lizzy replied, hating how sullen she sounded. "Why are you suddenly so interested in my career?"

"I just want you to be happy. Fulfilled, you know. Because you deserve it. You were such an amazing little girl. I remember thinking, *How could one little head hold so much information?* You made me wish I'd paid more attention when I was a kid and Althea was trying to teach me." Her mouth turned down at the corners, her expression somber again. "At least she had you. You had so many wonderful gifts—and you were nothing like me. I was always glad of that."

Lizzy wasn't sure which of Rhanna's revelations to respond to first. "I'm surprised you remember me as a girl."

"I remember more than you think, Lizzy. More than I ever wanted to."

Lizzy stared at her, annoyed. "I don't know what that means."

"It means you're not the only one with terrible memories. I live with them too. I've been living with them since before you were born."

"They weren't all bad," Lizzy reminded her. "There was the barn. You loved doing that mural."

Rhanna's face brightened at the mention of the mural. "Of all the paintings I've done, I never loved any of them the way I loved that mural."

Lizzy couldn't help grinning. "You loved it because it freaked people out."

Rhanna's eyes shot wide. "That's what you think? That I painted it to freak people out?"

"It's why you do *most* things, isn't it? Like the peace sign on the church. And the night you went skinny-dipping in the fountain."

"All right. You've got me there. But the mural was different. It was . . . personal. It's how twilight felt to me when I was a kid. That sliver of time between day and night, when the sky looks like velvet and the stars are just coming out. It always felt so magical, like the world was holding its breath, waiting to see what happened next."

Lizzy was too astonished to reply. She'd never seen Rhanna so filled with . . . What was it? Happiness? Yearning? Was it possible that beneath all that angst, her mother had actually tucked away some pleasant memories?

"You sounded almost happy just then."

Rhanna shrugged. "It wasn't all bad."

"Not all of it, no."

The silence spooled out. They sipped their coffee. "I didn't make it easy for you, did I?" Rhanna asked finally.

"No. You didn't."

"Is that why you left Salem Creek, because you were ashamed? Of me?"

Lizzy lifted her chin a notch, unwilling to concede the point. "I left to go to school, like I was always going to do. But you were a big part of why I stayed gone. The damage you did—the wreckage you left in your wake. You made sure there was nothing left to come back to."

Rhanna nodded, accepting the words as truth. "I never meant to."

Lizzy tilted her head to one side, trying to read her face. "Was that your idea of an apology?"

"Would you believe me if I said yes? If I fell down on my knees right now and asked you to forgive all the terrible things I've done, would you buy a word of it? Or would you think I was just saying it to say it?"

"There's history, Rhanna. That makes it hard."

"I know that." She wandered to the end of the worktable, quiet as she scanned the array of bottles and jars scattered over its surface, the FedEx box and discarded Bubble Wrap. "What's all this?" she asked, waving a finger.

"Just some supplies I ordered."

"Colloidal oatmeal, shea butter, lye." Her head came up. "You're making soap?"

Lizzy nodded, surprised she'd put it together so quickly. "I brought some headache tea to a woman who works the lunch counter at Wilson's. She told a friend. Now I'm making soap."

"You could have said no."

"They're old customers of Althea's. They stood by her when the rest of this town turned their backs. I felt like I owed them."

Rhanna picked up the package of oatmeal, peered at the label, and put it back down. "I could help."

The coffee. The chitchat. All at once, Lizzy understood. She was wrangling for more time. "We talked about this last night, Rhanna. I said one night."

"Please, Lizzy." Rhanna blinked several times, her gray eyes suddenly luminous with tears. "You can't send me away. Not like this. Not

213

until . . . well, I don't know, really. I don't even know why I'm here. I just know I had to come. I'll be good. I promise. If I screw up, you can kick me out. And I'll earn my keep. Let me help you make the soap."

"Why?" Lizzy asked flatly. "Why now?"

"The women," she said simply. "The ones who stuck by Althea—I owe them too. In fact, I owe a lot of people."

Lizzy studied her, wary of this new, softer side. Was she sincere, or was this just a new act?

Help her find her way back if that's what she wants.

"All right," Lizzy said reluctantly. "For Althea's sake."

"But only that?"

Lizzy met her gaze without flinching. "It's the best I can do."

Rhanna nodded, accepting the response at face value. "Thank you. For saying yes, and for letting me in."

"Tonight, after supper," Lizzy replied coolly. "And I'm not doing it for you."

TWENTY-NINE

The rain was coming down in buckets by the time Rhanna slid into the passenger seat of Lizzy's car, her purse clutched against an oversize denim jacket.

"Seat belt," Lizzy reminded her as she backed down the drive. "And tell me where I'm going."

"Go to the bottom of the hill. I'll tell you where to turn when it's time."

Lizzy's patience was already beginning to fray. "What's going on, Rhanna? Where are we going? And why in the world do we have to go now?"

Rhanna stared at the windshield, unblinking. "There's something I should have told you too. Something terrible."

Lizzy slid her a look, feeling the old familiar dread. She'd seen her mother in every state imaginable over the years—drunk, high, and just plain crazy—but never like this. Never terrified. "Talk to me, Rhanna. Tell me what's going on."

"You need to turn here."

Lizzy glanced at the street sign: OLD STAGE ROAD. "There's nothing up here but the cemetery."

"I know."

"Rhanna—"

"Go to the end and stop the car."

Lizzy did as she was told, parking just outside the cemetery gates. Granite monuments dark with rain stretched in all directions. They were spaced at irregular intervals, and varied in shape and size, giving them an oddly haphazard feel, like an ill-planned garden.

"All right," Lizzy said, over the slap of the wipers. "We're here. Now tell me why."

Before Lizzy knew what was happening, Rhanna was out of the car, lurching out into the cold, gray rain. Lizzy fumbled with her seat belt and set out after her. "What are you . . . Rhanna! Where are you going?"

She was soaked in seconds, struggling to see through the near-blinding rain. Rhanna was already through the gates, wending her way between the gravestones like a woman on a mission. Lizzy scrambled to catch up, slipping twice on the rain-slick grass. Finally, Rhanna stopped, coming to such an abrupt halt that Lizzy nearly piled into the back of her.

"Are you crazy? What are you . . ." Lizzy's voice trailed off as she followed Rhanna's gaze.

HEATHER & DARCY GILMAN.
BELOVED DAUGHTERS OF FRED AND CHRISTINA GILMAN
SISTERS IN LIFE AND IN DEATH.

Rhanna stood motionless, rain dripping from her nose and chin. "They were buried together," she said finally, over the steady drumming of rain. "In one coffin. Did you know that?"

Lizzy felt a chill crawl down her back. "What are we doing here, Rhanna?"

"It was white. Covered with baby's breath and pink roses. It rained that day too."

Lizzy blinked at her, stunned. *Rose petals and wet earth.* "You were here. The afternoon of the funeral, when you disappeared—this is where you were. You came home drenched and wasted, and never said a word."

Rhanna was shivering now, her gaze still locked on the headstone. "I had to come. I watched from a distance so no one would see me, but I had to come."

"Why?"

"Because it was my fault."

Lizzy went cold all over. "What was your fault?"

"All of it. Them. The water." She buried her face in her hands then, shoulders heaving. "I just . . . I had to see it finished."

"See *what* finished? What are you saying?" Lizzy grabbed both sleeves of her jacket, and yanked her hands from her face. "Look at me! See *what* finished?"

Rhanna stared back, gray eyes wide and unseeing.

She was somewhere else, Lizzy realized. Somewhere terrible. And she had no idea how to pull her back. But standing in the rain wasn't going to help. She grabbed a fistful of drenched denim, saying nothing as they marched through the gate and back to the car.

Rhanna remained mute as Lizzy opened the car door and gave her a shove. She landed in the passenger seat like a sack of seed, and was still staring blindly when Lizzy slid behind the wheel. Her skin was a pasty shade of gray, her teeth clenched tight to keep them from chattering.

Lizzy reached for the sweater she kept in the back seat and tucked it around Rhanna's shoulders. "It's okay," she said, rubbing Rhanna's arms briskly. "You're okay."

Rhanna blinked heavily, as if coming out of a deep sleep. "We're in the car."

"Yes. And I need you to pull yourself together. Can you do that?"

Rhanna shoved a hank of wet hair off her face, then nodded groggily.

Lizzy exhaled for what felt like the first time since arriving at the cemetery. The smell of roses was so strong in the shut-up car it nearly made her queasy. This was what she had picked up when Rhanna first arrived. The smell of the cemetery and funeral flowers. The smell of death.

"All right, Rhanna. I need you to explain some things for me. What did you mean when you said you needed to see it finished? What exactly did you need to see finished?"

Rhanna's eyes were glazed and slow to respond. It was how she used to come home sometimes, after a night of heavy partying, dulled by whatever combination of goodies she'd managed to score from friends. But there was no slurring now, no sharp reek of alcohol oozing from her pores. There was only fear.

"What haven't you told me, Rhanna?"

Rhanna sucked in a ragged breath and sagged against the seat. After a moment, her head swiveled in Lizzy's direction. "Do you want to know why I left? Why I really left?"

Lizzy swallowed uneasily. Suddenly she wasn't sure she *did* want to know.

"I see things, Lizzy," she said, closing her eyes. "Awful things no one should see."

Lizzy waited for the rest, afraid to push. The seconds ticked by as the rain continued to pelt the car roof. The windows began to fog.

"I see how people die," Rhanna said finally.

The hair on Lizzy's arms prickled to attention. "How people . . . die?"

"When I was a girl—fourteen, I think—Althea and I were downtown at the green. It was Easter Sunday, and there was an Easter egg hunt. There were kids everywhere, all dressed up in their new clothes. They were having so much fun. There was this little girl, a tiny thing in a stroller. She had these big blue eyes and strawberry-blonde curls. I can still see her face." Her gaze slid to her lap, her voice little more than a whisper. "I can see all their faces."

"Whose faces?"

"The dead people."

Lizzy felt goose bumps spring up beneath her sopping clothes. She grabbed the steering wheel, squeezing tight. "You were talking about a little girl."

Rhanna nodded, swallowing thickly. "She was holding this little stuffed lamb, hugging it the way they do. When she saw me watching, she held it out to show me. It fell out of the stroller and landed on the sidewalk. I bent down and picked it up. When I gave it back to her, our fingers touched. That's when I saw it—when we touched."

"What?" Lizzy prodded. "What did you see?"

"The girl. All of a sudden my head was full of noise—sirens and those horrible horns the fire trucks blow. And then I saw her. She was still in the car, in her car seat, covered with blood and broken glass. And the lamb. It was on the floor of the car. It was a split second, like a single frame from some hideous home movie, but it was her, Lizzy. It was real."

"It wasn't real, Rhanna. It was your imagination."

"No." Rhanna pressed a hand to her eyes, shaking her head in denial. "It was on the news a few days later. A mother and a little girl hit by a drunk driver on Spaulding Turnpike. They showed her picture. And the mother's. It was them, Lizzy. It was her. The girl from the park. Some guy in a Suburban got on going the wrong way. The drunk guy lived, but the mother and little girl died at the scene."

Lizzy fell back against her seat, trying to digest what she'd just heard. "And you saw it? You saw the accident?"

"Not the accident, no. I never see that part. Just . . . after, when they're already dead."

Her response was so matter-of-fact that Lizzy found herself groping for words. "I don't understand . . . how . . . You're saying it's happened more than once?"

Rhanna nodded miserably. "Yes."

The windows were completely fogged now, and the car felt steamy and claustrophobic. Lizzy used her sleeve to wipe the windshield, knowing she was stalling for time, knowing it wouldn't make any difference. "Do you know . . . how?" she asked finally.

"The first time—with the girl—I thought I caused it. That I'd made it happen. I felt like a monster. And then it happened again. A guy at the drugstore went home and had a heart attack after I bumped into him at the lunch counter. And then again, with a kid I went to school with."

"How many?"

"I don't know. After a while I lost count. Dozens, I suppose. And every one of their faces is burned into my brain. Do you have any idea how many ways there are to die?"

Lizzy remained silent. There was simply no way to answer a question like that.

"I get how crazy this sounds, Lizzy. Like something the old me would have said to get attention, but I swear I'm telling the truth. Even I wouldn't make up something this hideous."

"Did Althea know?"

Rhanna shook her head. "I was already enough of a handful. I didn't want to add crazy to my repertoire. Besides, it's not really the kind of thing you want to share, is it—that you're some kind of freak who sees dead people? They put you away for saying things like that, and I didn't want to go away. Not then. And in the beginning I didn't even know what it was. It only happened to people I physically touched, and even then it could take weeks."

Fourteen. She'd been about the same age when her own gift had appeared. But that was nothing compared to what Rhanna had just described. "I can't imagine . . . You must have been terrified."

"I never knew when it was going to happen again—or with who." A sob escaped her, like an unexpected hiccup. "So many faces. Every time I closed my eyes. And then Lonnie Welden introduced me to vodka, and I found a way to deaden the images. It helped for a while, until it didn't anymore. Then I had to find other things."

"Drugs?"

Rhanna shrugged. "Drugs. Booze. Guys. Anything to numb me. And then I found out . . ." She looked away. "And then you came along. A baby. How could I have a baby when I had this *thing* inside me? What if . . ."

"No, don't," Lizzy said, cutting her off. "We can do that later. Why are you telling me this now? And why did we have to come here for you to do it?"

Rhanna stared at her hands, palm up in her lap. "I saw them, Lizzy. I saw the Gilman girls."

It took a few seconds for the words to actually register. "What? How?"

"I don't know how. I've never known. It just . . . happens. It was a Friday night and I was with Jimmy Swann at the Dairy Bar. We were waiting for them to make our frappes when the girls showed up. They got in line behind us. All of a sudden the oldest one—Heather, I think—brushed up against me. And I saw them. Both of them."

Lizzy closed her eyes, trying to imagine the unimaginable.

"They were in the water," Rhanna said softly. "In the pond. I knew it was our pond because there was something shiny on the bottom. It was the charm bracelet I'd lost a few months before."

Lizzy stared at her, unable to blink. "You knew. All that time they were missing, you *knew* where they were."

"I wanted to be wrong, Lizzy. I wanted to be wrong so badly. And for a while, I thought I was. Two weeks later, nothing had happened. Then another week passed, and another. It took five weeks for them to even go missing."

The memory of Susan Gilman's tearstained face suddenly loomed. "How could you keep something like that to yourself? Their poor mother was out of her mind."

Rhanna pulled her knees up, curling in on herself. "You don't think I know that? Every day I had to watch that poor woman crying for her little girls, begging someone—anyone—to bring them back safely. And all the time I knew where they were—and that they were never coming back. But what was I supposed to say? That I'd had a premonition? And then what?"

Lizzy nodded, reluctantly conceding the point. No one would have bought that. Not coming from Rhanna.

"You can't imagine what it was like, Lizzy, knowing they were out there and having to keep it to myself. I was like the guy in that Poe story, hearing that heart beating under his floorboards, terrified I'd be found out, knowing what people would think when I was."

Bit by bit, it was falling together. "It's why you stopped going to the pond to swim," Lizzy postulated. "And why you got weird all of a sudden about being touched."

"Yes."

Rhanna's tortured whisper spoke volumes. Last night, when she asked about the episode at the coffee shop, Rhanna had bristled about people pointing fingers and acting like they knew what happened to the Gilman girls, when the truth was no one actually *knew* anything. No one except Rhanna. But she'd left that part out of last night's discussion.

Seeing the dead.

It was inconceivable. And yet she'd heard of such things. People who worked with police to find missing children, using the gift of sight to solve crimes and ease suffering. Was that what this was? A gift? Rhanna certainly didn't seem to think so.

"You could have told Althea," Lizzy said quietly. "She would have understood."

"Seriously?" Rhanna seemed genuinely stunned by the suggestion. "She would have gone straight to the police. You know she would have. Because that's who she was, always doing the right thing no matter what it cost, trusting things to work out like they should. But they didn't."

"No," Lizzy said, almost under her breath. "They certainly didn't."

"I'm not asking you to forgive me, Lizzy. I don't deserve that. Not after everything else that's happened. I just . . . needed you to know."

Lizzy remained silent as she studied Rhanna. She'd never seen her like this, stripped of her rebel's guise and shaken to the core—achingly raw. It wasn't easy to look at, but it was the first time she'd actually felt a connection to the woman who brought her into the world. Perhaps they weren't so different after all. They had both been born with *gifts* they never wanted, had both done everything in their power to run away from those gifts, and had both failed miserably.

"I can't believe you kept this to yourself all these years. I think I would have gone mad."

"I thought I might," Rhanna said, pulling in another shaky breath. "But I found a way to deal with it." She dragged her purse off the floor and, after a bit of fumbling, produced a black leather-bound book. "I drew them."

She laid the book in Lizzy's lap and slowly withdrew her hand, as if afraid it might explode. Lizzy recognized it immediately. She'd received one just like it the day she turned sixteen. And here, apparently, was her mother's.

"*The Book of Rhanna*," Lizzy said solemnly.

"We're supposed to use them for recording our journey, to write about our gifts and how we use them. I drew mine instead. So I could get the faces out of my head."

Lizzy wrapped her hands around the book but didn't open it. "Did it work?"

"Not as well as vodka."

Lizzy held her breath as she looked down at the book. It felt hot against her palms, the leather slick with perspiration. She wasn't sure she wanted to see what was inside, to know the kinds of images that had lived in Rhanna's head since that first premonition nearly forty years ago. But she had to see them, didn't she? To know they were real—to know *it* was real.

The first sketch was in pencil, crude but accurate enough to recognize what she was looking at: a little girl awkwardly slumped in a car seat, eyes closed. And the lamb.

The sketches improved as Lizzy continued to turn the pages, the details becoming sharper and cleaner as Rhanna's artistic skills improved over time. Bodies in every imaginable position, their faces eerily still in death. A heavyset man in a plaid shirt, crumpled on a kitchen floor. A runner sprawled facedown on what looked to be a jogging path. An old woman lying in a heap at the bottom of a staircase. It was terrible, like something from a nightmare. And for Rhanna it had been a nightmare. One she'd never shared with a soul.

Lizzy turned to look at her. "All of these?"

Rhanna nodded mutely.

"I'm so sorry," she said softly, because she was. And because she didn't know what else to say. So much made sense now. Her sudden withdrawal, the haphephobia. She couldn't fathom living with those kinds of images in her head.

She closed the book, unable to look further. "Are they in here? The Gilman girls?"

Rhanna shook her head. "I was afraid to draw them. What if someone found it? What would they think?"

Another valid point. A drawing like that would have raised a lot of questions—none of them good. "Does it still happen?"

"Sometimes, but not like it used to. I move around a lot, and steer clear of close connections. It's easier that way. I know it's not me *causing* it, that I'm only seeing what's going to happen whether I'm there or not. But it's hard not to feel at least a little responsible." She bunched her shoulders, then let them drop heavily. "Some gift, huh?"

"I'm sorry you had to deal with it on your own."

"It was my choice. And it's not an excuse for all the crap I put you and Althea through. Anyway, now you know."

"Now I know."

Lizzy started the car and flicked on the defroster to clear the windows. She was right. It wasn't an excuse. But she couldn't help thinking of Althea's words concerning Rhanna, and how eerily true they suddenly rang. *You made up your mind about her years ago, leaving no room for the possibility that there might be more to her story. More than either of us will ever know.*

Once again, Althea had been spot on.

THIRTY

Lizzy rolled down her sleeves as she stepped outside and headed toward the barn. The breeze was cool, on the verge of chilly as the sun slid low, reminding her again that summer was slipping away—and that she'd already been here too long. Chuck Bundy's son was on the mend, and they had an appointment the day after tomorrow to discuss options for listing the farm. Finally, she'd be able to stop dodging Luc's calls and tell him she was making progress. Sort of.

Human resources had responded to her request to use the balance of her accrued time off for extended leave. Years of skipping vacations and a generous rollover policy had allowed her to accumulate almost eight weeks, but she'd already burned through four of them, which left her with four. Not much time considering all she still needed to do.

A week had passed since Rhanna's revelation at the cemetery. It was a day neither of them was likely to forget, but it had clearly been therapeutic for Rhanna. She'd spent the next day, and a good part of every day since, out in the shop, experimenting with whatever she could find in the cabinets and drawers. She was also painting again. And perhaps most telling, the unsettling pong of damp earth that used to cling to her was beginning to dissipate, a sign that she'd begun to release the pain and guilt associated with Heather and Darcy Gilman. There was no way to know what the future would hold when they went their separate ways, but for now, at least, it felt good to think that Althea would be pleased. And maybe that would have to be enough for all of them.

Lizzy ducked into the barn, propping the door open behind her. Rhanna's question about missing the actual hands-on part of perfume making had gotten her thinking. She'd played it off at the time, but the truth was she *did* miss it. So much so that she'd been toying with the idea of re-creating the Earth Song scent Rhanna had been so fond of as a surprise. She was also mulling over ideas for a scent for Evvie. Something warm and subtle, with a hint of the exotic—a citrusy top note balanced with myrrh, neroli, and jasmine.

But first she'd need to clear her old workbench and sort through her equipment—see what was salvageable, trash what wasn't, then make a list of ingredients she'd need to get started. She'd also need to start hunting for just the right bottles, preferably vintage. They would be parting gifts, mementos of Moon Girl Farm's last summer. She wanted them to be special.

As she approached the workbench, she was surprised to see the old chambray smock she had filched from Althea still hanging from its nail, like an old friend waiting patiently for her return. It would need a good washing before she could wear it. She was about to pull it down when she heard the scuff of footsteps. She turned, surprised to find Andrew behind her.

"Hey." He raised a hand as he came toward her. "I pulled the window to work on the frame, so I had to put up a tarp. I came to see if it held after last week's downpour. I didn't expect to find you in here."

"I'm thinking of starting a new project, but I needed to clear my workbench first."

"What's the project?"

"A gift for Rhanna. A perfume she used to like. I'd like to make it a surprise if I can, so I'll need to work out here—in secret."

"So things are better with you two?"

Lizzy shrugged. "We talked through some things. It wasn't exactly a lovefest, but I understand some things I didn't before. Things she's never told anyone. I think it'll give us both some closure when we leave."

"Any idea when that'll be?"

"Not yet. I'm still mulling my options. Basically, I have two. Spend money I don't have to fix the place up, or list it as is and wait months—maybe years—for it to sell. Unfortunately, the property taxes are due in January. Which means I'm probably looking at a mortgage either way."

Lizzy smothered a groan when her cell rang, already knowing who it was. She slid it from her back pocket, checked the number to confirm, then tapped "Ignore." "My boss," she explained sheepishly.

"Luc?"

He'd pronounced the name with a swishy French accent. Lizzy dismissed the snark with a roll of her eyes. "Yes, Luc. I've been dodging him for days, so he's been leaving me messages. He wants to know how long it's going to take me to wind things up here, and I don't really have an answer."

"He's pressuring you?"

Lizzy half shrugged, half nodded. "It wasn't supposed to take this long. I thought I'd be done in a few days—a week at most. It's been a month and I've barely scratched the surface."

"You thought you'd be able to pack up decades of family history in a week?"

"I thought it would be . . . easier. Not just the packing, all of it. I didn't know the place was falling down, or that Rhanna was going to show up. And I certainly never planned on playing detective in an eight-year-old rerun of *Cold Case Files*. Luc's been incredibly patient, but at some point he expects me back."

"So what's the deal with you two?"

Lizzy blinked at him, caught off guard by the question. "There is no deal. He's my boss."

"Are you sure? Because the last time I asked, you fumbled your answer a little."

"Yes, I'm sure." She waited for a response. None came. He wasn't buying it. "All right. We were seeing each other for a while, but I called it."

"You make it sound like a baseball game—called on account of rain."

"I got a promotion. A big one. And I didn't want everyone thinking . . . you know. So I ended it."

A crease appeared between his brows. "You ended a relationship because you were worried about what people would think?"

"It wasn't a relationship," she corrected evenly. "Not in the way other people classify them. Luc isn't a commitment kind of guy, and that suited me just fine."

Andrew's eyes narrowed slightly. "You weren't looking for a commitment from *him*? Or from anyone?"

Lizzy turned away, feigning interest in a bottle of ylang-ylang oil, its contents long since evaporated. "Let's just say it's not part of my plan."

"So it's a career thing?"

"It's a me thing," she replied, tossing the empty bottle into a nearby trash can. "Some people are destined for the whole love-and-marriage thing. I'm not one of those people."

"Sorry. I didn't mean to overstep. I don't know anything about your life, or how you see your future. I just . . ." He paused, pushing his hands deeper into his pockets. "Why aren't you one of those people?"

The question made Lizzy's mouth go dry. Why were they talking about this? She looked down at her hands, wiping smudges of dust from her palms. "When your last name is Moon, you learn pretty quick not to want what other people have. Not because you don't want it, but because not everyone gets a choice." She closed her mouth, shook her head. She'd already said too much. "Sorry. Ignore me."

His eyes locked on hers, unblinking as a lazy grin lifted the corners of his mouth. "I've never been able to ignore you, Lizzy. I think you know that."

Lizzy took a step back, then another, until she felt the bench at the small of her back. He was too close, the smoky-amber scent of him too distracting. "Please don't flirt with me, Andrew."

"Why?"

Breathe. Just breathe. She put a hand to her chest, trying to quell the bloom of warmth beneath her ribs. "Because I might forget that I don't want to be flirted with, and I don't want to forget it. I'm not looking for a summer romance."

His grin slipped, his voice suddenly thick. "Neither am I."

She flinched when he touched her face, a single knuckle tracing the curve of her cheek. Suddenly it was hard to breathe, hard to pull her gaze from his. "I mean it, Andrew. This isn't me being coy. What I said before, about not letting myself want what other people have—it's real. I'm not like most women. I'm not chasing happily-ever-after. I'm . . . different."

Andrew dropped his hand to his side, but his eyes remained locked with hers. "You think I don't know that? That you're . . . *different?* I've lived next to you my whole life. How could I *not* know?"

"But you don't, Andrew. Not really. If you did—"

"You're wrong," he said, with a strange intensity. "I do know. I've always known. The first time I saw you, the first instant . . . I knew you weren't like anyone else."

Something about the way he'd paused for just a beat, the way he'd held her gaze when he said it, as if confirming something they both already knew, set off alarm bells in her head. "I don't know what you're talking about. I just meant . . ."

"I know, Lizzy." He relaxed visibly as the words left his mouth, as if he'd been holding them in for a long time, and was relieved to finally say them aloud. "I've always known. About you. About *all* the Moons. I know."

Lizzy froze. It was in his face, his eyes, his words. He *did* know. Somehow. *All* of it. Who she was. *What* she was. Who and what they *all* were. But how? Had Althea let something slip? Had Evvie?

"How?" she whispered. "*How* do you know?"

He shrugged. "I don't know. I just . . . do."

"For how long?"

"Honestly? I can't remember a time when I didn't know. It was just a fact, like the sun coming up in the morning. There's a light inside you, Lizzy. Althea had it too. And your mother. It's what makes you a Moon—that light."

Lizzy flashed him a look, stunned that they were talking about this at all. "You say it like it's a good thing, like I've been blessed or something. All I ever wanted was to be like other people, to have an ordinary life. Instead . . ."

Andrew cut her off with a shake of his head. "You'll never be like other people, Lizzy. Which is why you had me wrapped around your finger when I was eighteen." He took a step forward, cutting the distance between them in half. "And why you still have me wrapped around your finger."

Lizzy clenched her hands into fists to keep them from trembling. He was so close she could see the flecks of gold in his eyes, the subtle cleft in his chin, the glint of stubble along his jawline. How was this happening? She'd never planned for something like this—or for someone like Andrew. He knew. He knew, and he was going to kiss her anyway.

And she was going to let him—even if it cost her everything.

The ground fell away as his arms came around her, cinching tightly about her waist. She swayed against him, hands pressed to his chest, and briefly met his gaze. His lips were soft as they met hers, tentative, as if seeking permission. She gave it willingly, melting into him as the kiss sparked and caught fire. The consummation was both new and terrifying.

Stop. Stop this while you still can.

Lizzy heard the warnings but shoved them down. She needed this. Needed him. Now, for just this moment, she needed to be who he thought she was—the girl with the light inside her.

Except she wasn't that girl, and it wasn't fair to let him think she was.

She pulled out of his arms and dragged in a breath. "I'm sorry. I can't do this."

Andrew took a step back, eyes clouded with confusion.

Lizzy pressed a hand to her lips, mortified. How could she have been so stupid? "I'm so sorry, Andrew. I didn't mean for that to happen. I mean, I did obviously, but then I didn't. My life's just so upside-down right now. I don't need any more complications."

"No complications," he said, nodding stiffly. "Got it."

His tone stung, but he had every right to be annoyed. She'd given him the green light, then slammed on the brakes. "You think you know all about me, but you don't. Before, when I said I wasn't chasing happily-ever-after, I was actually talking about all of us—all the Moons. We don't get . . . attached. We have one job, to produce a daughter to carry on our legacy. Romance doesn't enter into it."

"So . . . no husband."

She swallowed hard, not sure she was ready to have this conversation, but he was waiting for an answer. "It's . . . less messy that way," she said thickly. "For everyone." She looked down at her hands, her shoes, anywhere but at Andrew. "You were right, we are different. But not in a good way. People call us wicked. They blame us for everything, and treat us like lepers. Sooner or later, that rubs off on the people we love—like a stain." She paused, shrugging. "It's only a matter of time until everything's poisoned."

"So why bother?"

Lizzy nodded. "Why bother."

Andrew blew out a long breath. "And you're okay with that? Raising a daughter on your own someday, in order to fulfill some ancient custom?"

"I'm not, in fact. Which is why the legacy will end with me."

The words seemed to hum in the charged air. "You're saying . . ."

"I'm saying I'm the last Moon girl."

"So no husband *and* no kids. Sounds pretty final."

"It's meant to."

"It also sounds lonely."

Lizzy shrugged. "Maybe, but it's the only fair thing to do. Women worry about passing on all sorts of things to their daughters—bad skin, wide hips, a latent crippling illness. I don't worry about those things. I worry about bringing a little girl into the world who has to hide who she is, who's afraid to make friends and doesn't fit in anywhere. I lived that life growing up. I won't do it to a daughter of mine."

"At the risk of sounding presumptuous, it *is* possible to marry and skip the kids. Lots of couples do."

"Yes they do, but it's not just about kids. It's all of it. Marriage is hard enough when both people are normal. But I'm not normal. My family's legacy isn't a liability I'm willing to foist on either a husband or a child. That's what I meant by complications. No . . . attachments."

Andrew arched a brow. "Luc wasn't a complication?"

Lizzy sighed, knowing just how bizarre all this must sound to someone like Andrew, who'd grown up in a family that always colored inside the lines. "Luc wasn't anything. He didn't have expectations about us, and neither did I. That's why it was safe. He didn't want the white picket fence and the minivan. But you're not like Luc. You want something I can't give. And I want something I can't have."

Andrew's face softened, and a slow smile appeared. "All I heard you say just then was that you want me. I did just hear that, right?"

"I was speaking figuratively."

"Were you?"

Lizzy stared at him without blinking. To falter now would be unfair. "Yes."

He touched her cheek, brushing it lightly before dropping his hand. "Just as well. This isn't exactly how I imagined our first romantic encounter—in a barn."

Lizzy felt her cheeks go pink. "You imagined a romantic encounter with me?"

"I was eighteen years old. And male. Of course I imagined it. I still imagine it. But not here. And not if it isn't what you want. But don't count me out. I waited twenty years for that kiss. I'll wait another twenty if that's what it takes."

He turned then and headed for the door. Lizzy watched him go, her response stuck in her throat. Had he not heard a word she just said?

THIRTY-ONE

August 17

Lizzy woke with a nagging headache and a knot in the pit of her stomach. Andrew had kissed her last night. And for one disastrous, weak-kneed moment, she had kissed him back. Until she remembered what was at stake. Her heart. Maybe his too. At least she'd put a stop to things before they went too far.

It would be weird between them now, because that's what happened when you kissed someone you shouldn't. Things got weird. And they stayed weird. Until you started inventing reasons to avoid each other.

But that wasn't what she wanted. Andrew was the truest friend she'd ever had—the kind who knew all your secrets and stuck by you anyway—and for whatever time she had left in Salem Creek, she wanted him to remain a friend. They'd go their separate ways soon enough. The farm would sell, and that would be that. She'd have nothing tying her here, no reason to ever return.

The thought evoked a hollowed-out sensation she preferred not to name. Labeling a thing made it real.

"That you, little girl?"

"Yes, it's me," Lizzy answered, rounding the corner to find Evvie seated at the kitchen table. "Have you seen Rhanna? I wanted to ask her about some of the stuff in the attic."

"Blew through here a little bit ago," Evvie mumbled from behind her paper. "Made a pot of that devil's brew y'all drink, then headed out to the shop. She's been working her backside off out there for days."

Lizzy filled a mug with coffee and joined Evvie at the table. "She's painting again, did she tell you?"

Evvie glanced up, her face stony. "There's another article."

Lizzy sighed into her mug. "Of course there is. What does it say?"

Evvie's brow creased as she scanned the article. "Let's see. Here it is. *A source familiar with the investigation told the Chronicle that lab results had proved inconclusive. Kerosene has been confirmed as the accelerant, but no fingerprints were found.*"

"Which means no suspects."

"There's more."

Lizzy rolled her eyes. "Do I want to know?"

"They've got a quote here from the organist at First Congregational— Miriam Summers. She says she's not surprised bad things are happening at Moon Girl Farm since it's bound to be haunted by the spirits of those poor dead girls. Actually used the word *haunted*. Can you imagine a newspaper printing nonsense like that?"

Sadly, Lizzy could imagine it. As fate would have it, Chief Summers's wife had been in the coffee shop the day of Rhanna's unfortunate outburst, and had heard it all firsthand. She'd been only too happy to fan the town's outrage back then, and it seemed time had done nothing to soften her opinion. Except this time she was the one causing the outrage, and not Rhanna.

"I've been thinking, Evvie . . ."

Evvie's eyes narrowed. "Thinking what?"

"That maybe I'm in over my head. I mean, who am I kidding, thinking I can do what the police couldn't do eight years ago? Maybe it's time to put my energy into getting this place on the market and forget the sleuthing. All I'm doing is pissing people off."

"You scared?"

Lizzy stiffened. She wasn't scared. But things were starting to get messy, and on more fronts than she'd counted on. "I'm not scared. It's just . . ."

Evvie folded her paper and tossed it to the end of the table. "There's no shame in being scared, little girl. Not with what's been going on around here. But if you're thinking of throwing in the towel because people are in a snit, that's a whole nother kettle of crawdads."

Lizzy would have smiled at Evvie's colorful turn of phrase if she weren't so distracted. "I'm not scared, Evvie. I'm just wondering what I'm really accomplishing. All I've managed to do so far is remind everyone why they don't like us. But as far as the actual case goes, what do I know now that I didn't know when I got here? That Heather Gilman was a wild child who broke curfew and drank with boys—like half the girls in Salem Creek. That she dumped her BFFs with no explanation, and one of her old friends thinks she might have been afraid to go home."

"It's more than the police managed to find out."

"Maybe, but what does it prove? Mrs. Gilman said herself that she doesn't believe her husband was capable of hurting their daughters. And let's not forget that he has an ironclad alibi for the night they went missing. No wonder the police won't reopen the case. If Fred Gilman is really in the clear, there's nowhere else to look."

"So that's it? You're going to quit? Just go back to New York?"

Lizzy's face softened. She reached across the table and laid a hand over Evvie's. "This was never supposed to be permanent, Evvie. You know that. At some point, I'm going to have to throw in the towel and go home."

Evvie poked out her lower lip. "This *is* home."

"It was—once upon a time. It's where I grew up. But sometimes growing up means growing out of things."

"You can't grow out of your home, Lizzy. Home is in your blood. It's not just where you live, it's who you *are*."

"New York is who I am now, Evvie."

There was a beat of hesitation before Evvie spoke again, as if she were weighing her next words. "What about Andrew?"

Lizzy withdrew her hand and picked up her mug, carefully avoiding Evvie's gaze. There was no way she could know about last night. And what if she did? It was a kiss. One innocent, ill-advised kiss. "What does Andrew have to do with anything?"

Evvie pursed her lips thoughtfully. "I wonder."

A ping from Lizzy's cell phone spared her from having to respond. She tapped the message open, already knowing it would be Luc.

Call me, Lizzy. I mean it.

Evvie's eyes narrowed. "Something wrong?"

"It's just work. I need to make a call."

She waited until she was upstairs to dial Luc's cell. She had nothing new to report, no return date she could give, but his message was clear enough. He'd run out of patience.

Luc didn't bother with hello when he answered. "Do they not have cell phone towers in New Hampshire?"

Lizzy suppressed a sigh. "Hello, Luc."

"I've been leaving messages for over a week. Were you *ever* going to call?"

"I'm calling now."

"To say you're coming back?"

"No. But I am meeting with the Realtor tomorrow. Then it looks like I'll be heading to the bank to arrange for a loan so I can swing the repairs and property taxes until we find a buyer. It shouldn't take long to hire the contractors once I have the funds. Andrew can give me some recommendations on who to use, and keep an eye on the workmen."

Luc huffed into the phone. "How 'bout I just write you a check for the taxes, and you leave today?"

"I'm not letting my boss pay the taxes on my grandmother's farm."

"It's your farm now, Lizzy. And we both know I'm more than just your boss. Stop being stubborn and let me help you."

Lizzy counted to ten, annoyed by his presumption. "I'm not being stubborn, Luc. It's a kind offer, really, but this is my problem."

"I'm curious," he said coolly. "You dragging your feet wouldn't have anything to do with Andrew, would it? It feels like maybe your attention's being . . . diverted. Please tell me you're not thinking of throwing away your career to chase some silly happily-ever-after with the boy next door."

Lizzy struggled to control her temper. He was pushing her buttons, bullying her because she wasn't jumping to attention every time he called. As if her salary somehow entitled him to a say in her personal life. "We agreed when we stopped seeing each other that we'd keep it professional, Luc. My happily-ever-after is none of your business."

"We didn't stop seeing each other. *You* stopped seeing *me*. But if you want to keep things strictly professional, I can do that too. I have a company to run, Ms. Moon. When I gave you that promotion, I expected to get my money's worth. And instead of gratitude, I get the runaround."

Gratitude?

Lizzy sat with the word a moment, stung by the transactional sentiment behind it, and by his condescending use of her last name. "You didn't *give* me anything, Luc," she said finally. "I earned that promotion, and you know it. Not because I was your girlfriend for six months, but because I worked my tail off. And because I'm good at what I do. According to HR, I have six weeks of vacation saved, plus ten days of sick leave. Which means I still have three-plus weeks left. Pay me for them. Don't pay me for them. However you want to handle it. But I can't leave here right now."

She didn't wait for a response before ending the call. Her hands shook as she stared at the blank screen. Had she just quit her job? Before she could examine the question further, the phone went off again. She expected to see Luc's number pop up, but the call was local.

"Hey, it's Chuck Bundy." His tone was overly bright, and vaguely annoying. "I know we're scheduled for tomorrow, but I'm wondering if we should maybe slow things down a little. I've been crunching the numbers, looking at what else is on the market, and my gut's telling me we should wait."

Lizzy felt her stomach drop. "Wait for what? We've been playing tag for weeks."

"I know, and I'm sorry about that. It's just that given the history of the farm and, well . . . the talk lately, maybe now isn't the best time."

"This is about the article in this morning's *Chronicle*, isn't it?"

"Ms. Moon." There was a pause, the flick of a lighter, a breath being pulled in, then let out. "I told you what we were up against the first time we spoke. There's already a glut of rural properties on the market, and let's face it, it was going to be hard enough to find a buyer when all we were dealing with was the Gilman girls, but throw in an arsonist and church ladies talking about ghosts, and we've moved into radioactive territory. I know you're in a bind, and that this isn't what you want to hear, but I have to be honest. We're moving too fast."

Moving too fast?

This was starting to feel like a breakup call, a fresh spin on the it's-not-you-it's-me line. "You're backing out?"

"Technically, there's nothing to back out of. We haven't drawn up a listing agreement yet, and frankly, I don't think we should right now. I'd be happy to refer you to someone else if you're determined to go ahead, but fifteen years in the business tells me it would be a mistake. If you list now, it's going to sit, and the longer it sits, the less it'll be worth. The prudent thing to do is let the dust settle, and take another look in six months, maybe a year."

Six months? She didn't have six months. And she certainly didn't have a year.

"Right," Lizzy said numbly, as she ended the call. "I'll let the dust settle."

~

Rhanna was standing over a stoneware bowl, pouring honey into a measuring cup, when Lizzy entered the shop. She had tuned Althea's old radio to the oldies station and was crooning along to "Monday, Monday," her gauzy skirt swishing around her ankles as she swayed to the music.

Lizzy stood quietly, watching her work. Evvie was right. She had been busy, and astonishingly productive. In less than two weeks, the shelves had filled with tonics, massage oils, and salt scrubs, each hand-labeled and finished with a raffia bow.

"This is amazing," Lizzy said softly, spinning in a slow circle.

Rhanna started, clearly surprised to find she had company. She reached for a towel to wipe her hands, then turned down the radio. "Sorry. I didn't hear you come in. I'm playing with a new oatmeal soak. It's a tweaked version of one I found in Althea's book. I'm going for something warm and spicy for fall—or maybe Halloween. We could call it A Wicked Good Soak. What do you think?"

Lizzy mustered a smile. She'd never seen Rhanna this enthused about anything. But she was forgetting that by Halloween none of them would be here.

Rhanna pointed to the wire racks where Louise Ryerson's soap sat curing. "The bars came out perfectly. Maybe we should make another batch. Apparently, the word is out."

"The word?"

"That the Moons are back in business. Evvie's been fending off customers left and right."

"We're not, though. You understand that, right? That this is just temporary?"

Rhanna wilted a little, then narrowed her eyes on Lizzy. "What's wrong? What's happened?"

"I had a call from my Realtor."

"And?"

"He's not my Realtor anymore."

"Why?"

"There was another article about the fire in this morning's paper and it's apparently left Mr. Bundy squeamish. *Radioactive* was the term he used. He says if I list now, it'll just sit and lose value. He says I should wait."

"How long?"

"Six months to a year is what he said."

"A year?" Hope flickered in Rhanna's eyes. "What are you going to do?"

Lizzy lifted a shoulder. "I don't know. Get a second opinion, I guess. And hope the bank will give me enough money to tide me over."

Rhanna startled Lizzy by briefly laying a hand on her shoulder, the first time she'd initiated any kind of contact in years. "I'm sorry you've had to carry the whole load around here, but I want to start helping. There's a guy I used to see back in the day—Billy Church. His family has this big real estate office in Somersworth, and he owes me a favor. Or maybe I owe him. I'm kind of fuzzy on the details. But I bet I can track him down. As for money, Evvie and I have been talking, and I think we've found a way to help out."

Lizzy eyed her warily. "Should I be worried?"

Rhanna feigned a pout. "I'm going to ignore that. There's a New Age festival coming up in New Bay, Connecticut. I called last week, and they had a few tables left. We thought we'd take some of Evvie's honey and some of this stuff, and make some quick cash."

Lizzy peered over Rhanna's shoulder, scanning the neatly labeled containers on the shelf. Gardener's salve made with dandelion flowers, lemon-mint salt scrub, almond-coconut body butter. There were even tiny pots of honey-vanilla lip balm. Not bad, considering the limited materials she'd had to work with.

"That's what you've been doing out here? Making stuff for a festival?"

Rhanna beamed. "We didn't want to say anything until we knew we'd have enough inventory, and we will by the time the festival rolls around. Evvie has her bracelets and her honey. I'll be doing readings too. It won't pay the property taxes, but it'll keep the lights on, and I did promise I'd earn my keep. I know it's not really your thing, but you don't need to go. Evvie and I can handle it while you do what you need to do here."

Lizzy shook her head, smiling. "Althea always said you had Roma blood in your veins. When is this festival?"

"This weekend. Ben from the hardware store is lending us a big umbrella and some stuff to hang up signs."

Lizzy's brows lifted at the mention of Ben's name. "How did he get involved?"

"I'm not sure. Apparently, Evvie mentioned the fair and he jumped at the chance to help. Sounds like maybe he's crushing on our Evvie."

"I think that street runs both ways," Lizzy said, grinning. "A couple weeks back, she was loading a box of honey to take to the hardware store, and she was wearing lipstick."

"Lipstick? Evvie?"

"Earrings too."

"Peter, Paul, and Mary," Rhanna breathed, a slow grin lifting the corners of her mouth. "A romance right here on Moon Girl Farm. I'm definitely going to have fun with this."

"Yeah, well, she buttoned up tighter than a deacon's wife when I brought it up, so don't expect her to admit it."

Rhanna tapped her lower lip thoughtfully. "On second thought, maybe I should leave it alone. I've just gotten in her good graces, and I'd like to stay there." A bead of perspiration trickled from her temple. She blotted it on the sleeve of her T-shirt. "Good grief, it's hot. Want to break for some ice cream?"

"Can't. I'm headed to the bank to pick up some paperwork and make an appointment with a loan officer."

Rhanna nodded grimly. "Right. Maybe later. We could go to the Dairy Bar and share a banana split. It's still there, right?"

"Yup. Still there. I was surprised how little downtown had changed, though we actually have a vape shop now, and a tattoo parlor."

"Wow. In a town like Salem Creek, that's progress. As I recall, there was never much of anything to do in this town. Unless you knew the right people."

"The right people?"

"Ahem . . ." Rhanna cocked a brow. "The Hanley boys?"

Lizzy frowned, bewildered. "I have no idea what you're talking about."

"I'm talking about the Hanley farm—the one right behind ours, with all the bright yellow No Trespassing signs posted all over the place. The old man liked to pretend no one knew what he was growing back there, but we all did. It was the worst kept secret in Salem Creek."

"What he was . . ." Lizzy's mouth dropped open. "You mean pot?"

Rhanna rolled her eyes. "Yes, honey. I mean pot."

"I thought they grew corn."

"Oh, they did. It's just not all they grew. Good thing too, or those boys wouldn't have had *any* friends. They were such an odd pair. Whatever happened to them anyway?"

"Hollis died in a car crash not long after he got back from Afghanistan. Dennis works part-time for Andrew, and helps take care of Hollis's daughter. I wouldn't have thought him the family-man type, but I guess we don't always know what someone's going through. Maybe it changed him."

Rhanna nodded, her eyes suddenly shiny. "Time has a way of doing that," she said softly. "And if you're really lucky, it gives you a second chance."

THIRTY-TWO

Lizzy was in and out of the bank in under an hour, leaving her plenty of time to run her final errand. Evvie had asked her to drop off another dozen jars of honey at the hardware store while out, and pick up a trellis for the honeysuckle vine she was planning to train for her bees. Lizzy hadn't been able to resist teasing her, expressing surprise that Evvie would pass up a chance to see Ben again. Evvie's response had been a grunt and a less than convincing scowl.

The hardware store parking lot was nearly empty when Lizzy pulled in. She chose a spot near the door and grabbed the carton of honey. A string of brass bells jangled as she pushed inside. She headed for the sales counter at the back of the store, where she was greeted by a stocky man with skin like leather and hair the color of freshly fallen snow.

"Afternoon."

"Are you Ben?"

"Guilty as charged. How can I help?"

Lizzy took a quick inventory as she slid the carton onto the counter. He was handsome in a gnarled, outdoorsy way, like weathered oak—deeply grained and worn smooth by time. "Evvie sent me."

"Oh." Ben blinked at the carton of jars, then back at Lizzy. He managed a smile but his disappointment was plain. "She usually comes herself."

"I know, but she's busy getting ready for the fair. Thank you, by the way. I heard you're helping her out with some signage. It was kind of you to offer."

Lizzy wouldn't have thought it possible, but Ben actually blushed. "She's a good woman, that Evvie. Wise and kind, and so funny. She's really something."

Funny?

It was official. Ben the hardware man had it bad for Evangeline Broussard. "Evvie tells me you sell quite a lot of her honey," she said, hoping to draw him out further.

Ben nodded, grinning like a teen. "That I do. Folks swear by the stuff. Claim it cures everything from psoriasis to the common cold." Ben held up a knobby finger. "Reminds me. I've got an envelope for her in back. And a trellis she asked me to set aside for her. Just give me a sec."

Lizzy watched him disappear through a set of swinging doors, then wandered toward a rack of seed packets. She was reaching for a packet of sweet william seeds when she saw Fred Gilman walking toward her with a spool of rope and a long-handled ax. Her throat seized as she watched him come toward her, the ax swinging like a pendulum at his side. Finally, he came to an abrupt halt, his eyes heavy lidded and unblinking as they locked with hers.

It was Lizzy who looked away first, relieved to see Ben pushing back through the swinging doors with a fan-shaped trellis in his arms. He threw an oblivious nod to Fred as he handed her the trellis, then fished an envelope from his back pocket. "There's her cash for the last batch of honey, and the trellis she wanted. Be sure to tell her I said hello, and that I'll be by with the umbrella tomorrow."

"Thanks. I will."

Lizzy stuffed the envelope into her purse, then headed back down the aisle to the door. Her hands were shaking as she fumbled with the key fob to open the trunk. It wasn't that she'd expected Fred Gilman to lop off her head right there in the hardware store, but there'd been no missing the icy fury he had leveled in her direction.

She blew out a breath, willing her pulse to slow as she dropped the trellis into the trunk and slammed the lid. When she looked up, Fred Gilman was standing in front of her, ax balanced on his left shoulder. She caught the smell of him, the tangy brine of sweat mingled with the stench of a festering wound, as if he were slowly rotting from the inside.

Stepping back, she ran a frantic glance around the lot, hoping for help, or at least a witness. There was no one. She squared her shoulders, determined not to let him see that she was afraid. "What do you want, Mr. Gilman?"

He flicked dull eyes down the length of her, then brought them back to her face. "Read in the paper you've had some trouble lately. Something about a fire. Said no one got hurt." The corners of his mouth twitched, the rictus of a smile. "Glad to hear it. My first wife died in a fire. Not a good way to go."

Lizzy opened her mouth, but found she couldn't manage a response. Instead, she pushed past him, heart thudding as she made a beeline for the driver's side door.

"Maybe you should be more careful about where you stick that nose of yours," he said as she slid in behind the wheel. "Be a shame if someone got hurt next time."

~

She was still shaking when she reached Andrew's office. She wasn't sure what she expected him to do, but he was the first person she thought of as she sped out of the hardware store parking lot.

She ignored Dennis Hanley's cold stare as she navigated the construction zone outside Andrew's office and knocked on the door.

"Come," he barked.

His head was still down when she stepped into the office. When he finally looked up, his expression was one of blank distraction. "Lizzy. What are you . . . What's wrong? You're as white as a sheet."

"I'm sorry to bother you." She was still clutching the doorknob, still trembling. "I didn't know where else to go."

He was on his feet and beside her in seconds, prying her fingers off the knob and leading her to a chair. He went to the watercooler, filled a paper cup, and put it in her hands. "Drink this. And tell me what's happened."

She felt silly suddenly. He looked so alarmed. What if she was overreacting? "I ran into Fred Gilman at the hardware store and he . . ." She paused, gulping down the last of the water. "He followed me out to the parking lot."

"Did he hurt you?"

"No. He never touched me. He just . . . talked. About the fire, and how lucky I was that no one got hurt. It was like he was taunting me. It didn't help that he was holding an ax."

Andrew stiffened. "He had an ax?"

"He wasn't wielding it. He'd just bought it. But he had to know I'd be terrified. He *wanted* me to be terrified. His eyes were like ice. Like he would have strangled me with his bare hands if he thought he could get away with it. And I just stood there, listening, while he all but confessed to setting the fire."

Andrew took the empty cup from her hand, crumpled it, and tossed it into the trash can. "I know he scared you, Lizzy, but talking about the fire—even taunting you about it—isn't the same as a confession. Think. Did he mention anything he shouldn't know about? Anything that hasn't been in the papers?"

Lizzy sank back in her chair. "It's all been in the papers."

"Did he threaten you? I mean *actually* threaten you?"

"Not in so many words, no. But it's what he meant. I could smell it coming off of him."

"You could . . . smell it?"

Lizzy pushed out a sigh, wishing she'd been more careful with her words. "It's a thing I have," she said quietly. "The way my brain's wired, I guess. I can smell what people are feeling, and he was definitely feeling rage."

Andrew nodded, absorbing this new information. "What does rage smell like?"

"Putrid. Like something was eating away at him. And he wanted me to know it. Why else would he remind me that his first wife died in a fire? Should I go to the police?"

"That's an option, though I'm not sure it's the most effective one. Without an explicit threat, there's not much the police can do. There are laws about making threats, but it's perfectly legal to be a bastard."

"Doesn't it matter that I *felt* threatened?"

"To the police? I don't know. But it matters to me." He clicked off his desk lamp and grabbed his phone and keys from the desk. "Go home. I'll call you later."

"Where are you going?"

"To pay Mr. Gilman a visit. I don't expect him to admit anything, but he'll damn sure know I'm watching."

THIRTY-THREE

Andrew looked up in time to see the traffic light go yellow. He stomped on the gas, gunning through the intersection, then caught himself. Perhaps a better use of his drive time would be to make a list of reasons *not* to throttle Fred Gilman senseless. Jail, for instance. Except, for every con he managed to come up with, he came up with two perfectly valid pros.

An ax.

The bastard had threatened Lizzy while holding an ax. A fact he'd be addressing as soon as he had Gilman in front of him. He didn't have an exact address, but he knew the trailer park where Gilman lived, and knew his puke-green Subaru. It might take a few turns through the park, but he'd find him. And when he did—

A goddamn ax.

He'd been more than a little surprised to find Lizzy hovering in his office doorway. After their aborted kiss last night, he'd expected her to keep her distance, although the more he thought about it, the more convinced he was that distance was actually the best thing for both of them. He'd laid his cards on the table, or had come pretty close to it. Lizzy had laid hers out too, making it crystal clear that her future plans didn't include him—or anyone else, for that matter. Safe was what she wanted, a life without complications.

He got it. He did. But he didn't have to like it.

The sign for Meadow Park loomed just ahead on the left. He turned in, winding through the maze of short streets until he found what he was looking for.

He swung into the driveway behind Fred Gilman's Subaru and cut the engine, but remained behind the wheel, grappling with his anger. He needed to be able to string together a coherent sentence when the man answered the door, to make it plain that Lizzy Moon was strictly off limits, and decide whether the guy was simply a bully or posed an actual threat.

After a series of deep breaths, he got out of the car, mounted the steps to Gilman's front door, and knocked three times. A moment later the door eased back.

"Yes?"

Andrew stood there blinking, trying to reconcile the grizzled, stubbled man staring back at him with the Fred Gilman he used to know. He'd been a tough guy back in the day, the kind who wore his anger close to the surface, but the man standing before him looked like a good gust of wind might flatten him.

"Fred Gilman?"

"Who's asking?"

The yeasty pong of beer floated through the open door, along with a host of other smells Andrew preferred not to identify. He resisted the urge to take a step back. "I am."

"Do I know you?"

"I'm Andrew Greyson. You knew my father."

"Right. Right. Owned the hardware store before Ben bought it. I was just there today."

"You were," Andrew replied curtly. "Which is why I'm here. I'm a friend of Lizzy Moon's."

Gilman's mouth hardened. "Go away."

Andrew checked him, wedging a boot between the door and the jamb before he could slam the door in his face. "Not until I've said what I came here to say."

"You've got nothing to say to me."

"I do, and you're going to listen. Unless you'd rather I say it to the police? I'm guessing you wouldn't, though." He paused, waiting for a response. When none came, he continued. "You confronted her today in the parking lot—holding an ax. You scared her."

"Scaring's what she needs."

Andrew's pulse ticked up. "You think so?"

Gilman puffed out his chest. "Damn right I do. Coming back after all these years, poking her nose where it doesn't belong. She deserves everything she gets, and then some."

"And you think it's your job to make sure that happens, right? That's why you got in her face today?"

"I went to buy an ax and some rope, to help a friend take down a tree, and there she was, walking around the store bold as brass."

"You don't think she had a right to be there?"

"Woman like that doesn't have a right to be anywhere. All she's done since she's been back is make trouble for folks."

"For folks? Or for you?"

"My girls are none of her damn business."

"And that's why you threatened her?"

Gilman's eyes rounded. "Who said anything about threatening her?"

Before Andrew could stop himself, he'd grabbed a fistful of Gilman's shirt. "You got in her face . . . with an ax in your hand."

For the first time, Fred Gilman seemed to realize he was in trouble. "I never . . . I only wanted . . ."

Andrew gave him a shake. "You wanted what?"

To Andrew's astonishment, Gilman's face crumbled. His body went next, his shoulders and chest caving in as a series of sobs bubbled up in his throat. "It was supposed to be over. When that old crone died, that was supposed to be the end of it." His breath was coming in ragged gulps now, tears streaming down his cheeks. "Now the other two are back, and the whole town's talking. No one wants them here. They need to know that."

"So you set fire to the shed and burned down their orchard—so they'd know."

Gilman's eyes flew open. "What? No! I had nothing to do with that!"

Andrew tightened his grip on Gilman's collar. "And the doll in the tree. The note. That was you too?"

"It wasn't!"

"Perhaps you need the police to jog your memory. What do you think, should I give them a call? Tell them you threatened a woman with an ax today? Because I think that's the kind of thing they might be interested in."

Gilman went pale, his body suddenly limp. "No. No police. Please. I don't know anything about any doll. And I had nothing to do with that fire. I swear it. I just wanted to scare her, so she'd leave us alone." He shook his head, blinking away a fresh rush of tears. "I wanted her gone is all. For the dead to stay dead and buried."

"I'm having trouble believing a word you're telling me, Mr. Gilman. But here's what I do believe—you're a bully. And bullies are just cowards who pretend to be tough guys. It's why you like to pick on women. But there are a few things you should know about the Moons, and about Lizzy Moon in particular. They don't scare easy, and they don't back down. The other thing you should know is that if I catch even a whiff of you around Moon Girl Farm, or anywhere near Lizzy, it won't be the police you need to worry about. It'll be me. Do you understand?"

Gilman stared back at Andrew, his mouth drooping mutely.

Andrew gave him a final shake. "Say you understand."

All Gilman managed was a nod, but it was enough. For now.

~

Lizzy was sitting on the front steps, sipping a glass of wine and watching night fall, when Andrew pulled into the drive. She lifted her glass in a half-hearted greeting.

"You're back," she said, as he came up the walk.

"What are you doing out here?"

"Counting fireflies," she said quietly. "I loved fireflies when I was a little girl. They looked like stars dancing in the treetops." She lifted her glass, sipping lazily. "We don't have them in New York. In the city, I mean. Once, I . . ."

The words trailed off and she fell silent. Andrew eyed the wineglass as he dropped down beside her, wondering how many she'd had. "You all right?"

"Just . . . a bit of a day." She waited a beat, then pulled in a deep breath. "My Realtor broke up with me this morning, I may or may not have quit my job, and I was threatened by a crazy man with an ax. On the bright side, the bank is going to let me mortgage my grandmother's farm." She frowned as she stared into her wineglass. "I think there might be a country song in there somewhere."

Andrew barely registered the quip. "You quit your job?"

"Maybe." She paused. Another shrug. "I don't know."

"I don't understand. How don't you know?"

"Luc and I got into it this morning, about me coming back. It didn't end well." She craned her neck, feigning interest in the darkening violet sky. "Let's talk about something else, okay? How was Fred Gilman?"

"The man's a wreck of a human being, that's for sure. But he's hard to read. I asked him about the fire and the note. He denied it all, of course. Claimed he had nothing to do with it. When I called him a liar, the bastard broke down crying."

Lizzy's mouth dropped open. "He . . . wait . . . did you say *crying?*"

"Like a baby. Honest-to-god tears running down his face."

She tilted her head back, studying him. "You almost sound sorry for him."

"I might be if I could get past the image of him holding an ax. But there were times when it felt like he was telling the truth. He talked about being relieved when Althea died, about how her dying meant it was finally over. And he looked genuinely horrified when I accused him of setting the fire. It might have been an act, but it didn't feel like it."

"You're saying you believe him?"

"I'm saying I don't know. For one thing, there are two different questions on the table. The first is whether Gilman is responsible for the fire and the note. The second is whether he's capable of harming his own daughters. And the truth is I don't know the answer to either. Like I said, the guy's hard to read. One minute he's all bowed up, talking like a big man; the next he's a sniveling, snotty mess. One thing I do know is that he doesn't want you here. He also doesn't want the cops involved. He looked absolutely petrified when I suggested calling them."

"So that's it? We're back to square one?"

"I wouldn't say that. I was pretty clear on what would happen if he bothered you again. I called Roger on the way back and ran the whole thing by him. He agrees that while Gilman was way over the line this afternoon, nothing he said or did was actually illegal, but he said it might be good to get it on the record. The police will send someone around to talk to him, take a statement, probably warn him to stay away. Gilman won't like it, but that's his problem."

Lizzy shook her head wearily. "I know I probably overreacted this afternoon, turning up like some hysterical damsel in distress, but he was just so angry. I didn't know what to do. You were the first person I thought of."

"I'm glad. And you didn't overreact. I know you hate anyone trying to protect you, but under the circumstances . . ."

She was quiet for a time, allowing the crickets and peepers to fill in the stretch of silence. Finally, she sighed, tipping her glass to him. "All right. You can be my bodyguard. But I'd appreciate you not mentioning this afternoon to Evvie and Rhanna. I don't want them freaking out on me."

Andrew nodded grudgingly. "Where are they, by the way?"

"Out in the shop, making one last push for the festival this weekend. I was out there for a while, but I bailed. I needed some time to clear my head."

"And count fireflies?"

She smiled sadly as she looked off into the distance. "Yes."

Andrew watched her from the corner of his eye. She looked so beautiful in the moonlight, so cool and still, and so very far away. But then she'd always had a talent for detachment, an ability to hold herself apart from the world around her—and from him.

"I'm glad you thought of me today, Lizzy, and that you felt you could come to me. You always can, you know. No matter what happens with us—or doesn't happen—I'll be here for you." He stood and shoved his hands into his pockets. A reflex to keep from reaching for her.

Lizzy blinked up at him, as if startled to find him on his feet. "You're going?"

"Have to. I'm off to Boston in a few days, and I need to finish the latest set of plans. If I don't see Evvie and Rhanna before they leave for the festival, tell them I said good luck."

"Andrew." She stood so that they were face-to-face, her eyes luminous in the moonlight. "Last night in the barn, when we . . ." She dipped her head awkwardly. "It's not that I'm not . . . I just . . . can't. You get that, right?"

He heard what she was saying. Maybe she even believed it. But as he met those silvery-gray eyes, he saw the truth: that if he wanted to, he could kiss her. She wouldn't stop him this time, despite all her careful explanations. The wine—and perhaps the events of the day—had softened her up, leaving her pliant and vulnerable. But he also saw that she would regret it. Again. And there'd be no coming back from a second rejection.

He took a careful step back. He could wait. Even if waiting meant never. "Good night, Lizzy."

THIRTY-FOUR

August 19

It was the quiet that woke Lizzy at 2:00 a.m., the prickly sensation that something wasn't right. There was no light bleeding out from under Evvie's door, no muffled Joplin or Creedence drifting down the hall from Rhanna's room. Then she remembered: Rhanna and Evvie had set out for Connecticut just after breakfast, headed for the fair with a load of salt scrubs and massage oils, and Ben's borrowed umbrella.

She'd spent the rest of the day in the barn, organizing her workbench and unpacking supplies, then experimenting with what she hoped would be a workable formula for the re-creation of Earth Song. But the work left her restless and unable to settle. It had taken a hot bath and a cup of valerian root tea to finally get her to sleep. And now she was awake again.

It felt strange being in the house alone, the darkness thick and inky, the silence absolute. She lay still, waiting for her eyes to adjust. It was there again, the niggling feeling that something wasn't right. There were no whirring appliances or ticking clocks, no creaky ceiling fans or whiffs of moving air, as if the house had suddenly stopped breathing.

She reached for the lamp, flicked the switch, once, twice. Nothing. Either the power was out, or the prehistoric fuse box had finally given up the ghost. Frustrated at the possibility of another expensive calamity, she kicked off the covers and groped her way out into the hall, vowing to make finding an electrician her top priority when the bank loan came through. She was halfway down the stairs when she suddenly went still. Had she imagined the creak of a floorboard somewhere below her?

She sucked in a breath, hand on the banister, letting the quiet spool out. Not a sound. What was wrong with her? She was a grown woman and acting like a big old scaredy-cat. Then she heard it again, another creak, louder this time, just below her in the kitchen. Her heart slammed against her ribs when she spotted the hunched silhouette sliding past the window.

It took everything in her not to shriek her head off. Instead, she flattened her back to the wall, a hand clamped over her mouth as she watched the shadow melt into the darkness below. One wrong breath and she'd give herself away. But she couldn't hold her breath forever.

With the kitchen phone well out of reach, she had two choices: make a run for the mudroom door and pray she reached it before the intruder did, or bolt back up the stairs to her cell phone, lock herself in, and hope he'd be too spooked to come after her.

The next second the decision was made and she was hurtling down the stairs, barely registering the startled grunt of the intruder as she shot past him toward the mudroom. He'd left the door ajar. She stumbled through it and out into the dark, landing hard on one knee before scurrying back to her feet and pelting barefoot across the yard, blurring past the vegetable garden, the greenhouse, Evvie's hives.

Her head filled with a dull thudding. Footsteps or her heart? She couldn't tell and didn't dare look back. The moon was high and nearly full, making her an easy target. If she remained out in the open, she'd be caught for sure, dragged down and set upon, like a fox run to ground.

Veering left, she plunged into the woods, zigzagging half-blind through the dark tangle of trees, heedless of the brush slashing at her shins, the low branches whipping her cheeks. A pain began to cut into her right side but panic kept her legs moving, feet pounding over tree roots and dew-slick leaves.

Her breath came in a sob when she finally broke from the trees and saw the light in Andrew's upstairs window. A few more yards and she'd be safe. It took the last of her strength to surge the remaining distance. She scraped a shin as she staggered up the steps and fell against the door. She pounded with both fists, tried the knocker, then the bell, then her fists again. His truck was in the driveway; he had to be home. She was thinking about smashing the sidelight window and reaching in when the porch light flicked on, and Andrew pulled back the door.

"My god, what . . . Lizzy!"

She sagged against him, panting. "Someone . . . in the house. In the . . . kitchen."

He caught her before she could slide to the ground, pulling her inside, then led her to a folding metal chair in one corner of the empty living room. "Are you hurt?"

She shook her head, strangely numb. "No."

"Did you see who it was?"

"Too . . . d-dark." Her teeth had begun to chatter as reality crowded in.

Andrew ran a careful eye over her, as if taking inventory. "You're sure you're not hurt? Maybe we should get you checked out."

Lizzy blinked down at her legs, bare and crisscrossed with a network of scrapes and welts. She had bolted out of the house wearing nothing but an oversize T-shirt, and her flight through the woods had left her rather the worse for wear. She ran her tongue over a stinging lower lip. Apparently, her face hadn't fared much better.

"I'm okay," she said, still winded. "Just nicked up. I came through the woods."

"Jesus . . ." Andrew scraped a hand through his hair. "Did you call the police?"

"I couldn't. He was in the kitchen, and my phone was upstairs." She closed her eyes, fighting down a shudder. "I had to run past him to get out of the house. I ran all the way here."

Andrew stepped away. Lizzy registered the sound of drawers opening, the clatter of ice. Moments later, he returned with a makeshift ice pack. "Hold this on your mouth. It'll keep the swelling down."

Lizzy did as she was told, wincing as the cold hit her throbbing lip. He went to the hall closet to fetch a blanket, then dropped it over her and tucked it in around her arms. She was shaking uncontrollably now, sobs of relief shuddering through her in waves.

"You're safe," he told her softly. "But we need to call the police. You said you saw him. Are you sure you couldn't identify him?"

She shook her head, sniffling, then mopped at her eyes. "I never saw his face. Just his silhouette. I think he cut the power."

"Right." Andrew grabbed his phone on the way to the door. "I'll be back in a bit. Keep the ice on your lip, and don't open the door."

Lizzy sat up abruptly. "What are you going to do?"

"I'm going to call the police, and then I'm going over there. It's time to put an end to whatever this is. They'll want to talk to you, I'm sure, but that can wait until tomorrow. For now, just sit tight. And I mean it. Don't open the door."

THIRTY-FIVE

By the time Andrew reached the house, a pair of squad cars were sitting in the driveway, blue lights pulsing eerily. They'd wasted no time, he'd say that for them, though the intruder was almost certainly gone.

He stood in the front yard, watching a pair of flashlight beams move past the curtained windows. A short time later, Ken Landry and Jonathan Clark appeared at the top of the drive. Their hands went to their holsters when they spotted Andrew.

Andrew held out his hands, palms out. "It's Andrew Greyson. I'm the one who called."

The taller of the two, Landry, switched on his Mag, aiming the beam straight at Andrew's face. When he was satisfied, he flipped it off again. "Hey, Andrew. Ms. Moon around?"

"She's at my place. She's a little shaken up. She didn't actually see the guy's face, just his silhouette, but it scared the hell out of her. She thinks he may have cut the power."

"Looks like he pulled the main disconnect at the fuse box. We can't reconnect it until the fingerprint team does their thing, but we went through the place room by room. No one inside. Probably took off the minute he knew he'd been seen. Most of them do. But he did leave us a souvenir."

Andrew felt an uneasy prickle slide up the back of his neck. "What kind of souvenir?"

"The sharp, pointy kind," Clark chimed in. "Must have dropped it on his way out. Nasty thing too. Come have a look."

Andrew followed Landry and Clark around back. The mudroom door was still open, presumably awaiting the print team. Landry flipped on his Mag again, aiming the beam at the base of the stone steps. "There ya go. Like I said, *nasty thing*."

Andrew followed Landry's light. *Nasty* was right. It was an unusual knife, nine or ten inches in length, slender with a stainless handle and a curved, sinister-looking blade.

"What the hell is that?"

"It's called a breaking knife," Landry supplied. "Hunters use them to butcher game. They're good for severing cartilage and bone."

Andrew shoved away the images suddenly flooding his brain. "And he was carrying it?"

"Unless it belongs to the Moons. It could, I suppose."

"They're vegetarians."

Landry cocked his head. "Come again?"

"The Moons—they're vegetarians. They'd have no need for a knife that breaks bone."

"Gotcha. I'll make a note of that. The techs should be here soon to process the scene. They'll take it with them, run it for prints, ID the manufacturer. We'll check out local suppliers, though I doubt it'll tell us much. This is deer country. There are probably dozens of these around town. Then again, we might get lucky."

A white SUV pulled in behind the squad cars and cut its lights. Clark nodded toward the drive. "I'll go brief 'em on what we've got."

Andrew watched him go, then turned back to Landry. "You guys know what's been going on, right? The threats Lizzy's been getting?"

Landry nodded. "Everyone knows. It's all over the papers. Summers isn't any too happy about it either. Says it's not good for the town's image." He paused, watching the print team file in through the mudroom door with their equipment, then turned his attention back to Andrew. "About Ms. Moon. I know you said she's all shook up, and didn't really get a good look at the guy, but we'll need a statement for the report."

"Sure. We'll set something up tomorrow. I'm going to try to convince her to stay at my place tonight. I don't think she should be alone."

"Good plan until we've got a better handle on what this was. Could just be some punk looking to pinch a stereo for meth money."

Andrew eyed Landry squarely. "It wasn't, though, was it?"

Landry's chin dropped a notch. "No. Probably not. We've got a car sweeping the neighborhood, but so far nothing. Tomorrow we'll knock on some doors. Maybe we get lucky and somebody saw something, but it's probably going to come down to whatever the scene techs find. We'll lock up best as we can when they're through, and have someone keep an eye on the place overnight. You never know, the guy might realize he dropped his knife and come back."

Andrew took his time walking back to the house. He needed time to digest what he knew so far. He couldn't get past the fact that the intruder had waited until Evvie and Rhanna were away. The break-in could have been random, but did a guy looking for stereos and pocket change go to the trouble of cutting the power? Or come equipped with a hunting knife?

No, this was personal.

Whoever it was had been hunting Lizzy, and he'd come much too close to catching her.

~

She was asleep when he returned, curled awkwardly in the chair with the blanket tucked under her chin, her face relaxed in slumber. He should wake her, fill her in on what he knew. But after the night she'd had, he wasn't sure he had the heart. There was nothing more to be done until morning. He was still weighing the decision when her eyes opened.

"You're back," she said, her voice thick with sleep.

"I'm sorry I woke you."

She sat up, wincing. "Did the police come?"

"Yes, but whoever broke in was long gone. They'll need you to go through the house in the morning, see if anything's missing. The fingerprint team was still there when I left." He paused, wishing he didn't have to tell her the rest. "They're pretty sure he was carrying a knife."

Lizzy wound her fists into the blanket, cinching it tight to her throat.

"The police found it on the ground. They thought it might be from the house, but I told them that was unlikely."

"Why unlikely?"

"It was a breaking knife. The kind hunters use to butcher deer after they shoot them."

Lizzy nodded slowly.

Andrew watched as her eyes glazed over, fairly sure he could guess what was going through her head. She was imagining what might have happened if she hadn't gotten away, if he'd chased her into the woods, if he'd caught her. He'd been imagining it too.

"You'll stay here tonight," he told her firmly. "The police will be watching the house for a few days, on the off chance that he comes back. No one thinks he will, but it's what they do after this sort of thing. Tomorrow we'll go down to the station and see what else they found. Summers has to take this seriously now."

"You think the man in my kitchen tonight killed Heather and Darcy Gilman."

Andrew's first instinct was to say no, but there was no point in sugarcoating things. "I think it's hard, given everything that's happened, not to put two and two together."

"And you think he wanted to kill me."

"I think what happened tonight was about more than just wanting to scare you, Lizzy."

Her eyes flicked away from his, but he could tell she thought so too. She may not have a name yet, but she'd apparently found her killer.

Or, rather, *he'd* found her.

THIRTY-SIX

Lizzy winced as she patted her skinned knee dry. It had begun to smart in earnest now. In fact, every inch of her seemed to be feeling the effects of her panicked dash through the woods. She was bone weary, her limbs sore and quivering like jelly, but at least she was clean.

And safe.

She hadn't bothered to fight Andrew on spending the night. Nothing short of a shotgun—and probably not even that—would have convinced him to let her go back to the house. Not that she'd wanted to. He'd been as solicitous as any nursemaid, offering to make her tea, or scrambled eggs and toast. She had declined both; the mere thought of food left her queasy. But he'd hit on something when he suggested a long, hot shower.

He'd shown her to the guest room and bath, then bid her good night, only to reappear moments later with a pair of men's pajamas, a toothbrush, Band-Aids, and antibiotic ointment. Now, as she buttoned herself into his borrowed pajamas, she found herself wishing she'd taken him up on the eggs. Not because she was hungry, but because she wasn't ready to turn off the light and close her eyes. She was too skittish for sleep, her nerves like overtuned violin strings.

A man in her house. And a knife. The kind used to butcher deer. What if she hadn't awakened when she did? She shoved the thought away, looking around for a distraction, something to help her wind down. Sadly, Andrew's guest room had little to offer. She went to the door and peered out. A slice of light showed beneath one of the doors at the end of the hall. Andrew's room, presumably. She padded down the hall, pajama bottoms clutched in her fist to keep them from sliding down around her ankles.

The door opened as soon as she knocked. "Is something wrong?"

"No. I just . . ." She glanced away, feeling awkward at having encroached on his personal space. "I don't think I can sleep. I was wondering if you had something I could read. A magazine, maybe."

"Sure. Yeah." He scraped a thumb back and forth over his chin, darkened now with a shadow of stubble. "Most of my books are packed up in the basement, waiting for me to build some shelves, but I should have something lying around. Come on in while I look."

Lizzy stepped into the room, making a quick and—she hoped— discreet survey. It was sparsely furnished: a king-size bed with a tufted suede headboard, a single nightstand and lamp, a chest of drawers with a mirror to match, and, stationed near the window, a drafting table with an adjustable lamp clamped to one end.

"Slim pickings, I'm afraid," he called over his shoulder, as he sorted through the stack of magazines on the nightstand. "You have your choice between last month's *Architectural Digest* or a dated issue of *Old-House Journal*, which features an absolutely fascinating article on brownstone restoration."

Lizzy put a finger to her lips, pretending to weigh her options. "Let's go with *Old-House Journal*. I adore a good brownstone restoration article."

"Well, then." Andrew handed her the magazine with a flourish. "You're in luck. Though I feel I should warn you. It's pretty steamy stuff."

"Thanks," Lizzy said, suddenly shy. "I was surprised your light was still on. You've got Boston tomorrow."

"I had a few last-minute details to clean up."

"At four in the morning?"

He shrugged. "I do some of my best work late at night."

"Right. Sorry. I'll leave you to it."

She was almost to the door when he stopped her. "You could stay if you want. Stretch out with your magazine and read for a while. You won't bother me."

Her eyes slid to the bed, then back to Andrew, hating that he'd sensed her reluctance to be alone. "Are you sure?"

"I am. As long as you promise to turn the pages quietly."

Lizzy smiled, grateful for his attempt at levity. "I promise."

She waited until Andrew was back behind his drafting table to lie back against the pillows and open the magazine. She wouldn't stay long. Just until she felt drowsy. As it turned out, it wouldn't take long. She struggled through the benefits of in-kind repair versus patching, and the various components required to create a proper patching mix, but when it came to the specific parts of lime versus mica, her eyes began to glaze over.

She looked at Andrew, head bent over his blueprints, the stubby end of a drafting pencil caught between his teeth. He was the hero she never wanted, the friend she had come to trust, the risk she was still afraid to take. And yet there was a part of her that found the thought of him—of *them*—tantalizing. With Andrew, there would be no need to keep any part of herself hidden. He knew exactly who she was—and he wanted her anyway.

He was staring at her, she realized, a crease between his brows. "Everything okay?"

Lizzy felt her cheeks color, embarrassed to have been caught staring. "Everything's fine." She closed the magazine, set it aside, and swung her feet to the floor. "I think I'll be able to sleep now." She pushed to her feet, preparing to leave, then stopped. "Thank you, Andrew."

He stood and came around to the front of the drafting table wearing a lopsided smile. "Glad it did the trick. Next time I'll try to have something a little more interesting on hand."

"I didn't mean for the magazine. I meant for tonight. And the day before yesterday, at your office." She glanced down at her toes, peeking out from under the borrowed pajamas. "And for the night at the fountain. I never said it, and I should have."

"I meant what I said on the steps last night, Lizzy. About being here for you. You never have to say thank you to me."

"But I want to." She looked away, speaking quickly, before she lost her nerve. "The other night in the barn, you said you'd waited twenty years. Did you mean it, or were you just flirting?"

"You told me I wasn't allowed to flirt with you."

"So . . ."

"Yes. I meant it. I have been waiting, and I'll keep waiting, because I can't seem to help myself."

Lizzy held up a hand, afraid of what else he might say, and even more afraid of what *she* might say. How had it happened? She'd been so careful, so determined to keep him at arm's length. But it *had* happened. Somehow, while she wasn't looking, she'd dropped her guard and let him in.

"Talk to me, Lizzy."

Her eyes skittered away from his. What was there to say that she hadn't said already? And yet none of it had mattered, because here she was—here they *both* were. She shook her head, trying to comprehend what was happening. "It feels like I've been pushing you away for half my life. You'd come over with your dad and I'd disappear until I knew you were gone. The night at the fountain, when you pulled me away from the crowd, and I said all those terrible things. The time at homecoming assembly when you came and sat next to me, and I bolted like you had the plague." She shook her head again, cheeks warming at the memory. "You were always trying to rescue me."

He smiled sheepishly. "I wasn't trying to rescue you. I was trying to pluck up the courage to ask you out. Never got around to it, though. You had a real knack for shutting me down."

"You scared me to death. I guess you still do. The idea of you—of us. I don't think I knew that until tonight. But I know it now, and . . ." Her eyes shifted back to his, mere inches from her own. "What if it turns out to be a mistake, Andrew? What if *we* turn out to be a mistake?"

"We might. But I think it's worth finding out, don't you? If I'm not what you want, I'll walk away, and that's that. But not because it's scary." He paused, reaching for her hand. "We're all scared, Lizzy. And we all make mistakes. That's how it works. We just keep trying until we get it right."

"What about you?" She searched his face, not sure what she was looking for. "Have you ever . . . gotten it right?"

He glanced down at the carpet, then back up again. "Almost."

It wasn't the answer she'd been expecting. "What does *almost* look like?"

"Like a girl I met in college. Dianna. She was smart, pretty, fun. Perfect, really."

"What happened?"

He shrugged. "She wasn't you."

Lizzy stared at him, too startled to reply. He'd said it without batting an eye.

"It's always been you, Lizzy. Since the day I saw you coming out of the woods with your hair full of leaves, like something from a fairy tale. You didn't say a word. You just stood there staring at me. And that was it. I was in love with the girl next door."

"Andrew, I can't . . ."

"I know," he said quietly. "I'm not asking you to. But stay with me. Even if it's just for tonight."

Lizzy looked down at their hands, his fingers and hers warmly woven. It would be so easy to let this happen, to simply disappear into him for the night. "Just for tonight," she whispered. "That would be enough for you?"

"No. But it's more of you than I ever thought I'd have." He touched her face, his palm warm against her cheek. "Stay with me."

He kissed her then, with bone-melting slowness, laying waste to the last of her resistance. Something in her let go, like the snick of a lock springing open, the moment of decision suddenly behind her. It was happening. This reckless, glorious, disastrous thing was happening.

His hands were in her hair, his breath a ragged half moan as his mouth blazed a slow, sweet trail down the slope of her neck, the soft, pulsing hollow of her throat. She reached for his shirt, dragging it up over his head, then let her hands roam his chest, the hard, flat planes of his belly. He smelled of soap and shampoo, but there was no missing the earthy musk of sandalwood and warm amber radiating from his skin. She breathed him in as he undressed her, pausing to kiss her between buttons, until the pajamas he'd lent her an hour before lay puddled on the carpet. There was only desire between them now, a searing hunger that left no room for words.

They eased down onto the bed, a tangle of need and clinging limbs. His eyes never left hers as he laid her back, palms, smooth and warm, skimming the hollow of her belly, the curve of her hip, the smooth, soft slope of her inner thigh, as if he were trying to memorize every inch of her. She closed her eyes, wanting to pretend none of it meant anything, but it would be a lie. This wasn't Luc. Or any other man she'd ever been with.

She heard her name, and felt it too, rasped warmly against her throat, pulling down the last of her barriers. She would regret it all in the morning. Perhaps they both would. But in this moment there was nothing but the feel and smell and taste of him. And the abandon of a moment that might never come again.

THIRTY-SEVEN

Andrew pulled the truck to the top of the drive and cut the engine. "Sit tight while I go in and look around. Until we know more, I think we should err on the side of caution."

Lizzy watched as he disappeared around the side of the house, relieved to have a moment alone with her thoughts. The last twelve hours were still such a jumble. Waking to find a prowler in the house, her panicked flight through the woods, falling into bed with Andrew.

Her cheeks tingled as she remembered their bodies in the darkness, the dizzying sense of inevitability, like a tide rushing toward shore. She'd been swept away, drowned in the moment. But now, in the light of day, the tide had gone out again, leaving her to navigate the aftermath of last night's weakness.

He had awakened her with coffee and a plate of scrambled eggs. She'd never had a man make her breakfast, let alone bring it to her in bed, unless she counted Luc showing up on the occasional Sunday morning with bagels from Luesden's bakery.

They had eaten in silence at first, sitting cross-legged on Andrew's bed, with her doing her best to keep her mouth full, and Andrew sneaking sidelong glances between bites of toast. He was being tactful, she realized, waiting for her to bring up what had happened between them. Because at some point they would need to talk about it—about what it meant, and what it didn't—but so far, she'd been spared that conversation.

Andrew had barely finished his eggs when his cell went off. One of the contractors on the Boston job had called to tell him they'd discovered an issue with the foundation, one that would require both plumbing and wiring redos. The clients needed to see him ASAP, to talk options and costs. There had been a flurry of calls after that. He had apologized profusely, but the truth was she'd been grateful for the diversion.

Lizzy glanced out the passenger side window in time to see Andrew reappear and wave the all clear. She felt a frisson of dread as she climbed out of the truck and made her way to the back of the house. She'd been preparing herself for this all morning, but a chill prickled down her spine when she saw the mudroom door standing ajar. The lock plate had been pried from the jamb, the jamb itself visibly gouged.

"He jimmied his way in," Andrew said, pointing out the damage. "Then apparently found the fuse box."

Lizzy nodded mutely, eyeing the powdery black residue smearing the doorknob and jamb. She'd heard about fingerprint dust, about the mess it made and what a nightmare it was to clean up. Now she'd get to see it firsthand. For the second time in eight years, Moon Girl Farm had been designated a crime scene.

Andrew reached for her hand. "You okay?"

"Yeah. It just gives me the creeps, thinking about what could have happened."

"Me too." He gave her fingers a squeeze. "We don't have to stay long. You'll just do a quick walk-through, see if anything's missing, and get into some proper clothes. Although, I have to say, you look a lot better in my boxers than I do."

Lizzy mustered a smile. He'd lent her a T-shirt and a pair of his boxers to wear. She'd had to roll the waistband several times to keep them up, but they'd done well enough.

"Ready to go in?"

She nodded, swallowing a groan.

Inside, the mess was even worse than expected. Lizzy did her best to ignore it as she moved from room to room, looking for rifled drawers and cabinets, but it was hard when virtually every surface was smeared with sooty residue, a stark reminder of the intruder's presence.

"Well?" Andrew said when she made her way back around to the kitchen.

"Nothing's missing down here. I guess he wasn't here to steal the silver."

"Looks that way."

"I'll have a quick look upstairs, then throw on some clothes so we can get this over with. I'd like to get a few hours of work in out in the barn when I get back, and then I guess I'll have to start cleaning up this mess."

Upstairs, she was relieved to find nothing disturbed. There were no ransacked closets or tousled drawers, and her purse and phone were both on the dresser where she'd left them. That the intruder hadn't ventured upstairs should have been comforting. But it seemed only to confirm the suspicion that the break-in had been motivated by something other than robbery.

After swapping Andrew's boxers for a pair of jeans, she ran a brush through her hair, slid her phone into her purse, and headed back down. She'd check in with Roger when she finished with the police, to fill him in and see where things stood.

She found Andrew in the front parlor, roaming from window to window, scribbling on the notepad Evvie usually kept by the phone. He turned when she entered the room, brows raised. "So?"

"I don't think he made it upstairs at all. And if he did, it wasn't to steal. My purse was on the dresser in plain sight. What are you doing?"

"Counting windows. I'll replace the lock on the mudroom door this afternoon, and then the minute I get back from Boston, I'm fitting all these windows with new locks."

Lizzy looked around the room and sighed. "I don't even want to think about what's coming when Evvie and Rhanna get back and see all this. Evvie isn't going to let me out of her sight."

"I wouldn't blame her. In fact, I'm thinking a security system might not be a bad idea."

"People in Salem Creek don't have security systems, Andrew. Half of them don't even lock their doors."

"They'll start once word of this gets out."

Lizzy was about to respond when her cell phone pinged. She pulled it out of her purse, frowning when she saw the text from Luc.

Do you still work for me or what?

Andrew was watching her. "Everything's okay?"

"Luc," she said flatly. "He wants to know if I still work for him."

"Do you?"

Lizzy let out a sigh. She knew what he wanted her to say: that she wasn't going back. But she couldn't say it. If last night had proven anything, it was that the best thing she could do was get herself back to New York before she caused any more confusion—for Andrew and for herself. She'd been trying all morning to figure out how to have this conversation. It seemed Luc had forced her hand.

"I worked hard to get where I am at Chenier, Andrew. I have a future there. I can't just walk away from that."

"So that's a yes."

"I suppose it is." She looked away, groping for words that would make this easier, but there weren't any. "I know what you want me to say, that last night changed everything, and I'd be lying if I said that wasn't true. But it also made me realize why I've been pushing you away for so long. It's because you make me forget. The things I promised I'd do—and the things I promised I wouldn't. Why I came back, and why I can't stay. But there's one thing I can't forget, especially after last night. This town doesn't want me here. And that's never going to change. No matter how many questions I ask, or what I prove. Salem Creek has been trying to get rid of the Moons for two hundred years. It's time to give them what they want."

Andrew had been listening with arms folded. He shifted his feet now, and squared his shoulders. "Is that all?"

Lizzy blinked at him. "All?"

"Three days ago you told me you *might* have quit your job. I asked when you'd know for sure. You shrugged it off, like it was no big deal. Now, all of a sudden, you're crystal clear about all the reasons you need to go back. At the risk of sounding paranoid, are you sure this isn't about last night?"

"I'm going back because it's what needs to happen, Andrew. I'm still who I am—still *what* I am. I let myself forget that last night. Because I wanted to feel how I felt. I wanted to be with you. I wanted it more than anything. But it wasn't fair to you. I was wrong to let last night happen."

"So I was a mistake?"

"No," she said evenly, hating that he'd thrown her own words back at her. "I was. I knew it couldn't be anything more than one night. I just . . ."

"How long did it last with Luc?"

"Luc was nothing. He was a distraction, someone to fill up my nights and weekends. He wasn't . . ." She closed her eyes, letting the rest dangle.

"What?"

"You," she said softly. "He wasn't you." She resisted the urge to reach for him. Touching him now wouldn't do either of them any good.

"All I did last night was make things harder for both of us, and I'm so sorry for that. You deserve the whole white-picket-fence thing, and you'd never have that with me. I told you I'm not happily-ever-after material. I was wrong to let you think I might be—and wrong to let *myself* think it."

"Who said anything about a white picket fence? I don't need kids, or even a ring if that's how you want it. I don't care about all the trappings. I care about you. And last night I thought you cared too."

"I do. I care enough to step back, to not ask you to live half a life. I was always clear about that."

Andrew nodded, his face suddenly shuttered. "Yes, you were. I guess part of me thought I could change your mind. Apparently, I overestimated my powers of persuasion." He turned away, running his eyes around the kitchen. "I suppose we should get to the police station."

Lizzy picked up her purse, clutching it to her chest like a life preserver. "Maybe it would be better if I went alone. You need to get down to Boston, and, really, I can do this. I have to stop at the bank and the market on the way back. You don't need to hang around for all that."

"You shouldn't be alone. Not after last night."

"The police told you they'd keep an eye out. I'll be fine."

"You could come with me to Boston. Give the police a few days to do their thing. A break might be a good idea. You could hang out by the pool, or poke around Newbury Street."

Lizzy forced a smile. "There you go again, trying to rescue me."

"There was a man with a knife walking around this kitchen last night. What am I supposed to do?"

"You said you were going to put a new lock on the mudroom door, and if it makes you feel better, I'll sprinkle salt on the doorstep for protection."

He glowered at her, clearly frustrated. "I can't tell if you're kidding."

Lizzy managed a half smile. "Only a little."

She understood his concerns for her safety, but the truth was she couldn't think of anything more dangerous than spending two or three days with Andrew in Boston. It would be too easy to backslide, to surrender to the delicious pull of memory. She needed to keep her distance and give her resolve time to jell.

Andrew pulled his keys from his pocket, removed one from the ring, and laid it on the counter. "You'll stay at my place again tonight."

"Andrew—"

"Don't worry. I won't be there. From the sound of things, I'll be gone several days, which means you'll have the place to yourself. There isn't much in the fridge, though, so you'll still need to hit the market. Make sure you drive over. Don't cut through the woods. And make sure everything's locked up once you're in."

Lizzy looked at him, stung by his frosty tone. She wished there was something between icy aloofness and the hot sting of rebuff, some middle ground where they could coexist in the wake of last night's brief lapse in judgment. Again, she found herself casting about for something to say—for *anything* to say. But they'd already said it all. Except perhaps goodbye.

~

It was nearly three by the time Lizzy arrived at the market. It was a relief to have the trip to the police station behind her. She understood the need, but she'd known before setting foot in the station that nothing would come of it.

Detective Hammond had run her through the questions. No, she hadn't seen the intruder's face. No, there was nothing she recognized about him. No, nothing had been taken from the house. The only detail she felt confident in sharing was that the intruder appeared to have been male, and even that was speculation.

The entire interview had taken less than an hour and had ended with Hammond handing her his card, encouraging her to call if she happened to remember anything else. He'd promised to keep her apprised of future developments but hadn't sounded especially optimistic. Perhaps because the knife had turned up negative for prints.

The market was relatively quiet. Lizzy wandered the aisles, picking up enough to get her through the next few days at Andrew's, then turned down the household aisle. A Google search on how to clean up fingerprint dust had suggested microfiber cloths and a multipurpose cleaner with ammonia. She grabbed several of both, then headed for the checkout, eager to get back to her work in the barn before tackling the mess in the house.

Unfortunately, there was only one cashier working, and three people already in line. Lizzy scanned the tabloid headlines to pass the time, played peekaboo with the sticky-faced toddler in the cart in front of her, browsed the display of gum and mints. Finally, the mother of the toddler paid for her groceries and told her son to wave goodbye to the pretty lady.

Lizzy fumbled in her purse for her debit card while the cashier scanned her items. About halfway through, the woman looked up. Her hand stilled, her pasted-on smile slipping as she locked eyes with Lizzy. Her hair was different, pulled back in a lank ponytail, and she was wearing a heavy layer of foundation, but there was no mistaking the woman who, a few weeks back, had given her a chilly once-over from the customer service desk. Lizzy glanced at her name badge—Helen.

Helen dropped her gaze and resumed her work, avoiding eye contact until it was time to collect her money. "Thirty-seven twenty-six is your total."

Lizzy slid her debit card into the reader, tapped in her PIN, then waited for Helen to bag her order. Getting the cold shoulder wasn't new, but her nerves were still raw after the events of the last twenty-four hours, and it irked more than usual.

"Have a nice day," Lizzy huffed as she lifted the pair of paper bags into her arms. She didn't realize Helen had stepped from behind the checkout until they collided, dislodging a pair of peaches from one of the bags and sending them skittering across the floor.

Before Lizzy could bend down to retrieve them, Helen beat her to the punch. She met Lizzy's gaze squarely as she dropped the peaches back into her bag, her brown eyes flat and unblinking. "You should be more careful, Ms. Moon. I'd feel awful if you ended up getting hurt."

Lizzy gaped at her, preparing to point out that it was *she* who had caused the collision, and not the other way around, but something in Helen's gaze brought her up short. The seconds stretched, awkward and bristling, until Lizzy finally stepped around her and headed for the door.

In the car, she replayed the incident as she pulled out into traffic, wondering if she'd misread the look on Helen's face, and overreacted in the wake of her recent run-in with Fred Gilman. There'd been nothing inherently threatening about Helen's words. Quite the opposite, in fact. She'd merely warned her to be more careful.

Warned.

The word sent a chill through her. Was it possible Helen had smashed into her on purpose, manufacturing an opportunity to speak to her? Or was she simply being paranoid because a man with a knife had crept into her kitchen last night?

At the next traffic signal, Lizzy made a U-turn and headed back to the market. She parked near the entrance and left her purse on the seat. She was probably about to make a complete fool of herself, but she didn't care. It wouldn't be the first time a Moon had made a public spectacle of herself.

She was nearly to the door when Helen came out, almost causing a repeat of their earlier collision. Lizzy froze, her hastily rehearsed words suddenly caught in her throat. Helen stared at her, wide-eyed and mute as the seconds ticked by, her hands clamped so tight around her purse strap that her knuckles blanched white. After a moment she seemed to collect herself and stepped to her left. Lizzy checked her, then checked her again when she tried to change direction.

"A little while ago, when you bumped into me, you said I should be careful, and that you'd feel terrible if I ended up getting hurt. What did you mean?"

"Nothing," Helen shot back, eyes lowered. "I didn't mean anything."

"Was it a threat? Were you threatening me?"

"Please. Leave me alone. Leave *all* of it alone."

"*All* what?"

Helen shook her head, as if trying to shut Lizzy out. "You shouldn't be here."

"I'm not going anywhere until you tell me what you meant when you said I should be careful."

"Please," Helen murmured hoarsely. Her eyes skittered over Lizzy's shoulder, her face suddenly chalky beneath her too-dark foundation. "I don't need any trouble. I only wanted . . ."

Lizzy saw it then, the purple-green shadow along Helen's jawline, not quite hidden beneath the heavy makeup. "Your face—"

Helen cut her off with an almost imperceptible shake of the head. Seconds later, Lizzy heard footsteps and turned.

Dennis Hanley stood glowering behind her, holding a little girl with hair the color of corn silk in his arms. Her face was a mirror of her mother's, pale and heart shaped, but her yellow-blonde hair was all Hanley. *Helen.* Of course. Andrew had mentioned her name once, when Hollis came up in conversation.

"Mommy!" The child held out both arms, trying to launch herself out of her uncle's grasp. "Want Mommy!"

Helen managed a smile as she reached for her daughter, but Dennis stepped away, keeping the child just out of reach. He turned to Lizzy, an eye cocked against the afternoon sun. "Something you need?"

Lizzy felt her spine stiffen, an instinctive and visceral recoiling. He was wearing a long white coat smeared with what looked like dried blood, and there was another smear on the side of his neck. The stench of blood came off him in waves, so thick she could nearly taste it. Salty. Coppery. Sharp. He was glaring at her over the top of the child's head, still waiting for a response.

Helen rushed in to fill the gap. "I was just apologizing. I wasn't watching where I was going when I came out just now, and we sort of collided."

Dennis's eyes never left Lizzy's face. "That right?"

Lizzy did her best to look sheepish. "It was actually me who wasn't looking where I was going. Sorry. I've always been a bit of a klutz."

Helen was about to reply when Dennis silenced her with a look. He jerked his head toward the parking lot, where a rust-riddled Bronco sat with the driver's door open. "Time to go."

Helen moved to his side like a dog to heel, leaning in to drop a kiss on her daughter's pale head. Her bruised jaw glinted in the sunlight, a bull's-eye of purples and greens, and Lizzy found herself unable to look away. Helen must have sensed her gaze because she ducked her head, a brief but telling gesture. She was ashamed. Someone—almost certainly Dennis—had hurt her, and *she* was ashamed. The thought sickened Lizzy.

She watched as they walked away, Helen lagging a step behind. She turned her head briefly before climbing into the Bronco. For an instant, their eyes met. A plea or a warning? Lizzy couldn't be sure.

THIRTY-EIGHT

Lizzy's first impulse on the drive home was to call Andrew and tell him Dennis Hanley was battering his sister-in-law and should be fired immediately. But did she know that for sure? That Helen was afraid couldn't be denied. She'd caught the faint tinge of urine on her breath—an ammonia-like odor she'd always registered as fear. And the bruise on her face was real enough. But did the two necessarily add up to assault?

There was no sign of Andrew's truck as she pulled up, either in her driveway or his. Inside, she found a pair of shiny silver keys on the kitchen counter, along with a note.

Mudroom door lock has been replaced. Off to Boston—A.G.

Lizzy read the note several times. It was hard to ignore the clipped tone, the use of initials—first *and* last—instead of his name. Cool. Distant. But that was what she wanted, wasn't it—distance? She considered calling him, running her suspicions about Dennis by him, but if she was serious about closing the door between them, he couldn't be her first phone call every time something went wrong. If she was determined not to want him, she wasn't allowed to need him.

Resolved, she began unpacking her groceries, separating what she would take to Andrew's, and what would stay. Her stomach rumbled as she pulled out a parcel wrapped in white deli paper and opened it. She rolled a piece of swiss cheese and clamped it between her teeth, then rolled another. She hadn't eaten since Andrew's scrambled eggs this morning.

Had that really been only this morning?

She pushed the thought aside, focusing on her to-do list instead. It was a little after three. If she played her cards right, she could spend an hour in the barn, then another hour or two scrubbing fingerprint dust, and still make it to Andrew's by dark. It would feel strange sleeping alone in Andrew's bed, an uncomfortable reminder of just how careless she'd been with his feelings—and her own. But the truth was, she was still a little jumpy after last night.

She was rewrapping the cheese when she paused. Something—*what was it*—had caught her attention. Something she should be noticing or remembering. She looked down at the deli paper she'd been refolding with a sudden flash of clarity. Not art paper. Butcher paper. The kind that might be used at a meatpacking plant.

On impulse, she tore off a small square and held it to the light. Heavy but not expensive. No watermark. She closed her eyes, remembering words scrawled in red crayon.

Thou shalt not suffer a witch to live.

The floor seemed to tilt as the pieces shifted and fell together.

Call Andrew. No, not Andrew. Roger.

Voice mail picked up on the fourth ring. Lizzy smothered a groan, praying she wouldn't have to wait days for a return call. "It's Lizzy. Call me the minute you get this. I need to run something by you."

She waited, staring at the phone, willing it to ring while her brain continued to tie itself in knots. Was she grasping at straws? Seeing bogeymen where none existed?

When ten minutes stretched to thirty and Roger still hadn't called, she slid the phone into her pocket, and headed for the barn. She needed to get out of her head, to do something productive instead of standing around, dwelling on her runaway thoughts.

The barn was cool and dark as she stepped inside. She flipped on the lights, then rolled up her sleeves, eager to see how the oil blend had aged. She unscrewed the cap from the small amber bottle, dabbed a bit on her wrist, and inhaled, slow and deep. Next, she held her wrist about an inch from her mouth, closed her eyes, and inhaled through her parted lips, allowing the scent to pass over her tongue and into her throat, a kind of back door to the nasal passages.

Dark, woody, moist, and green.

Not a perfect re-creation of the original, but as close as possible with nothing but memory and her nose to guide her. It was time to begin the dilution phase. Then two weeks to rest, and she'd be ready to bottle.

She pulled her phone from her pocket and laid it on the workbench, then scared up a pen and set to work on her calculations. She was thinking an eau de toilette at an 85 percent dilution. Not only would it lighten the overall fragrance; it would also increase her yield. She made a mental note to calculate how many bottles she'd need to order.

She had just finished her calculations and was unscrewing the cap from a bottle of perfumer's alcohol when her cell rang. She pounced on it. "Roger. Thanks for calling me back."

"I just got off a call. Heard you had a visitor last night. Are you okay?"

"Andrew called?"

"No. A friend at SCPD. I asked if you were okay."

"Yeah. I came down the stairs, saw him, and bolted. But never mind that. What do you know about Dennis Hanley?"

There was a pause while Roger shifted gears. "Why?"

"Maybe I'm just being paranoid, but I had an odd moment at the market today. Helen Hanley rang up my groceries. As I was leaving, she bumped into me—hard—then told me I should be careful, that she'd hate to see me get hurt. I thought she was just being rude. But the more I thought about it, the more it felt like something else. When I went back to talk to her, I saw that she had a bruise on her cheek. She'd tried covering it with makeup, but I could still see it. And then Dennis showed up. She was terrified of him, Roger. And I don't blame her. He was wearing a white coat smeared with dried blood. He must have just left his shift at the meatpacking plant. I didn't put it together until I got home and unwrapped a package of cheese from the deli."

"Cheese?"

"It was wrapped in white paper. Butcher paper—like they'd use at a meatpacking plant."

There was another pause while he connected the dots. "The note," he said finally. "You think Dennis wrote the note."

"I'm crazy, right? Putting two and two together and coming up with five?"

"Maybe not. In fact . . ."

Lizzy waited for him to finish. When he didn't, she prodded him. "In fact what?"

"It's something I heard from a buddy right after Hollis died. New guy got the call—Steve Gaffney. He was a good guy, but he bungled it a little bit."

Lizzy's pulse ticked up. "Bungled how?"

"He claimed there was a note at the house, a suicide note essentially. Hollis's wife found it tacked up on the refrigerator, and gave it to Gaffney when he showed up to tell her about the wreck. He said she was crying, but didn't seem that surprised by the news."

"What was in the note?"

"The kind of stuff a man writes when he's on the edge. According to Helen, he came back from Afghanistan pretty wrecked. She begged him to get help, to join a support group, but Dennis put a stop to that. Said the Hanleys deal with their own problems."

"Spoken like a true expert on PTSD," Lizzy muttered.

"That's the thing. Hollis was never actually diagnosed with PTSD."

"Maybe not officially, but something must've happened over there. A year after he comes back he commits suicide? What did the note say?"

"Nobody knows. Gaffney screwed up and left the note behind. Rookie mistake, I guess. Your first DRT can shake you up pretty bad, especially if it's messy, which this one was."

"DRT?"

"Sorry, it's police slang for *dead right there.*"

"Nice."

"Not really, no. But it's a coping thing. Anyway, when they went back for the note, it had disappeared."

"How does a note disappear?"

"With help. By the time they got back to the house, Dennis was there and Helen had developed a severe case of amnesia. Claimed she never saw the note. When they pressed her, Dennis stepped in. Said Helen had been through enough, and he'd be handling things going forward. There was no suspicion of foul play, so they let it go. People are funny about suicide, squeamish. But the disappearing note rubbed Gaffney wrong. There were a few lines that stuck with him, about how some people deserve what happens to them, while others just get caught in someone else's nightmare, and how he was going to hell for what he'd done."

"Well, it fits, doesn't it? He must have seen some awful things in Afghanistan—maybe even did some awful things—and it obviously haunted him. Maybe Dennis knew too, and didn't want anyone poking around and finding out."

"That's how it reads if you don't know the whole story. But Gaffney couldn't let it go. He knows a guy Hollis was stationed with, and the way he tells it, Hollis Hanley never fired his weapon. First mission out, their unit got into a mess. They were pinned down in some shelled-out building, taking heavy fire. Hollis shouldered his weapon, and then . . . nothing. He froze. A couple of guys managed to drag him down before he got himself killed. They found him a noncombat role, but it was no good. Something in him was broken. He wound up getting separated. Sorry, it means discharged."

Lizzy digested Roger's words, laying the pieces end to end. "If Hollis didn't kill anyone in Afghanistan, why did he think he was going to hell?"

"Now you see where I'm going."

The gears turned slowly, eventually clicking into place. "You think he committed suicide because of Heather and Darcy—because he killed them. And Dennis knew."

"It was years after the murders. Not likely anyone would have connected the dots back to Heather and Darcy. But now I think it bears looking at. It would explain Dennis getting rid of the note. He was always Hollis's protector. Maybe that didn't end when Hollis died. Maybe he wanted to make sure no one would ever ask the kinds of questions we're asking now. Then you show up and start digging."

Lizzy sat with that last part. The note. The fire. The silhouette in the kitchen. "Helen was trying to warn me. She knew Dennis was behind everything that was going on."

"It's just a theory, but it fits."

"So what do we do?"

"*We* don't do anything," Roger told her pointedly. "If we're right, and there's a good chance we are, Dennis Hanley is a dangerous man. Summers can't bury it this time. Where's Andrew?"

"In Boston. On a job."

"You might want to give him a call. Let him know what's happening. I've got a few calls of my own to make. Stay near your phone."

Lizzy put down her cell and splayed both hands on the workbench. Andrew had enough on his plate in Boston. She'd call him tonight, after she heard back from Roger. In the meantime, she'd get some work done, and try to wrap her head around the possibility that Heather and Darcy Gilman's killer might actually be brought to light, if not to justice, that at long last Althea's name might be cleared.

Things were beginning to tie up, the pieces of what she'd come here to do all nearly in place. The loan had come through. Once she lined up the repair work, and signed with Rhanna's real estate friend, there'd be nothing keeping her here. Rhanna and Evvie could stay until the farm sold, and see to the contents of the house when the time came. It was time to call Luc and commit to a return date. And finish the Earth Song for Rhanna. She'd make it a going-away present.

The thought brought an unexpected heaviness as she reached for a glass beaker and began filling it with alcohol. She had one eye on her phone, the other on the pad she'd used to jot down her calculations, when she suddenly stopped pouring. There'd been no sound, no movement caught out of the corner of her eye, just a subtle shift in the air around her, alerting her that she was no longer alone.

THIRTY-NINE

She recognized Dennis's silhouette the instant she turned.

He stood motionless in the doorway, arms hanging slack at his sides. Her heart thudded against her ribs as she waited for him to speak, but he just stood there, eyes flat, and yet strangely riveted. Finally, he pulled the door closed and began moving toward her, his steps slow but deliberate.

Lizzy's mind whirred as she calculated the odds of escape. There was zero chance that she'd get past him this time, and consequently no hope of reaching the door.

"You've got no business here," she said, fighting to keep the panic from her voice as she edged toward the end of the workbench and her cell phone. "Leave. Now."

Dennis continued to advance. She could see his face now, ruddy and sweating, his lower jaw shot forward like a bulldog's. He had swapped the blood-smeared coat for a bulky camouflage jacket that seemed all wrong for a sticky August afternoon.

She caught a whiff of him, the now-familiar mud-and-blood stench, mingled with alcohol. He'd been drinking since she'd last seen him, heavily if she was any judge, though she wasn't sure whether that worked in her favor or against it. The alcohol might have slowed him by a step. Or it might have just stoked his temper. Her money was on the latter.

"You," he slurred, as he continued to close the distance between them. "You think you're so smart. Coming back here after all these years, poking around in things that are none of your business. Like you're goddamn Columbo or something."

"Heather and Darcy Gilman *are* my business."

"And my sister-in-law—she your business too? And my brother?"

Lizzy sidled to her left, another step closer to her phone. "I never really knew Hollis—"

"Don't you say his name to me! Don't you ever say his name!" He dropped his head as if suddenly exhausted. "You should have stayed gone."

"Is that what you came to tell me last night? That I should have stayed gone?"

Dennis lifted his head, eyes glittering. "I didn't come to *tell* you anything."

"I know," Lizzy said quietly, unnerved by the admission. He'd said it without blinking. Like a man with nothing to lose. "The police found your knife."

"I gave you three chances!" he bellowed at her. "Three chances to leave it alone. That stupid doll and the note. Burning down the shed. When none of that worked, I showed up with a knife. But you just kept poking, asking your questions. That stops now." He was sweating heavily, and paused long enough to drag a sleeve across his face. "A man protects his family. My old man taught me that. Took a while, but I get it now. A man does what he has to."

Lizzy squared her shoulders, refusing to be cowed. "So does a woman."

Dennis's mouth curled unpleasantly. "I wonder if you'll think it was worth it."

The glint in his pale eyes turned Lizzy's blood cold. She wasn't sure what the remark meant, but she wasn't sticking around to find out. She darted to her left, grabbing blindly for her phone, then wheeled back to her right, ducking as he lunged for her.

She was almost in the clear, her eyes on the door, when Dennis caught her arm and jerked her back. Terrified, she flailed at him with both arms, managing to land a solid blow to his chest, another to his left cheek.

In the end she was no match for his size and strength. Her head snapped back as his fist connected with her jaw, the white-hot crack of pain all but blinding her as she went down. She lay sprawled on her back, her jaw throbbing like a pulse, the taste of blood metallic on her tongue. Black spots danced at the edges of her vision as she attempted to get up. At some point during the struggle she'd lost her phone.

Dennis stood nearby, his face sheened with sweat, a welt already forming on his left cheek. He looked on dispassionately as Lizzy struggled to get to her knees. He craned his neck, running his eyes around the barn, finally coming to rest on the workbench. He stepped closer, picking things up, putting them down again.

"Some setup you've got here," he said with a lazy smile. "Some flammables, I see." The smile widened as he reached into his pocket and pulled out a lighter. He flicked it briefly for effect. "Be a shame if there was an accident."

Panic fizzed through Lizzy's limbs, the hot-and-cold prickle of adrenaline surging through her arms and legs. The room spun as she dragged herself to her feet. There seemed to be two of everything, like binoculars out of focus. For a moment she thought she might be sick, but the sensation vanished when she saw Dennis unzip his jacket and reach inside.

Her throat convulsed when she spotted the bottle of red liquid, a rag stuffed into its neck. The investigators had found one just like it among the ashes of the shed. He inverted the bottle several times, soaking the rag. Lizzy caught the oily reek of kerosene as some of the liquid trickled through his fingers, down his sleeve, and onto the floor.

"Dennis, please." The pain in her jaw was so excruciating she thought she might black out. She grabbed the edge of the workbench to steady herself, willing herself to stay conscious, to keep him talking. "You don't want to do this."

He looked at her with a twisted smile, then took a step back. "Don't I?"

"The police know everything," she blurted, scanning the bench for something, anything, she might use as a weapon. "They know why Hollis killed himself. They know about the doll and the note, and that you burned the orchard. They have one of the torches you used to start the fire. If you do this, they'll know it was you. They'll put it together, and they'll come for you."

"It won't matter by then." Lizzy was stunned to see tears in his eyes. He blinked hard, but they spilled anyway. He smeared them away with the heel of his hand. "We paid enough, Hollis and me. Hollis most of all. It was supposed to be over. Paid in full. Now here you are, wanting us to pay all over again. Only that ain't how this is going to go." He paused, staring through her suddenly, his eyes dull and far away. "They say the only way to kill a witch is to burn her." He paused again, taking another step back, then gave the lighter a flick. "A man does what he has to."

"Noooo!"

Lizzy watched in horror as Dennis brought the kerosene-soaked rag toward the flame, aware in some terrified corner of her mind that she had slipped into one of those fractured moments when nothing seems real, when everything speeds up, and at the same time slows down, flickering one horrifying frame at a time.

The beaker felt cool as her fingers closed around it. An instant's hesitation, a ribbon of fear, and then it was airborne. She watched, transfixed, as it arced cleanly toward its target, a tail of alcohol in its wake, then erupted in a rush of blue flame as it connected with the lighter in Dennis's hand. His sleeve caught first, quick tongues licking up the spilled kerosene. He stared at it, eyes wide and blank, as if he were stunned to find himself on fire. Eventually, he began to flail, beating wildly at his jacket as the flames spread, blue-orange and hungry.

Lizzy opened her mouth to scream but there was no one to hear, no one coming to help. And it was already too late. She registered the sound of shattering glass as the milk bottle crashed to the floor, then a burst of heat and light as the kerosene flashed.

Dennis was engulfed in seconds, shrieking as the flames swallowed him whole. He thrashed briefly, then folded to his knees, a macabre marionette whose strings had been cut. He writhed a moment more, facedown in the flames, like a swimmer out of water, then went still.

Lizzy gulped back panicky sobs as bile swam up into her throat. She covered her nose and mouth, the stench of kerosene and charred flesh suddenly overwhelming. The flames were spreading rapidly now, devouring swaths of bone-dry timber as they crawled across the floor and up one of the walls. In minutes her only path to safety would be blocked.

Breath held, she dropped to her knees—something she'd learned in grade school fire drills—and scurried past the lapping flames. The barn had grown strangely dark as clouds of greasy smoke swallowed the wavering firelight. Lizzy groped her way to the door, fumbling frantically with the latch.

There was a deep huff of air as she burst through the door, like a sharply indrawn breath, and then a searing burst of wind that sent her sprawling into the dirt. She lay there a moment, choking down mouthfuls of clean air. The barn was engulfed now, moaning and crackling as the flames continued to feed, churning inky smoke into a pristine blue sky.

The sight should have gutted her, but she felt strangely numb as she watched the devastation, as if her mind had somehow become unmoored from her body. She should *do* something, call someone, but she suddenly found herself incapable of stringing two thoughts together. In the distance the wail of sirens, thin at first, then louder, closer. She closed her eyes. Someone had seen the smoke. Someone was coming.

FORTY

Lizzy shifted the disposable ice pack on her jaw and opened her eyes, willing her vision to clear. Blurred vision. Vomiting. Confusion. All consistent with a blow to the head, and all signs of a concussion, according to Janie, the paramedic who had advised her in the strongest terms possible to go to the ER, get herself X-rayed, and have her pulmonary function assessed. At least the ringing in her ears had subsided. She'd even gotten most of the assessment questions right, fumbling only the name of the current president.

Somewhere in the middle of the assessment, she had blurted out that they would find Dennis Hanley in the barn. Janie's partner, Hal, had disappeared soon after, presumably to inform whoever was in charge that they would need to call the ME's office.

"All set?" Janie asked, as they prepared to load her into the back of the medic rig. "Hal's playing chauffeur. I'll be in back with you."

Lizzy nodded, looking down at the straps securing her to the stretcher. It wasn't like she had a choice.

"Wait! Please!" It was Rhanna, wild-eyed and breathless, churning up the driveway. "Let me see her, please! Lizzy, baby—" She broke off with a gasp, her eyes swimming with tears. "My god—your face."

Lizzy narrowed her eyes, struggling to focus. "What are you doing back?"

"Never mind that! What happened to you?"

"I'm okay," she mumbled around the ice pack. "They just want to check me out. Where's Evvie?"

"She's behind me somewhere. We had to park on the street. We saw the smoke . . ." She reached for Lizzy's hand, her face crumpling. "Oh, baby . . . how did this happen?"

Janie stepped in before Lizzy could respond. "Sorry. We need to take her now. She'll be at Memorial."

"Right. Sorry." She smiled at Lizzy as she stepped back, but her chin began to wobble. "We'll be right behind you."

"No. Wait. Will you ride with me?" Lizzy's eyes slid to Janie's. "Can she? She's my mother."

Janie hiked a shoulder. "Works for me. What do you say, Mom—ready to roll?"

Rhanna brought Evvie up to speed while Janie and Hal loaded Lizzy into the rig and prepared for transport. When Hal gave the signal, Rhanna climbed in and settled beside Janie.

Lizzy reached for her hand as the rig started down the driveway. "Thanks for coming with me."

Rhanna wiped her eyes, a smile trembling at her lips. "Sorry to be such a Weepy Wilma. It's just . . . before, when you asked if I could ride with you, did you say I was your mother because you thought she'd say no if I weren't?"

Lizzy was surprised to feel the prickle of tears behind her own lids. "I said it because it's who you are. I saw your face just now, when you saw me strapped to this stretcher. You were scared—for me." She closed her eyes, swallowing convulsively as Althea's words drifted back. *Bridges can be built across the widest chasms, even when all we have to build with are broken pieces.* "It's time to stop punishing you."

~

Lizzy squinted at the vision chart tacked to the trauma room wall until the double images finally resolved into one. The glare from the overhead fluorescents wasn't doing her headache any favors. Unfortunately, in the case of concussion, most pain meds were contraindicated. They'd given her acetaminophen, but so far it hadn't helped much.

After much pleading, the doctor had agreed to let her go home, but only because Rhanna had promised to keep her still, wake her every few hours, just to be on the safe side, and strictly prohibit all electronics, which shouldn't be difficult now that her cell phone had been reduced to ash.

Lizzy looked up as the vinyl room divider slid back and Evvie appeared. She faltered as her gaze settled on Lizzy.

"Oh, my little girl. All broken up, and black-and-blue. I knew something was wrong. I could feel it. That's why we packed up early. I knew . . ."

Lizzy touched the butterfly closure on her lip. "It's not as bad as it looks. Just some bruises and a little concussion."

"Humph. I'm guessing you haven't seen yourself. And there's no such thing as a *little* concussion. They said your jaw might be broken."

"It's not. Just a bone bruise, which looks worse than it is. I might be living on Cream of Wheat for a while, though."

Evvie rolled her eyes as she pulled a tissue from her handbag and blotted her eyes. "You could have been killed."

"But I wasn't." Lizzy pulled in a shaky breath, fingers pleating the thin hospital blanket, as the seconds ticked by on the black-and-white wall clock. "It was Hollis Hanley, Evvie," she said finally. "He killed the girls, and Dennis was afraid I'd find it out. The note, the orchard, all of it, was to protect Hollis."

Evvie nodded, her face grave. "Your mama told me. Have you talked to the police yet?"

"They sent a detective to take my statement. The same guy I spoke to about the break-in. Apparently, he's a friend of Roger's."

She'd been surprised to find Michael Hammond waiting for her when they wheeled her back from X-ray, until he explained that Roger had given him a heads-up after their conversation. He let her know that Dennis's remains had been recovered from the debris. Unfortunately, with only dental records to go on, it would probably be several days before they had a definitive ID.

"I told him about the paper the note was written on, how it reminded me of the stuff butchers use to wrap meat. He's going to the plant where Dennis worked tomorrow to see if it matches, and to compare the knives they use with the one the police found the night of the break-in. We still won't have solid proof linking Hollis to the murders, but the circumstantial evidence certainly points to him."

"It's enough," Evvie told her evenly. "And past time for it all to be over."

Lizzy thought about that, about what it would feel like for it all to be over, to finally have the questions answered, the pieces all neatly linked. This didn't feel like that. There was no rush of relief. No sense of closure. There were only more questions.

"I hope so," she said, quietly.

"What aren't you saying?"

"Nothing, probably. But it's ironic, don't you think? Dennis spent years trying to cover up what happened that night, and all he ended up doing was ruining his life. Why? Hollis was dead." She paused, probing her swollen lower lip. "I can't help thinking . . ." She closed her eyes, fighting a shudder. She'd heard about death by fire—all their kind had—but seeing it with your own eyes was something else entirely. "The last thing he said was *A man does what he has to.* It was like he thought he had no other choice."

"Hush," Evvie hissed. "You did what you set out to do, and that's an end to it."

Lizzy nodded, silent. She wanted it to be true.

FORTY-ONE

Andrew smelled smoke long before he spotted the fire trucks. His gut twisted when he turned the corner and saw the emergency vehicles clogging the road, the reflective orange-and-white barricades blocking through traffic. He parked as close as the barricades would allow, not bothering to pull the keys from the ignition, and hit the ground at a run.

The house was fine. So was the shop. Which left the barn. He followed the trail of flaccid fire hoses up the drive, faltering briefly when he spotted the plain white van sitting with its back doors flung wide.

No water in the hoses. No medic rig on the street. ME already on scene. Whatever had happened was winding down—and someone was dead.

The thought hit him like a fist.

A fug of smoke and wet ash hung in the air, turning the evening sky a filthy shade of gray. He could taste soot at the back of his throat, and his eyes were beginning to sting and blur. He slowed long enough to wipe his face, then cut across the field, climbing to the top of the rise where he could see the back half of the property.

He saw it then, beyond the rise, a blackened shell where the barn should have been. The roof was gone, the charred walls splayed open like an overripe seedpod. Against the darkening sky, it looked like something from a nightmare.

A handful of firefighters were milling about, masks removed, poking through the steaming wreckage with shovels and axes. The mop-up team. Andrew made a beeline for the guy closest to him and tapped him on the shoulder.

The man swung around, his sooty face a mix of surprise and annoyance. "No one's supposed to be in this area, pal. Not until the reflash team gives the all clear."

"I need to know . . ."

Andrew's words dangled as he spotted two men dressed in navy coveralls emerging from the wreckage, a black body bag stretched between them. Another gut punch.

"Who . . ." The saliva in his mouth was suddenly thick. "I need to know who . . ."

The firefighter turned his head, following Andrew's gaze to the body bag. He leaned on his shovel, glancing down at his boots, as if suddenly uncomfortable. "Can't help you there. Above my pay grade. But maybe somebody else can." He cupped a hand around his mouth. "Tammy!" He waited until Tammy came over. "Any idea on the fatality?"

She pulled off her helmet, pushing back the sweaty blonde strands that had escaped her ponytail. She ran her eyes over Andrew, sizing him up. "You family?"

"No. I'm . . . a friend."

She nodded, her face softening. "At this point, we don't know. The body was . . . pretty bad. I'm sorry. I'm guessing the police will send someone to the hospital to talk to the girl."

Andrew felt a wave of dizziness wash through him. "Girl?"

"The one who lives here. I don't know her name."

Andrew thought his legs might buckle. "Lizzy Moon? She's at the hospital?"

"Memorial. She was lucky to get out."

"Was she . . ." He let the word dangle, unspoken. *Burned. Was she burned?* "How bad was she hurt?"

Tammy's eyes were full of sympathy. "I don't know. I'm sorry. We had our hands full at that point. All I know is the medics took her away."

Andrew threw a *thank-you* over his shoulder as he turned away, already churning his way back to the street, feet keeping time with the words pounding in his head.

Not dead. Not dead. Not dead.

~

The emergency room was a study in controlled chaos. Patients in various states of illness and injury were stacked into rows of green plastic chairs, wearing facial expressions that ran the gamut from bored discomfort to genuine misery.

Andrew moved past them to the admittance desk. A nurse in faded pink scrubs greeted him brusquely, eyes already assessing him for life-threatening conditions. When she found none, she reached for one of the preloaded check-in clipboards.

Andrew waved it away. "No. I'm looking for a patient. Lizzy Moon. The medics would have brought her in a couple hours ago. There was a fire . . ."

The nurse scanned the computer screen to her left. "Yup. She's in trauma room four. Are you family?"

"I'm a friend of the family. Is she all right?"

"I'm sorry. I'm afraid I can't tell you anything more. Her mother's with her. If you'd like to have a seat, I'll let her know you're here."

Andrew dropped into the nearest chair, wondering what Rhanna was doing here. She was supposed to be in Connecticut. Moments later, she appeared. He shot to his feet, trying to read her face. She looked shaken and exhausted but not grief-stricken.

She captured both his hands, squeezing hard. "She's all right. She's got a concussion, but it sounds like they're going to let her go home."

A hundred questions crowded into his head as the initial wave of panic began to ebb. "I went to the house, saw the fire trucks. They were taking someone out in a body bag, and I thought—"

"She got out," Rhanna said, cutting him off before he could say it out loud. "She's safe." She pulled her hands free, dropping them to her sides. "Dennis Hanley's dead."

The body bag. Dennis. He let it sink in. "Did she tell you what happened?"

"She was out in the barn. Dennis showed up with a bottle of kerosene—like the ones they found in the orchard. He was going to burn the barn with her in it, to keep anyone from finding out what his brother did to Heather and Darcy Gilman." Her eyes had gone shiny. She blinked away the unshed tears, suddenly focused again. "She threw something at him as he was about to light the rag—some alcohol, I think—and his sleeve caught fire. When he dropped the bottle of kerosene, the whole place went up. She barely made it out."

"Is she . . ."

"No," Rhanna answered quickly. "No burns. But he hit her. Her face is a mess."

Andrew squeezed his eyes shut, the sudden rush of fury so strong he could taste it. For a moment he found himself wishing Dennis Hanley wasn't already in a body bag.

Rhanna put a hand on his arm. "Do you want to see her? I'll tell them it's okay."

She didn't wait for an answer, just stepped away. A short time later, she returned. "They said you can go in. I'll take you. Evvie's with her now, but I'll pull her out."

Lizzy was holding an ice pack to her face when he walked in. She lowered it when she saw him and met his gaze. He had tried to prepare himself for his first glimpse of her, imagining how she might look, what it would feel like to see her hurt, but it hadn't been enough. There was no way he could have prepared for the angry bruise already forming on the left side of her face, the swollen mouth, the bandaged lip. Anyone looking at her would swear she'd gone twelve rounds with a prizefighter—and lost.

"Look who I found, Lizzy," Rhanna said, breaking the awkward silence. "And just in time too. The doctor wants you to hang out a little longer, but she said if nothing changes, you can go home in a few hours. I've been wondering how we were going to get you home with Evvie's wagon packed to the roof. Now you can ride with Andrew." She looked at Evvie, crooking a finger. "You and I need to step out. The nurse said only one at a time."

When they were alone, Andrew stepped to Lizzy's bedside. "Jesus. I'm so sorry."

She blinked at him. "For what?"

"For being an hour and a half away when this happened. For disappearing in a huff because my ego was a little banged up. I should never have left for Boston."

"I told you to go, Andrew. You had work to do, and I had . . ." She paused, cocking an eye at him. "Come to think of it, what are you doing here?"

"Roger called me. He said he told you to stay by your phone, but you weren't picking up. He called me to see if we'd spoken. He told me about your run-in with Dennis, said he had a bad feeling. So I started calling. When you didn't answer, I came home. Then I got to the house and saw the fire trucks . . ." He paused, remembering the sinking feeling in his gut when he saw the ME's van.

"I'm okay," Lizzy said, waving off the rest before he could get it out. "But let's not talk about it anymore right now. I'm tired."

She lay back and closed her eyes, and for a moment he simply watched her breathe, grateful for the steady rise and fall of her chest. She looked small and pale in her faded hospital gown. Fragile. The memory of the body bag being carried from the remains of the barn made his throat tighten as he stared at her face, bruised and streaked with soot. He'd nearly lost her. Except she wasn't his to lose.

FORTY-TWO

August 20

Lizzy opened her eyes to watery light and the scent of coming rain filtering through the parlor windows. She was groggy and stiff, her neck painfully kinked after a night spent propped up on the settee, where Evvie and Rhanna could take turns keeping an eye on her.

It had been well after midnight when they finally returned home. Rhanna had helped her out of her clothes and prepared a warm bath scented with chamomile, then helped her bathe and wash her hair. Afterward, she'd been bundled into a pair of soft flannel pajamas and tucked up on the settee with a pillow and blanket, the way Althea had done when Lizzy was little and down with a stomachache or a cold.

She could hear Rhanna in the kitchen now, talking with Evvie, their voices lost amid the sound of running water. It wasn't hard to guess the topic of their conversation. She threw back the covers and sat up gingerly. The room swayed as she pushed to her feet. She waited for the dizziness to pass, then padded toward the kitchen.

Rhanna flashed her a look of disapproval as she reached the doorway. "What do you think you're doing?"

"Getting some coffee."

"I'll bring you coffee. You lie back down. There's enough of a mess in here with all this black dust everywhere. We don't need you on the floor to boot."

"You know there's nothing wrong with my legs, right? I'm perfectly capable of standing."

"And perfectly capable of falling down and cracking your head again," Rhanna shot back. "Let's go."

Lizzy allowed herself to be steered back to the settee. Rhanna gave her pillows a quick plumping, then pulled back the blanket. "Down you go."

"Thank you," Lizzy said as Rhanna retucked her blanket. "For taking care of me."

Rhanna's lips curved, a soft, fleeting smile. "It's me who should be saying thank you. After all the years, and all the mistakes, I've been given a second chance. And then yesterday I almost lost you. It made me realize how much I've missed." She shrugged heavily. "I guess I'm trying to make up for lost time."

Lizzy swallowed the sudden lump in her throat. "You look tired. Did you get any sleep?"

Before Rhanna could respond, there was a knock on the front door. Rhanna stepped away to answer it, returning a moment later with Andrew in tow.

"You've got company," she announced cheerfully. "And perfect timing too. He can make sure you stay put while I brew a fresh pot of coffee."

Andrew watched her go, then turned to Lizzy. "You look better."

Lizzy rolled her eyes. "Liar."

"Okay. You look *cleaner*." He eased into the armchair nearest the settee, forearms propped on his knees. "Seriously, though, how are you?"

"Sore. I feel like I've been pummeled with a baseball bat. Other than that, I'm okay. Rhanna's doting on me like I'm an invalid. She's been wonderful, actually."

Andrew's gaze strayed to the coffee table. This morning's copy of the *Chronicle* lay folded in half, presumably where Evvie had left it after reading it. Lizzy had already seen the headline. SECOND BLAZE AT MOON GIRL FARM TURNS DEADLY.

Andrew picked it up, scowling at the photo of the collapsed barn. "Have you read it?"

"I don't have to. I was there."

He tossed the paper down with a look of disgust. "I should have seen it coming."

Lizzy stared at him. "How? Dennis wasn't on anyone's radar."

"Maybe, but he should have been on mine. He said something once, about you having the nerve to come back here and stir up talk about the murders. He trash-talked the Moons in general, but it was mostly you he focused on. I should have put it together."

"Why would you? It's nothing half this town hasn't said at one time or another. And there were things we didn't know, Andrew. Things no one knew—and never will now that Dennis is dead. But it's over. No one will ever be charged. But we know what happened, or at least who was to blame. And the Gilmans will know too. And the rest of Salem Creek can believe what they want. They always have."

Rhanna appeared holding a mug with a paper straw in it. She handed it to Lizzy, then turned to Andrew. "Can I get you one before I head to the market?"

"Thanks, no. I've already had more than my share this morning."

Evvie came bustling out of the kitchen, wearing a pair of bright-yellow rubber gloves. "Not so fast," she said to Rhanna. "I need to add some more cleaning stuff to that list of yours. The more I scrub, the more that mess spreads. It's like the *Exxon Valdez* ran aground in there."

Lizzy ducked her head sheepishly and slid her eyes to Andrew. "I forgot to warn her about the fingerprint dust last night before we got home."

"Oops."

Another set of raps sounded on the front door, this time with the knocker. Rhanna pocketed her list and went to answer it. After several minutes of muffled conversation, she returned.

"It's Helen Hanley, Lizzy. She's out on the steps, asking to talk to you."

Lizzy stared at her. She knew Helen had been notified of her brother-in-law's death, but had no idea how many of the details had been shared, or how she'd taken the news.

Andrew pushed out of his chair. "You don't need to talk to her if you're not up to it, Lizzy. I can send her away."

Lizzy flashed back to yesterday's confrontation at the market, the silent plea in Helen's eyes, the bruise she had tried, and failed, to cover. She had one of her own now to match it.

"No. Don't send her away. I'll talk to her."

Evvie and Andrew exchanged glances but said nothing.

A few moments later, Helen stood in the parlor, her little girl perched solidly on one hip. Her eyes were puffy and red rimmed, and she wore no makeup. The yellow-green bruise stood out in ugly relief against her cheek.

"I'm sorry I had to bring Kayla. I couldn't get a sitter on short notice, and I didn't want to wait." Her hand came to her mouth, her eyes pooling with tears. "Oh my god . . . your face. This is all my fault."

Lizzy sat up and patted the settee beside her. "Why don't you sit down?"

Helen eased down onto the settee and folded her daughter into her lap. She was crying softly, swallowing sobs as she pushed the words out. "The police came last night. They told me about Dennis—about what he tried to do. I came to say I'm sorry."

"It was Dennis, Helen. You have nothing to apologize for."

"I do," Helen sobbed brokenly. "I've been a coward. All these years, I've let him bully me into keeping quiet, and last night he almost killed you." She sniffled loudly, using the collar of her shirt to blot her tears. "I'm going to the police when I leave here. I should have done it last night, but I wanted to talk to you first, to look you in the eye and say I'm sorry. For what happened to you yesterday, and what happened to your family all those years ago. I should have ended it when Hollis died. I should have, but I didn't."

Andrew leaned forward, forearms braced on his knees. "You're talking about Heather and Darcy Gilman."

Helen hung her head. "Hollis was a good man. He was simple and gentle, but he was broken too. Even before Afghanistan. But he was worse when he came home. He was withdrawn, and he had nightmares. He started drinking. I begged him to get help, to see someone, but he wouldn't. Then I found out about a group that met over in Rochester. PTSD sufferers dealing with the things they'd seen and done. I finally convinced him to go. Then Dennis got wind of it, and that was that. He made it clear that I didn't get a vote. It didn't matter that my husband was a basket case, or that there was a little girl who needed her daddy to get better."

She had begun to cry again. She wiped her eyes, flashing Kayla a *Mommy's all right* smile before going on. "I was furious at him for letting Dennis push him around. One night he got drunk and we had a horrible fight. That's when it came out."

Lizzy knotted her hands in her lap, willing herself to be patient. She'd waited eight years to learn the truth. She could wait a few minutes more.

Kayla had begun to squirm in her mother's lap. Helen jiggled her gently, then pressed a kiss to the top of her blonde head. When she was quiet again, Helen went on. "The summer the girls disappeared, Hollis and Dennis had started hanging out with them. Hollis was never a ladies man, so Dennis hooked them up. The four of them would go out riding around. Dennis would bring along a few bottles of smash."

Lizzy frowned, unfamiliar with the word. "Smash?"

"A concoction of hard cider and homemade hooch. It's cheap, and you don't need an ID to buy it. Plus, it gets you drunk pretty fast. And according to Hollis, Heather liked to get drunk. She was kind of screwed-up. Had a lot going on at home, apparently. Dad stuff."

Lizzy seized on the offhand remark. "Dad stuff?"

"She told Dennis she woke up one night and found her father standing over her bed, and that he was always walking in on her when she was getting dressed. He'd pretend it was an accident, but she said it happened all the time. One time, she came right out and told Dennis that's why she was hanging out with him, because it drove her daddy crazy. Anyway, one night the four of them were riding around. They ended up back at old man Hanley's place. Heather and Dennis went off on their own. Darcy stayed with Hollis in the car. But when Hollis started getting friendly, she got spooked. She said she needed to pee and wandered away. When she didn't come back, Hollis went looking for her."

Evvie had been standing in the doorway. She stepped forward now, clearly troubled by what she was hearing, but perhaps more uncomfortable with the fact that there was a little girl in the room. "Maybe Kayla would like to go out to the garden with Rhanna and me," she suggested pointedly. "While the grown-ups talk?"

Helen looked confused at first, then glanced at Kayla and seemed to understand. "Oh, right. Are you sure you don't mind?"

"She'll be fine with us," Rhanna assured her, smiling that smile women reserve for children under three. "Kayla, is it? What a pretty name."

Helen mouthed a silent *thank-you* as she relinquished her daughter. "That's a good girl. Go with the nice ladies. Mommy will be right here."

"We'll be right out back if you need us," Evvie called as they headed for the mudroom.

Helen looked suddenly bereft without her daughter. She glanced from Lizzy to Andrew, and back again. "I'm sorry. I should have thought about Kayla. She won't remember her daddy, but she doesn't need to hear the rest of this. I'm just so . . . I haven't been sleeping well since Dennis moved in."

Lizzy didn't bother to hide her surprise. "You and Dennis were . . ."

"No." Helen shuddered visibly. "Nothing like that. But he moved in a few weeks ago. He said it was so he could help with Kayla, but I think it was to make sure I stayed quiet."

"Dennis knew that you knew what happened to the girls?"

"He did. Hollis told him about getting drunk and spilling everything. Dennis was furious. That's when he started watching me."

"You said Hollis went looking for Darcy when she didn't come back," Lizzy prompted, wanting to get back to the night the Gilman girls died.

Helen closed her eyes, as if preparing herself. After a few minutes, she blew out a breath and squared her shoulders. "It took a while, but he finally found her. She was bent over, throwing up from all the smash. She started crying when she saw him, and took off running. Hollis went after her. Not to hurt her, just to keep her from going where she shouldn't. But it was too late. By the time he caught up to her, she wasn't in the cornfields anymore. She was in the back fields, where Hollis's daddy didn't let anyone go."

"Because of the marijuana," Lizzy said quietly, stealing a glance in Andrew's direction. Not a flicker of surprise. Had everyone known?

"Yeah," Helen said, nodding. "The pot. There was this big shed out there where they used to dry the stuff. Darcy ran toward it. I guess she thought she could hide. All of a sudden the door opened and out came Mr. Hanley, drunk as a skunk and waving a shotgun. Darcy started screaming. The old man didn't bat an eye. He just stepped up behind her and smashed in the back of her head with the butt of his rifle. She went down like a ton of bricks." She paused, a hand to her mouth. "Hollis said he used to hear the sound of her skull cracking when he closed his eyes at night."

Lizzy fought an unexpected wave of queasiness. Helen's story fit perfectly with the coroner's findings. *Blunt force trauma to the occipital and parietal regions.* But that was what killed Darcy. The ME's report said Heather had been strangled. "What about Heather?"

"She and Dennis must have heard Darcy screaming, because they came running. Heather took one look at Darcy facedown in the dirt, and started wailing her head off. Even drunk, the old man could see he was in trouble. He told Dennis to shut her up. When Dennis didn't move, his father pointed the gun at him. He said if Dennis didn't shut Heather up, he'd do it himself, and then he'd shut the boys up too. Dennis didn't realize the old man was serious until he pointed the gun at Hollis. He knew Dennis's weak spot."

Andrew's mouth dropped open. "He threatened to shoot his own son?"

Helen nodded. She looked paler now than when she'd first arrived, drained and shaky. "He would have done it too. Dennis knew it, even if Hollis didn't, so he wrapped an arm around Heather's throat and just . . . squeezed. She fought but he was too strong. Hollis was horrified at how long it took—nothing like it happens in the movies—but finally she stopped fighting."

Lizzy remained silent, shaken by the gruesome scene Helen had just painted—and by the realization that Dennis's determination to keep the truth buried had more to do with his own guilt than with either his father's or brother's.

"The pond," Lizzy said numbly. "How did the girls wind up in the pond?"

"Mr. Hanley told them to fill the girls' pockets with stones from the wall behind the shed, and then drag them into the pond. When they didn't snap to, he told them to stop acting like girls. He said a man does what he has to. I guess it worked, because they did what he said. Not that they had much choice. They were in it too by then. It was Dennis who called in the anonymous tip, to make the police think it was your grandmother who'd killed them."

A man does what he has to.

Lizzy suppressed a shudder. Dennis had used the same words yesterday. His father's words. That had been his father's legacy—the murders of two young girls and then covering up the evidence. She frowned suddenly. "You said *they* were in it—Hollis *and* Dennis—but Hollis wasn't in it. He didn't hurt either of the girls."

Helen stared down at her hands, her fingers so tightly laced that her knuckles had gone white. A tear slid down her cheek, then another. Finally, she lifted her head. "They loaded the girls into an old cart and wheeled it to the pond. Dennis waded in with Heather first, and watched her sink. But when Hollis picked Darcy up, she let out a moan."

Lizzy's stomach did a slow, queasy roll. She'd forgotten the rest of what Roger had said. One of the girls—Darcy—had shown evidence of drowning. She looked at Helen, unable to find words.

"Dennis didn't say anything but Hollis knew. They had to finish it. Dennis took hold of Darcy's legs, and they dragged her in. They waited, just to make sure, but she stayed down."

Salt and stagnant water . . . like a mud flat at low tide. Or a pond.

"She was alive when she went into the water," Lizzy whispered, registering the horror of it. "She might have survived the blow to the head if she hadn't been dragged into the pond."

"Hollis never forgave himself."

And there it was. The reason Hollis had driven his car into a tree. Lizzy closed her eyes, trying to blot out the image in her head. "When he . . . died," she said haltingly, "there was a note. You gave it to the police, but they left it behind. Then it disappeared."

Andrew pulled several tissues from the box Rhanna had placed nearby for Lizzy and passed them to Helen. She took them with a grateful nod. "That was Dennis," she said, dabbing at her eyes. "He told me to burn it, to say I never saw it. He was afraid people would tie what Hollis wrote back to the girls."

"It was never about Hollis. All of it—the note, the fire—was about protecting himself. Because he killed Heather."

"I'm not sure Dennis knew the difference anymore. His whole identity was wrapped up in being Hollis's protector. When Hollis died, he lost that. Then he lost the farm. And then he heard you were back, and asking questions. That's when things got bad. When the stories started showing up in the paper, I knew it was him, but I couldn't say anything. He said he'd take Kayla, and I'd never find her."

"Did he mean he'd take her and run, or that he'd hurt her?"

Helen's eyes flashed with remembered panic. "I don't know. I just knew something terrible would happen if I went to the police. That's why I bumped into you yesterday and said what I did. I didn't know what else to do. And then last night, the police came to the door, and I thought . . ." She paused, pressing a hand to her mouth. "When they told me you got out, that you were okay, I knew I had to tell the police everything—and give them the letter Hollis wrote before he died."

Lizzy gaped at her. "You *have* the letter?"

"It was the last thing he ever wrote, and he wrote it to me. I couldn't just burn it. I'm going to take it to the police and tell them everything. But I needed to see you first. I felt like I owed it to you—and your grandmother. I know I can never be sorry enough, but I had to say it anyway."

"Thank you for that," Lizzy said quietly, knowing just how hard today must have been for her. "The bruise on your cheek—that was Dennis?"

She touched the discoloration gingerly. "He came home drunk, making a lot of noise. I had just gotten Kayla to sleep and I asked him to be quiet."

Andrew blew out a slow breath, like a pressure cooker releasing steam. "I know Dennis was helping you financially. Will you and Kayla be able to manage?"

Helen shrugged, wadding the tissues in her hand. "I don't know. I haven't had time to think about it. My parents are in Florida. They'd probably let me come, but I have to talk to the police first. I might end up in jail for not telling them what I knew."

Andrew scrubbed a thumb over his chin as he mulled over her response. "Why don't you wait a day before talking to the police? Lizzy and I have a friend, a detective, who might be able to offer some advice. And you need to get yourself a lawyer before you say anything."

Helen's face fell. "I can't afford a lawyer. Especially now."

"Let us worry about that."

Helen blinked at him, genuinely stunned. "I don't know what to say. After everything . . . I don't deserve that sort of kindness."

Lizzy met Andrew's eyes briefly, then laid a hand on Helen's. "There's been enough harm done, Helen. You ending up in jail won't undo any of it. Let us help you if we can."

"All right then. Thank you." Helen stood, sniffling, and pushed her crumpled tissues into her pocket. "I'd better find Kayla and go. I work at two, and I have things to do. Should I just wait to hear from you?"

"I'll make a call. It shouldn't be long."

Andrew took Helen out to the garden to find Kayla. Lizzy remained on the settee, drained and numb. She'd wanted the truth, and she'd gotten it. All of it.

The twisted lives of the Hanley boys, the by-product of a drunken and morally bankrupt father. Two girls brutally murdered, because one of them was afraid to go home. Her skin crawled at the thought of Fred Gilman standing over his daughter's bed. At some point, she'd need to call Susan. She deserved to know the truth, and not from a headline in the *Chronicle*.

After years of heartache, she would finally know what happened to her girls, but the grief and the questions would never end. How could they when the loss was so inexplicably cruel?

There was no way to know if her husband had ever acted on his fixation with Heather, but it was hard to look at the chain of events and not conclude that it had played a role in the behaviors that ultimately led to her oldest daughter's death. And poor Darcy had been collateral damage.

As for Fred Gilman, he'd soon have a new demon to wrestle—himself. He'd spent the last eight years accusing Althea Moon of murder. Now he could live with the knowledge that to some extent at least, he'd been culpable in the deaths of his daughters. But then he'd probably known that all along. And maybe that was the most fitting punishment of all. Guilt was a cruel and relentless jailer.

FORTY-THREE

The sound of the mudroom door jolted Lizzy from her musings. She met Andrew's eyes as he reappeared. "Is she gone?"

"Yeah. And Evvie and Rhanna are on their way to the market. You okay?"

"It's just so much to wrap my head around. I'm still digesting."

"I should have asked you before I volunteered to help Helen. I'm sorry I didn't."

"No. I'm glad you did. I saw the look on her face yesterday at the market. She was truly terrified of him. I can't blame her for staying quiet. I would have done the same thing if I had a little girl to protect."

"So should we give Roger a call? I can put my phone on speaker."

"The sooner, the better. You know this town. Word's going to get out, and it'll be better for Helen if she goes to the police before they come to her."

"I agree." Andrew pulled out his phone and scrolled through his contacts, hit the call button, and set the phone down on the table between them. It rang three times before Roger picked up.

"Hey, it's Andrew. Have you got a minute? I need to run something by you."

"I do, but first, how's Lizzy? I just got off the phone with Michael Hammond. He told me about last night. Jesus."

"She's here with me. She's pretty banged up, but she's got plenty of nurses. I think we might need another favor, though. A big one this time."

"Okay. Let me have it."

"Let's say, hypothetically, that I have someone who can tell the police exactly what happened to the Gilman girls, but that someone is afraid of going to jail for not coming forward sooner. If she was afraid for her life, or the life of someone close to her—a child, for instance—is there a chance the police would cut her some slack?"

"I'm assuming we're talking about Helen Hanley?"

Andrew caught Lizzy's eye, brows raised. Lizzy nodded, giving him the go-ahead.

"She spilled everything, Roger. About Hollis, Dennis, even the old man. They were all there, all part of it. She's going to the police either way, but I was hoping there might be a way to help her, maybe someone you could talk to. She didn't come forward because Dennis was threatening her. She has a little girl, Roger."

There was a long pause. Lizzy held her breath, waiting.

"I need to hear her story," Roger said finally. "If I'm satisfied, I'll ask my brother to arrange a meeting with someone in the DA's office. She could be looking at accessory after the fact. She didn't just protect her husband. She protected his brother and her father-in-law, and there's no privilege for in-laws. But if she really was afraid for her life, or her daughter's, there might be a deal to be had. Give me a couple hours to make some calls and take some temperatures. I'll call you back when I know something. We can set a time to talk if we need to. Until then, she shouldn't talk to anyone."

"It sounds like there's at least a chance," Lizzy said when Andrew ended the call. "I'm glad. Even if she did have a legal obligation to come forward, the police can't blame her for protecting her child. And she's doing the right thing now."

"I think they'll see her as credible. All you have to do is look at her to know she was scared silly. I had to help her get Kayla in the car seat. Her hands were shaking so bad she couldn't do the straps. I told her I'd call her tonight after I hear back from Roger."

"Speaking of phones, I guess I'll need a new cell phone."

Andrew eyed her sternly. "No driving for you yet. I'll take you in a day or two. Right now you need to rest."

"I am a little worn-out," she admitted, sensing a potentially awkward shift in topic. "Maybe I'll try to nap while the house is quiet."

"Can I get you anything? Jell-O? Soup?"

Lizzy flashed back to something Evvie had asked once. Did she have someone to fix her soup? She'd said no at the time, but she did have someone now—if she wanted him. And she did want him. More than she had allowed herself to admit. But letting him stay and play nurse was a bad idea. For starters, she'd be sending mixed signals, not to mention the very real possibility that she would drop her guard again. She'd hurt him once. She wasn't doing it again.

"Thanks, but I'm good." She managed a smile, wincing as the butterfly closure over her top lip pulled. "You need to get back to Boston. You have a business to run, clients to keep happy."

Andrew glanced away briefly, clearing his throat. "I'll stay, Lizzy. All you have to do is ask."

Be strong. Don't falter now. Say what you need to and let him go.

"I can't, Andrew."

"Can't or won't?"

"Both. You've done so much already. I need to let you get back to your life."

"So you can get back to yours?"

Lizzy forced herself to meet his gaze. "I had an email from the bank. The loan went through, which means I can start lining up the repairs, and Rhanna knows a real estate agent who owes her a favor. I should be able to wrap things up in about a week."

"Right," Andrew said, pushing to his feet. "Sounds like you've got it all worked out. I'll make you a list of reputable contractors before I leave town."

"Thank you." She blinked against the threat of tears, afraid some part of her would break open if she tried to say more. She watched, throat aching, as he headed for the door.

Let him go, Lizzy.

FORTY-FOUR

August 26

Lizzy braced herself as she caught sight of the barn—the first time since it had burned to the ground. Seven days had passed since the fire; four since Helen Hanley had spoken to the DA in exchange for immunity; three since Andrew had left for Boston.

The concussion symptoms had finally subsided, the bruising along her jaw had mellowed to an iridescent mix of violets and greens, and her lip was healing well, thanks to the salve of comfrey and geranium Rhanna had whipped up in the shop.

Rhanna walked beside her now, her face solemn beneath her fading California tan. They'd come to say a goodbye of sorts. The demolition crew Andrew had contracted to remove the remains of the barn had called to say they'd be arriving soon.

They stood silent for a time, shoulder to shoulder, looking down from the top of the rise. There wasn't a trace of Rhanna's mural left. It was just a charred hull now, scorched and jagged against the bright morning sky. It had been a landmark to some, an eyesore to others, and in a few hours it would be gone, scrubbed from the landscape.

The thought rocked Lizzy more than she cared to admit. She wasn't even gone yet, and it was already happening. Little by little, the Moons and their way of life were disappearing, the links of Althea's precious chain beginning to give way. It shouldn't matter. She was leaving soon. But it did, somehow. It was a piece of her past, a piece of all their pasts, and soon it would be nothing but a memory.

Lizzy and Rhanna turned in unison at the sound of gears grinding up the driveway. Another few minutes and the bulldozer was lumbering in their direction. A man in a hard hat and bright-orange vest kept pace a few steps behind, a clipboard in his hand.

Lizzy held her breath as the dozer came on, then breathed a sigh of relief when it halted just short of the barn, as if an eleventh-hour stay of execution had been granted. "I suppose I need to go down and give them the green light, or whatever it is I'm supposed to do."

The dozer operator had climbed down and joined his counterpart. They stood with their backs to Lizzy as she approached, gesturing now and then as they worked out a plan of attack. The man with the clipboard noticed her first.

"We're supposed to talk to Elzibeth Moon. Would that be you?"

"Yes. I'm Lizzy Moon."

He handed her the clipboard, pointing to the signature line at the bottom of the work order. "We'll need you to sign off—here."

Lizzy signed and handed back the clipboard.

"Anyone currently inside the structure?"

Lizzy eyed the charred ruin dubiously, but she supposed there were policies to follow. "No. No one."

"Good then. It shouldn't take long. The removal truck will be by later to clean up and haul it all away. We'll need you to move back, and stay clear until we wrap up."

Lizzy felt numb as she walked back up the rise to join Rhanna, her arms folded tight to her body. "We need to stay clear while they work. He said it won't take long."

Rhanna sank down onto the grass, sitting cross-legged. Lizzy sat beside her, knees hugged to her chest, watching as the men slowly circled the barn.

"I still can't believe it," Rhanna said, shaking her head. "It's just so horrible."

"I'm sorry. I know how much you loved that mural."

Rhanna's head snapped around. "I wasn't talking about the mural. I was talking about you—about what almost happened. What on earth were you doing in the barn anyway?"

Lizzy thought of the Earth Song, so close to completion—lost now. There wouldn't be time to re-create it before she left, so there really wasn't any point in keeping it a secret. "I was making perfume."

Rhanna's eyes widened. "You were not."

"The Earth Song you used to like—I was trying to re-create it. I wanted to surprise you with it before I left."

"Oh, baby. What a lovely thing to do."

She shrugged. "It's gone now. The fire . . ."

"No," Rhanna said, catching Lizzy's hand and holding it tight. "Don't you dare. You're here. I'm here. That's all that matters. Just knowing you wanted to do that . . ." She glanced down at their entwined hands and smiled. "I've been trying to figure it out since I've been back. Why I'm here, after the way things went down, all the messes I made. I thought it was to pay my dues, you know, like a penance. Now I know it wasn't that at all. I came back for *you*, Lizzy. I came back here to learn how to be your mother." She paused, smiling wistfully. "I know. My timing stinks. I'm about thirty-six years too late. But I'll always be grateful for these weeks with you."

Lizzy felt something let go in her chest as she met Rhanna's gaze, a bloom of emotion unfurling like petals under a warm sun. They'd come a long way in only a few short weeks, unpacking years of baggage, opening old wounds. Rhanna had laid herself open, owned her mistakes, and paid her penance. But what about her own wounds? A lifetime of resentment and blame, the ache of abandonment she'd never allowed herself to admit. Perhaps it was *she* who'd had the longer road to travel.

She laid a hand on Rhanna's arm, tentative about risking the unsolicited contact. "When you showed up . . . I was horrid to you. I didn't want you here because I didn't want to admit that it hurt that you never wanted me. I'd spent too many years pretending not to care to just let it all go. Growing up, I used to hope that one day you'd learn to like me, that we'd finally be a family, but you never did. Then you took off, and that was that. I guess I was trying to punish you. Now I understand why you did what you did, and I'm glad you came back, glad we had this chance to reconnect."

The bulldozer cranked up again, and they fell silent.

Lizzy raised a hand to block the sun, her throat constricting as the dozer moved in for its first pass, then backed up, repositioned, and advanced again. The fresh gouge in the earth left a hollow in the pit of her stomach. Time marched on, it seemed, even in Salem Creek.

Thirty minutes later, the remains of the barn had been reduced to a heap of charred timber, and the dozer was gone. Rhanna plucked several blades of grass and began to braid them together. "You're leaving soon, aren't you?"

Lizzy wasn't surprised by the question. There'd been a sense of finality in the air all morning. Apparently, Rhanna felt it too. "Yes."

"When?"

"A day or two."

Rhanna's face fell. "That soon?"

"I called Luc to let him know things were wrapping up. Andrew helped me line up a roofer and an electrician, and Billy Church emailed me the listing contract first thing this morning. Thanks for calling in that favor, by the way. You and Evvie are welcome to stay until the farm sells. That'll give you time to make plans. There'll be some insurance money from the fire. Not much, but that and the loan money should keep you afloat until we find a buyer."

"You're really going to do it," Rhanna said quietly.

"You thought I wasn't?"

Rhanna lifted a shoulder. "I guess I hoped you'd have a change of heart, that we'd reopen the shop and run it together. I thought you and Andrew might . . ."

"Live happily ever after?"

Rhanna smiled sheepishly. "Something like that, yeah. I was surprised that he left for Boston without saying goodbye."

"We already said our goodbyes."

"When? I didn't see him."

Lizzy blew out a breath. She'd been hoping to avoid this conversation. "The night of the break-in—when I wound up at Andrew's—we spent the night together."

"Oh, Lizzy . . ."

"The next morning I realized I'd made a mistake, and I slammed on the brakes. It wasn't fair to let him think we were ever going anywhere. I was trying to make things easier."

"Easier for who? The man's in love with you. And unless I miss my guess, you're in love with him too. How is any of that a mistake?"

"It just is," Lizzy shot back. "This isn't an episode of *Bewitched*. The happily-ever-after thing—the honeymoon, the kids, the Disney vacations—that's for other people. Normal people. And we both know that's not who we are. Andrew knows it too."

Rhanna stared at her. "You told him . . . about us?"

"I didn't have to tell him. He knew. He's always known, apparently. He swears it doesn't matter, and I think he even believes it. But eventually it will matter. He deserves the kind of life I could never give him."

Rhanna shook her head slowly. "Peter, Paul, and Mary. I knew you were stubborn, but I never realized you were stupid. You have a shot at something amazing, and you're just going to walk away? Because of some moldy old family tradition? Or because it might be messy? Times change, Lizzy. Even for people like us. The days of the solitary crone ended a century ago. There's no reason we can't have someone in our lives if we want to."

Lizzy threw a pointed glance at Rhanna's left hand. "I don't see a ring on your finger."

"No," Rhanna said softly. "You don't. I missed my window. But don't think for a minute that if I ever have the chance you have right now, I won't grab it with both hands. To have a man look at me the way Andrew looks at you? A man willing to take me on, in spite of my bizarre family baggage? You bet your sweet ass I would. Because I'd know how lucky I was, and just how rare a man like that is."

"You don't think I know what I'm walking away from? Of course I know. But there's more to it than that. There's my job, and this town—"

Rhanna caught Lizzy by the sleeve, cutting her off. "Lizzy, honey, this is your chance. *He's* your chance. And the rest of it's just crap."

Lizzy bit her tongue, unwilling to test their fledgling truce. It was easy for Rhanna. Until three weeks ago, she'd never committed to anything in her life, and especially not a man. She had no idea what it meant to risk her heart and lose. Come to that, neither had she. Until now.

She pulled free of Rhanna's grasp and stood. "I'm sorry. I need to get back. I still have things to pack."

She was halfway down the rise when she heard Rhanna call after her. "You're allowed to be happy, Lizzy."

～

Back at the house, Lizzy was greeted by the aroma of white sage smoke. She found Evvie in the parlor, a smoldering sage bundle in one hand, a saucer of spent ashes in the other.

"Thought it was time to give the place a good clean," she said, wafting white smoke up into the corners. "I did the upstairs first, and made sure all the windows were open. Let all the bad juju out."

Lizzy forced a smile, recalling their first meeting, face-to-face in this very room, the prickly words and hard glances. She would miss Evvie. Her gruff wisdom and fierce loyalty. Her homegrown honey and Creole lullabies. She claimed to have plans for after the farm sold—for both herself and her bees—but thus far had kept those plans to herself. Perhaps she would return to Baton Rouge. Or head to Texas to be with her sister. Both were viable options. Still, it was hard to imagine her anywhere but the farm.

As far as Lizzy knew, Rhanna hadn't made any plans for the future. Apparently she'd been holding out hope that Moon Girl Farm would remain in the family, and together they'd reopen the shop. She hoped their conversation had squelched any further thoughts in that direction.

"Where's your mama?" Evvie inquired through a scrim of pale smoke.

"I left her up on the rise," Lizzy said, not quite meeting her eyes. "I told her I'd be leaving in a few days."

Evvie lowered her smudge stick and nodded mutely.

"I know you wanted this to end differently, Evvie. And for a while I think I lost sight of the promises I made when I decided to come. But now I've done what I came to do, and it's time to go back. I wish you'd tell me what you plan to do, so I know you're going to be okay."

"I'm a grown woman. I'll be fine."

"Yes, all right. But I can't help worrying. Will your car even make it to Texas?"

Evvie blinked at her. "Who said anything about Texas?"

"I just thought . . ."

"Nope. Not going to Texas. Or back to Baton Rouge either. I'll be right here in Salem Creek if you must know."

It was Lizzy's turn to stare. "You're staying here in town? I just assumed . . ."

Evvie resumed fiddling with the smudge stick, eyes carefully lowered. "I found myself a roommate."

Lizzy narrowed her eyes, taking in the uncomfortable posture and averted gaze. She'd seen her like this before, sheepish and evasive, when she'd teased her about being sweet on Ben. "This roommate wouldn't happen to own the local hardware store, by any chance?"

Evvie squared her shoulders, struggling to keep her face blank. "He might."

Lizzy experienced a fierce stab of joy, the first she'd felt in a long time. "Oh, Evvie! I'm so happy to hear it. I had a feeling there might be something going on there, but I had no idea it was this serious. Why didn't you tell me?"

Evvie offered one of her grunts. "Folks my age don't run around bragging about shacking up."

Lizzy barked out a laugh. "Shacking up?"

"That's what we called it in my day. Anyway, that's how it is. You're looking at a lot of alone when you're my age. No one to talk to you, or do for you—or remember you. We're both on our own, and we get on. Makes sense to set up house together."

"But you care for him?" Lizzy prodded, worried that circumstance and not genuine affection had pushed Evvie into accepting Ben's offer.

Evvie smiled, eyes clouding. "My husband, Archie, was like a clap of thunder. Liked to knock me flat the first time he kissed me. Ben's a warm blanket, a bit frayed at the edges, but cozy and safe, which is exactly what I want at this point in my life. Truth is, at my age a thunderbolt's likely to kill me. I can help him in the store, and I'll have a place for my bees and my vegetables. But yes, little girl. I care. He's a good man."

"He'd better be," Lizzy said somberly. "You've been so kind to me, to Althea, and to Rhanna. You've become part of my family. I want you to be happy."

"And Andrew?"

"What about Andrew?"

"Don't you want him to be happy?"

"I do, Evvie. Which is why I can't stay. He wouldn't be happy with me, with what I wouldn't be able to give him—he only thinks he would. But eventually he'd resent it. And me. And I won't do that to either of us."

Evvie let the subject drop. "When will you leave?"

"I'm not sure. A few days, maybe. As soon as I finish packing and tie up the loose ends." She ducked her head, her throat suddenly tight. "I know you're disappointed in me."

Evvie's face softened. "Not if this is truly what you want. And only you can decide that. You did good, little girl. What you did for your gran—for your family—it was good. Now it's time to live your life. Even if that life isn't here. Go on up now, and do what you need to."

Upstairs, the aroma of white sage smoke still hung in the air, the telltale traces of Evvie's smudging. Lizzy picked up a pair of empty boxes in the hall and carried them to Althea's room, then crossed to the bookcase and dropped to her knees.

The key turned with a metallic snick, the brass hinges rasping dully as she pulled back the glass door. She slid the first book free—*The Book of Sabine*—and was briefly tempted to open it. Instead, she laid it in the bottom of the box, then removed the others, one at a time, and carefully packed them away. There were eight in all—not quite the full set. Althea's book was still out in the shop. She would leave it with Rhanna for now, to use until she left the farm. But what about Rhanna? Would there ever be a book with her name on it? One filled with recipes and scraps of wisdom rather than macabre sketches?

And what of her own book?

She rose and retrieved her suitcase from the corner. The journal was still in the front compartment, untouched since her arrival. She pulled it out, thumbing briefly through the clean white pages—*The Book of Elzibeth.*

But was it *really* a book if its pages remained blank? The thought was strangely unsettling. Was that how her life would be remembered? As a blank? Come to that, would it be remembered at all? In the end, it really didn't matter. There'd be no one to read it, no one to care what she'd done and not done. It was the necessary end to the bargain she'd made with herself, to leave behind a blank slate and end the Moon line once and for all.

She laid the empty journal in the box with the rest, then slid her gaze to *The Book of Remembrances* on the bedside table. What about *it?* Did it belong with the others, boxed up and forgotten at the back of some closet in her apartment? She knew the answer even as she asked the question—no. Althea might have shelved it beside the others, but it was different. It hadn't been penned for future generations, but for her, and her alone.

And what about the rest of Althea's things? The ebony trinket box on the dresser, the sterling silver hand mirror on the dressing table, the vintage Dresden plate patterned quilt at the foot of the bed, items lovingly collected over the course of her grandmother's life. What was she supposed to do with all of it?

The plan had been to pack up the books and a few personal items, then contact an estate agent to handle the rest. Now she realized that was impossible. Because they weren't just things. They were her grandmother's most cherished possessions, many of them passed down to her from other Moons. From Aurore, Sylvie, Honoré, Dorothée. Perhaps further back than that.

Suddenly, she could feel them around her, like the portraits on the parlor wall, a collective presence reminding her that once upon a time they had lived here, and left their mark. They had defied convention, weathered the elements, wrested a living from a rocky patch of soil, created art, raised daughters, healed generations of Salem

Creek's sick, and no doubt endured all manner of whispers before finally giving their ashes to the ground.

The Moons stuck.

Until now.

She'd be the last of them, the end of her line. But that had always been the plan, hadn't it? To end the line and slip into the life of anonymity she'd always craved. The last of the Moon girls.

How simple it sounded—and how hollow.

Overcome by a wave of claustrophobia, she pushed to her feet. There were too many people in the room with her suddenly, the shadows of all those other Moons, invisible, but there just the same, leaning against her heart.

But there was only one Moon she wanted at the moment.

Abandoning the half-packed carton, Lizzy crossed to the nightstand, tucked the *Book of Remembrances* under her arm, and headed downstairs. There was no sign of Evvie or Rhanna as she passed through the kitchen. She was grateful for that. She needed quiet and fresh air, a space free of guilty reminders.

She settled for the garden bench beneath Althea's favorite willow tree and laid the book open on her knees, startled to realize that she'd reached the final entry. But perhaps that was as it should be.

The waxed-paper packet she had come to expect was there. Keenly aware that it would be the last, she teased it open, stared at what lay pressed within—a simple dandelion with its roots still intact.

Dandelion . . . for resilience.

Dearest Lizzy,

It seems we must part sooner than expected. You mustn't be sad. We each have our little portion of time, and I have had mine. Harder than some perhaps, but sweeter too, in ways most forget to count. To say I have no regrets would be untrue. Choices have consequences, after all, and there are some I would make differently if I could have them back.

Still, there's a kind of peace at the end of a life well lived, knowing that you've given what you had to give, loved where you were free to love, that you've left nothing unsaid or undone. And with this final entry, that part at least will be true.

But this isn't meant to be about my story, Lizzy—it's meant to be about yours. Each of us comes into the world with a story to tell, a book of blank pages we're given to fill. How we choose to fill them is up to us, but fill them we must—with our truths or someone else's.

History hasn't been kind to women in general, but it has been especially hard on our kind. We've been both revered and reviled, sought for our wisdom, yet spurned for our otherness. We've been cast out, hunted, tortured, and killed, blamed for everything from dead cows and failed crops, to hailstorms and stillborn babes. We remember the burning times, and because we remember, we've learned to be careful, to keep our own company and trust no one.

But there can be a cost to keeping your own company, a cost I know all too well. Over the years I've seen that cost at work in you. You've been hiding for as long as I've known you, playing small as they say nowadays, afraid of making others uncomfortable. The world has always been afraid of a singular woman—as it is of most powerful things. It would much rather keep us in the shadows, where it needn't acknowledge our gifts. But the world has no right to keep us in the shadows, Lizzy. Not without our permission. At some point, we must step into our stories, and claim them for our own.

Anything else is half a life.

It won't be easy. Stepping into the light never is, but it's what we're all called to do. To find our truth— whatever that may be—and live it without apology. Each generation has had its burdens to carry, and you will almost certainly have yours. But you will never be alone. When life is hard, when your soul is parched, look to your roots for sustenance—like the dandelion pressed between these pages—and remember those who came before you, their strength and their resilience, their refusal to remain in the shadows and not bother anyone.

How I would love to say I'm one of those strong, resilient women, that I have always lived according to my own truths, but I am not—or wasn't when it mattered most. What I tell you next, I have never told anyone. I have kept it hidden, locked up tight in the deepest reaches of my heart. But there is a lesson in it—a lesson for you, Lizzy—which is why I must tell it now, before my pages run out . . .

FORTY-FIVE

Lizzy stared at the book, still open on her lap, the world as she knew it—or thought she'd known it—suddenly and irrevocably unshaped by Althea's parting words. The lines from the journal's final page continued to echo, a confession, but a cautionary tale too, about the choices we make and how they echo down through the years, until the sand in our hourglass eventually runs out.

She had wondered once about the thread of wistfulness that crept into Althea's entries from time to time, but had shrugged it off, unable to imagine her grandmother needing anything more than the farm and her work. It never occurred to her that there might once have been another dream, or a yearning for something lost.

Lizzy blinked away tears as she traced her fingers over the thinly scrawled lines, Althea's pen strokes achingly fragile, yet indelible somehow. *Each of us comes into the world with a story to tell.* Was her grandmother right? *Did* she have a story to tell? A book she had yet to begin? And could she begin it here?

It would mean leaving Chenier. Walking away from everything she'd worked for, and toward everything she'd sworn she never wanted. And maybe a few things she believed she could never have. It would mean stepping into the light, being seen for who and what she was—or at least who Andrew thought she was—the girl with the light inside her.

The wind lifted suddenly, rustling the leaves around her feet into tiny whorls. It was there again, Althea's earthy-sweet scent, swirling in the warm breeze. Lizzy closed her eyes and tipped up her face, reveling in the soft caress of it against her cheeks. And this time she knew. It wasn't wishful thinking. It was a call to follow her heart.

FORTY-SIX

Andrew checked the dashboard clock as he exited the Spaulding Turnpike. Nearly six o'clock. Five hours since his phone had pinged with the text from Lizzy's new cell.

It's Rhanna, so don't reply. Our girl's getting antsy. Get home ASAP if you want to say goodbye.

Goodbye. The word had left him gutted, as if a door he'd been feebly propping open had suddenly and irrevocably slammed shut. Not that there'd ever really been a door. She'd made her position clear from the get-go. Her life was in New York, and there had never been a chance that she wasn't going back to it.

And yet there'd been a flicker of hope, a flimsy thread he'd chosen to cling to, that something, anything, would change her mind and convince her to stay. He'd been a fool. And now he was playing the fool again, navigating rush hour traffic with a knot in his gut, asking for one more kick of the mule.

He hadn't replied to the text. Or dropped everything to hurry home. He'd wrestled with it a bit, playing their last words over in his head, searching for the slimmest hint that there was some opening, something he could say to make her stay. He'd come up empty. He couldn't make her feel what he felt, or want what he wanted. If slipping out of town while his back was turned was how she wanted to end things, so be it. But he wasn't letting her go without seeing her one last time.

His stomach did one of those roller-coaster plunges when he turned the corner and spotted her car still in the drive. He hadn't been quite sure how to interpret the word *antsy*, and was afraid she might already be gone. Now, as he pulled up and cut the engine, he realized he should have given some thought to what he actually planned to say.

He was holding his breath when the front door pulled back. He let it out when Rhanna appeared instead of Lizzy. She grabbed his sleeve, pulling him over the threshold and into the foyer.

"I'm sorry about the text, but I didn't know what else to do. She's been packing all afternoon. I was afraid she'd be gone by the time you got back."

"Where is she?"

"Out back last time I saw her. What are you going to say?"

He shrugged. "Goodbye, I guess."

Rhanna's face fell, making it clear that she'd been hoping for some grand MGM ending, where the hero drags the heroine into his arms for a bruising kiss as the credits roll.

He stepped around her, headed for the mudroom door. From the steps, he scanned the yard, the fields, the ridge overlooking the place where the barn had stood. There was no sign of her. But there was a book lying open on the wrought-iron bench. He was moving down the steps, making another scan of the yard, when he saw her coming out of the woods, her head down as she moved toward him. It was the third time he'd come upon her like this, but the effect was no less startling, the way the sun filtered through the trees, bathing her in light, the brief moment of confusion as her head came up and she saw him.

"You're back," she said, going still.

He nodded stiffly. "I heard you're heading back soon. I thought I'd come say goodbye, wish you good luck, or safe travels. Whatever it is neighbors do when one of them moves away."

"Andrew . . ."

He shook his head. He didn't want to hear all the reasons she was going, any more than she wanted to hear all the reasons he wanted her to stay. They'd done that to death, and he'd come out on the losing end. He had no claim on her. He got that. But it stung that she'd intended to go without a word.

"It's not that you're leaving," he said, fighting to keep his voice even. "You never made any secret of that. It's the way you were going to do it. Blindsiding me. I'd come back, and your car would just be gone. Maybe there'd be a FOR SALE sign in the yard, just to make sure I got the message."

She stood there looking at him, as if he were some exotic species of wildlife she hadn't expected to encounter. "Who told you I was leaving?"

"Rhanna sent me a text from your new phone. She said if I wanted to say goodbye, I'd better get back here pronto. I wasn't going to come at first. I tried to talk myself out of it. I thought if that's how you want it—" He broke off, leaving the rest unsaid. He'd promised himself he wouldn't do this, wouldn't try to guilt her, wouldn't ask her to stay. "I wasn't going to come."

She blinked hard, as if fending off tears. "Why did you?"

He dragged a hand through his hair. *Why?* It was a ridiculous question. And he had absolutely no idea how to answer it. "When I left for Boston, I didn't know . . . I thought you'd still be here when I got back, that there'd be time. If I had known you wouldn't be . . ." He dropped his hands to his sides, abandoning the pretense. "I came because I needed to see your face one last time."

~

The tears Lizzy had been fighting finally spilled down her cheeks. How had she ever thought it would be easy to leave this man? Or that skipping town while he was gone would be less painful for either of them? It seemed incomprehensible now.

But then, so much seemed incomprehensible after what she'd just read. She should say something, make him understand, but she couldn't seem to find the words.

"I wasn't trying to hurt you, Andrew." She reached for him, but he pulled away. "I was trying to make it easier."

"You thought this would be easier?"

"Andrew . . . listen to me."

"I've *been* listening. I've heard everything you said. Every single time you said it. Did I hope you'd change your mind? Yeah. But I get it now. So I came to say goodbye."

She put a hand to his lips, cutting him off. "I'm staying, Andrew. I'm not going back to New York."

"You're . . ." He grabbed both her hands, as if afraid she might run away. "But Rhanna said . . . What made you change your mind?"

Lizzy smiled up at him. "Nine generations of Moon women, a dandelion—and you."

He frowned, clearly puzzled. "I don't understand."

"The things you said—about me planning to slip out of town without saying goodbye, the part about the For Sale sign—it's all true. That's exactly what I was going to do. But this afternoon I was packing some of Althea's things, and it hit me. I can't walk away from what those women built, what they made, who they were, what they endured so that I could be here. They're part of my story—and I'm part of theirs. I don't think I understood that until today. *They're* my legacy. Not this place—not the buildings or the land—the *women*."

"What about your job?"

"I can make perfume here."

Andrew stared at her, his expression guarded. "You're going to just walk away from your life in New York?"

"I am. I've spent the last hour walking in the woods, trying to reconcile what I want with what I promised myself all those years ago, and here's what I realized. My mother was right. I'm allowed to be happy, and this is my chance. *You're* my chance. And the rest of it's just crap. I'll call Luc tomorrow and tell him he needs to find a new creative director." She reached up to touch his face, inhaling the warm amber scent of him. "I want to write my story here, Andrew—with you, if you'll still have me."

His arms went around her, his breath warm against her mouth as he pulled her close. "I love you, Elzibeth Moon. I loved you when I was eighteen, and I'll love you when I'm eighty. Those are just the facts."

He kissed her then, his mouth achingly tender as it closed over hers. She had nearly walked away from this—from him. From everything they could have and be together, to return to what her grandmother called *half a life*. How could she have ever considered it? Althea had spoken of blank pages, reminding her that how her own pages eventually got filled was a choice only she could make. And now she *had* chosen.

"I plan to hold you to that," she whispered between kisses. "The part about loving me until I'm eighty, I mean."

He stepped back just a little, grinning down at her. "What happened to not being cut out for happily-ever-after?"

Lizzy slid out of his arms, took his hand, and led him to the shade of Althea's favorite willow tree. "This happened," she said, picking up *The Book of Remembrances* from the bench and handing it to him.

Andrew glanced at the handwritten page, then back at Lizzy. "This is the book you told me about, the one Althea left for you, with all the pressed flowers."

"It is," she said, smiling softly. "Read the last page."

Gardenia . . . for secret love.

Dear Lizzy,

I was twenty-two when I met Peter Markey. We met
at the fair one day when he nearly ran me over with a
handcart. I thought he was the most beautiful boy I'd
ever seen. Dark haired and blue eyed, with a smile that
made me go weak at the knees. He was there with his
father, a photographer working one of those dress-up
booths. He asked if he could buy me a cider. I knew
my mother wouldn't approve, and that I should say
no, but I didn't. The next day we met again. By day
three, I was in love.

We saw each other as often as we could. He lived
in Somersworth, so it was hard. But we managed,
sneaking off whenever we both had a free hour. We'd
go to the pictures—that's what we called it in those
days—or dancing at this little place in Dover, where
no one knew us. I told my mother I was with my
friends, but she figured it out. I think she knew about

the baby before I did. When I told her Peter wanted to marry me, she forbid it.

She reminded me of Sabine's story, and why our kind must never marry—because no man must ever be allowed to rob a Moon of her power. Our loyalty, she said, must be to our legacy and our land. And to our daughters, who must be raised to be strong, self-sufficient, and solitary. She told me that if I followed my heart, I would be betraying that legacy, that our line might be weakened, perhaps even lost—because of me.

I broke it off, and never told Peter about the baby. If he had known I was pregnant, he would never have gone away. But he did go away. Two weeks later, I learned that he joined the marines and shipped off to Vietnam. I hurt him so badly, and he never knew why, never knew he had a little girl—or that her name was Rhanna. He was killed just before she was born.

I've never spoken of him to anyone, but I've never forgotten. You'll find a cigar box at the back of my closet, where I've kept a few small treasures from our time together. A photo he took of me the day we met. A beaded bracelet he gave me for my birthday. Ticket stubs from the first picture we ever saw together—Katharine Hepburn and Spencer Tracy in *Guess Who's Coming To Dinner*. And a lock of his hair, given in exchange for one of mine. It seems silly now, but that's how it is when you're young and in love. Perhaps I should have gotten rid of these things—Rhanna should have been remembrance enough—but I couldn't bear to let them go.

So there it is. I've told you all of it. I should have told Rhanna. He was her father, after all. But she was always so distant. And then you came along. By the time you were old enough, I wondered if it even mattered. I've been ashamed for so long. Not because I'd been ready to break faith with all the Moons before me, but because I did break faith with Peter—and with myself. I broke a good man's heart—a man I loved—for the sake of someone else's beliefs. I let someone else write my story.

Not a day goes by that I don't wonder how things might have been if I'd followed my heart instead of the rules. We've been taught that to love is to give ourselves away. But that's wrong. We lose nothing when we love. It's only in refusing to love that we pay, and lose the most precious part of ourselves. That's why we've come—to love. Because that's all there is. It's all love—and it's all magick.

I'm tired now, and my Circle has drawn to its close. I must lay down my pen. But I leave you with these last words. Love, my Lizzy. Love wherever it may lead, and write your story. Write it with your whole heart, and give it a happy ending.

A—

EPILOGUE

January 24

Lizzy smiled as she switched on the lamp and sat down at Althea's writing desk, warmed by the faces peering out at her from the collection of silver frames scattered over the polished surface. A candid shot of Rhanna at work on one of her sketches, her hair fastened geisha style with a pair of paintbrushes. A black and white of Althea at twenty-two, clutching an enormous stuffed poodle—the kind won at fair booths by lovestruck young men. A grinning Peter Markey, Althea's lost love and the man Lizzy now thought of as her grandfather, boyishly handsome with his Brylcreemed wave of dark hair. And the most recent addition, taken on her own wedding day, her hair woven with a chain of wildflowers, her smile radiant as she slid the ring onto Andrew's finger.

She had borrowed an embroidered hankie from Evvie, and carried her grandmother's cherished copy of Rumi's *The Book of Love*, as her something blue. Althea hadn't lived long enough to see her married, but the mingled scents of lavender and bergamot had filled the air as they spoke their vows on that sunny afternoon.

A distant hammering broke the quiet: Andrew working in the new drying barn. It would be finished by spring, and then a new mural would appear. Moonflowers this time, Rhanna had decided, with lots of stars and indigo sky as their backdrop.

The landscape of Moon Girl Farm was already changing, reinventing itself for the next generation. Salem Creek was changing too. A pair of commemorative benches had appeared in the park last fall, anonymous gifts to the town of Salem Creek, complete with neat bronze plaques. The first honored the memories of Heather and Darcy Gilman. The second, inscribed with the words HARM NONE, was dedicated to the life and good works of Althea Moon. Eight years ago, the names Gilman and Moon had become inextricably linked, but at long last the whispers were over.

Lizzy lifted her pen, then paused to peer out the window. The sun had been down for hours, the winter sky a velvety, unbroken black. It was the first new moon of the new year, the sacred space between waxing and waning, between nothingness and becoming. It felt right, somehow, to begin it tonight, at the beginning of the moon's birthing cycle. She smiled softly as she turned back the cover of the journal, blank for so long, and began to write.

The Book of Elzibeth

My sweetest baby girl,

When I was very young, I asked your great-grandmother—her name was Althea—what we were. Her answer was a kind of fairy tale, the kind with magick potions and powerful queens, because it was all I could understand at the time. She promised to tell me more when I was old enough to grasp it. But by then, I no longer wanted any part of that fairy tale. I had become afraid of myself, afraid of my own power, and I tried to run away. And then, when Althea died, I came home. Not just to the farm, but to myself.

A wise woman—the woman who will be your aunt Evvie when you arrive this spring—once told me that home isn't where you live, it's who you are. I know now just how true that is. Your grandmother, Rhanna, knows it too. She taught me to forgive, to open my heart to all that has been, and all that can be.

And so, today, I begin this book, for you, my dearest daughter—the next Moon girl.

There are a hundred names for what we are—and all of them are wrong. Because we're not one thing. We're many things. Each endowed by Spirit with a gift that is ours and ours alone. That gift is the work we're meant to do in the world, the blessing we're meant to be to others. It starts searching for us the moment we're born, and when it finds us we know, because we hear its call with our heart. Sharing that calling with others is our gift back to Spirit.

The Circle is complete.

We need no church, no graven image, no rules scratched on stone tablets or ancient scrolls. No sacred ritual or initiation is required to become what we already are—bits of god and stardust held together by divine breath and pure love.

That, my dearest daughter, is what I want you to know when you arrive. You are not here to work magick—you ARE magick.

L—

ACKNOWLEDGMENTS

Most writers will tell you that some books are more challenging to write than others. Some enter the world with seeming ease—a few twinges and it's done—while others come breach, doubling us over in their struggle to be born. They make us question our abilities and say naughty words. But these are the books that stretch us as writers. As people too, I suppose. Perhaps because from the moment of conception, we have such high hopes for them. We know what we want our words to convey, what we want the book to stand for. And anything else feels like failing.

And so begin the birth pangs—the wailings and moanings, the whimpers of exhaustion. But if we're very, very lucky, we don't go through it alone. There are people—wonderful, talented, amazing people—who are there from first twinkle to last push, who hold our hands until the panic and sweating are over. For me, those hand-holders are:

Nalini Akolekar and the entire team at Spencerhill Associates, who took on a rookie writer eight years ago and taught her how to be an author. Gratitude doesn't begin to express it.

Jodi Davis Warshaw, my wonderful editor, and the entire Lake Union/APub team, for the tremendous support and careful shepherding of my book babies, with a special shout-out to the art department for this gorgeous cover!

Charlotte Herscher, my developmental editor, who always knows how to pull the best from my characters, and who is an absolute joy to work with. I couldn't have asked for a better creative partner. And finally, to Paul, my amazing copy editor, whose keen eye and attention to detail make me look far smarter than I am. Always a pleasure, sir.

The members of my wonderful and ever-expanding author community, who blow me away every day with their talent, wisdom, and unfailing generosity. I'm limited to a collective thank-you here, because your names and kindnesses are too many to list.

The book bloggers, reader page owners, and reviewers—you know who you are and how much you are loved. For your voices and your support, I'm more grateful than I can say.

Patricia Crawford, a.k.a. Mom. For believing in me when my confidence is down around my ankles, and for reminding me always to remember who I am and where I came from.

Tom Kelley—husband, life coach, beta reader, masseur, and the best hand-holder any wife could ask for. You taught me what happily-ever-after truly looks like. Thank you for every single minute of every single day.

And of course—my cherished readers. You're my tribe, my village, my book family, and I'm continuously humbled by the time you take to read and reach out. Thank you, thank you for sitting on my shoulder every day as I write.

LAVENDER & LEMON
SUGAR SCRUB

- 2 1/2 cups granulated sugar (white or raw)
- 1/4 cup coconut oil (olive oil or almond oil will also work)
- 6–8 drops lemon essential oil
- 6–8 drops lavender essential oil
- Freshly grated zest from 1 lemon (optional)

1. Measure the sugar into a mixing bowl and set aside.
2. Measure the coconut oil into a microwave-safe bowl. Heat until melted (30 seconds).
3. Pour the coconut oil into the sugar. Mix until well combined. Add in the lemon and lavender oils.
4. If desired, zest the rind of 1 lemon and add to the mixture. Stir to combine.
5. Additional sugar may be added to thicken the mixture to the desired consistency.

SILKY BEDTIME BATH TEA

- 1/4 cup dry milk powder
- 1/4 cup organic oats
- 1/3 cup Epsom salts
- 1/3 cup Dead Sea salt
- 1/2 cup dried lavender buds
- 1/2 cup dried chamomile flowers
- 5–10 drops lavender essential oil
- 1 tablespoon coconut oil
- Mason jar
- Muslin drawstring bags

(All ingredients are available at Amazon.com or other herb supply dealers.)

1. Mix all the ingredients in a large mixing bowl until well combined.
2. Spoon into a mason jar (or other airtight container) for storage.
3. To use, fill a muslin bag and pull the drawstring tight. Add to bathwater. Rinse the bag well and allow to dry for future use.

BOOK CLUB QUESTIONS

1. Rhanna's revelation about her own gift helps Lizzy understand her mother's experiences, and paves the way for reconciliation between mother and daughter. Has there ever been a time in your own life when some bit of information coming to light has helped heal a long-standing rift?

2. One of the key themes of the book deals with the importance of owning our own story rather than living by someone else's rules. To live our truths without apology. In what ways has society tried to impose its own rules on women over the years? Do you believe it's still happening today? If so, in what ways?

3. What do you think Lizzy needed to learn about herself and her place in the world before she could make the shift from a "safe" relationship to one that required her to let down her guard and let herself be vulnerable?

4. Another theme running through the book is that of vocation, a personal calling instilled in us by a higher power, or by our higher self. Althea referred to it as the thing we're meant to do in the world. Do you believe we each have a personal calling?

5. In the last line of the book, Lizzy tells her unborn daughter that she is not coming into the world to *work* magick, but to *be* the magick. What do you think she meant? What does everyday magick look like?

6. In one of Althea's journal entries, she tells Lizzy that hate is always rooted in fear. Do you believe this is true? Can you give examples?

7. In our patriarchal society, legacy is often thought of in masculine terms. Property passed from father to son. Lineage followed through the male bloodline. But the Moon legacy is passed from mother to daughter, its traditions traced through story and the written word. In your own family, would you say it's the men or the women who are the true guardians of your family legacy and traditions? In what ways does this manifest?

8. There are references throughout the book about being invisible, making ourselves small, and not bothering anyone. Can you identify with these kinds of thoughts, and if so, how and why do you think we manifest these feelings in our everyday lives?

ABOUT THE AUTHOR

Photo © 2015 Lisa Aube

Barbara Davis spent more than a decade as an executive in the jewelry business before leaving the corporate world to pursue her lifelong passion for writing. She is the author of *When Never Comes, Summer at Hideaway Key, The Wishing Tide, The Secrets She Carried,* and *Love, Alice.* A Jersey girl raised in the south, Barbara now lives in Rochester, New Hampshire, with her husband, Tom, and their beloved ginger cat, Simon. She's currently working on her next book. Visit her at www.barbaradavis-author.com.